P9-CCX-208

Free Public Library of Monroe Township
713 Marsha Ave.
Williamstown, NJ 08094

Monroe Township Public Library

3 4201 10165111 Q

BREAKING POINT

Also by Dana Haynes

Crashers

DANA HAYNES

BREAKING POINT

 MINOTAUR BOOKS ✹ NEW YORK

This is a work of fiction. All of the characters, organizations, and events portrayed in this novel are either products of the author's imagination or are used fictitiously.

BREAKING POINT. Copyright © 2011 by Dana Haynes. All rights reserved. Printed in the United States of America. For information, address St. Martin's Press, 175 Fifth Avenue, New York, NY 10010.

www.minotaurbooks.com

Design by Philip Mazzone

Library of Congress Cataloging-in-Publication Data

Haynes, Dana.
  Breaking point / Dana Haynes.—1st ed.
      p. cm.
  ISBN 978-0-312-59989-8
  1. United States. National Transportation Safety Board—Fiction.   2. Aircraft accidents—Investigation—Fiction.   3. Government Investigators—Fiction.
I. Title.
  PS3558.A84875B74 2011
  813'.54—dc23

                                                        2011026222

First Edition: November 2011

10   9   8   7   6   5   4   3   2   1

Free Public Library of Monroe Township
713 Marsha Ave.
Williamstown, NJ 08094

To my editor, Keith Kahla, who made this book possible.
To my agent, Janet Reid, who made Keith possible.
To Katy King, who makes all the rest of the universe possible.

PROLOGUE: THE CRASH

D R. LEONARD TOMZAK WAS a modern American male. He knew it was considered inappropriate to stare openly at a pretty girl with long legs as she approached. Especially in public.

He decided to throw caution to the wind. Tomzak—"Tommy" to his friends—gave a wolf whistle as Kiki Duvall stalked down the corridor toward the waiting area of gate A15 at Reagan National, two lidded coffee cups in her hands.

"You're too kind, sir," she said, bending at the waist and kissing him on the lips.

"I'm a pathologist. Nobody pays me to be kind. They pay me to be accurate. And I accurately find you to be hot."

She wound herself into the thermoformed chair like a shoestring being lowered into a tight pile. A tall, athletic woman with hair the color of pennies, it was her lithe grace that had first attracted Tommy to her. Her pianist's hands were large enough to carry two creamer packets along with the coffee cups. She handed him one of the packets and a stir stick. As she sat, she glanced around the waiting area, which was all but empty.

"Ooooooh," she purred. "Leg room!"

"Leg room?"

She waved the other coffee cup to encompass the gate. "It's not a full flight."

"Cool. Wanna make out?" Tommy asked, the Texan in his voice ramping up a bit.

"When do I not?"

He opened his cup and blew on the surface. As he did, a curved hank of black hair fell across his left eyebrow. Kiki brushed it back.

"D'you even know what kinda plane we're flying in? Could be this is full up."

"Claremont VLE, twin turboprop." She snapped a bubble with her gum. "Seats sixty-five with four crew. State-of-the-art avionics courtesy of Leveque Aéronautique Limited out of Quebec. Twin Bembenek engines. Came off the line fifteen months ago and is due for a checkup in five cycles."

A cycle is one trip: takeoff, flight, and landing.

Before Tommy could razz her nerdiness, an appreciative, two-tone whistle sounded to their left. A man in the familiar brown-and-gold uniform of Polestar Airlines had been using a Nerf football to play catch with an eight-year-old passenger. He smiled at Kiki. "Even I didn't know all that, and I'm the copilot. You an aircraft lover, ma'am?"

Kiki smiled. "Something like that."

Neither Kiki nor Tommy felt a burning need to identify themselves as crash investigators for the National Transportation Safety Board. Pilots often were squeamish about flying with "crashers" on board. It felt like tempting fate.

"Pilot's flirting with you," Tommy said for her ears only.

"That's because, as you pointed out, I'm so hot."

Tommy lifted his coffee cup and tapped it silently against hers in agreement. He checked his battered, digital Timex. It was going on 8:00 P.M.

"So where the hell's Grey?"

"He'll be here. Probably checking his luggage."

Tommy blinked at her. "We're only staying over one night."

"Have you ever known Isaiah to pass up a golf course? In fact, if he even shows up for our panel discussion, I'll be surprised."

Tommy laughed and pointed to the right. Isaiah Grey, a wiry, African American pilot, rounded the corner and waved to the couple. He was wearing flying clothes: comfortable chinos with loafers and a polo shirt under a denim jacket.

Isaiah shook his head and peered out the terminal's window at the

Claremont aircraft, which was being readied by both a fuel truck and a food-services truck. "Somebody wanna remind me why we're taking a freaking red-eye *and* a damned prop-job three-quarters of the way across the continent?"

"I booked the flight," Tommy said brightly. "You should see how much I saved."

Isaiah glanced at him. "It's not your money!"

Tommy said, "It's the taxpayers' money."

Isaiah sat and shook his head at Kiki. "He's your man, you explain it to him."

Kiki said, "Love, we're federal bureaucrats. We don't actually like the taxpayers."

As they bantered, Tommy noted a dark-skinned man with wild hair and a Roman nose—perhaps Middle Eastern—sitting with two others, one Caucasian and the other from somewhere around the Indian Subcontinent. As Tommy watched, the three men leaned forward in their chairs and began whispering.

It was completely wrong and indefensible to suspect fellow airplane passengers just because they look Middle Eastern. Tommy knew this. He would never mention his suspicions out loud. Not even to Kiki. He took extra pains to smile pleasantly at Middle Eastern passengers, if only to assuage his silent guilt. But, since September 11, 2001, Tommy had harbored those precise suspicions and he was secretly aghast at himself.

Tommy looked up as a second man in the brown-and-gold Polestar uniform walked into the waiting area, wheeling luggage in his wake. The newcomer pretended to be shocked to find his copilot tossing around a ball with an eight-year-old. "What's this?" The newcomer turned to the young boy. "Okay, that means you have to fly the plane."

"Nuh-huh!" the kid reeled back.

"Just having a catch, boss." The copilot grinned, then turned to the boy's parents. "But your son can come look at the flight deck before we take off, if that's all right with you." His parents beamed.

The pilot nodded to Tommy and his two cohorts, then headed toward the ramp.

The copilot gathered the passengers' attention. "Folks? If we could get you to stand on line and punch your tickets, we'll get everybody seated on board. No need to wait for your row to be called. We've got a light load today."

With that, the pilot and copilot exited through the door onto the jetway leading to their plane. Tommy returned the lid to his coffee, stood, and gathered his battered leather portmanteau.

Flight attendants Andi Garner and Jolene Solomon studied the computer screen behind the counter as the last of the Flight 78 passengers trudged down the gangway toward the amidships door.

"When was the last time you saw a half-empty plane?" Andi asked.

"Pre-nine/eleven," her partner Jolene replied. "Pre-Travelocity and the other sites. This is weird."

The petite blonde, Jolene—in her twentieth year as a flight attendant—picked up the phone behind the counter and hit three numbers.

"Central." The voice came from Polestar Airlines' headquarters in Cincinnati.

"Hi. Jolene Solomon, FA-7, calling from Reagan. Hey, can someone check the computers for—"

The Cincinnati voice said, "Flight Seven-Eight to Sea-Tac?"

Jolene looked at her younger cohort, both eyebrows rising. "Yes."

"Yeah, we figured you might call. We got hit by some sort of computer virus. Nobody's been able to book that flight for the past day and a half. They just get kicked out of the system. And some of your ticket-holders got rerouted to Dulles. We got 'em booked on the three ten to Sea-Tac."

Jolene winked at her friend. "We're not complaining! This'll be the easiest flight we've had all year."

She started to say her thanks and hang up, when another thought flickered. "Hey. How many other flights are affected?"

"None," Cincinnati said. "Just you guys."

Tommy, Kiki, and Isaiah lined up with the others, boarding passes out.

The flight from Reagan National to Sea-Tac takes eight hours, more or less. Less, if there's a tailwind. This particular flight was scheduled to stop in Helena, Montana. And Kiki had guessed right: only twenty-two of the sixty-five seats were filled. After a boxed snack had been served—once free, Polestar charged nine bucks for it these days—several people shifted their seats to have rows to themselves.

Halfway over southern Montana, Pilot-in-Charge Miguel Cervantes handed the stick over to Second Pilot Jed Holley. It was past ten o'clock mountain time. Cervantes had absolutely no qualms about giving up the stick: he would trust any aircraft to Holley. Both men had served in the navy, where they'd studied to be aviators. Both had gotten out with the rank of captain. They were a year apart, age-wise, and both enjoyed playing touch football. Even their wives knew each other. Cervantes had been named PIC—*Pilot-in-Charge* and *Second Pilot* being the terms used at Polestar Airlines for captain and copilot—a year earlier. Holley would take the test in five months.

Cervantes used the lavatory and washed his hands. He flirted with both flight attendants, good-naturedly, and they flirted right back. He returned to the flight deck and struck the door with the knuckle of his middle finger: *tap, tap . . . tap.*

Inside, Holley flipped the toggle on the center control panel, unlocking the steel-reinforced door. "I changed course for Vegas. Hope that's okay."

Cervantes sat, adjusted his two-strap safety harness. "Fine by me. I lost five bucks on the Mariners last night. To heck with Seattle."

The Claremont VLE was in the mountain time zone, 105 degrees west of the prime meridian: 1330 hours Zulu time in the air, 10:30 P.M. on the ground.

They were forty-three minutes out of Helena.

Sitting in an aisle seat, Tommy studied his notes for the Helena lecture, using the next-to largest font size available on his e-reader. Public speaking was one of the highlights of his job as a pathologist. He always prepped rigorously to be able to rattle off a frightening array of statistics without glancing at his notes. "It's how I pick up chicks," he'd once explained to Kiki Duvall.

"Yes." She had patted his arm. "That's usually what does it for us."

A few minutes earlier, the pilot had announced that they would be descending into Helena, Montana. Tommy glanced to his left. Kiki slept in the window seat, wearing the earbuds of her iPod, Vivaldi softly canceling out the susurrus of the twin Bembenek Company engines. She was two inches taller than Tommy but, by sitting at an angle, she could stretch her legs out under Tommy's seat, ankles crossed, barefoot. Claremont aircraft were configured in a two-seats-on-the-left, two-on-the-right formation. Tommy studied her for a moment: the freckles across her nose, the swell of her breasts under her sweater. He smiled, feeling like the luckiest guy on earth.

He turned to his right. Isaiah Grey slept across both seats on the starboard side, back against a window, knees up, feet on the aisle seat. He'd fallen asleep with reading glasses perched low on his nose, a novel open on his lap. That wouldn't last long: attendants had just started making their way down the aisle, waking people up and urging them to push their seat backs to their upright position.

Tommy checked his watch: 11:15 P.M. mountain.

Pilot-in-Charge Miguel Cervantes adjusted the voice wand, keeping it clear of his mustache. In his ear, he could hear air traffic control in Helena describe the QNH, or the barometric settings on the ground that can cause an altimeter to read incorrectly.

"Roger, QNH," Cervantes replied. "We are on descent. Over."

"Confirm, Flight Seven-Eight." It was a woman's voice. Unusual. The great majority of air traffic controllers were guys. "You are thirteen miles from the outer marker, over."

"Thank you. We have the localizer. Over." He nodded to Jed Holley. "Speed good. Flaps one selected."

Holley hit the switch. "Flaps to one. You want extra light in here?"

Miguel said, "I think we're good." He toggled the internal PA system. "Ah, flight attendants, cross-check and prepare for landing, please."

To Holley he said, "Extend the slats."

"Slats are good."

"Okay. Slowing down a bit. Flaps eleven, please."

"You got flaps at eleven, boss."

Cervantes smiled at that *boss*.

"Altimeter."

"Checked."

"Speed brakes."

"Armed green," Holley chanted back. "Good to—"

Thump.

Jed Holley said, "What in hell . . . ?"

Both turboprop engines died, simultaneously. Every light on every monitor on the flight deck shut off as well. The sound of air whooshing around the airframe grew loud.

Miguel Cervantes said, "Hey, hey, hey. What's this . . . C'mon!"

Glow-in-the-dark decals on many of the flight deck's surfaces infused them with a sickish green glow.

Cervantes began walking through the emergency ignition system.

Nothing happened.

He did it again.

Holley said, "Jesus . . ."

Tommy brought his head up sharply. He'd heard something go *thump*. He turned back to the notes on the e-reader, just as the device died.

Zip. Nada. Totally blank screen.

Tommy whacked it. "Piece a shit . . ." he whispered.

And only then did it dawn on him: the engines had died, too.

Both flight attendants turned and dashed for the flight deck. Tommy glanced out the window. Trees were close. Very close.

"Fuck!" He grabbed Kiki by the shoulders, pulled her forward and down, and climbed on top of her.

Kiki woke with a shock. Someone was on top of her, pushing her down, her chest against her legs.

Her first thought was: *If this is an assault, the bastard is going to be more sorry than he could ever imagine.*

Her second thought: *I'm still on the plane. Oh, dear God . . .*

Tommy shouted, *"Isaiah! Get down get down get down!"*

The former fighter pilot snapped awake. Isaiah blinked, taking the scene. In a second, he realized they were powerless. He craned his neck, sweeping away his reading glasses and looking out at the slowing propellers.

He turned back and saw Tommy piling onto Kiki, pushing her down between their row and the seat backs ahead of them: rows 10 and 11.

One of the flight attendants rushed down the aisle but lost her footing. Her head panged off one of the aisle-seat arms. Isaiah reacted quickly, grabbing her and rolling to the floor, he on the bottom, covering her head with his arms.

Flight attendant Jolene Solomon looked back and didn't see Andi. At that moment, a dark-haired man with a hawk nose leaped from his seat, grabbed two cases from an overhead bin, and sprinted down the aisle toward the empennage, or tail cone. One of his friends stood, too.

Jolene shouted, "Sir! Sit down! Now!"

Jed Holley shouted into the dead radio, "Mayday! Mayday! Mayday! Polestar Seven-Eight declaring an emergency! Repeat: emergency!"

Miguel Cervantes tried the ignition sequence three times. It obviously wasn't going to work. He switched to hauling on the yoke for all he was worth, fighting desperately to keep the nose of his powerless aircraft up.

The Claremont VLE began slicing through the fir and pine trees, the tallest trees ripped savagely by the once-powerful Bembenek engines that hung beneath the eighty-five-foot wingspan of the plane. Cervantes and Holley both struggled with their yokes in the bizarrely quiet, green-tinted flight deck.

Through gritted teeth, Miguel Cervantes said, "Jed?"

Jed Holley said, "I know, man," as a towering Douglas fir caught on the port wing and tore it loose from the airframe.

As the port wing sheared free, the Claremont yawed madly, the starboard wing dipping, hitting more trees, thicker branches. Most snapped and splintered away. A massive pine caught the starboard turboprop, breaking the downward-facing propeller like a toothpick, before ripping away the entire wing.

The Claremont rolled over, starboard windows facing the ground, port windows the moon. The great ship slid lower into the trees, momentum tanking, ablating bits of aluminum and glass and losing altitude but still not nosing over.

A lone lodgepole pine shattered the flight deck windshield, tearing the copilot's chair out of its floor restraints, sending the chair and Jed Holley into the back of the flight deck.

Tommy, his head near the floor, saw a man's legs flash by, struggling to negotiate the off-axis aisle toward the empennage.

Beneath him, Kiki hissed, "Oh God!" He felt her tense up.

With her ear to the industrial carpet, she was the first to hear the *snap! snap! snap!* of treetops hitting the underside of the airliner.

Most of the screaming passengers in the left-hand seats dangled to their right, hanging by their seat belts. Passengers in the right-hand seats pressed against the wall of the fuselage. Some sobbed. Some prayed. Others swore. Overhead bins opened; coats and laptops rained on passengers' heads. The three crash investigators, wedged near the floor, stayed in place.

Still reeling over on its right side, Polestar Flight 78 hit the ground almost horizontally and slid, screaming, another hundred yards, snapping trees and sloughing off bits of both aircraft and bits of passengers.

HELENA REGIONAL AIRPORT (HLN)

Air Traffic Controller Jennifer Westphalia frowned at her radar monitor in the darkened air traffic control tower. "Hey. Where'd my Polestar go?"

The swing-shift supervisor popped a Nicorette out of its blister pack, walked over to Jennifer's station, and slid on the half-glasses that hung from a lanyard around his neck. "What?"

Jennifer pointed to her screen. "Polestar Seven-Eight. TRACOM gave me the plane about ten minutes ago. It was seven minutes out. It just fell off my screen and I can't raise them."

The supervisor wore a headset, unplugged. He plugged it into the jack beneath Jennifer's terminal. "Polestar Seven-Eight, this is Helena Regional. Please state your status. Over."

They waited. "Polestar Seven-Eight, please say your status. Over."

They waited three beats.

Jennifer said, "Uh-oh."

Kiki was crushed to the floor under Tommy's weight. Doubled over, her face and knees to the floor as she was wedged tightly between rows 10 and 11, Kiki feared her ribs would cave in under Tommy's weight.

She squeezed her eyes shut, listened to the hellish shriek of aluminum being rent asunder. She felt the insane vibrations under her cheek and knees. Part of the seat undercarriage dug viciously into her thigh.

She suddenly smelled fresh air and pine trees. She got a face full of dirt, bitter and foul. She had it in her mouth, up her nose. She coughed, relieved not to have Tommy's weight crushing her anymore—then suddenly realizing he wasn't there. Still wedged between the seats, Kiki screamed, *"Tommy! Tommmmmmmeeeeeee!"*

BOOK ONE

THE DEVICE

1

SIX DAYS EARLIER

Renee Malatesta's mobile thrummed. She ignored it.

She snugged the starched, white sheets around her and burrowed into the warm depression made by the German tourist she'd allowed to seduce her. He'd come to Segovia via bicycle. He had iron thighs and funny little ears and he smelled delicious. He slept the sleep of the just as Renee's mobile thrummed again on the white-painted, faux-Victorian side table.

Renee's nut-brown arm emerged from the eggshell-white sheet. She turned the phone so she could see the LED.

Andrew.

She glanced at the German biker, easily a dozen years her junior. He smiled in his sleep. She glanced around the havoc of the apartment, looking for her clothes. She found his bike jersey, decided it would do. She sat up, pulled it over her head, and freed her shoulder-length hair. She grabbed the phone and stepped out onto the ornate, wrought-iron balcony overlooking the plaza, thinking to herself, *You could take the call in the apartment. It's not a videophone.*

Although, with Andrew, one never knew.

Four stories below, the nightlife of Segovia, Spain, was just getting started. It was 10:00 P.M. on a Friday, and everyone was in the plaza. Renee figured she was high enough that no one could really tell what she was wearing, and the big man's jersey covered all the important bits.

She flipped open the phone. "Hello?"

"Hi." He sounded chipper, but Andrew Malatesta always sounded chipper. "Sorry to bother you on vacation. I wanted to warn you."

Renee stared down at the canopy of trees that dominated the center of the plaza. From the sounds of it, hundreds of people were out for the warm evening. "Warn me?"

"I'm at the AVE station in Madrid." He pronounced it "abbey," Castilian-style. "I'll be there in thirty minutes or so."

She blinked. "You're in Spain?"

"I didn't know if you had company. See you in a half hour."

He hung up.

Renee tugged at the hem of the thin, blue shirt. Andrew was on his way. And he was in a mood to talk.

The German biker was agreeable about the rush. He dressed quickly, pecked her on the lips, and didn't ask questions.

Renee took a long shower, washing all his cologne out of her hair and her skin.

She and Andrew weren't living together, true, but they were still husband and wife. And they were business partners. She didn't mind his suspecting that she'd taken an occasional lover but there was no point being cruel.

She'd carefully dried her wavy, shoulder-length hair with a diffuser. She pulled a white sundress out of her closet that would show off her tanned skin. Naked, she checked out her reflection in the full-length mirror, pronounced herself satisfied. *Not bad for thirty-eight,* she thought. Her eyes changed focus in the mirror, took in the rough, white-painted walls, the oak bedroom furniture, the five hundred-thread-count sheets, the spectacular view outside the open double doors to the balcony, and she smiled.

As Renee Noel, she had grown up in abject poverty in Haiti. She hadn't owned shoes until she was twelve. Looking around, she fired off a quick prayer of thanks to God. As she did most mornings.

She pulled the sundress over her head, tied the string behind her neck, and padded barefoot into the apartment's living room. Andrew was just setting down his ever-present saddlebag in the attached kitchen. He smiled up at her, his black hair askew.

"Care for a cava?"

She said, "Why not?"

They went down to the Plaza Mayor de Segovia and joined the revelry. Andrew went to the Bar Juan Bravo for two flutes of the good Spanish brut while Renee sat on the ornate, nineteenth-century bandstand, watching the city come to life. Everyone was out on this Friday night. Children chased one another. Young couples flirting. Senior citizens telling stories they'd told a thousand times before. The night was clear and the moon almost full.

Andrew returned with the sparkling white wine, handed one flute to her, and stepped up onto the octagonal bandstand, leaning against the ornate iron railing. With his Sicilian roots, jet-black hair, and aquiline nose, he looked like a local.

"Cheers."

"Cheers." They sipped. The wine was good; not sweet. They couldn't see the fourteenth-century wall or the much-older Roman *acueducto* from here but knew that a younger crowd would be gathering beneath its shadow tonight, to drink and laugh and skateboard. To the west, the great *catedral* glowed rose-colored at night, throwing ruby-tinted shadows across the revelers.

"I assume you weren't just passing through."

He gave her that brilliant Andrew Malatesta smile. The one that raised the ambient temperature in any given room a couple of degrees. He had deep-set eyes. That smile still made Renee's heart flutter, even though she realized that everyone got the same one. A handsome man at forty, his hair remained untouched by gray and more than a little wild. He had a clean-shaven face and the body of an avid runner and soccer player.

"Darling"—he sipped his wine—"is someone, somewhere, working on the device?"

Fuck! she thought.

Children raced by, screaming laughter and dodging the young couples necking. Renee said, "Creating or even testing that device is prohibited by the Bruges Accord." She smiled back over her shoulder at him. "Why do you ask?" Although she knew. She knew.

A *futbol* descended onto the bandstand from out of nowhere. Andrew shifted position, caught the ball with his raised left knee to bleed off its momentum. He glanced around, found the players. He dribbled the ball with his loafer, then side kicked it straight back to one of them. The boys howled with laughter and applauded. He didn't spill a drop of his wine.

"There are footprints in the files." He spoke with his back to her, watching the scrimmage. "Someone's been in our backup server."

"It was probably Antal looking up—"

He turned quickly. "It wasn't Antal." He crossed to her, sat on the steps, too, so they were shoulder to shoulder.

"Send Tichnor a message for me, honey."

"I haven't spoken to Barry in weeks."

"Tell him, if he touches the device or any of my designs without my express permission, I will go to the press. About everything."

Renee stared into his eyes. He didn't yell, didn't even raise his voice. But his anger seethed under the surface. There were maybe six people on Earth who could tell the real emotions behind his smile. Andrew's wife was one of them.

"No one's touched the damn thing," she said. "You're being paranoid."

He smiled, his mahogany eyes cast down.

He'd been home in Maryland the last she'd checked. To fly all the way to Spain and take the high-speed AVE train to their vacation apartment in Segovia meant he wasn't guessing. He knew. For sure.

When he didn't respond, she decided to press his buttons. "How is your mom?"

He glanced up. "My mom?"

She sipped her wine. "This is delicious. Thank you. Did you bring running clothes? I was going to jog around the walled part of the city later, get—"

"Mom is fine. I don't want to run. Halcyon/Detweiler is experimenting with my weapon designs." He spoke in the same calm, even voice as always. His smile was ironic.

She sipped the brut, bought time. "You work sixteen hours a day down in your lab, coming up only for beer or to kick around a football. You're growing mad."

"There have been three breaches. I have them documented. The blueprints and their specs were downloaded in increments, hoping I wouldn't notice. After the second breach, I added a little something of my own. For the third breach, the terminal they used was in the Halcyon/Detweiler main research facility, outside Reston. I don't know if it was Barry's fat little fingers on the keyboard but, hey, I've got logs of when he used his parking pass and when he used his swipe key to get into that very room."

Her blood froze. "Trojan horse?"

"Inside the specs. Of course. The bastards are real, dear. Barry Tichnor is real. They're studying my prototypes, trying to create the device."

The blood drained from her face. She set the flute down next to her gladiator sandals. "Andrew? Andrew, this isn't just breaking some contract. This is corporate espionage against a Fortune 200 company!"

Andrew sipped the cava.

When Renee was angry, her Haitian accent tended to kick in. "Go home. Go invent a better mousetrap. Go invent a better windmill; it'll give you something to tilt at. Go fuck Terri and leave homeland security to patriots."

Andrew smiled. He finished his wine in a gulp. "Patriots," he repeated, whispering.

"You think America doesn't have enemies? You think the Barry Tichnors of the world are just pesky capitalists?"

He set his glass down on the step. "If you provide access to the device or any of our prototypes for Barry or anyone else, be they Halcyon or even the Pentagon, I will go to the media. I'm not kidding here, honey. When have you ever known me to bluff?"

Her anger snapped. She stood, stepped down onto the flagstones of the plaza. "When you said, *I do!*"

Andrew smiled his smile. "I'm not, you know. Fucking Terri. And it's difficult to maintain the moral high ground when there's a condom wrapper in the kitchen garbage."

Renee paced, her mind racing. "I'm your lawyer. Go to the media and you'll be breaking your nondisclosure agreement. Halcyon's lawyers would crush us!"

He ran his hand through his always-askew hair. "I've written depth-charge programs into our backup server. Tell Halcyon if they go scrounging in there they'll release a virus that will fry their mainframes. I swear to God, it's the most malleable virus ever. It'll send Tichnor's corporation back to the Stone Age. They want to sue me, they'll have to scrounge up a manual typewriter to do it."

"Now it's treason and corporate espionage plus sabotage! Andrew, goddammit! Stop being so pig-brained! This is a matter of national security!"

"It's not, you know. It's the military-industrial complex putting itself above international law."

She scoffed. "International law?"

He smiled. "Spoken like a true lawyer."

"You never understood the importance of Malatesta, Inc. being a Pentagon subcontractor. It's not just the millions you pissed away, you holier-than-thou bastard! Your designs are brilliant! They're revolutionary! The security of—"

Andrew belted out a laugh.

Renee flinched. "What?"

"The irony, baby, is that you're not wrong. I have more than sixty patents to my name, and the weapon-design stuff is some of my all-time-best work. And it's awful. Awful."

Renee couldn't hear the sheer anger in his voice. But she could read it in his eyes.

"It was hubris. It was ego. And, fuck, yes, it was greed. Halcyon/Detweiler and the Pentagon dangled millions of dollars in our faces and I had visions of sugarplums and Maseratis. I admit it. It was the high of the dollar. But, baby? I'm not a weapons builder. I'm not."

She glanced around the plaza. Two hundred people out and all were ignoring their spat. Couples fight in public in Spain. It was no big deal.

She steeled her jaw. "Except you *are* a weapons builder. And America needs you."

Andrew stood and dusted off the back of his trousers. "Baby?"

She said, "It's Renee," and glowered.

"Renee?" He stepped closer to her, his hands on her shoulders. He kissed her and she stood her ground, not kissing back but not averting her lips, either. "I love you. I'm sorry about . . . you know. Everything. Tell Tichnor I'll strafe his mainframe if he takes any files off our server. Tell him I'm out."

He turned and walked the length of the plaza back to their pied-à-terre.

2

FIVE DAYS EARLIER

"Your argument," said Susan Tanaka, "is perfectly clear. I see your points clearly."

She had met the three men in a conference room in Washington, D.C.'s L'Enfant Plaza, home of the National Transportation Safety Board. It was a Saturday but the concept of *weekend* is often lost on federal agencies. The men sitting on the other side of the wide conference-room table smiled and nodded at her. The man in the middle said, "This is great. We knew the NTSB would see reason. We felt it highly likely that—"

"Don't get me wrong." Susan smiled serenely. "We're going to ignore your recommendation in its entirety. I just wanted you to know I understand the basis of it."

Susan Tanaka wore a black pencil skirt and black Max Mara tunic jacket over a shimmering ruby-red blouse with four-inch Kate Spades, a double strand of pearls and matching earrings. She was the very essence of fashion, and that probably led the representatives of Homeland Security, the Transportation Safety Administration, and the Federal Aviation Administration into the false sense that this would be a fair fight. The men were all around six feet tall and wore severe business suits. And they were used to getting their way.

The representative from Homeland Security blinked. "Ma'am?"

The National Transportation Safety Board's senior-most intergovernmental liaison, Susan Tanaka, was neither an engineer nor a pilot. She couldn't tear apart an airplane wing or conduct an autopsy. That was not where her gifts lay. If a crash occurred anywhere in the United States or its territories, her job was to ride herd on the local, state, and federal agencies that tended to gum up the works. Sometimes that took dexterity, sometimes that took quick thinking and teamwork, and sometimes that took leg-breaking ruthlessness. Susan Tanaka could muster all three.

She batted her lashes, smiled sweetly, and watched the three men across from her glower.

"Miss Tanaka, we are hoping you'll take this to Wildman. We think he should make the call."

"It's missus," she said, smiling. "And it's *Delevan* Wildman or Chairman Wildman to those who are not his friends. The chairman has given me the authority to decide on this issue. Your idea has the rare combination of being both more expensive and less efficient than the status quo."

The representative from the TSA shook his head ruefully. "Listen, honey, this is the right thing to do. Come on, just take it up to your boss, please. We really do insist."

Susan Tanaka ratcheted up her smile enough that one could read by it.

"Gentlemen?" She slid the cap onto her Mark Cross pen. "From your perspective, there's good news and there's bad news. The bad news is: your recommendation for altering safety protocols in high-density corridors is dead on arrival. At first blush I thought there was a kernel of merit in there somewhere, but the more you explained it, the worse the idea got. Now, alas, I would categorize it as *silly*."

She closed her portfolio, stood, and buttoned her formfitting tunic. She adjusted her sleeves. "I would sooner play handball in a tutu than bother Delevan Wildman with a silly idea. That said, I think our meeting is adjourned."

The FAA representative adjusted his tie. "You said there was good news . . . ?"

"We validate parking."

.   .   .

Susan Tanaka returned to her office to find Kiki and Tommy waiting for her. She hugged them. Susan had to rise up on the balls of her feet to reach Kiki, despite the four-inch heels.

Tommy Tomzak drawled, "Suze. So, you really doing this?"

"I really am."

Kiki winced. "This place can't handle you being gone for a month! It'll fall apart!"

"They'll get along just fine. Kirk's back surgery went better than we could have hoped but he's got a long recovery period ahead of him. And we're going to go through it together."

Tommy gave her a lopsided grin. "Yeah, in Italy. Tough assignment, Tanaka."

"Hey." She laughed. "I'm taking one for the team. Shall we?"

Susan led the way into the office of Delevan Wildman, longtime director of the NTSB. The office was clean but a little cluttered.

Del sat on one of three deep-green couches clustered around a maple-and-glass coffee table. He twisted around and waved in Susan, Tommy, and Kiki. Beth Mancini was already seated. Kiki poured coffee for herself and Tommy.

Tommy, in chinos and an untucked cotton shirt, shook his head ruefully at the attire of Wildman, Susan, and Beth. "Any of y'all understand the concept of *Saturday*?"

Del smiled. "I've heard the term."

"Swear t'God, if I said, 'Hey, the Jets are playing,' you'd wanna know if they landed safe."

"We were explaining," Kiki interrupted, "that we don't for a minute believe Susan is taking an actual vacation. I need to see photos, with Susan in them, mind you. Oh, and, Susan? I know how Photoshop works. Don't even try."

Susan unbuttoned her form-fitting jacket as she sat. "It's not Siberia. It's the Italian Lake Region. You can reach me if you need me."

"We won't," Del said in his baritone Tennessee accent. A bear of a man, his years in the military and years as a chief pilot for the airlines left him with a gravitas. "Beth will be acting senior intergovernmental liaison for the four weeks you'll be gone. She's ready for it. Aren't you?"

"Sure." Beth Mancini gave a little, self-deprecating shrug. She was always self-conscious around Susan. It was partly Susan's I'm-in-charge demeanor. It was partly a wardrobe thing. Beth's jacket and pants had

Free Public Library of Monroe Township
713 Marsha Ave.
Williamstown, NJ 08094

looked perfectly fine in the mirror that morning, but as soon as Susan walked into the office, Beth found her own outfit frumpy.

Susan waved away the conversation. "Beth isn't the concern. I only worry about getting my job *back* from her. No, the problem, as always, is Dr. Tomzak."

"Bite me," Tommy said without rancor.

Susan ignored him, per usual. "Since the Oregon incident, the NTSB's profile has never been higher. And Idiot-Boy here is a national hero."

Tommy snorted a laugh. "You're meshuggener. I served in Kuwait. I know from real heroism. I didn't do jack-shit in Oregon."

"And you can't pull off Yiddish with a Texas twang. Look, we got great national coverage, but that was almost nine months ago. Budget hearings are starting up on the Hill. We're out of the spotlight, and I don't think that's a good place to be right now. I want to do some more media. I want us to consider a nonfiction book. And I need Tommy."

"Get Isaiah," Tommy said. "He actually stopped the bad guys."

"Isaiah's as stubborn as you. Kiki, talk sense into this man!"

Kiki held her cup to warm both hands. "Yes, because of the vast history of Tommy actually listening to me. That tactic *always* works."

She reached out and tousled his hair. Tommy shot her a cocked eyebrow and a lascivious wink. "You could always try coercing me."

Beth Mancini cleared her throat. "Here's a thought."

The others turned to her. It had taken Beth years to get over her fear of public speaking. Her trick: she pretended to be Susan Tanaka.

"Northwest Tech."

Tommy shrugged, lost.

"It's one of the big technology expos," Kiki explained. "Thousands of geekazoids go each year. More to Beth's point, so do a lot of technology-oriented media."

Beth immediately warmed to Kiki, whom she didn't know well. "But it's like Comicon for technology. Mainstream media covers it, as well. Imagine putting together a panel discussion: Dr. Tomzak—"

"Tommy," Tommy grunted.

"Tommy," Beth corrected, " Isaiah Grey, and Kiki. You could talk about the technology that brought down CascadeAir 818. You could talk about the way the Go-Team untangled the mystery. No one person has to play the hero. It was a team effort. I have a friend on the executive committee this year. I called her. I can make this happen."

Tommy started to protest as Kiki beamed, "I'm in! So is Tommy."

"Whoa, honey! I'm in? Since when?"

"You are." Kiki patted his knee. "We'll talk Isaiah in, too. Beth: good call!"

Beth beamed.

Del sat back, hands clutched over his solid middle. "See? I just shut the hell up and let you youngsters sort it out. That there's leadership."

Susan reached across the maple table and squeezed the back of Beth's hand. Then she smoothed her skirt and stood up. "Good. *Now* I'm on vacation."

3

The Wild Boar Brigade was ginned up for the Big Sell. Today was make-or-break time for the entire op.

Two agents waited in a dilapidated GM pickup with an off-color trunk lid and left-rear quarter panel; a dead coyote carcass was bungeed to the dented hood. One more guy waited across the street, kneeling next to a '74 Harley, a tool kit and a repair book open on the battered sidewalk. They had two guys inside the bar with La Chica—the bartender and a fifth agent knocking around balls on the tattered and madly canted pool table.

La Chica sat at the bar in a very short denim skirt and cowboy boots and a flouncy blouse, unbuttoned low. She drank Cerveza Preparada and nibbled on peanuts. She looked like she could be Mexican. By the time she'd been there forty minutes, she had turned down four dour efforts at amorous communication ranging from *you're new here* to *how much, honey?*

As she neared her forty-fifth minute on the bar stool, the guy kneeling next to the Harley said, "Tango Tango Tango" into his collar mike. A six-week-old, cherry-red Cadillac Escalade glided up to the front of the bar, braced by twin steel-sided Humvees, dust rising in their wakes. All three drivers glared, alert to the streets of Juarez.

Two hard guys in crisp jeans and snakeskin boots climbed out of the lead Hummer. Both wore sunglasses and Wrangler jackets long enough to hide holsters. They checked out the two agents in the GM pickup, who had a map of Texas unfolded on the dashboard and were arguing loudly in Spanish. The dead coyote on the hood was a nice bit of business. Who had ever heard of *federales,* regardless of which side of the border they hailed from, rolling with a carcass on the hood?

J. T. Laney, head of ATF's Joint Intelligence Task Force on Mexican Weapon Procurement, had thought up the thing with the coyote. He'd shot it, too. The night before the big sell, pissing drunk, they'd outfitted the carcass with Ray-Ban knockoffs, an ear jack, and a shield. They'd shot photos of it and dubbed it "Special Agent Wiley."

Now, the gun-hands from the Hummer dismissed the arguing cowboys as drunks and ignored them. Perfect.

J. T. Laney, kneeling next to the Harley, said, "You got two bucks."

La Chica likely would get scanned for electronics, so she wore no communication gear; Laney's words were for the agent behind the bar and the guy at the pool table.

The rear door of the Escalade, with its smoked windows, remained closed.

One of the agents in the GM pickup said, "Any day now, Carlos."

Which is when the X-factor rolled into town. In this case, the X-factor was represented by a brown-haired American in a rented Toyota pulled up next to the Escalade.

A big man—six-two, midforties, and broad-shouldered—undid his seat belt and climbed out of the rental. He coughed dust and walked toward La Chica's bar.

One of the guys in the truck swore. "Who's this Boy Scout? The fuck's he doing?"

J. T. Laney said, "Hold positions." He was used to X-factors. Every field operation included surprises.

The big man ignored the watchers on the street and opened the saloon door. At that exact moment, the right rear door of the Escalade opened and Carlos "the War Dog" Ramos stepped down. He wore a fifteen-hundred-dollar white suit and five-hundred-dollar Tom Ford sunglasses. Two more of his men left the Hummers, but not the drivers, who idled their rigs and glared at the dusty street.

Carlos and his boys began strutting toward the bar.

"Boss? The Boy Scout?"

"No time," J. T. hissed. The big American's timing couldn't have been worse. He was in the saloon and the War Dog was about to enter, so the die was cast.

J. T. Laney stood next to the Harley and brushed off the knees of his beat-up jeans. The War Dog glanced across the street at him but J. T. wore his Jose Cuervo baseball cap low enough to obscure his eyes. "No choice. We are green for go," J. T. said, hardly moving his lips.

La Chica could have been Mexican, but in fact she was half Israeli, half Palestinian. She glanced in the mirror and froze as Ray Calabrese from the Federal Bureau of Investigation walked into the bar. Ray moved directly to the bar, picked a stool five down from Daria Gibron, La Chica, and ordered a Bud. He turned to Daria with a polite smile across his rectangular face. *"Buenos días, señora."*

Ray turned away, reached for a bowl of shelled peanuts.

Daria began swearing inside her head. Ray must have been staking out the saloon.

Carlos Ramos and his soldiers appeared in the mirror behind the bar.

The bartender grabbed a bottle of Gran Patron and set it near the cash register: the signal to Daria that the big sell was a go.

She crossed her shapely legs and turned slightly on her bar stool.

Carlos the War Dog walked straight to her. He took a seat next to Daria, four seats from the big American, eating peanuts and minding his business. Daria smiled languidly at the drug kingpin and sipped her spiced drink. She wore her black hair very short and spiky, shaved close at the back of her neck.

Carlos said, "Tonic water."

The agent poured him one over ice with a lime wedge.

Two of the four guards took tables at the left-front and the left-rear side of the bar, flanking the room. A third took the last stool at the bar, to the right of Ray Calabrese, and spun the stool so he faced the room at large. The bar was laid out in a reverse L shape; Daria, Carlos, Ray Calabrese, and the guard sat on the long side. The fourth guard took a stool on the short end of the L, to the right of the bartender.

The guards' positions had the flair of a well-executed military maneuver. All angles and exits were covered, and the few other patrons were all in sight.

Daria had no choice but to play out the scene. She leaned toward the dapper man in the spotless white suit. "Did you like the samples?"

He nodded, eyes on the mirror behind the bar and thus on everything that happened behind him. He glanced at the man smacking pool balls on a table that badly needed adjustment.

"The weapons were splendid. But there's a problem."

Daria tensed up without showing it to anyone. It was a trick she'd learned in the Israeli army and intelligence services.

"Tsk. I am not a woman who does *problem* well."

"Alas." He shrugged within the spotless white suit. "We have an infestation problem."

"Infes—"

"Federales," Carlos the War Dog said, smiling.

The ATF agent behind the bar had excellent hearing and an even better poker face. He fiddled with the cash register. He put his weight on his left boot, which rested on the innards of an electric guitar foot pedal the Wild Boar Brigade had turned into a silent alarm. He stepped on it twice.

The power pedal created a specific tone of interference in the ear jacks of the ATF team. Two hisses of static, one second in duration, meant *Trouble.*

Carlos sipped his tonic water. "Do you know how to spot federal agents, señorita?"

"Yes. I have been in this business awhile."

But Carlos wasn't interested in her response. He nodded to his right, toward Ray Calabrese with his beer and growing pile of peanut shells half filling the plastic bowl before him. "This fellow, for instance?"

Daria reached languidly to her left boot and slid a palm-size folding knife into her hand. She pretended to look past Carlos at Ray, who minded his own business.

"Is he an agent?" Carlos asked.

A flick of her short thumbnail, and the wide, two-inch-long blade whispered out of its hinged sheath.

"Most certainly not," Carlos answered his own question. "The hair, the clothes . . . He *looks* like a cop. Thus, he is not a cop. But the bastard pretending to play pool . . . ?"

The agent at the pool table had been staring at the back of the War Dog's head. His eyes flickered to the bar mirror and he realized the drug dealer was staring right back.

Carlos turned in his seat and motioned to the ATF agent by the pool table. "Excuse me. Señor?" He made a *come here* gesture. His four soldiers braced.

The agent's eyes flickered nervously. "Um . . . Sorry, man. Just playing pool."

Carlos switched to English. "Come here."

Daria glanced behind Carlo's head. Ray's eyes were on the dwindling pile of peanuts.

The stunned agent at the pool table shrugged. He looked far too sweaty to carry off *just playing pool.*

Carlos smiled languidly. "Trujillo."

The man at the left-front table stood and drew a Colt Python.

The bartender stepped hard on the foot pedal. *Trouble.*

Daria slid off her stool, drawing Carlos's attention back her way. He turned to her, brows rising in question.

Daria's left arm was a blur. Seemingly out of nowhere, she produced a short, fat knife. She slashed out, her arm arcing horizontal. The guard sitting on the short end of the L flinched away, wondering why she'd almost slapped him. He went for his gun. But his brain began to register a problem. He hadn't yet realized his neck had been sliced open from windpipe to spine.

Ray Calabrese hadn't appeared to be paying attention, but as soon as Daria stood, he brought his right arm up and smashed his bent elbow into the temple of the guard nearest him. The man's eyes rolled up and he fell as if boneless, flopping to the floor.

Daria stepped close to the War Dog. In swift, coordinated moves, she had one hand in his hair, and with the other she shoved the short, fat knife against the drug lord's throat. The blade was still clean because her arcing attack to the first guard had been far faster than his blood spatter.

"*¡Nadie se mueva!*" she barked.

The last two guards froze.

The ATF agent with the pool cue did likewise.

Ray hadn't entered with a weapon—the professionals would have spotted it. Instead, he decided to borrow a SIG-Sauer from the guard he'd clocked.

As Ray started to draw it, the guard sitting at the far-left table gambled. He shoved away from his table, fist coming up, long steel barrel clearing his holster. The man climbed to his feet but cried out and dropped like a guillotine as Ray shot him through the thigh.

Everyone in the saloon flinched at the boom of the SIG.

The bartender reached for a sawed-off shotgun under the cash register. Daria's back was to him, eyes on the last guard with the Python, but she heard him move.

"Bartender's good," she said in English.

Ray said, "Okay."

He lined up his borrowed gun on the last guard. The man hadn't aimed the Python yet, but he hadn't set it down, either. His eyes flickered from his boss's throat to Ray and back again.

J. T. Laney burst into the saloon, the two agents from the pickup behind him. The ATF agents stepped between Ray and the standing guard.

"Freeze! Nobody move! No—"

No longer in Ray's line of fire, the guard stepped forward and tucked the Python under J. T.'s jaw.

The agents from the pickup aimed at the guard, shouting *"Down! Put it down!"* almost drowning one another out. The guard pointed his weapon at their boss; the agents pointed their weapons at him. He made no move to obey their shouts.

The first guard lay on the floor, hands around his throat, gagging on his own blood. The second had crumpled to the fetal position under his stool. The third held his thigh, keening in misery. The men on the ground were the only ones moving.

"I have committed no crime here," Carlos the War Dog said loudly and in English, feeling the battle knife against his throat. "We were attacked. Shall we call the local police, ask them to clear up this misunderstanding?"

A beat, and the bartending agent said, "Boss?"

J. T. licked his suddenly bone-dry lips. "Carlos? I keep your men. Especially the fucker who drew on me. You walk."

The guard increased the pressure of the barrel against J. T.'s jaw.

Still, nobody moved but the wounded.

"Daria . . . ?" J. T. let his eyes travel to hers without moving his head.

A beat, and she released her hold on Carlos. He took two steps away from her, turned, eyes burning with rage. He made fists but felt, more than heard, Ray step to his back.

Carlos looked around at the three downed men. He turned back to Daria, then to J. T. "Deal."

The last guard let his Python swing on the fulcrum of his trigger finger, the handle falling, barrel rising to the ceiling. One of the agents from the pickup took it from him.

Carlos the War Dog Ramos adjusted his white suit, his open shirt collar. He nodded once to Daria—"Señora?"—and turned to the saloon door.

4

THE EXPEDITIONARY UNIT OF the U.S. Bureau of Alcohol, Tobacco, Firearms and Explosives made three arrests in the small Mexican town and contacted its indigenous counteragency to handle the legal details. Three high-level soldiers of the Ramos cartel would be held at the nearest Mexican Army garrison: one man concussed, one leg wound, one uninjured. A fourth drug-runner bled to death on the scene.

The true objective of the sting operation, Carlos the War Dog Ramos, walked away.

In the dusty street outside the saloon, locals emerged from hiding—some underground telegraph alerting them the gun fighting was over. At least for now.

J. T. Laney spoke on his cell phone with the unit's headquarters in Tucson. He paced, his men and Ray Calabrese watching him, the men darting acid glances at the FBI agent who had donned sunglasses and leaned against the ATF pickup. After a mumbled conversation, J. T. hung up and turned to the FBI agent.

"You screwed the pooch, you dumb son of a bitch! We worked this case—"

He was cut off as Daria Gibron emerged fast from the saloon, stepped into the throng of federal agents, and stepped up to the young agent who had pretended to play pool.

"That was amateur!" she spit. "You could have gotten me killed!"

The young agent gave her a cocky grin. "Don't get your panties knotted, babe. You weren't—"

Daria pivoted and delivered a roundhouse kick, boot heel as high as her head. It was not a ladylike strike in a miniskirt. Her heel connected with the now-stunned agent. The blow lifted his cowboy boots off the sidewalk. He was unconscious before he landed.

Daria rode the spin until she faced J. T. "Ray didn't blow anything! That idiot did!"

She broke into thirty uninterrupted seconds of obscenities, standing right in J. T.'s face. The insults were primarily in Hebrew but everyone got the gist. She eventually stopped to gulp air.

J. T. blinked at the five-foot-six human tornado standing toe-to-toe with him.

The agent who played bartender raised one hand, as if he were in a classroom. "Um, boss? Yeah. FBI dude didn't fuck up. Perkins there, did. Thugs woulda killed him for sure and Daria, too, wasn't for this guy." He jacked a thumb in Ray's direction. Ray seemed to be studying his dusty loafers.

J. T.'s face turned red. The young ATF agent lying on his back moaned, one leg twitching.

"You're saying it was Perkins's fault?"

Ray stepped away from the GM pickup with the dead coyote bungeed to the hood. "No, it was your fault."

J. T. shot the taller man a combative grin. "Really, Boy Scout? 'Cause the way I see it—"

"You're Laney. I've been doing some research on you. You've gotten three undercover agents killed in a little over seven months."

"This is a dangerous job we—"

Ray plowed through him. "Lovely operation here. Real pro. You've got two agents in a beat-up truck out front of the bar, but the truck's got four brand-new, expensive four-ply treads. Perfect for chasing someone across the desert. If that didn't look suspicious enough, you've got two guys inside. Only thing is, you've got one behind the cash register and one at the pool table. Which puts Daria in a perfect crossfire position. And all of that would be bad enough, Agent Laney, but to make matters worse, your pupils are so dilated I can hardly see them. You're working stoned."

J. T.'s face went from red to purple. He drew his Glock 9 from his belt holster. As his hand cleared his hip, Ray Calabrese's fist darted out, and somehow he ended up holding the Glock. His eyes never left those of J. T. Laney. Ray ratcheted the slide and quickly, expertly, dismantled the auto, dropping its component parts contemptuously at J. T.'s feet.

The other agents glanced at one another. None of them actually saw Ray take the gun. It had happened too fast.

The unit leader tried to regain his cool. "Daria's here because she wants to be here, asshole! She chose the job. She's fucking outstanding at it. You got no rights, you got no say in it!"

"Justice Department might have a different take on it. Let's you and me—"

But Daria touched Ray's arm. He stopped, turned to her.

"Go home, Ray."

He looked down at her. She kept her hand on his forearm, very dark eyes locked on his.

"You don't have to be doing this."

"I know," she said. "I'm choosing to do this."

"This asshole is going to get you killed!"

Daria offered Ray a sad little half smile. Her Israeli accent was back now. "It wouldn't be a war if that weren't one of the outcomes. Thank you, Ray. Now go home."

He studied her. She looked up into his eyes, unflinching.

And after a while, Ray walked to his rental, pulled out, and left a dust trail in his wake.

J. T. spit on the sidewalk. "What a fuck—"

Daria's voice dropped an octave. "Don't," she warned, eyes on Ray's car. "Not ever."

5

RENEE MALATESTA KITTED UP and did her run around the walled city of Segovia, her anger thrumming like a guitar string. Andrew had returned to the States.

Malatesta, Inc., was a small firm. Andrew and four other designers were the engineering heart and soul. Renee was the chief financial officer. They had four employees, all clerical.

The company had started with the first circuit boards Andrew had designed in a U-Store-It facility they'd turned into a makeshift lab. There had been times, at the beginning, when he'd had to stop designing and tend bar to help pay for Renee's law school. They had started as two people in love, with doctoral degrees and debt. They'd survived a bankruptcy. They'd survived a miscarriage. When they were in their late twenties, Andrew's first patent was bought up by Apple for eight hundred dollars and they'd gotten mad drunk on tequila and made love until dawn.

Andrew made the cover of *Wired* magazine at thirty and Renee gave up a partner-track position at a law firm to serve as general counsel and CFO. Their first million-dollar contract was followed ninety days later by a seven-million-dollar contract.

The more successful they were, the less time they spent in the same room. Neither of them noticed at first.

Renee moved the company to Maryland, lured by a lush state-tax incentive. They had become a company swirling around a nucleus of Andrew and his uncanny ability to design *the next big thing.*

She jogged around the massive Alcázar de Segovia, the strangely Disneyesque stone castle built on a Roman foundation. The day was gorgeous and the sun glinted off the sea. Keeping up a grueling pace, she passed into a dodgier neighborhood outside the walled city.

Last year she and Andrew had met Barry Tichnor, a managing partner at the nation's largest defense contractor, Halcyon/Detweiler. Barry oversaw the research-and-development arm of the multinational. He'd taken the couple out to dinner at a two-story French restaurant on Connecticut Avenue in Washington, D.C. Over hors d'oeuvres, he'd told them that Halcyon/Detweiler, with $317 billion in profits that fiscal year, was looking to subcontract some research-and-design work for the Pentagon. The name Malatesta had come up in more than one board meeting.

"Our plants are designed to gin up jet fighters and battle tanks," Barry told them over a savory tourtière. "The . . . devices we're talking about are a bit smaller." The money would be more than their firm had made since its inception. And since it would be classified defense work, there would be almost no congressional oversight.

Andrew had wanted no part of it at first. But Renee knew this was their big break. This was the brass ring. It took three months to persuade her husband. In the end, it had been the challenge, not the profits, that brought him around.

She returned to the older section of Segovia and the massive Roman aqueduct looming over everything. She bought a bottled water and stood on one leg, stretching the other, her cross-trainer up against her bum, then stretched the other leg. She watched the well-to-do of Europe, Asia, and America joking, taking photos, consuming conspicuously. She lived in Segovia sixty days a year, more or less, and had learned fluent Spanish, which meant that, like every other ex-tourist, she had come to loathe tourists.

After the initial meetings with Tichnor, Andrew had been in The Zone. She hadn't seen him for days at a time. He'd set up a kind of apartment in the basement of their leased building and slept there more nights than not, near his computers and drafting board and three-dimensional, holographic-design computers.

She remembered the day she had arranged the lunch with Barry Tichnor and Andrew and herself. Andrew had brought his vade mecum, a nicked and scratched saddlebag he'd found in an antique shop in Santa Monica, the same year he and Renee met, and which he'd carried with him everywhere ever since. Between courses of dim sum, Andrew dragged out his sketch pad and showed it to Barry.

Barry removed his eyeglasses and peered at the sketches. "Is that . . ." He flipped a page. "My lord . . ."

Andrew had actually blushed and had taken his book back, shoving it into the saddlebag with its hokey leather fringe. "Ah, it's just a couple of ideas. Things we might try."

"No, no." Barry slipped the glasses back on. "Those ideas are revolutionary. I've never . . . I mean, I've worked in this field my whole adult life. I've never seen designs like that."

Andrew had just smiled the Andrew smile, the one that served as a siege wall; the one nobody got through. Renee might not have been sleeping with him on a regular basis, but she was his wife. She could tell that he was in.

Malatesta, Inc., signed a contract worth $128 million with the mighty Halcyon/Detweiler, Inc., and nobody in the outside world knew about it. The contract was backed by the Pentagon and was classified. Renee arranged for new headquarters, purchased the land not far from the National Geospatial-Intelligence Agency in Bethesda, near Potomac Palisades Park. The crew broke ground at the end of summer. A month later, Andrew rented a condo two blocks from their old headquarters and moved most of his clothes there. He and Renee never talked about it, as such. They never went to a marriage counselor and they never spoke of divorce.

One of the worst days of her life came on a Tuesday in July, when Barry Tichnor met the Malatestas at a bar in Glen Echo. Andrew ordered a glass of Evian for himself and a straight Barbancourt Haitian rum for her, without asking. It was her favorite. Barry had a glass of cheap, lethargic Chablis.

"I've been monitoring Bruges," Barry began, removing his glasses to clean them, only to realize that he just had.

Andrew wore a frayed sweater and jeans, his black hair tousled. Renee wore Chanel and wore it well. Andrew said, "The city in Belgium?"

"The weapons summit," Barry said, blinking in surprise. "You don't know about this?"

Andrew just shrugged.

"An international weapons summit is being held there. They, ah, have been discussing a ban on research and development of devices such as yours."

Renee drained the rum in a gulp, did not feel the burn going down.

Barry said, "It's by far your most promising endeavor. We might have to . . . ah, add a level of security to your work, Andrew. Keep it on the hush-hush for a while."

Andrew smiled his Andrew smile and said, "No."

"Excuse me?"

He turned to his wife, not to Barry Tichnor. "We've seen this coming for months. The device is too dangerous, too destabilizing. If I had a vote in the Bruges Accord, I'd vote to ban it, too."

"Honey, let's not get ahead of ourselves," she counseled. "Barry's not saying they have been banned, only that there are talks under way. We don't—"

"We've talked about it. Me and the others." The *others* being the rest of the Starting Five, his longtime engineering partners: Terri Loew, Antal Borsa, Vejay Mehta, and Christian Dean. Andrew was the fifth. "The whole direction we're going. The device. It's destabilizing. No, Barry, I'd have brought this up if you hadn't mentioned it first. It's a game-changer. It's too much."

He'd stood and peeled a twenty-dollar bill, left it on the table and walked out.

"That did not," Barry Tichnor said, adjusting his untouched glass of Chablis, "go as well as I'd hoped."

"This isn't over," Renee told him. "Not by a long shot."

6

Early Monday morning, Renee Malatesta came back home to the States and took a cab directly home. She walked in to find Andrew baking.

Andrew enjoyed the precision of baking, and he was good at it. He just hadn't done much of it, in their home, for a long time.

Renee kicked off her heels, studied the ingredients. Andrew wore a chest-to-knee apron and efficiently whisked batter in the largest of their clear glass nesting bowls. "What are you making?"

He turned and smiled his Andrew smile. The state-of-the-art coffeepot burbled by the wooden chopping board. "Hi. Madeleines."

"Yum."

Renee changed into jeans and a cranberry cashmere sweater. She removed her jewelry and washed off her makeup. Barefoot, she stepped back into the kitchen. "I saw on the calendar that you're going to Seattle?"

Andrew stirred the pale batter. Facing the stove, his back was to her. "Yeah."

"Northwest Tech?" Renee stood on the far side of the granite-topped island.

"Yeah. Coffee?"

"Yes, please."

He got down two mismatched cups and poured. He turned, hair tousled more than usual, handed her a cup. He had a little flour on his left cheek but she didn't say anything.

"You hate tech expos." The preheated oven dinged.

Andrew returned to stirring. "You remember the device? Barry Tichnor's dream project?"

"Of course."

Andrew measured butter on a plate, slid it into the microwave to soften it. "I modified the device, couple days ago."

She sipped the strong, black coffee. "I thought you were through with that thing."

"I designed a Mark II version on our mainframe. Same as the first, but I added a circuit board made by Hammerschmidt Systems."

"Colin's company?" Colin Hammerschmidt had been a classmate of theirs at Stanford.

"Yeah. The circuit board is called a Jabulani. I noted that it would improve the throughput of the device by twenty percent."

Renee sipped her coffee, hackles rising.

"Colin called this morning from Fresno. The high-and-mighty Halcyon/Detweiler Company contacted him, asked about buying the patent for the Jabulani circuit board."

Renee knew where the story was going but kept a straight face. "Can I help? With the Madeleines?"

"I could use some lemon zest."

She placed a box grater on a strip of paper towel and retrieved a lemon from the refrigerator. "This Jabu—"

"Jabulani."

"It doesn't exist, I assume."

"Very good, love. *Jabulani* is a kind of soccer ball. I warned Colin he might get the call and to stall them."

Renee and Andrew stood back-to-back, he at the stove, she at the island. She began gliding the lemon over the grater, careful to avoid her knuckles. "They're still inside our mainframe."

"You missed the point, Counselor. Barry didn't call and ask for a fictional circuit board. He asked to buy the patent for it. He's not just looking to make a prototype, he's looking to go into mass production."

She concentrated on grating, turning the lemon a few degrees, grating, turning it again. "What are you going to do?"

Andrew added a little more sugar to the slurry. "Burn Barry's house down."

"Andrew—"

"I'm going to cancel all contracts with Halcyon/Detweiler. I'm going to out them. The whole nasty story."

Renee braced herself with both hands on the granite, her knees almost buckling. They stood back-to-back, like some sort of Victorian dance set on Pause.

"Andrew. Don't."

"I took it to a vote of the engineers. It was three-to-two."

"You can't."

"I have. The zest?"

"Then my vote makes it three-to-three!"

The microwave sounded. Andrew retrieved the soft butter. He remained facing away from her. "You let them into the mainframe. On this topic, you no longer have a vote."

Barry Tichnor called a noon meeting of Halcyon/Detweiler's Infrastructure Subcommittee on Deferred Maintenance. "We have a ploughshare problem."

Barry's actual government affiliation was somewhat difficult to pin down. When he'd been brought on at Halcyon as a partner, it was understood that he had long served as an unofficial adviser to the CIA and NATO. But no specific agency laid claim to him. He was on no agency's payroll. He had served for a dozen years as a sort of ex-officio cabinet adviser to specific members of leadership in the Pentagon, and also as an off-staff adjunct to the NSA. He knew, thanks to the suite of surveillance equipment at Malatesta, Inc., that Andrew Malatesta referred to him as "that damn spook." Barry actually liked the nickname.

The Infrastructure Subcommittee on Deferred Maintenance had been given its name under the theory that no congressional investigator or crusading journalist would think twice about such an excruciatingly dull, corporate work group. The members included Barry, whose personal org chart was a bramble bush of dotted lines and deniable culpability, along with Liz Proctor, director of the Aircraft Division (with oversight of both jet fighters and gunships) and Admiral Gaelen Parks, retired, formerly of the Joint Chiefs of Staff and now director of Halcyon's Military Liaison Division. They met in an office in a building owned by Halcyon but leased out to the Department of the Interior, an office that was swept for passive and aggressive surveillance daily.

When Barry said they had a "ploughshare" problem, Gaelen Parks growled, "Malatesta."

Barry cleaned his glasses, nodded.

Liz Proctor, a willowy blonde in her fifties, said, "We all saw this coming. He's been the weak link from the start."

"Of course." Barry nodded, slid his glasses back on, and the lenses picked up glare from the overhead lights. "But his designs are revolutionary. We didn't have all that many choices, and the wife has been gung-ho from the start."

"Typical for an immigrant who makes it big," Liz said. "They tend to be überpatriots." She started to light up a cigarette, then remembered they were in a federal office. She turned to Barry. "The prototype?"

"Up and running. We really need to talk about field tests."

The admiral grimaced. He carried the same squat, square build that made him a tackle at Annapolis thirty years earlier. "We start testing the damn thing, we're going to get caught. I'm speaking for the Pentagon here. I'm saying, if we get caught, we get no cover from the military. They cannot be seen making the commander in chief a liar, just days after he signed the accord."

Coward, Barry thought and smiled. "Sure. Understood. Liz: any word on China?"

She crossed her knees and smoothed her linen skirt. Her linen looked crisp while Barry's no-ironing-needed polyester sport coat was badly creased. "My sources at the NSA say they're almost certainly testing a similar weapon. Pakistan, too," she said.

Gaelen Parks looked sour. "China gets it, it means North Korea gets it. Pakistan gets it, it ups the chances of al Qaeda getting its hands on it. Then we're in the shit storm."

Barry said, "Hence the field tests. We'll schedule a batch of them on the hush-hush. We'll—"

His phone vibrated and he pulled it out of the pocket of his ill-fitting suit. "Speak of the devil. Renee Malatesta just sent me a text. She wants to meet."

Liz said, "Is this good news or bad?"

Barry smiled behind his thick lenses. "I suppose we'll see."

"Washington Post. Dreyfus."

"Amelia Earhart's living in my mom's basement."

Just past noon on a Monday, Amy Dreyfus had a Sprite in one hand and a fuchsia stress ball in the other. She sat at her desk with her butt barely in her chair, legs up on her desk and crossed at the ankles. A business reporter for the *Washington Post,* she'd been scanning the wire services—AP, *New York Times, Los Angeles Times, Washington Post,* and Reuters—to see what was going on in the world.

She grinned. "Andrew? Hey. Loan me some money."

She heard him laugh. "How do I know you won't just blow it on food and shelter?"

She used a headset for her phone so she could talk and type two-handed. Or, in this case, squeeze a stress ball and sip a soda. At only five feet, she sat with an upturned box in front of her chair so that her feet didn't dangle. Her curly red hair constantly threatened to abandon whatever hairdo Amy attempted each morning. She sat up straight, feeling herself smile. "What's up?"

"Do you ever go to the Northwest Tech Expo?"

"Couple of times. Last year, in fact. It rained like . . . I don't know, Old Testament rain."

"I'm going this year."

"'Cause you invented the Next Big Thing? Again?"

"No. Because there will be a big audience. And media. Hey, ah, Amy? I need your advice."

She leaned forward. There was something odd in his voice. He sounded as if he were smiling, but Andrew *always* sounded as if he were smiling. Amy was his de facto big sister. They had lived with three other undergraduates for a couple of years at Stanford and Amy had introduced him to Renee, who frankly, everyone agreed, was way, way out of his league.

Where others would have heard just the smile, Amy caught tension. "The only time Mister I Got My First Patent in Junior High needed my advice, it involved girls. Are you and Renee okay?"

He laughed. "We're . . . not. But it's bigger than that. It's about the media. I need your help with a thing."

"Sounds serious."

"Life-and-death serious. I need to let the world know about this thing."

Amy said, "A press release?"

He chuckled. "A little bigger than that. Look, come to the expo on Thursday. Let me buy you a beer. I want to do something and do it right. And I want you to have first crack at it. Okay?"

She set down the soft drink and the squeeze ball. "Andrew, it's Ezra's birthday. I can't."

She waited.

"Sure," he said. "Hey, say hi for me. Look, I'll call you when I get to Seattle. I still need your advice."

"Sure, of course. But what is so important you—"

And he abruptly hung up.

The dayside city editor looked over from his adjacent desk. "Trouble?"

"Huh? Oh. No. I mean, maybe. It's my little brother acting all cryptic."

He said, "Since when did you have a little brother?"

"Since Stanford." She went back to scanning the wires, only now working the stress ball just a little harder.

A junior member of Halcyon/Detweiler's security division tagged the call from Andrew Malatesta's cell phone, downloaded the digital recording to a flash drive, and called out to the room, "Has anyone seen Mr. Tichnor?"

RESTON, VIRGINIA

Monday around 1:00 P.M., Renee asked Barry Tichnor to meet her in a D.C. bar just off K Street. Neither of them lived or worked nearby.

The place was dark and almost empty. They had plenty of privacy, sitting under photos of baseball teams from the 1920s and '30s.

She ordered Barbancourt rum and Barry ordered a Bud Lite. She turned her glass in small circles, never lifting it off the table. "Andrew knows you're still in the backup servers."

Barry sighed. "Our hackers assured me otherwise."

"He also wants out of the Pentagon contract, in toto. He's converted two of the Starting Five. They're going to the Northwest Tech Expo on Thursday, in Seattle."

Barry sipped his beer, light glinting on his oversized lenses.

Renee played with her glass, never lifting it.

"Andrew loves the coup de theatre. The big, grandiose display. He intends to out himself as a Pentagon subcontractor at the Tech Expo. And to denounce the Halcyon contract, the Bruges Accord, and . . . I don't know. Maybe more."

Barry thought, *Shit! Shit! Shit!* and let the opening of the bottle's neck touch his lips, not letting any beer enter his mouth. He nodded occasionally. He didn't push her. He waited for her to get there.

"Andrew is going to out the device. And you."

Barry set down his beer and patted his lips with the bar napkin. He spoke softly, overhead lights glistening off his wide, round glasses. "We have a . . . strong need for this to go the other way. We've made certain agreements with the Pentagon. China and Pakistan are testing similar weapons."

She said, "Pakistan is an ally," but her voice trembled, as if she were pleading.

"In that part of the world? The word has no meaning. Pakistan means the Taliban. Pakistan means al Qaeda. Al Qaeda with the device means dead Americans."

Renee leaned forward, her shoulders hunched, head down. Her wavy black hair obscured her face. She stayed like that for almost two minutes. Barry tipped his beer, not drinking, said nothing. He let it stew.

"He had a Trojan horse virus hidden in the device's specs. He's inside Halcyon's computer. He knows about you contacting Hammerschmidt Systems. That was a ruse, by the way. There is no Mark II version of the device. This isn't about him suspecting anything, anymore. It's about him having solid proof."

Barry Tichnor had fleeting thoughts about smashing his beer bottle into her skull again and again until she lost consciousness but, instead, he just nodded. "About thirty minutes ago, your husband called a journalist. He's asked her advice regarding going to the media."

She squinted, peered at him. "You're monitoring our phones?"

"Of course we're monitoring your phones. It's part of our security protocols. But then, you suspected as much. If he goes to the media, not only do we lose the race against China and Pakistan, but he could set back other highly secret weapons projects. Renee? At this stage, a threat to Halcyon/Detweiler is a threat to the Pentagon. A threat to America."

She wiped tears off both cheeks with the back of her hand, sat up ramrod straight.

"I grew up in Haiti." She whispered still, but fiercely.

Barry sat quietly.

"My father didn't make it past the fourth grade. He died of cholera when I was thirteen. I came to America and America took me in. Because of America, I have a law degree and a thriving company. I am a patriot, Barry!"

"Yes," he said. "I wouldn't have approached you if I hadn't known that."

She drained the rum in one shot. She stared into the glossy, reflective lenses that hid his eyes.

She stood up and snarled, sotto voce, "Fuck you to hell, Barry Tichnor. Fuck you and your company."

Barry took off those glasses, let her see his eyes. He stared directly into hers. When she neither flinched nor turned away, he nodded.

He said, "Okay then."

He slid the glasses back on.

7

EARLIER ON MONDAY, AN engineer at Halcyon/Detweiler had typed in the word *Jabulani,* which she assumed was a type of circuit board.

The word had another, hidden purpose. At 11:55 A.M. exactly, the Halcyon/Detweiler mainframe holding the Malatesta prototype information had spooled up. Perfect backup files were created for everything on the mainframe. The backup files then were chopped up into moderate-size chunks of data and distributed throughout the corporation's less-secure computer servers.

At just a little past noon, the Information Technology Department started getting calls about slow-downs on the mainframe. The engineers answering the calls said they'd look into it, but they already knew the answer.

At noon, close to a fourth of the Halcyon/Detweiler staff began logging on to Facebook, or ESPN, or YouTube, or Netflix, or Amazon, or eBay. Or porn. This happened almost every day at noon. Everyone in IT knew it. They ignored the calls, knowing their bandwidth would be restored by 12:30 or so.

Throughout the main headquarters building, silently, simultaneously, computers went online and the weapons documents slipped out of the building. All the information was routed to the personal computer of Andrew Malatesta.

. . .

Directly from the meeting with Barry, Renee went to the company head-quarters. She got there before two in the afternoon and went looking for Andrew. She found him in his lab, where he was studying the polygonal mesh model on his thirty-two-inch screen. It showed a 3-D illustration of one of his latest microelectronic circuits. He adjusted it on the X-axis, fifteen degrees, then typed in a minor modification. The CAD software instantly adjusted the circuit accordingly.

He wore earbuds for an MP3 player and Renee had to knock twice on the doorframe before he heard her. He smiled that luminous smile and yanked out the earpieces. "Hey. Sorry. Shostakovich."

He adjusted the microcircuit on its Y-axis. He picked up a well-chewed pencil and scratched a note on his sketch pad.

Renee's gold suit was impeccable and hung elegantly off her athletic frame. The off-center V in the skirt showed a triangle of taut, tanned skin on her left thigh. He liked her hair shoulder-length. "You look good."

"Thank you. Don't do this."

He ramped up the lopsided smile and brushed his hand through his unruly hair. "I've thought about it. A lot. I prayed. I think it's pretty much the only thing left to do."

"Andrew, if you want out of the contract with Halcyon, then we can get out. We will be left with . . . some significant debt, and that's if they don't sue us. But we can get out. Or at least renegotiate. You don't have to burn down the village."

He thought about that. "No. I think you're wrong. Tichnor's R-and-D people have downloaded enough of my specs, they can still probably build a prototype. And you know these people by now. No international treaty will stop them. Going into mass production means they won't just test the device, they'll sell it. To any country that has the cash and can get away with it secretly."

She hadn't realized she was making fists until her nails threatened to cut into her palms. "So you expose Barry Tichnor. You expose Halcyon/Detweiler, or at least Barry's division of it. You make your big theatrical display, in front of all the technical journalists in America. That's the big plan?"

"That is, as you say, the big plan."

"The Justice Department will come after you. They'll come after our company, based on RICO statutes."

"This isn't a racketeering deal. No way they—"

"So now you're our general counsel. Fine. Let's assume I know more about the law than you do. You do this, you will ruin this company. Antal. Terri, Christian. Vejay. They've been with you for fifteen years, you self-centered bastard!"

"And they got to vote. I have money set aside for them. I brought some of the Madeleines. Do you want—"

"Don't do this," she almost whispered. "Andrew. I'm serious. Destabilizing the nation's largest defense contractor isn't just catastrophically stupid. It's un-American!"

He laughed, picked up his saddlebag. "No, baby. Making a banned weapon and selling it for profit is un-American."

He closed his sketch pad, shut down the 3-D CAD software. He stood and kissed her on the forehead.

"Don't," she said. "Don't do this."

Andrew smiled.

It was five hours before Barry's cell phone chimed and Renee's name popped up on the screen. It was 7:00 P.M. Barry was watching Animal Planet. He put his DVR on Pause and picked up his work cell phone, which rested by his side between his beer and the remotes.

"Hello?"

He listened to the hiss on the telephone line. He knew who'd called, although his LED screen was blank. He had the house to himself. He waited, listened to the hiss. A juniper tree rustled outside the den window. The family's calico sauntered into the room, vaguely curious, wondering if the call might lead to a belly rub or food. Barry sat.

Renee Malatesta said, "Ah . . ."

Barry inhaled, held it.

"We should . . . turn this around," she whispered into the line.

Barry said, "Yes."

And Renee hung up.

Barry Tichnor set down his work cell and left his recliner. In slippers, he stepped out into his garage and dug around in the box of Christmas ornaments for the other cell phone he had stored there. He took it plus his beer and walked out into his backyard, far from the house. He dialed a ten-digit number he'd memorized.

An answering machine beeped.

"A-fourteen-dash-C," he said softly, then sipped his beer. "Day code: Orange. Meet me, usual place."

He hung up and returned to the house.

8

TWO DAYS TO GO

At dawn on Tuesday, Barry Tichnor met a man calling himself Calendar in a parking lot three blocks from Metro Center on Pennsylvania. It was close to vacant.

Calendar was a tall man, early fifties, with close-cropped silver hair, wide shoulders, and a military bearing: a sharp contract to Barry's egg-shaped body and ill-fitting clothes. Barry had used him a few times before and found his professionalism and perfectionism reassuring. Not to mention his quick wits in the field.

They did not sit, nor did they shake hands. Calendar scanned the horizon, turning to Barry before he spoke, his eyes the last thing to pivot Barry's way, as if direct, one-on-one eye contact was painful. He spoke softly. "I've selected a target. Nova Scotia, six days from now. The collateral will be five geologists, three Canadians, two Swedes. We didn't want to test the device on American citizens, naturally, so—"

Barry said, "There's a new target. It will take place in forty-eight hours."

Calendar absorbed this without showing any emotion. He scanned the horizon. "Where?"

"On American soil."

The big man raised his eyebrows. "Are you sure?"

"We are. You'll have only one shot at this. It pays triple the amount we agreed to."

The two men were silent for a time. Calendar, without emotion, said, "So, essentially, you think I'm a whore."

Barry blinked. "Sorry?"

"You think this is about the dollar amount. You think I act out of love of money."

"No, I—"

"The price I set for this mission covers my associates' time and my own. It covers transportation. It covers weapons and supplies. I am not a mercenary, Tichnor. I'm a professional. The price is the price."

"Okay," Barry said. "I'm sorry. I didn't—"

"The price . . . is . . . the price." Calendar's blue eyes never changed, never took on any emotion. But he pressed his point. "Don't forget that."

"I won't. I'm sorry. I didn't mean to suggest anything else."

Calendar studied him for a moment. "And the target?"

"A man. A man who plans to leak sensitive information on the very weapon you're beta-testing."

Calendar's pale blue eyes scanned the vicinity. "That would be bad."

"Yes."

A beat, and the big man said, "Done."

Barry Tichnor said, "Thank you," and turned to walk away.

He didn't mop his forehead until he was out of Calendar's sight.

On his way back to the office, Barry Tichnor made a call to one of his contacts at the CIA. They agreed to meet at Rock Creek Park.

Agent Jenna Scott was six feet tall and her hair was so blond that it appeared white from a distance. Today, she wore black jeans and riding boots and a suede, aviator-style tunic with epaulets and brass buttons. She was standing by the driver's door of her sedan and smiled at Barry as he crossed to her.

That woman would stand out in any crowd, Barry thought. *That's a handicap for a spy.*

"Barry," she said, smiling.

"Ms. Scott. I want to give you a heads-up."

They walked away from her car. Barry had brought a lidded coffee. Jenna didn't speak.

"We are using a freelancer to perform a function, on U.S. soil, that will result in the loss of lives."

She stared down at the shorter man. Barry pried off the lid and blew on the surface of his coffee.

"You're serious."

He nodded. "It will involve an airplane. A commercial jet. It flies on Thursday. I need you to use your magic."

She stared at him, then shoved her fingers in the back pockets of her jeans and squinted up into the sky.

"Does this involve the device?"

"Yes."

She pondered some more. "And our friend, the designer?"

"He has evidence to out Halcyon/Detweiler. And he claims to have evidence regarding the device. Actually, we suspect he's attempted to gain access to our R-and-D mainframe. I have come to believe that he may have evidence of other . . . extracurricular research."

Jenna Scott pinched the bridge of her nose. "Aaaah, Barry . . ."

"I know." He sipped coffee. "It's a pickle."

She turned on her low heels, squinting at the bald, pudgy man who never quite seemed to generate the correct emotional response.

"There will be a price."

He nodded.

"The Agency gets the device. Not the Pentagon."

Barry certainly had seen that one coming. "No problem."

"And you don't sell to any other country unless I give you a green light. That's *I,* as in *me, personally.*"

Barry nodded.

Agent Scott jutted out her lower lip and let out a puff of air. She held out her hand, palm up.

Barry Tichnor gave her the details of Andrew Malatesta's flight.

VIRGINIA

Calendar sat in a modest hotel room just off the 66 near Falls Church. The room was sterile and devoid of originality, but he'd swept it for bugs.

He'd bought a mint tea at a Starbucks earlier. Now he stripped to his boxers and ran through five hundred crunches and five hundred push-ups, the last fifty one-handed. Sweating but feeling loose, he sipped his cooled tea, sitting at the cheap-ass writing table and booting up his custom-built laptop. He used a sixteen-bit encryption code to get to his Web site. He'd put together a solid enough team for the device's beta test in Nova Scotia. He trusted the men. But staging a mission on American soil, in a little under forty-eight hours, would require a whole different level of teamwork. He'd need men he'd worked with before, the best of the best. Calendar contacted five top-of-the-line independent agents and queried them to see if they were free. One was former British SAS and expensive but quite good. One was an ex-Green Beret. One was ex-Mukhabarat—Syrian intelligence—who'd seen the light of capitalism and had put up his own shingle. One was a former SEAL. The fifth was an ex-Israeli spy currently working for the U.S. ATF in Mexico.

He left them all a coded message: *Looking to hire. Two days from now. U.S. soil. Collateral damage unfortunately guaranteed. Top dollar.*

He posted the message, then opened another window. He contacted the Nova Scotia team and told them they had a red light: the mission was off.

His cell phone vibrated. He unfolded it but didn't speak. The mechanical tones told him the antimonitoring software was powering up.

When the noise stopped, Barry Tichnor's badly distorted, mechanical voice said, "You've been sent a download."

Calendar turned back to his laptop. Sure enough, a pdf file appeared on the desktop.

"Confirmed."

"This is the site. It has to happen here."

"Understood."

He folded the phone, set it down, then double-clicked on the pdf file.

A map of Montana popped open.

Calendar sipped his room-temperature tea. Montana. Close to Coeur d'Alene, Idaho.

It would be an ideal time to visit home.

SOCORRO, TEXAS

Daria Gibron poured Fortaleza Tequila Blanco into a chipped coffee cup and took her BlackBerry out to the *balcón* of the hotel. She'd showered and slipped into a red sheath dress that tied behind her neck. She was barefoot and sat on the railing.

J. T. Laney, enjoying the cool breeze on the balcony, three rooms down, saw her. He sipped from a can of Coors and smiled. "Nice night," he called out.

Daria looked up from the BlackBerry. She raised her coffee cup in his direction, nodded. She was showing five inches of tanned thigh. She'd been pinged by a Web cloud frequented by mercenaries. She typed in the thirty-two-key password as J. T. moseyed her way. The breeze was soft, the bougainvillea fragrant. "Can't sleep?" he asked.

She shrugged, eyes on her screen. "Not after a job. *Keyed up,* you Americans say?"

J. T. sipped his beer. "Yeah. Me, too. " She was looking down, so he took the opportunity to study her breasts. They were worth studying. "Things went good this week. We got the War Dog where we want him."

It was bullshit, obviously. The entire mission was blown and all they had to show were three high-level soldiers and a cadaver. But Daria kept her opinion to herself and her eyes on the smart phone.

Two days, she noted. *Collateral damage.* She recognized the coded ID as the man she'd run into twice before. The last time in Helsinki. She'd been Shin Bet at the time. He'd been U.S. Military Intelligence. Genus and family unknown, but allies nonetheless, and the Powers That Be in Tel Aviv and Washington had needed an arms merchant dead. The man had seven bodyguards. Getting to the arms dealer meant going through his men. No other way to play it.

The American worked under the name Calendar. Daria was not tempted to take his offer today. He was decidedly good but a bit mental. She saw it in his lack of emotions in the heat of battle. And when taking a life.

J. T. had walked over and now stood next to her. He ran the backs of two fingers along her bare, muscled shoulder. "One surefire way to blow off steam . . ." He smiled.

"Agent Laney?" She began erasing the message.

"It's J. T., darlin'."

She reached for the coffee cup she'd set on the railing, took a sip. She smiled up at him. "Remove your hand."

He rolled his eyes. "Moon-filled night. You, me, hours to kill. *Keyed up.* We could make this memorable."

He grinned.

Daria did, too.

"Remove your hand," she said. "Or I will. And when I say *remove . . .*"

9

Susan Tanaka slid her Prada sunglasses up into her straight, black hair and stared at the *Michelin Motoring Atlas*. She pursed her lips. "It doesn't look like two hours."

Her husband, Kirk Tanaka, stood on the other side of the rented Nissan SUV. "MapQuest says Varenna is a two-hour drive."

Susan studied her map. "I can get us there in an hour. Hour-fifteen." She turned to him. "Can you handle that?"

"Standing on my head," he said and winked.

She wasn't fooled.

Kirk Tanaka hadn't sat still for ninety minutes straight since he'd undergone low-back surgery to repair a ruptured disc. It was the kind of injury, and the kind of surgery, that could have ended his career as a lead pilot for United. But the surgeons told him there was a high likelihood of a full recovery. Given time.

Meanwhile, Kirk couldn't sit for ninety minutes. He couldn't stand for ninety minutes. He couldn't lie down for ninety minutes without the help of codeine. He was in more or less constant pain.

The trip had been Susan's idea and she'd mapped it out with her usual methodical eye for detail. Train from Virginia to Miami, so Kirk could stand and sit at intervals. A cruise-line ship from Miami to Rome, where, blessedly, Kirk could walk. Walking didn't hurt.

They left the cruise ship in Lido di Ostia and took trains north and west to Milan. The next hop would be in a car. This part couldn't be helped.

"I'm good," he said, popping a Vicodin with a slug of bottled water. Susan still looked worried.

Kirk winced and lowered himself into the passenger seat of the SUV, glancing at the piles of luggage in the rear. A very, very small proportion of it was his. He said, "Get in, woman! And have my dinner on the table by six!"

Susan laughed and tossed her leather Louis Vuitton satchel into the pile of bags. "Bite me, flyboy. Hour-fifteen, tops."

10

THE DAY

Tommy Tomzak opened his cup and blew on the surface. As he did, a curved hank of black hair fell across his left eyebrow. Kiki Duvall brushed it back.

"It's a Claremont VLE, twin turboprop." Kiki checked her watch. It was a bit past 5:00 P.M. on Thursday. "Seats sixty-five with four crew. State-of-the-art avionics courtesy of Leveque Aéronautique, Limited, out of Quebec. Twin Bembenek engines. Came off the line fifteen months ago and is due for a checkup in five cycles."

They heard an appreciative, two-tone whistle from a man in the familiar brown-and-gold uniform of Polestar Airlines. "Even I didn't know all that, and I'm the copilot. You an aircraft lover, ma'am?"

"Something like that."

"Pilot's flirting with you," Tommy said for her ears only.

"That's because I'm so hot."

ANNAPOLIS

Renee Malatesta had every intention of going into the office that afternoon, after announcing via e-mail that she would be working from home in the morning. She did a half hour on the elliptical, showered, and had a banana and a yogurt. Her left knee—she'd twisted it badly playing tennis a year earlier—was acting up so she palmed three ibuprofen tablets. She eyed them for several moments, then cupped them back into the amber bottle. She dug under the bathroom sink and found the Vicodin she'd been given after the fall on the tennis court. She dry swallowed one, donned her Armani armor and low sling-backs.

She had a five o'clock meeting with two of the company's engineers.

Renee sat in her Prius for twenty minutes, adjusting mirrors, fiddling with the satellite radio, checking and rechecking her wavy, neck-length hair. She tapped a strange little tattoo on the steering wheel with her fingernail. She checked e-mail on her iPhone.

She climbed out of the car and paced in the living room. She went to the bathroom cabinet, found the vial of Prozac, which she used sparingly. She took two, drinking a full tumbler of water, refilling it and draining it again. She tried to pee.

She shot an e-mail to two of the engineers, Antal Borsa and Terri Loew, to tell them she was caught up in a conference call and would have to reschedule their meeting.

She poured a fingerful of fifteen-year-old El Dorado rum from Guyana and downed it in a gulp.

VIRGINIA

Barry Tichnor used a secure phone. "Any communication?"

The surveillance unit parked a half block from the Malatesta home was using parabolic mics as well as the surveillance suite inside the house. "No, sir. She hasn't called his number. And if she does, we're preset to block the call."

REAGAN NATIONAL

Andrew Malatesta couldn't help but notice the tall, languid redhead with the freckles across her nose, curled up in one of the thermoformed chairs in the terminal. She was casual in a sweater, jeans. and canvas mocs, but you could still tell she had a killer body.

She was spoken for, too: the guy with the cowboy boots and black hair going salt-and-pepper around his ears, sitting to her left, shoulder-to-shoulder, smiling.

The redhead and the guy in cowboy boots looked like they were in love. Andrew, an unrepentant romantic, liked that. The guy in the scuffed boots said something and the redhead belted out a most unladylike laugh.

When was the last time he and Renee had been together, laughing? Andrew couldn't remember. It had been . . . some time. He missed her. He missed the notion of *us*.

Andrew reached into his ever-present saddlebag-shaped pack and pulled out a leather portfolio. It contained a legal pad with the speech he was still spiffing up—a speech he was going to deliver tomorrow at the Northwest Tech Expo in Seattle.

He sat with two of the Starting Five: Vejay Mehta to his right, doing Sudoku, Christian Dean across from him, devouring an enormous sweet roll and flipping through the *Annals of Biomedical Engineering* the way other travelers were flipping through *Us Weekly*.

Andrew had told these guys—with whom he had toiled for a decade and a half—that he didn't want to make weapons. Christian had sighed with relief. "Dude. Me, either." Vejay, ever the pragmatist, mentally watched his profit sharing drop, but shrugged and said, "It's your call."

The other two chief engineers—Terri Loew and Antal Borsa—had been angry. They had embraced Renee's idea of turning the company into a Pentagon subcontractor. In the end, they, too, acknowledged that Malatesta, Inc., was merely an extension of Andrew Malatesta's genius. As he went, so went the company.

And in about thirty hours, the rest of the microelectronics world would find out at the Northwest's largest high-tech trade show.

Upon landing, Andrew planned to call his college roommate and old friend, Amy Dreyfus, and get her take on how best to burn Barry Tichnor and Halcyon/Detweiler for screwing, illegally, with his weapons designs.

LANGLEY, VIRGINIA

Barry used his swipe card and an eight-digit alphanumeric code to enter the computer room buried deep within CIA headquarters. That he even owned such a swipe card would give heartburn to most of the Agency brass.

The room was empty save for a bank of computers, a communications array, and Agent Jenna Scott.

The tall blonde removed her narrow, red-framed reading glasses, looked up from the piles of official reports she had been scanning. Barry noted the pencil marks in the margins. She wore a padded headset, but removed it when she saw him.

"Hi. Thanks for coming over."

He pulled up a chair, adjusted his limp, brown necktie. "Do we have the plane?"

The agent nodded. "I handled the hacking myself. I've owned the booking computer for a couple of days. Anyone buying a ticket before that, I can't control. I did manage to alert TSA about a possible drug-runner on board. It means all of the luggage will be removed, checked, and reloaded. If I've calculated right, some of the passengers will opt to take another, quicker flight to Seattle. I can't keep everyone off, but I should reduce the body count quite a bit." She shrugged.

"Very good. Thank you. You wanted to tell me something, but before you do, I need to make sure you are fully aware of the situation."

Jenna had been cheating, sitting forty-five degrees away from him. But she swiveled her chair fully now and nodded.

"Some Americans are going to die."

She nodded again. "We understand that."

"If we thought there was any other way to stop this self-centered bastard, we would have."

"Of course. Still, this does give you your beta test."

"Exactly. Thank you. I knew you'd understand." Barry cleaned his thick lenses. "Now, what's on your mind?"

Jenna smiled. "I'm running Calendar."

Barry stared owlishly at her, glasses frozen in the wide end of the tie that he'd wrapped around the lens. *Calendar? How does she even know his name?*

She kept smiling but her forehead knotted, just a touch. She was one of those beautiful women whose age is difficult to guess. In her thirties or forties, he thought.

"Barry? I've been running Calendar since before you met him. When you had him sabotage the McDonnell Douglas drone tests? I green-lit that. Two years ago, when it was necessary to have Senator McMenwick's wife killed? We made the sign of the cross."

Barry stared at her. His eyes, usually hidden, bulged normally. Jenna

Scott touched his knee with one manicured fingernail. "You didn't know we knew about those incidents. Of course we do. Frankly, there aren't that many men who do this sort of freelance work."

With the door closed and security activated, Barry thought it would be easy enough to grab one of the headset cords in the room and whip it around her throat. He could crush her windpipe before she could even struggle.

Jenna smiled a languid smile and leaned forward, now resting her hand on Barry's knee. "This is not now, nor will it ever be, an Agency mission. You understand that. If things go south—"

He opened his mouth and she squeezed his knee, just a little.

"Shh. Barry? If things go south, you are not going to be able to blame the Agency. You'll find that the communication protocols you have with Calendar have been terminated. If you communicate with him, at all, it will be through me. That's the way it works. Do you understand me?"

Now, Barry thought. *The windpipe is so easily crushed.*

"Well, of course," he told Jenna Scott, and smiled.

REAGAN NATIONAL

The pilot turned to the eight-year-old boy. "Okay, that means you have to fly the plane."

"Nuh-uh!" the kid reeled back.

"Just having a catch, boss." The copilot grinned, then turned to the boy's parents. "But your son can come look at the flight deck before we take off, if that's all right with you."

The copilot spoke louder. "Folks, if we could get you to stand on line and punch your tickets, we'll get everybody on board. No need to wait for your row to be called. We've got a light load today. Sorry about the delay."

There had been something about the luggage. TSA had allowed the ground crews to load the bags, then had unloaded them and let drug-sniffing dogs do their thing. Eventually it had ended and the baggage was reloaded. The Polestar crew never did find out what that was all about. A United flight to Seattle departed first, and about a dozen passengers opted to take that flight instead, as the others cooled their heels in the terminal, the NTSB crashers among them.

. . .

Flight attendants Andi Garner and Jolene Solomon studied the computer screen behind the counter as the last of the Flight 78 passengers trudged down the gangway toward the fore entry point.

"When was the last time you saw a half-empty plane?" Andi asked.

"Pre-nine/eleven," Jolene replied. "Pre-Travelocity and the other sites. This is weird."

As Andrew and his engineers stood to board the plane, he remembered to turn off his cell phone.

"This'll be an interesting expo," Christian said.

Andrew and Vejay nodded.

11

THE FLIGHT FROM REAGAN National to Sea-Tac takes eight hours, less if there's a tailwind.

It was going on ten o'clock mountain time as Pilot-in-Charge Miguel Cervantes stepped out of the flight deck and into the head. Flight Attendant Andi Garner was making a new batch of coffee as he stepped out and flirted with her. She flirted right back. They'd flown together many times over the years and shared an easy camaraderie.

She watched him rap on the flight-deck door with the knuckle of his middle finger: *tap, tap . . . tap.*

They were forty-three minutes out of Helena.

Sitting in an aisle seat on Polestar Flight 78, Tommy was using his new e-reader to study his notes for the Tech Expo lecture. He glanced to his left. Kiki slept in the window seat, wearing the earbuds of her iPod. She'd kicked off her Top-Siders and stretched her long legs and bare feet under Tommy's legs.

Isaiah Grey slept across both seats on the starboard side, back against a window, knees up, feet on the aisle seat. He'd fallen asleep. That wouldn't last long: attendants had just started making their way down the aisle, waking people up and urging them to push their seat backs to their up-right position.

Tommy checked his watch: 11:15 P.M. mountain.

The Malatesta team sat together, Andrew and Christian on the port side, Vejay to the starboard. By tradition, they played Trivial Pursuit us-ing the question cards only, not game pieces or the board. Nobody kept score.

Vejay Mehta said, "Ah, science . . . Okay, this is the hardest material in the human b—"

Andrew said, "Enamel."

"Right." Vejay looked up from the card. "Hey, check it out."

He'd noticed that one of the flight attendants was keeping an eye on them. This happened all the time when they flew: Vejay was Indian but could pass for Pakistani. Andrew was Sicilian but often mistaken for Middle Eastern. It was annoying, but, since September 2001, they had gotten used to people staring at them on airplanes.

Christian said, "So. We're really going to do this?"

Andrew said, "We are really gonna to do this."

Christian said, "At the expo?"

Andrew smiled at the gangly engineer. "In for a penny . . . We're giving up the Pentagon contract and we're outing Tichnor and Halcyon for swip-ing the prototypes to a banned weapon. I've got all the evidence proving they did it."

Christian Dean shook his head. "Renee is not going to be happy."

Andrew kept smiling but something in his voice changed. "That's my problem."

On the ground, Calendar found a spot to park his stolen SUV on the pe-riphery of a state park. He checked his position using the Global Positioning System application in his laptop.

He reconsidered, turned over the engine, and drove another three hun-dred yards south. He checked the GPS again.

Better.

He climbed out and opened the top-hinged rear door of the sturdy vehicle. Inside were two metal boxes. Calendar pulled one of them nearer to him and popped both of its clasps. The box opened at the top. Calendar whistled a tuneless ditty and began assembling metal pieces.

He pulled forth the second box, unclasped it.

He took the opportunity to marvel at the content.

In less than thirty minutes, he began to hear the drone of an airplane.

Miguel Cervantes adjusted the voice wand, keeping it clear of his mustache. He toggled the internal PA system. "Ah, flight attendants, cross-check and prepare for landing, please."

To Holley he said, "Extend the slats."

"Slats are good."

"Okay. Slowing down a bit. Flaps eleven, please."

"You got flaps at eleven, boss."

Cervantes smiled at that *boss*.

"Altimeter."

"Checked."

"Speed brakes."

"Armed green," Holley chanted back. "Good to—"

Thump.

Jed Holley said, "What in hell . . . ?"

Both turboprop engines died, simultaneously. Every light on every monitor on the flight deck shut off as well. The sound of air whooshing around the airframe grew loud.

Miguel Cervantes said, "Hey, hey, hey. What's this . . . C'mon!"

Cervantes began walking through the emergency ignition system.

Nothing happened. He did it again.

Holley said, "Jesus . . ."

Tommy brought his head up sharply. He'd heard something go *thump*. He turned back to the notes on the e-reader, just as the device died.

Zip. Nada. Totally blank screen.

Tommy whacked it. "Piece a shit . . ." he whispered.

And only then did it dawn on him: the engines had died, too.

. . .

Both flight attendants dashed for the flight deck. Tommy glanced out the window. Trees were close. Very close.

"Fuck!" He grabbed Kiki by the shoulders, pulled her forward and down, and climbed on top of her, shouting, *"Isaiah! Get down get down get down!"*

Isaiah Grey snapped awake when his sleeping brain realized the seats beneath him were no longer vibrating. He craned his neck, swept away his reading glasses, and looked out at the slowing propellers. He took in the lack of lighting in the cabin.

He saw Tommy piling onto Kiki, pushing her down between their row and the seat backs ahead of them: rows 10 and 11.

One of the flight attendants rushed down the aisle but lost her footing. Isaiah reacted quickly, grabbing her and rolling to the floor, he on the bottom, covering her head with his arms.

The three designers from Malatesta, Inc., stopped playing Trivial Pursuit.

Antal said, "What . . . just happened?"

Andrew Malatesta's eyes grew large as the midsize aircraft grew quiet. "Jesus. Oh, Jesus," he whispered.

Christian gasped. He had reached the same conclusion as Andrew. "Is . . . is this your . . . it can't be!"

Andrew was ripping at his seat belt. "Fucking . . . motherfuckers . . ." He shot up, clawed at the overhead bin, hauled down his saddlebag.

Vejay rose, too.

A flight attendant shouted, "Sir! Sit down! Now!"

Andrew grabbed Vejay's locking, titanium attaché case and sprinted for the back of the plane. In a crash, that's statistically the safest place to be.

At least, he thought he'd read that somewhere.

His two senior engineers sat and gaped.

Calendar broke down the launch tube into its component parts and slid each into the proper slot carved into the black foam rubber that filled the carrying case. He closed the lid, slid the case back into the rear of the Dodge Durango he'd stolen, slammed down the hatch.

Another man might have brought a team for this kind of job but Calendar disliked teams. A solo operation greatly simplifies the questions: Whom can I trust? Who will carry his own weight?

Not that he was working alone. Someone in Tichnor's shop had taken care of the Polestar Airlines booking computers, reducing the collateral damage as much as possible. He had brought on two good soldiers, working under the names Cates and Dyson. He'd worked with them before and trusted them with his life. More important, with his country. They had their tasks cut out for them, later. But for this—for the wet work— Calendar preferred solitude.

He climbed in, hit the ignition, and watched the Claremont VLE glide silently toward a copse of lodgepole pines, Douglas firs, and spruce, a mile in the distance.

At less than one hundred feet over Calendar's head, Jed Holley shouted into the dead radio, "Mayday! Mayday! Mayday! Polestar Seven-Eight declaring an emergency! Repeat: emergency!"

Miguel Cervantes tried the ignition sequence six times. It obviously wasn't going to work. He switched to hauling on the yoke for all he was worth, fighting desperately to keep the nose of his powerless aircraft up.

Kiki, head to the floor, saw a man's legs flash by, sprinting toward the empennage. With her ear to the industrial carpet, she was the first to hear the *snap! snap! snap!* as treetops hit the underside of the airliner.

The Claremont VLE sliced through the fir and pine trees, the tallest trees ripping savagely at the once-powerful Bembenek engines that hung beneath the eighty-five-foot wingspan of the plane. Both Cervantes and Holley struggled with their yokes in the bizarrely quiet flight deck.

Through gritted teeth, Miguel Cervantes said, "Jed?"

Jed Holley said, "I know, man," as a towering Douglas fir caught the port wing and tore it loose from the airframe.

As the port wing sheared free, the Claremont yawed madly, the starboard wing dipping, hitting more trees, thicker branches. A massive pine caught the starboard turboprop, breaking the downward-facing propeller like a toothpick, before ripping away the entire wing.

The Claremont rolled over, starboard windows facing the ground. The great ship slid lower into the trees, momentum tanking, ablating bits of aluminum and glass and losing altitude but still not nosing over.

A lone lodgepole pine shattered the flight-deck windshield, tearing the copilot's chair out of its floor restraints, sending it and Jed Holley into the back of the flight deck.

Most of the screaming passengers in the left-hand seats dangled to their right, hanging by their seat belts. Passengers in the right-hand seats pressed against the wall of the fuselage. Some sobbed. Some prayed. Others swore. Overhead bins opened, coats and laptops rained on passengers' heads. The three crash investigators, wedged near the floor, stayed in place.

Andrew braced himself, literally standing on the downward-facing wall of the jet, and managed to wedge the attaché case under one of the locked-down food trolleys before losing his balance and slamming against the starboard-side wall, his head banging hard against the airframe.

Still reeling over on its right side, Polestar Flight 78 hit the ground almost horizontally and slid, screaming, another hundred yards, snapping trees and sloughing off bits of both aircraft and passengers.

Doubled over, face and knees to the floor, wedged between rows 10 and 11, Kiki feared her ribs would cave in under Tommy's weight. Part of the seat undercarriage dug viciously into her thigh.

She suddenly smelled fresh air and pine trees. She got a face full of dirt, bitter and foul. She had it in her mouth, up her nose. She coughed, relieved not to have Tommy's weight crushing her anymore—suddenly realizing he wasn't there. Still wedged between the seats, Kiki screamed, *"Tommy! Tommmmmmeeeeeee!"*

BOOK TWO

THE CRASHERS

12

JUSTIN OAKES, A MEMBER of the Montana National Guard just back from a tour in Afghanistan, was first out of his tent, wearing boxers and a Crimson Tide T-shirt. He'd grabbed his hunting rifle by instinct. "What was that!"

His two buddies, with whom he'd played high school and college football, came barreling out of their tents, both men grabbing their rifles.

A geyser of smoke and debris, lit by the full moon, rose out of the forest less than two miles away and about one hundred feet lower than their bivouac.

"Jesus," Pete said. "I think an airplane just hit!"

Calendar left the Durango a good hundred feet from the crash site, parked on an outcropping of rock. He ran with deft balance through the forest, dodging trees like tackles, comfortable moving at full clip through a forest at night. The full moon and cloudless sky played to his favor.

Steam hissed from vents. Fire crackled nearby. He could hear the *tec tec tec* of expanding metal.

Thirty feet from the on-its-side fuselage, he found a piece of sheared-off steel, the size and length of his forearm. Perfect. He picked it up.

He heard someone crying. A man sat up against a tree, blood flowing from his nose. His right leg was bent at the knee in an impossible angle.

Calendar knelt. "Sir. Are you okay?"

The crying man turned, dazed. "What . . . I . . ."

"Sir." Calendar laid a hand on the man's shoulder. "What happened here? What happened to the aircraft?"

"I . . . I don't know. I don't know. I was asleep. . . ."

Calendar patted the man's shoulder. "Don't worry. We'll get you some help. Stay calm."

He stood and stalked closer to the fuselage. He found a young man, maybe nineteen, maybe twenty, on his back, struggling to rise. The guy was still belted into the bottom part of his seat, which clung to his ass. The rest of the seat was nowhere to be seen.

"Are you all right?"

The kid said, "Jesus, do I look all right?" He spat out a tooth, hands clawing at the belt. "The goddamn plane crashed!"

"What happened to it?"

"I don't know, man." He finally got the belt unhooked, savagely shoved the seat away from him. Calendar helped him rise to his feet. "The engines just fucking died! All the lights. My iPod, just boom: like flipping a switch!"

His answer was disappointing. Calendar glanced around, saw no on-lookers. Lightning fast, he smacked his steel rod against the kid's windpipe, swinging it like a baton. The blow knocked the kid off his feet, hands on his throat, eyes bulging.

It would take him a minute or two to die. The autopsy would show that something from the aircraft had hit the kid at a high rate of speed.

Should have stuck with "I don't know, man," Calendar thought and moved on.

Miguel Cervantes hung limply to his right, body constrained by his harness. He grunted, eyes snapping open, the pain in his side bringing him fully awake.

His right arm hung toward the ground, a scary amount of blood drooling out of his brown-and-gold jacket, pooling in his palm, then dripping down to the combination of starboard wall and forest floor below him. Landing right where Jed Holley's seat should have been. Miguel tried to close his palm into a fist. His fingers disobeyed.

Bleeder, he thought. *Deal with that first. Get that, then get to the passengers.*

A grunt sounded behind him. He heard thrashing. He froze.

Jed!

"Hey. Hang in there," he gasped, ripping at his harness buckle with his good, left hand. "Jed? Hang on, man. I'm . . . I've gotcha."

Miguel's words were slurred, almost unintelligible to his own ears. Concussion or blood loss? Hard to say.

The harness buckle gave way. Miguel winced when he tried to move. The harness had broken his clavicle. His left leg hurt, too, but not badly. The pain actually helped sweep away some of the cobwebs in his brain. He rolled to his right, his weight tipping over the starboard armrest. He fell like a sack of cement, past the central control panel, past the place where Jed Holley's seat should have been. He landed with no grace, the wind knocked out of him. He saw stars, blue and red lights at the periphery of his vision.

But he heard the grunting again. "J-Jed," he croaked, and forced himself up on his knees, left hand down for support. His right arm hung useless. "It's okay . . . I got you . . . all right . . ."

Miguel crawled on his knees and one good hand toward the back of the flight deck. He'd thought Jed Holley was dead for sure. But if he survived, what a miracle. If Miguel could get to him—

He pulled himself with his left arm around the captain's chair and came face-to-face with a deer, lying on its side in the ruined deck, its torso caved in, legs flailing, eyes mad.

The deer stared at him until it died.

Kiki levered herself out of the space between rows 10 and 11. The plane rested on its side, she realized, the interior dark and filled with floating particulate, obscuring her vision. Steam hissed in the darkness. The entire fuselage groaned and vibrated. Moonlight beamed in from the left-hand windows, displaying the madcap Brownian dance of the dust particulate. Struggling not to fall, she rested her bare feet against the right armrest of Tommy's seat.

Peering down, she discovered seats 11C and 11D were missing. She bent low, peered toward the tail section. Rows 12, 13, and 14 were missing, too.

Isaiah Grey had been sleeping across seats 11C and D.

. . .

"What happened to the plane?"

The elderly woman in the hand-knit blue sweater blinked up at Calendar. *"Ya niz niyou,"* she said.

Calendar spoke Russian. She didn't know. Good. He rose, moving on.

Kiki lowered herself to the fuselage floor, which was actually a wall. And partly it was dirt. She stood on curved plastic-on-metal but also on earth and pine needles, littered with in-flight magazines and blood. She heard moaning in the dusty dark, heard the snap of electrical cables arcing. Smelled the electricity in the air.

She did a quick inventory of herself: left thigh bleeding under a three-corner tear in her jeans. Raising her arms hurt like hell and inhaling was no fun. At least one broken rib on her left. Nothing life-threatening.

She heard a cough near her feet. She inched forward toward the empennage. A hand grasped her ankle.

She knelt. "Tommy!"

He lay on his back. She touched his face, her fingers coming away tacky.

He coughed. "The . . . fuck are the odds . . ." he slurred. "Seriously! What are the . . . fucking odds that . . . *we'd* be in a crash?"

She peered through the dust and darkness, suddenly remembering that Tommy always carried a penlight in his khakis. She dug through his pockets, found the little light. She clicked it. Nothing happened. She tossed it aside.

Tommy squinted. His hair was matted with blood on the right side of his skull. She checked the rest of him, found no obvious wounds. No *obvious* ones.

It was too dark to check the dilation of his eyes, but given the head wound, she made an assumption.

"Sweetie? You're concussed."

"Yeah," he muttered, struggling to rise. "Probably . . . caused . . . by the concussion."

"Shh. No, baby. Lie here. Rest."

But he pushed himself to a seated position, leaned over, and puked up the coffee he'd drunk at the airport. "C-can't . . . skipper didn't . . . he didn't have time to dump his fuel. We gotta . . . get folks the fuck outta Dodge."

Kiki helped him to his feet and he staggered like a drunk. She had a degree in electrical engineering; she knew nothing about treating concussions, about how smart or stupid it would be to walk around. But she also smelled the sulfur from the arcing electrical circuits. Tommy was right.

She'd been asleep, so her eyes were already adjusted to the dark. She realized there were gaps in the fuselage easily large enough for them to duck through. "C'mon, baby. Let's get you out of here."

HELENA REGIONAL

The swing-shift supervisor for air traffic control called the Lewis and Clark County Sheriff's office. "Hey, it looks like we lost an airliner, five minutes ago. Possibly somewhere in or near Helena State Forest."

The voice over the line said, "No way! Okay, we're airborne tonight. We'll get the chopper heading over that way right now!"

The supervisor hung up, searched the wall for the red acrylic clipboard and a telephone number, and called the National Transportation Safety Board emergency number in Washington, D.C.

13

PAUL MCKINNEY'S CELL PHONE rang at 12:02 A.M. Friday. He was up anyway, hunting for an antacid and angry at himself because that bowl of chili at 9:00 P.M. had been a dumb idea and he'd known it at the time.

"McKinney here."

The voice on the other end said, "Chief? State police. Helena Regional reports they may have an airliner down in the state forest, not two miles from Twin Pines. Figured you'd want to know."

"No kidding! Are you guys airborne tonight?"

"Sure are. Chopper's outbound, heading your direction."

The police chief of Twin Pines, Montana, brushed back the curtains in his kitchen and saw the running lights of the state police helicopter heading straight over his little town.

"Thanks for the call. I'll get on up there, see if I can help."

ARLINGTON, VIRGINIA

Her BlackBerry chimed to life. Beth Mancini jerked awake. She sat curled on the love seat, realizing she'd fallen asleep halfway through *All About Eve*. Dammit—that was two nights in a row! She contemplated holding it for a third try but—given that her special work phone was buzzing at her—decided just to send it back to Netflix. Chances were, she'd be on a flight within two hours.

She connected the line, knowing it could only be her assistant. "Hey, Rick."

"Beth? We've got reports of a Claremont down over central Montana. It went down after eleven P.M. their time."

"Okay," she said, reaching for the remote and shutting down the TV. "Meet you in the office."

Her heart raced. This would be her first major crash as intergovernmental liaison.

MONTANA

A mile from the fuselage, one of the dismembered engines hissed. Electricity arced between two wires, and a pool of kerosene—airplane fuel—ignited. In less than forty seconds, the engine, its propellers, and the intact section of the wing were on fire.

Being August, the underbrush in the vicinity caught fire, too.

The blaze began feeding itself with a long line of jet fuel that stretched about half a mile to the second engine. And from there to the fuselage.

Kiki half carried Tommy out through a great gouge in the ceiling of the fuselage, about halfway back. Outside, in the forest, she gasped: a trail of downed trees and debris stretched as far as the eye could see.

She found a freshly created stump and helped Tommy sit. "Okay, I'm going to go find survivors."

"Hey," he gasped, the blood on his scalp glinting in the moonlight. "Love you."

"I love you, too."

She limped back into the fuselage, stepping gingerly on the balls of her bare feet, knowing that shattered glass and shards of aluminum would be everywhere.

Tommy sat, dizzy, gasping, nauseated. He heard someone moan to his left. He staggered to his feet, stumbled a half-dozen steps, came to a girl, a teenager, lying on her stomach. Tommy dropped to his knees. He felt her pulse. "Ah shit," he muttered, seeing that her left sleeve was black with blood.

He ripped her T-shirt, revealed a sweet bleeder just below her shoulder. The brachial vein.

Tommy shrugged out of his sport jacket, used the sleeve to tie a pressure bandage around the girl's arm. She spit leaves out of her mouth. "Am I dead?"

"Nope," Tommy said. "Course, your doctor's got a concussion, so . . .'"

A man crouched by Tommy's side, laid a hand on his shoulder. "Hey. What happened to the plane?"

Tommy blinked blearily. The guy was a little out of focus. He had silver hair. He held a piece of broken steel.

Tommy's mouth was too dry to swallow. "The hell should I know. Hey, put that shit down, man. No souvenirs. This is a crash scene."

As he spoke, Tommy turned the girl over. Beyond the bleeding right arm, she appeared to be okay. The silver-haired man knelt, brushed blond hair from her eyes. "Do you know what happened to the plane?"

She shook her head. "W-where are we?"

"Okay," the stranger said, and smiled with confidence at Tommy. "Stay with her."

"Sure," he slurred, as the man stood and strode off.

Kiki found the body of the boy who'd been playing Nerf football with the copilot at Reagan. He had a large gash in his abdomen. Kiki stared at him, then turned and bent at the waist and threw up, holding her hair back. Her eyes teared up. He had died quickly, she noted. That was probably a blessing.

She heard sobbing. A largish woman in her sixties hung sideways from one of the portside seats. The woman wore pink velour sweats with MAL-IBU across her bosom in cursive. Kiki helped her unbuckle her seat belt and supported her as she climbed down. The woman's eyes bulged as she stepped down out of her seat. She was sobbing, hysterical. "My leg! Oh my god, my leg!"

Kiki—who rowed in San Francisco Bay and played beach volleyball—put the woman's arm over her shoulder, her own arm behind her. "Not a problem. Lean on me."

Once they were out of the airliner and twenty feet clear, Kiki helped the woman sit. They both peeled back the cuff of her sweat bottoms to find a fragment of white anklebone protruding from the skin. The woman took one look at the bone fragment and her eyes rolled up in her head. She passed out.

. . .

Kiki returned to the fuselage, stepping gingerly to avoid glass, and found another survivor in seat 7C. It was the first survivor she'd found in any of the left-hand seats. It was a man, unconscious. He was small, maybe five-two, and appeared Middle Eastern, wearing a tweed suit, a black tie, and a white shirt. He looked professorial, she thought, peering at him through the dusty dark.

A bright light engulfed the unconscious man. Kiki turned. A man stood behind her with a Maglite, holding it up near his left shoulder. "Hey, are you okay?" he asked. He wore dark clothing and good hiking boots, his hair silver and cut very short.

"Yeah. Help me get him up." She bent over, unbuckled the man.

With the seats cocked at a ninety-degree angle, it was tough to do. The stranger helped lift the man up, took him by his shoulders as Kiki took his knees. As the stranger began walking backward toward the hole in the fuselage, he said, "So what happened to the plane?"

She had forgotten to ask Tommy. "No idea. I was asleep."

Tommy knelt over the surprisingly calm teenager, his fists in the soil, fighting the urge to puke again. His vision blurred and his arms shook.

"You okay?" the girl lying on her back asked.

"Yeah. Hit my head."

"I know," she said, and pointed to Tommy's face. He reached up to touch his temple. His fingers came away tacky with blood. "It looks scary."

He mustered up a wobbly smile. "Nah. I'm okay. You're awful calm."

The girl said, "I'm on Prozac."

"Your doctor's got you on Prozac? How old are you?"

"Fifteen."

Tommy said, "Your doc's an asshole."

She said, "Yeah." After a beat, she raised her good arm, stuck out one finger. "Can you help that guy?"

Tommy followed her finger. A man lay on the ground, on his side, curled up and moaning.

"Shit." Tommy breathed deeply, steadied himself, rose to his feet, fell to one knee, and tried it again. "Don't move, darlin'."

He staggered like a punchy boxer, made it to a pine tree. He leaned against it, caught his breath. He slid to his knees by the wounded man's side.

"Hey. Buddy. You okay?"

He reached out and shook the man's shoulder.

"N-no," the guy replied, his teeth chattering. "I'm . . . I'm fucked up."

Tommy shuffled his knees closer. He touched the man's hunched back, his neck. The man lay in the fetal position, arms pressed against his torso, knees up.

"I'm a doctor, man. Let me get a look."

Tommy lifted the upward-facing arm—the man lay on his side—away from his gut and saw a large puncture in his abdomen. A portion of the man's lower intestines was revealed.

"Well, shit . . . Okay, hold on."

Tommy looked around in the moon-glow gloom, found an airline pillow. He shuffled on his knees through the leaves, grabbed it. He brought it back, put it within the moaning man's line of vision.

"We're gonna make a pressure bandage. Okay?"

The guy nodded. He unwound a little from the tight fetal position, hissed as Tommy pressed the pillow against the gaping wound in his gut. Tommy whipped off his own belt, passed it around the pillow and the guy's waist. He cinched it tight, buckled it in the back.

"Okay, buddy. Just . . . Cavalry's comin'."

Kiki and the silver-haired stranger set the unconscious man down about twenty feet from the fuselage. Kiki went to work touching his arms, legs, and torso, looking for obvious wounds. She found none. She wasn't aware that the stranger had walked away.

The fire reached the second engine, which ignited in a great *whoooosh!* A spear of flame continued moving toward the fuselage.

From where he knelt, next to the man with the gut wound, Tommy heard *tak!*

Tommy froze. "You hear that?" he asked.

The guy in the fetal position moaned.

Tommy tried to shake his head, but that produced nausea. "Coulda swore I heard—"

Tak!

He froze again. "You heard that, right? The fuck is that?"

Tak!

A dozen feet away, a wounded, forty-foot-tall Douglas fir went *tak! tak! tak-craaaaack!* and fell over. It crashed three feet from Tommy and the gut-wound guy. Leaves and dirt blossomed. A dead bird thumped against Tommy's chest.

Tommy coughed as the leaves and dirt whirled past him.

Tommy blinked, then pulled a Star of David on a silver chain out of his shirt and kissed it. "Fuckin'-A!"

Far apart in the ruined fuselage, both Kiki and Calendar turned at the sound of the tree falling. Kiki flinched at the loud crash. Calendar did not.

As the rustling ended, Tommy heard more moaning. He grunted, rising, stumbling sideways, climbing over the newly felled fir tree. He circled two more trees, found another survivor, on her back, keening in pain. She seemed to be drifting in and out of consciousness.

Tommy collapsed to his knees beside her. She was maybe sixty, heavy-set with big, fleshy arms, in a Malibu sweatshirt. She wore ankle socks but no shoes. "Hey. You okay?"

She stirred, eyes fluttering open. "Who . . . who are you?"

"I'm a doctor. Where does it hurt?"

"My . . . my ankle." She began crying. "I can see the bone!"

Tommy wiped sweat off his brow with his sleeve. He lifted the cuff of her sweats: the ankle was broken, a chalky white stick of bone protruding. She had to be in some serious level of shock not to be screaming.

"This woman pulled me out. She saved me."

"Gorgeous redhead?"

The woman with a portion of her ankle outside her skin said, "God oh my god oh my god oh my god . . ."

"Okay. Just . . . here."

She lifted her pant cuff, looked at the bit of bone. She cried harder.

Tommy found a man's sweatshirt in the dirt. He brushed it off, looped it softly around her leg. He looked into her eyes—she wasn't in focus, thanks to his concussion. "'Kay, now, I'm gonna push this bit of bone back through the hole in your leg. Breaking the ankle hurt, I know, but this next bit's gonna hurt worse."

Sweat beaded on her jowly face. She nodded.

Tommy used his thumb to shove the bone back through her skin and she shrieked, eyes squeezed shut. Tommy grabbed both ends of the discarded sweatshirt and yanked them tight around the bleeder. Her mouth fished open but no more sound emerged.

"You okay?" he asked, but she fell back, limp, unconscious.

"For the better," he mumbled to himself. He wobbled to his feet and stumbled back to the fifteen-year-old girl.

That's when he saw the fire in the not-too-far distance. He was so dizzy, he couldn't be sure, but he thought maybe it was moving their way.

He collapsed to his knees by the girl.

She said, "Did you see that tree fall?"

"That . . ." Tommy huffed, "was fucked *up*."

Calendar stepped back into the fuselage and moved forward. He came upon a man strapped into his seat and dangling to his right. He recognized Vejay Mehta, a senior designer at Malatesta, Inc . He was unconscious and unresponsive, but alive. The engineer's chin rested on his chest. Calendar grabbed the man by the scalp, lifted his head, and slammed the length of pipe into his throat.

He looked at the seats across the aisle. They were empty but there was enough blood in the left-hand seat to suggest that it had been occupied and the passenger hadn't survived. He knew from the computers that Christian Dean had been assigned the seat.

The other seat should have held Andrew Malatesta. It was empty, too.

Calendar wouldn't leave until he found both engineers.

He walked up toward the flight deck, stepping over luggage and bodies and bits of the airliner's aluminum skin. He found no more survivors. He stepped over the body of a blond flight attendant. The door to the flight deck had come unhinged, hung at a funny angle. He shone his Maglite through the gap.

A man in the pilot's uniform of Polestar Airlines rose unsteadily to his feet. "Hey. Get me . . . get me outta here."

Calendar pulled the steel bar out of his belt and placed it near the one hinge still intact. He applied pressure, put one boot up on the cabin wall. The door clanged open, fell on top of the flight attendant's body.

"Thank you," the pilot said. "God bless you."

Calendar stepped into the flight deck, put an arm around Miguel Cervantes's neck, and twisted fast. His spine broke. Miguel died instantly, his body falling back into the sideways ceiling of the flight deck and sliding down to the ground.

Calendar looked around, saw the dead deer. *How odd,* he thought. He moved to the side, lifted part of the right-hand pilot's seat, which had been destroyed. He found part of Jed Holley's cadaver. Satisfied, he stepped out of the flight deck.

Tommy checked the eyes of the fifteen-year-old girl. In the moonlight, it was tough to tell, but they looked good. "How many fingers," he said, holding up two.

"Two." She lay as he'd moved her, not trying to get up.

"Straight A's. Okay, you just lay there and be good."

She said, "'Kay."

He felt around the makeshift pressure bandage he'd kludged together and didn't feel much blood. He looked around, squinting in the dark. To his right, six aircraft seats sat; three rows of two, each in the right order. The entire deck beneath them must have slid out, keeping all the seats together.

Only one seat was occupied. Tommy forced himself to stand, staggered over to the six seats. A woman sat in the third of three rows. Or most of a woman. She'd been decapitated.

Tommy leaned against the second, or middle, row.

"Tommy?"

He peered down between the first and second row of seats that sat so abstractly on the forest floor. He saw a woman lying there, facedown. But the voice he'd heard was Isaiah Grey's.

"Tommy . . . I tried to save her. Jesus, man . . ."

Tommy felt the woman's neck. No pulse. He realized Isaiah was wedged beneath her corpse.

"I know," Tommy said. "Let's get you outta there."

. . .

Calendar walked the length of the fuselage. He moved past the gaping gash in the roof and disappeared into the dust just as Kiki stepped back into the nightmarish tube of metal and plastic and glass and death. They were back-to-back, moving in opposite directions, she toward the flight deck.

Calendar found Christian Dean's head, neck, and one shoulder halfway back. The rest of the corpse was missing, but Calendar hadn't any more use for it than Christian, himself, had now.

In the food-services nook, back by the toilets, Andrew Malatesta struggled to sit up. He'd hit his head very hard. His back was killing him and he was pretty certain his left leg was broken. He wiped stinging sweat away from his eyes, looked around for anything that could be used as a crutch.

A light shone on his face. He squinted up into it. "Gimme a hand."

The stranger, oddly enough, sat on the sideways wall next to him. He turned the Maglite on himself, revealing his placid features, his tightly cropped silver hair. "Hello. Andrew Malatesta?"

After a beat, Andrew's shoulders sagged. The whole truth was so obvious. He spoke with sorrow and resignation. "You fucking bastard."

Andrew's rage began to overcome his pain. No longer looking for a crutch, his eyes cast about for a weapon.

Calendar's light fell on an aluminum attaché case under the food trolley. He leaned forward, pulled on the handle. It didn't move. He tugged again and it came free.

He checked. It was locked.

"This is the sketch pad I've heard so much about?" Calendar said, his voice soft, almost drowned out by the hiss and spark of severed wires. "Word is, you're the sorcerer's apprentice."

"It was a plane full of . . . innocent people!" Andrew growled.

"All threats," Calendar said with true regret, "foreign and domestic."

"You leave my wife alone . . ." he gasped.

Calendar nodded. "Oh, I can pretty much guarantee you we'll leave her alone."

Andrew stared into his eyes. The silver-haired man smiled a slight, almost timid smile. After a time, Andrew shook his head. Just a little.

"No," he whispered. "No."

Calendar slammed his elbow into Andrew's windpipe. He sat with the electronics designer until he died. Then he stood, grabbed the titanium case, and headed out.

Isaiah Grey pushed while Tommy pulled and they got the woman out from between the seats. Tommy realized she'd been one of the flight attendants.

Isaiah had lost both of his loafers. "God. Tried to save her . . ."

Tommy fell to his knees, rolling over on his side. Dizzy, he pushed himself back up, then reached between the seats and ran his hands up Isaiah's legs and torso. "Okay, no blood. No blood's good."

He stood. "Okay. We gotta . . . we . . ." He swayed.

Isaiah said, "Doc?"

"Hey. Ah, sorry . . . I'm about to—"

And Tommy's eyes rolled up into his head as he keeled over, poleaxed.

Isaiah said, "Doc? Yo, Tommy!"

Nothing.

Isaiah's back was on fire and he was pretty sure he'd broken every bone in his left hand. He shoved against the seat in front of him, groaning in agony. Nothing. He tried again, crying out now.

The seats in front of him gave. A little. He started to pull himself out with his left hand.

A strong arm appeared out of nowhere, lifting Isaiah up easily.

"Here you go." It was a stranger carrying an attaché case—how odd.

Isaiah winced, the pain in his back serious now. It wasn't his spine. It was low, to the right of his spine. "Damn. Thank you." He gasped, the pain sending sparks down both legs. "You all right?"

"I'm fine," the stranger said. "What happened to the aircraft?"

Isaiah took short, tight breaths, cradling his left hand against his chest. "P . . . powerplant," he said. "Full shutdown in midflight. Engines, lights, ev . . . everything."

The silver-haired stranger seemed saddened by that news. "Oh," he said.

Kiki found the dead crew members up front. She also saw the dead deer. She turned to the back end of the plane, found several dead, including a man on the floor by the food trolleys with his throat staved in. That was it; no more survivors. She headed for the gap in the fuselage ceiling.

. . .

Calendar circled the aircraft, going to the underside. Near the still-stowed tricycle landing gear he found the clay lump adhered to the aluminum skin. If he hadn't fired it himself, he never would have recognized this as the weapon he'd pulled out of the back of the SUV. He used his ragged-ended piece of steel to pry it loose. The size and shape of a deflated basketball, it fell to his feet, inert; the binary chemicals within were now spent. He picked it up and rounded the fuselage, returning to the stolen Dodge Durango just as a surplus U.S. Army jeep screeched into the clearing, not fifty feet away. Three big, white guys dressed for hunting started climbing out.

They hadn't noticed the Durango, their headlights on the few straggling survivors. And just then, Calendar heard the first *whup whup whup* of a helicopter.

He tossed in the titanium case and the misshapen lump of clay. Time to leave.

Kiki limped from the fuselage and her right foot slipped on something. She peered through the gloom and realized it was her own blood, dripping down her calf, ankle, and foot. *Not good,* she thought. But also not the priority.

She heard a jeep's engine and saw the bouncing headlights before she was even in open air. She trudged painfully in their direction, waving her arms, broken rib punishing her.

A spotlight blinked on from above. She shielded her eyes, saw a helicopter hove into view.

She looked at the stump. Tommy wasn't there. Where? She raked the now-well-lit scene, took in the teenager with something wrapped around her arm. Saw a man lying on his side, in the fetal position, with some kind of belt wrapped around his gut. She caught sight of the six seats, sitting neatly and uniformly on the forest floor. Tommy lay on the ground beside them.

She limped up to him, falling to her knees. She started to check his pulse but he groaned. Thank God! He lay with two women, both dead.

Kiki looked to the three rows of seats.

Isaiah Grey sat up in one of them.

He was dead.

14

WHEN AN AIRLINER CRASHES in the United States or its territories, a series of calls goes out from the NTSB headquarters to an amazingly dissimilar cast of characters. The first group called up would be the nine team leaders. Beth would be one of them, leaving eight other initial calls.

But before those calls were made, the very first call went to the designated Investigator in Charge, the person who would lead all the subgroup leaders.

Beth Mancini burst into her office and shouted back out through her door to one of her aides, "Hey! Who's on the rotation for IIC?"

"It's . . . hang on . . . ah, Peter Kim."

Beth winced. "Oh, swell," she mumbled, keeping her opinion to herself.

PENSACOLA

Peter Kim said, "What are you saying?"

At his home in Pensacola, Florida, Peter was packing his luggage, moving quickly, glancing repeatedly at his watch.

"I'm saying I know how you are. You get obsessed. Especially when you're in charge. You say you'll call every evening, but pretty soon it will be every other evening, or every third. You say you'll come home on weekends, but something will come up. A witness, a clue."

Peter placed three neatly folded white dress shirts into the bag. He turned to Janice, his wife. "When I say I will do something, I'll do it. I would expect you of all people to know that."

"Oh, me of all people. Yes, Peter, I know you better than anyone. And . . . well, I don't want you to go."

He snorted an unkind laugh. "This is my first crash as Investigator in Charge. It will get off to a bad start if I don't actually go to the crash."

He added four ties, matching pocket squares. Peter and Janice had had this discussion before. Several times before. He could repeat her lines.

"I just think Pete needs you right now. Needs a father figure."

That stopped him. "Kids who need a father figure don't have a father. He has one. And thanks to my laptop and camera, he'll see me. Every night. I'll be able to check his homework."

"Will you be able to attend the Little League games?"

"Janice!" He closed the bag. "Look. This is my job. This is what I do."

"You're a civilian engineer working for the navy. This isn't your job. This is . . . I don't know. This is an obsession with you."

"Okay, that's it." He inhaled, held it, exhaled. "Honey? I will call. I will come home on weekends. I will be a good father. Okay?"

She sat on the bed and chewed her right thumbnail.

Peter waited. "What?"

"I think we need to talk. About, you know. Us. Our family."

Peter sat, too. He took her left hand. "Our family is fine. It is. Honey, I have to go."

He stood, gathered his bags, and walked out of the bedroom, internally marveling at his wife's singular timing.

HELENA NATIONAL FOREST

The state police helicopter radioed in the unbelievable news: a midsize airliner, sans wings, was lying on its side amid the trees, and survivors appeared to be ambulatory.

Eight ambulances from Helena scrambled to the all-call, beginning their trek into the mountains. Sheriff's units screamed down Highway 287, heading east, lights casting ice and lava in the night sky. Paul McKinney, chief of police of Twin Pines, led the procession, steering wheel in one grip, radio in the other, arranging for on-duty personnel to head to the forest and off-duty personnel to replace them in town.

He set aside the car radio and used his cell phone to call Art Tibbits, mayor of Twin Pines. He checked the dashboard clock: nearly 1:00 A.M. Friday.

"Hello?" Art's voice sounded groggy and thick. Paul McKinney explained the situation quickly.

"Damn!" The mayor sounded awake enough now. "Okay, thanks for calling. Rescue teams are likely to need a staging area, you think?"

The chief drove with one hand. "Makes sense."

"Okay, I'll call, see about getting one of the closed businesses opened up."

"Thanks, Art." The chief hung up.

The three hunters who arrived first wanted to help, but Kiki had managed to get all survivors out of the fuselage. "Well, I could drive some folks into the city," one of them offered.

"Look, this man is a doctor." Kiki knelt in the leaves, Tommy's head in her lap. "If he were awake, he'd know if these people can travel. But I just don't know."

The three friends stood, uncomfortable, wanting to help but not knowing how.

Kiki wiped tears from her eyes. "Can one of you guys check the skid path?"

The hunter just back from Afghanistan scratched his head. "Ma'am?"

"The path behind us. Before the plane skidded to a halt. We're missing the wings, which means we're missing the engines. And that's where the fuel was . . . is. I'm worried about a fire."

One of his high-school buddies thumped him on the chest. "C'mon, dude."

It was *something to do*. That's all they were asking.

DULLES INTERNATIONAL AIRPORT
Three of the Go-Team leaders lived or were working close enough to the D.C. area that it made sense to drive to Dulles and take an NTSB charter

jet to Montana. Beth Mancini, the intergovernmental liaison, waited at the airport for Dr. Lakshmi Jain and Gene Whitney to arrive.

Dr. Lakshmi Jain was a New York City resident who, as luck would have it, was in Washington, D.C., testifying before a Health and Human Services subcommittee. Each of the essential subunits of the so-called Go-Team had a leader, and the leaders were on a rotating on-call list. Dr. Jain just happened to be at the top of the list for the pathology team.

She would oversee the postmortems and the injured. In a truly bad crash, some of the most vital evidence ends up inside the victims. It's precision work, and the tense, reserved Jain was perfect for the job.

Beth hopped into the hangar's bathroom to pee, checked herself in the mirror; as always, not satisfied with her weight. At thirty-five, she was just about willing to admit she'd never be a twig. She blew mousy brown hair away from her eyebrows in despair.

Stepping back out into the dark, her cell vibrated. The LED screen showed it was a few minutes shy of 3:30 A.M. Eastern—then answered. "Hello?"

"Beth?"

She smiled. Despite the hour, Delevan Wildman always called the liaison before a major investigation.

"Hey, Mr. Wildman."

"You got yourself good crashers, girl?" A sixty-eight-year-old black man from Tennessee, Delevan Wildman could get away with *girl*.

"Yes, sir. We'll do you proud."

He chuckled, a low, musical sound. "That's what I like to hear. How many souls?"

"Twenty-six. Remarkably low. It's a Claremont VLE, seats sixty-five."

"Okay. Peter Kim is IIC."

Standing outside the hangar, she watched her pilot do a walk-around of the Citation X. "He sure is."

"That man is as smart as you and as tough as me. He's tenacious and will follow the evidence where it leads. But in my life, I've never met a fella more full of himself and lacking in what you young folks call *the human touch*."

In the distance, she saw a very large man step out of a taxi, then haul out a suitcase and a backpack. "Yes, sir," Beth said. "He can be a handful."

"This is his first crack as Investigator in Charge. Don't rightly see how that's going to make him any sunnier."

She smiled. "I'll handle him, sir. I'll keep the locals out of his hair and the media at a safe distance. I'll make him look good."

She heard the low, lyrical laugh again. "My money's on you, girl. I'll back you up."

"Thank you, sir." She recognized the big man approaching her as Gene Whitney, one of her section chiefs.

"You have the passenger manifest yet?" Del asked.

"No." Her annoyance crept into her voice. "Polestar is having trouble with their computers. I'm hoping to get the manifest before we reach Montana."

"All right, then. Good luck out there."

Beth said, "I'll take it. Bye," and hung up. She reached out to shake Gene's hand but he was busy getting Tums out of his pocket. She didn't know him well but others described him as dour and not terribly communicative. Good at his job, though. This would be their first crash together.

"Gene Whitney. You're Beth. Hi." Now he shook her hand. He winced and chewed four of the stomach pills. "Let me guess: Del Wildman's famous pep talk?"

She said, "Yeah. He's worried about Peter Kim being IIC."

Gene nodded. "Me, too. The problem with being a really smart prick is, end of the day, you're still a prick."

Gene Whitney was a former military and commercial pilot. His job would be to study the flight crew, the grounds crew, the air traffic control crew, and to see if anyone had screwed up.

Not that many people chose to lie to Gene Whitney. The muscles that had earned him a full-ride football scholarship to the University of Kansas had long ago turned into fat, but he still looked disproportionately large, as if somehow he took up more space than his three-dimensional body should. He also wasn't that friendly. He lived alone, didn't pal around with anyone, and worked hard to keep it that way. He would fly to Montana, like the rest of the team leaders, do his damn job, write his damn report, and fly back home. Go-Teams almost always generate after-work cliques: the poker players, the golfers, the people who were in a foreign state or country and wanted to turn off-hours into minivacations. Gene Whitney wasn't those folks. He'd do his job, then he'd head home.

Beth Mancini called her aide, who would be pulling an all-nighter getting the teams ready, and asked him to check on an ETA for the passenger manifest.

Peter Kim had cut a deal with his employer, the U.S. Navy: he'd be ferried to the site of the crash on board an F-15E Strike Eagle and would be the first team member on site.

Jack Goodspeed, the airframe team leader, flew commercial out of Salt Lake City. He'd arrive second.

Teresa Santiago caught a flight north from Albuquerque. It would be Teresa's job to supervise the flight data recorder, one of two "black boxes" on board the Claremont VLE.

Hector Villareal, who'd focus on the cockpit voice recorder, was coming in from LAX.

And Reuben Chaykin, powerplant-team leader, was standing in a line at O'Hare as Beth, Lakshmi, and Gene lifted off the tarmac at Dulles.

CRASH SITE

Kiki knelt on the forest floor, Tommy's head in her lap, his hair spiky with blood. She held Isaiah Grey's lifeless hand in hers. One of the hunters had brought her a bottled water, the lid pried off. She wiped her cheeks with a sleeve bunched up into her fist. She poured water onto the sleeve in her fist and began cleaning the blood off Tommy's skull.

The three hunting buddies circled the fuselage and immediately saw the glow of fire in the distance. About a mile away, a straight line of fire moved toward them on a highway of fuel. Trees had caught fire, too. The friends hauled ass back to their Jeep, retrieved the shovels they had used to put out their campfire the dusk before, and ran back toward the blaze, to create a firebreak of freshly dug soil.

They then jogged back to where Kiki was. "You called it, ma'am," Justin

Oakes said. "It looks like you left the first engine about a mile east, and it's on fire. Fire's more or less heading in a straight line. Stinks of gasoline. We built a firebreak between us and the second wing."

Tommy's now-clean head rested in Kiki's lap. He had stopped bleeding. One of the hunters picked up a piece of thermoformed plastic the size of a Frisbee.

Kiki said, "Hey? Can you put that down, please?"

The hunter blinked, then set the thing down where he'd found it. "What is it?"

Kiki shrugged. "I don't know. It doesn't matter. A crash team is coming. Every piece of this plane, where it landed, its condition: it all means something."

The guys looked at one another. "Yeah?"

"Yeah. It's what we do." She patted Tommy's shoulder gently. She took Isaiah's limp hand again and kissed his knuckles.

The ambos couldn't drive into the forest so the EMTs grabbed med kits and stretchers and hiked in the last half mile. The going was only slightly uphill and relatively easy for the athletic crews.

The first EMT on the scene radioed back to Helena at 2:15 A.M., "Get a fire crew up here. We got smoke in the air."

Tommy wove in and out of consciousness. At one point, as the shouting paramedics arrived, he opened his eyes and said, "Kiki?"

"Hey."

"We in trouble?"

"Shh. No, baby." She rubbed her knuckles over his cheek. "We're safe."

"Okay." His eyes fluttered. "Don't tell Mom . . ."

Kiki surprised herself by releasing a short, tight little laugh. She felt the laugh turn to a sob but also felt a strange gratitude that Tommy, even in delirium, could make her laugh.

HELENA REGIONAL

At better than sixteen hundred miles per hour, Peter Kim's Strike Eagle chewed up the distance nearing northwest. The gunship hit Montana airspace around two in the morning and the pilot was given permission to land at Helena Regional.

"You're NTSB?"

Peter Kim walked from the Strike Eagle to a sedan that awaited him. A tall woman in jeans, dusty boots, and a Montana State sweatshirt stood by the sedan. Her black hair was pulled back into a complicated braid and she wore no makeup.

Peter wore an air force jumpsuit and carried a suit bag over his left shoulder. He checked his TAG Heuer: it was going on 2:30 A.M. mountain.

"Yes."

The woman opened the back door of the sedan and Peter tossed both of his bags in. "Peter Kim, Investigator in Charge. I'll be running the show."

"Adrienne Starbird," she said. "Operations manager for Helena Regional. I'm your liaison to the airport."

He shook her proffered hand. "That's a peculiar name." He climbed into the sedan and closed the door.

Adrienne Starbird paused, whispered, "Oooookay . . ." and circled the car. Then she climbed in.

"I can take you to the site."

"I need to change first. Take me to the terminal."

She shrugged, did as he asked.

Five minutes later, Peter Kim emerged from the men's room in a natty Martin Gordon suit, white shirt, and a narrow tie, raincoat over his arm. Adrienne had been expecting an NTSB windbreaker and baseball cap.

They returned to her vehicle and she drove around the terminal building.

"What's the situation on the ground?"

"State police have a helo in the vicinity. They report an airliner is down in the Helena State Forest. It apparently landed on its side and sheared off both wings. They report a forest fire, too. And they can see survivors. First responders are at the scene or should be any minute." She checked the dashboard clock to confirm that. "It's a Claremont VLE."

"Souls?"

"Unknown."

Peter checked his watch. "Why 'unknown'? Plane's been on the ground for three hours. Surely we have the manifest."

Adrienne Starbird shrugged. "We've contacted Polestar headquarters in Cincinnati. They're reporting some kind of computer malfunction. They're trying to get us a manifest."

"Unacceptable," he said. "I'll let our intergovernmental liaison deal with it. I need my primary team on site as fast as humanly possible. Do you have helicopters for us?"

"Yes. I've arranged for three to ferry your group out."

That news satisfied him, so Peter said nothing.

"Here." He handed her a business card. "We use specialized communication units, but they tie in to the cell-phone system. This is my number. You stay here and handle getting my people to the site. Call me and let me know when they're inbound."

"Okay." She circled the terminal building. A helipad came into view with a vehicle parked in the center that could be called a helicopter. But only just. Peter showed the first sign of emotion.

"What is that?"

"Aerospatiale Three One Three," Adrienne said, smiling at Peter's horrified expression. "Circa, oh, I'd say 1960. Trust me, they fly."

Peter said, "I wasn't even born in 1960."

CRASH SITE

"Fellas? Everyone? Hold up!"

Kiki lowered Tommy's head to a pillow she'd made out of a stray, cushioned computer case. She stood, waved her arms over her head, her busted ribs bitching her out.

The just-arrived paramedics turned to her. "Kathryn Duvall. National Transportation Safety Board. Look, this is a potential crime scene. Leave everything where you find it."

The EMT nearest her touched her arm gently. "We know. We're trained for this. Let's get you sitted down, ma'am."

Kiki gently lowered herself onto a stump. The medic knelt and used long-nosed scissors to cut her pant leg from the cuff to her midthigh.

.   .   .

The well-lit scene grew even brighter as a television station's helicopter took position overhead. A microwave truck from KXLH arrived ten minutes later and got footage of paramedics, two-by-two, carrying stretchers back down to the waiting ambulances.

TWINS PINES

Art Tibbits, mayor of the town closest to the fire, played poker with the managing editor of KPAX TV in Helena. He found the guy's phone number and called, glancing at the red-and-white art deco clock in his kitchen. He hated like hell calling at three in the morning but he had an idea.

"Um . . . yeah . . . ?"

"Stan? It's Art Tibbits, from out in Twin Pines."

"Um . . . okay?"

"Stan, an airliner crashed tonight. Helena State Forest, not five miles from my town."

"Holy crap!"

"The way I figure it, national media will be here by dawn. I figured you'd want to know so's you could—"

"Yeah, yeah. No kidding, Art, really. Thank you. I'll get a crew there now. Hey! I owe you!"

"Tell them I'm putting together a staging area for the media in the old Save-More Store on Main. It's wired for the Internet and there'll be plenty of coffee."

"We owe you! Thanks."

Art Tibbits hung up the phone. He stood for a moment. He'd been mayor of this town for twelve years and a resident for sixty-two. He loved Twin Pines. But it was dying. Everyone knew it.

He poured a splash of bourbon into a coffee cup, then filled it with coffee. He turned to the plat of the downtown core he kept taped to his kitchen cupboard at eye level. It showed a *city center*, if you could call it that, five blocks wide by seven blocks deep. There were roughly 130 commercial buildings downtown and he'd penciled Xs into 61 of them. Those were the vacancies.

Timber had built Twin Pines. And the timber industry today was a ghost of its former self.

Art Tibbits had seen an air accident once. It was in Boise. A plane had skidded off the tarmac. No one had been injured, but he remembered that a federal agency had set up shop and run operations for weeks. What had they been called? He could see their blue windbreakers in his head, plain as day.

NTSB. That's right. They were the NTSB.

He went to his eight-year-old Dell, booted it up, and googled the letters.

HELENA REGIONAL

Peter Kim's ancient chopper arrived at almost exactly the same moment as the NTSB charter touched down at Helena Regional. Beth Mancini stood in the aisle, BlackBerry to one ear, the other cupped in her palm, and shouted, "What? . . . Say again!"

"We finally got the manifest! From the Claremont!"

"Rick? It's really noisy here. Did you say we got the manifest?"

"Yes!" her aide bellowed from the office in Washington.

"Okay, ship me a pdf as soon as—"

"Beth? It's bad!"

"What?"

"*It's bad!* We got people on board! Isaiah Grey, Leonard Tomzak, and Kathyrn Duvall! They were on the goddamn Claremont!"

15

PETER KIM WALKED TO the on-its-side fuselage, a Maglite the length of a police baton over his shoulder, lighting the way. When he got close to the scene, he found six paramedics lifting three people on stretchers.

"Hang on." He showed them his badge. "Peter Kim, NTSB."

The paramedic nearest him said, "What, again?"

"Listen, please! It's vital that you do not move any—"

"Dude, it's cool. Your partner gave us the lecture." He knelt; another medic did, too. They counted silently to three, then hoisted a stretcher into the air.

"Partner?"

Kiki Duvall, on the stretcher, reached out, took his hand. Her voice was muddy with morphine. "Oh, Peter . . . Oh my god, Isaiah's dead. . . ."

The men carried her away, Peter thinking, *Wait. I know her. From the Oregon crash. It's what's-her-name.*

A mile from the crash scene, the fire staggered to the west, with plenty of fuel to burn along the path but too little wind to spread sideways. It remained a thin, ruler-straight path of destruction, heading toward the fire-break created by the three hunters.

Throughout the night, Go-Team leaders arrived and took the offer to be airlifted by antique helicopters to the crash scene.

Beth Mancini didn't go. Adrienne Starbird, ops manager for Helena Regional, gave up her own office for Beth. Not knowing what sort of office space awaited her, Beth had taken her office with her in the form of a backpack overstuffed with a tablet computer, extra batteries, a plug-in charger, and a portable printer that doubled as a fax machine.

She also whipped out a laminated to-do list, drawn up by Susan Tanaka, and went into full-scale attack mode: hotel rooms for her team, morgue space for the bodies, transportation, a place to store the pieces of the Claremont VLE—a space large enough that, if necessary, Jack Goodspeed's airframe team could reassemble the turboprop airliner. A full reconstruction often wasn't necessary but you never knew going in.

Two of her three aides were back home in Washington. They had begun the process of contacting the right people from the various businesses and agencies who would be called in to help: Claremont Aeronautics, Bembenek Company (maker of the engines), Polestar Airlines, the pilot's union, the mechanic's union, Leveque Aéronautique, Limited. Plus law enforcement officials from the city of Helena, Lewis and Clark County, the state of Montana, and—because of the unusual crash site, a state forest—the Montana Department of Fish, Wildlife and Parks.

Beth decided she could wait until morning to get someone to book the main auditorium at the Burton K. Wheeler Memorial Conference Center for the All-Thing: Delevan Wildman's storied enclave, in which representatives of all the companies, agencies, and organizations would have a chance to introduce themselves and to discuss ways they would be participating in the coming investigation. Which, past being prologue, was likely to take anywhere from one to two years to complete.

Well, last year's infamous seventy-hour investigation into the Oregon crash—crashes—being the exception to the rule.

She received a text from one of her three assistants that the mayor of Twin Pines, Montana, had called and offered a staging area for the Go-Team. Beth called in Adrienne Starbird and consulted with her.

"Twin Pines? Closer to the crash but it's a wide spot on the highway. I'd be surprised if it has five hotel rooms, total."

"Thank you," Beth said, then touched the tall, dark woman's sleeve. "Seriously. You've been great."

"And I can't tell you how much I hate the fact that you're here," Starbird said.

"Yeah. We get that."

She called Peter in the field using the team's dedicated communication devices: satellite radios attached to their belts, with ear jacks.

"We have an offer to set up headquarters in the nearest town, but the hotels will be back here in Helena."

"As will the bodies and the autopsies." He sounded as if he were in the room with her, the transmission loud and clear. "No, we'll work out of Helena."

"Okay. Hey: there are three crashers on board! It's—"

"I know," he cut in. "Duvall and Tomzak are injured. Isaiah Grey died." He sounded unemotional, a newscaster reciting facts of a story.

"Oh, God. Oh, no. Are you okay?"

Peter said, "Yes," and disconnected the line.

At 4:00 A.M. exactly—6:00 A.M. in D.C.—just as Delevan Wildman was sitting down at his desk in L'Enfant Plaza, Beth called him and told him what she knew.

Gene Whitney hiked up into the crash site, breathing heavily. Peter Kim saw the big man from afar and gave him a quick head-bob greeting. Gene wore an earpiece with a voice wand, a communications rig clipped to his belt. Like the other team leaders, he wore boots, a blue windbreaker with NTSB stenciled on the back, and a matching NTSB baseball cap. Only Peter Kim stood out, in his two-piece suit and London Fog raincoat. Peter stood on a rocky outcropping twenty feet from the fuselage, hands jammed into his trouser pockets, Maglite in his coat pocket, and silently watched his Go-Team leaders arrive.

Gene walked his way. "Coulda been much worse."

Peter nodded. He pointed to three rows of seats. "You worked with Isaiah Grey before?"

Gene looked in that direction. After a few beats, he walked over, squatted next to Isaiah's body.

He stayed like that for a while.

Eventually, Gene rose and walked thirty paces into the forest. When he was sure no one could see, he pulled out a flask of vodka and half drained it.

One of the EMTs turned to see Paul McKinney, Twin Pines' chief of police, come running from the direction of the engines, wings, and the fast-growing fire.

"How's it look?"

McKinney said, "Wind's in our favor. The fire's sticking to the path this thing dug." He nodded toward the fuselage. "But, hell, that could change before dawn."

SUBURBAN WASHINGTON, D.C.

Liz Proctor, director of the Aircraft Division of Halcyon/Detweiler and a member of Barry Tichnor's so-called Infrastructure Subcommittee on Deferred Maintenance, walked on her treadmill, scanning the *Washington Post* and listening to National Public Radio. Reports were coming in from Helena, Montana, that a commercial airliner had crashed overnight.

Liz finished her workout, drained the last of her ritual breakfast—a can of Coke Zero—then picked out a Donna Karan outfit for the day. She walked into the office, picked up her cell, and called Donny, her assistant.

"Hey, it's me. A commercial airliner went down last night in Montana?"

Donny said, "I'm working on a manifest."

"Okay. See you in about twenty minutes." She hung up.

Halcyon was the nation's largest military contractor. But almost every civilian airliner in the Western world carried some bits of Halcyon technology, be it in the airframe or avionics.

Liz Proctor would have the specs for that particular aircraft by the time she got to the corporate headquarters.

CRASH SITE

Three hours later, Hector Villareal, a compact, neatly fit man in khakis and the requisite NTSB windbreaker and ball cap, knelt amid the debris near the gaping hole carved into the top of the Claremont. Between his akimbo knees sat a metal box, twenty-five-by-twenty-five-by-twelve inches. It was a vivid orange and known without any intended irony as a black box. It was one of two black boxes on the flight. Hector and Reuben Chaykin had just retrieved the box from the empennage, or tail cone, of the aircraft. They'd had to move the food carts and the body of Andrew Malatesta to get to it.

Inside the well-padded box was a computer with an MP3 recording of the last half hour of the pilots' lives. It was the CVR—cockpit voice recorder.

Hector ran a hand over the steel box. It appeared undamaged. If so, it would tell them a great deal about the crash. Maybe everything.

He used his palm-size Canon PowerShot to take photos of the CVR's exterior.

Hector had small hands and narrow fingers, his nails trimmed. His mustache and beard, too, were neatly trimmed.

"Excuse me?"

Still on his haunches, Hector turned to find a man in a fur-trimmed bomber jacket, jeans, and boots. "Hector Villareal?"

Hector dusted off his palms, rose to his feet. "Yes?"

The stocky man—blond with an army haircut—showed him a folded leather case and a federal shield. "U.S. marshal. I was told to find you."

That was standard procedure, although Hector was impressed by how quickly the deputy marshal had arrived to pick up the black boxes and deliver them to their destinations. In the case of the CVR, that meant the nearest contracted recording studio, where the MP3 player's content would be uploaded to an NTSB Web site for Hector's ears within just a few hours. The marshal's job was to maintain the chain of custody, in the event that the crash turned out to be a crime scene.

Hector pointed to the steel box. "This is one of them," he said, then pointed thirty feet to his right, to Teresa Santiago, who was down on her haunches in exactly the same position Hector had been in, over another steel box.

"That's Teresa Santiago. She has the flight data recorder," Hector told the deputy marshal. "Mine goes to Portland, Oregon. Please—"

"Yes, sir," the blond man cut in with a small smile. "We know the procedure. Can you sign this?"

He handed Hector a clipboard. With a signature, Hector gave up his legal possession of the box.

Teresa Santiago watched Hector Villareal sign a sheet on a clipboard. The tall, ruggedly handsome Jack Goodspeed jogged up to her, also watching Hector.

"U.S. marshal?" he asked.

She shrugged. "I guess. I didn't expect them to get here so soon."

Tall and rangy, with a distance runner's legs and long fingers, she was physically the opposite of Hector. His neatly trimmed hair contrasted to her own wild mop. She had kinky lightning bolts of black hair that hung to the middle of her back, a leather string trying to keep that mane in check while stray, jagged shards of bramble-hair hung into her eyebrows.

"Fast is good," Jack said. "That should help."

A veteran flirt, Teresa winked at him and threw an arm over his shoulders. "Ah. I know you want to play pick-up sticks with all your shiny new toys." She gestured to the debris field. "But our black boxes will whisper their secrets to us long before you get this plane out of the forest."

HELENA REGIONAL

Gene Whitney's voice came through, loud and clear: "First, um, Isaiah Grey's dead."

Beth Mancini sat on the edge of Adrienne Starbird's desk, feet in the chair, and hugged her knees to her chest, eyes squeezed shut.

"Peter told me. You knew him better than I did. I am so, so sorry."

"Yeah. He was . . . He had a wife. *Has* a wife."

Beth said, "I'll contact her."

"Okay."

Beth waited. All she heard was static. "Gene?"

"Um, sorry. I poked around in the fuselage and found the flight crew's copy of the manifest. Right now—and these are early, early numbers—we're looking at twenty-six souls, estimated eighteen dead, eight survivors. From all accounts, Tomzak and Duvall ran the rescue. The site's goddamn pristine."

Beth said, "Crew?"

"Two and two," he said, meaning two pilots and two flight attendants. "None of them made it."

"Okay, thanks. Gene? I am sorry."

He said, "Yeah," and rang off.

Beth dialed 1.

"This is Kim."

CRASH SITE

Peter stood on his rocky outcrop, hands in his pockets, observing. He had touched nothing. He had hardly spoken. His team seemed good, solid.

His ear jack chimed. "This is Kim."

"It's Beth. Gene gave me the rundown. Were you and Isaiah close?"

"No," Peter said. "One crash together. Oregon." He didn't need to elaborate. That crash was legendary within the NTSB.

"I've set up the All-Thing for eleven on Saturday. There's no way we could get the stakeholders to Montana today."

"Acknowledged." He checked his watch; a bit past seven. For all Peter cared, they could have the damn thing on New Year's Eve. He considered the meeting of every conceivable stakeholder a monumental waste of time.

He rang off as Jack Goodspeed, the airframe-team leader, jogged over. A strapping, affable guy with jet-black hair worn short and a perpetual smile, Peter thought he looked like he'd played football in college and likely dated the homecoming queen. Upon arriving, he'd jogged east with a bright LED flashlight snugged into his palm, checking the debris trail. Now he was back, shaking his head.

"It's pretty much a straight line of wreckage, boss. Goes back a little better than a mile. You can see where both wings sheared off."

"The engines?"

"The one closest to us looks pretty chopped up. The other one's where the fire started. I couldn't get close enough to see it."

Peter nodded. "The fire?"

"Somebody dug a firebreak, quarter mile back there. The fire's not a threat right now but that could change quick. One option is for us to stay out here, get as much info out of that bird as we can before our luck turns. Besides, it'll be light soon." The day had dawned but the state forest remained in shade behind a mountain range to the east.

Peter said, "We've got the black boxes. There isn't much else to do until our teams are assembled. Get the others. We're heading in. I want everyone up and briefed by ten hundred."

But Dr. Jain walked up at that moment. "Peter? I don't know about the airframe, but I want to get all of the bodies out of here, in case the fire turns."

"All?"

"Absolutely. It wasn't a full flight. And I definitely want to autopsy every one. I can't do that if the forest fire expands."

Peter blinked. "It's seven A.M., in the middle of nowhere. Where would we even secure eighteen cadavers?"

"Excuse me?" A stocky man with a doughy, Irish face, in a bomber jacket and police hat, stepped up. "Paul McKinney. I'm chief of police, next town over. Twin Pines. Not five minutes away from the ambulance staging area. You need to store bodies?"

Lakshmi Jain said, "Yes, please."

"The mayor just called me, said he's set up a market, went bankrupt a month ago. Plenty of storage, and it's ice cold in there." Secretly, McKinney was wondering what had magically happened overnight to the lead in Mayor Art Tibbits's ass. He'd never seen the mayor mobilize anything bigger than a backyard barbecue.

Lakshmi turned to Peter. "Perfect. I've spoken with the paramedics. The fire could change direction today."

Jack said, "I'm with her, boss. We got bad clock here."

Peter nodded, turned to McKinney. "Chief, we're going to need help getting these bodies out of this field and transporting them to your town."

In response, McKinney reached up for the police radio clipped to his epaulet. "McKinney to base. Over." To Peter, Lakshmi, and Jack, he said. "I'll whistle up something."

Jack said, "If Lakshmi's staying, I want to help Reuben get as much of the avionics off the flight deck as we can. Same as the bodies: if the fire whips around, we'll lose a lot of evidence."

Peter agreed. It seemed that his people, or at least some of them, wouldn't be getting any rest. But he had to admit, he liked their professionalism.

HELENA REGIONAL

The supervisor for Helena Regional's air traffic control tower paged Adrienne Starbird, suspecting she had pulled an all-nighter due to the crash.

"Adrienne? We've got seventeen chartered flights booked for Helena tomorrow and more being filed every few minutes. And not small ones, either. Last two were a Gulfstream 550 and a Challenger S.E. What in the world is going on here?"

Adrienne Starbird took the question to Beth Mancini, who was using her office. "It's the All-Thing," Beth said, rubbing at a kink in her neck. "Everyone who had a hand in putting that plane together is going to want to help us figure out how it came apart. And I mean everyone. The airframe manufacturer, the wing manufacturer, the engines, the avionics, on and on. Then we get into Polestar Airlines and the pilot's union and the flight attendant's union."

Adrienne said, "And they're coming here?"

"Yes. My boss invented this event and dubbed it the All-Thing. Basically, we take two or three hours in the first few days to figure out who the players are. Establish a roster. Then, and I know this is counterintuitive, we actually take them up on the offer to help. If you've got a mental image of foxes guarding a henhouse, you're right on the mark. But when it comes to doing a full postmortem on, say the flight deck avionics package, we're going to need the experts of Acme Avionics or whoever it turns out to be. Which means your tower will receive a lot more flight plans in the next few hours."

HALCYON/DETWEILER, DUPONT CIRCLE, WASHINGTON, D.C.

Liz Proctor's new aide, Donny, handed her three manila envelopes and a cup of coffee. "Our friends in Islamabad have asked for twelve MKK-17s," he said, following her into her office.

Liz frowned. "Going fishing?" The MKK-17s were Halcyon's helicopter gunships, rigged for antisubmarine warfare. They were outfitted with both extremely low-frequency sonar and sonobuoys. "India's not going to like that."

"True."

She set the first folder on her oak desk and opened the second.

Donny gave her the highlights. "A Turkish Cypriot suicide bomber took out five people in a terminal at Larnaca International last night using—"

Liz said, "Suicide bomber in Cyprus? Jesus, Donny."

"I know. That's an escalation. No one saw it coming. I talked to my guy at the CIA. He says MI-6 has people on site now and they're sharing . . . for once. The Nicosia station chief is moving assets into position."

She sipped the coffee. Donny was twenty-seven and a total hottie. Blond hair, tall and slim, and favored Hugo Boss trim-fit shirts. Liz Proctor could have licked him. It didn't hurt that he had a master's in public administration and a doctorate in foreign policy and an IQ slightly higher than that of the Vulcan High Council.

"Okay, I need face time with Deitrich, before noon," she said, doffing her jacket. "Who's good on Cyprus. Jennings?"

"Jennings's water broke last night," Donny said, smiling. "Sorry. I'll get Craig Sutter up here."

"Okay." Liz looked at the third manila folder, opening it.

"Manifest from that crash in Montana."

Wow, he was good. She had forgotten all about it by the time she'd made the commute in. "Anyone interesting?"

"Unfortunately, yeah. A guy on the payroll. Subcontractor vetted by Mr. Tichnor's office. An Andrew Malatesta. Near as we can tell, he and . . . Liz? Are you okay?"

Her cheeks were burning. She made a hand gesture toward the door and Donny didn't hesitate. The moment the door closed, she sat and dialed Barry Tichnor's extension. The line rang twice. Liz heard the click of a receiver being lifted and didn't wait for Tichnor to identify himself.

"What the fuck, Barry? Seriously! What the fuck!"

CRASH SITE

The sun was close to rising from behind the mountain range but the forest remained dark.

Reuben Chaykin had flown from Chicago to take command of the powerplant team. He stood at the empennage end of the downed plane and stared forlornly to the east, at the fire that had started with the portside wing and engine and had chewed its way due west—straight as a Texas highway—to the starboard wing and engine.

The Claremont featured those two engines, two starter generators for direct-current power, three transformer units in the cargo deck, and three nickel-cadmium batteries. They, along with an engine-driven AC generator to supply variable-frequency power, made up the allied powerplant of the Claremont aircraft. It was Reuben's job to see if something within the powerplant had brought down the plane.

Much of his "evidence" was a fiery, mile-long mess. This was going to take a long, long time. Many months.

Reuben Chaykin was a squat, muscled little bantam of a man with a half-moon of hair the color and texture of steel wool. He wore half-glasses at the end of his nose, attached to a lanyard around his neck. He stood there, hands jammed into the back pockets of his dungarees, and sighed deeply.

Teresa Santiago, the flight data recorder expert, threw an arm over his shoulder and gave him a little hip check.

"You're powerplant?" She stood five inches taller than Reuben and they were both in their early forties.

"Yeah," he admitted.

"Bummer."

He removed his glasses and let them hang against his chest from their lanyard. "You're tellin' me."

The tall, curvy Latina bombshell and the morose Jewish fireplug made a sharp contrast. "How's your black box look?"

"Pristine. U.S. marshal's already been here and gone."

"This could be an easy catch for you," Reuben said, and shrugged, turning again to the fire trail.

"Yeah. But I think you're well and truly screwed."

He signed yet again. "I am so fakaktah."

Jack Goodspeed jogged in their direction. He'd been around to the belly side of the plane to see if the pilots had deployed the retractable tricycle-style landing gear. They had not.

"Reuben? Peter gave us the okay to try to get the avionics suite out of the cockpit. As much as we can, anyway."

Reuben said, "You're worried the wind will change direction, that fire biting us in the ass?"

"Yeah. You?"

Reuben gave his signature sigh. "Sure. God hates me. Why not?"

. . .

Chief Paul McKinney got the superintendent of the Twin Pines/Martins Ferry Unified School District out of bed. "Chip, I want to borrow your buses. All of them."

"Um . . . sure." The superintendent sounded half asleep. "When?"

"Now."

Chip Ogilvy climbed out of bed so as not to wake his wife. "Paul? What's going on?"

"A midsize aircraft crashed into the state forest, couple miles outside of Twin Pines. The damn thing started a forest fire. The feds are here, and they want to transport these people into town as quickly as they can."

Chip agreed, hung up, called his director of transportation, and got the buses rolling. It was early August and the buses weren't in use anyway.

Paul knew Chip well enough to know that he would have said no if the request had been to transport eighteen dead bodies. That's why Paul had worded it *these people*.

CLANCY, MONTANA

Calendar ditched the stolen Durango into a creek outside Clancy and walked a quarter mile to the motel he'd rented under a false name, paying cash. He let himself into the room, tossed the titanium case on the bed. He stripped off his clothes, took a two-minute shower, very hot. He scrubbed himself thoroughly. He disliked killing civilians.

He toweled dry. Naked, he brought the locked attaché case to the bathroom, studied it under the lights. The lock was a ten-key pad. Unpickable. He grabbed the case, turned it over, wedged it between the toilet and the bathroom wall with the hinges facing upward. It was a tight fit.

He padded into the main room, knelt, reached under the cratered bed with the threadbare cover, pulled out another locked case, dialed the combo, and withdrew an HK45, matte black and solid, with an Advanced Armament silencer. He screwed them together, returned to the bathroom, and put two bullets through the hinges, *phut phut,* barely audible if you'd had your ear against the motel-room door. A fine dust of steel filings, bullet fragments, and titanium littered the none-too-clean linoleum floor.

Calendar lifted the case away from the toilet, set it up on the cabinet, and opened it.

It was empty.

AIRBORNE

En route back to Helena via helicopter, Peter Kim called his intergovernmental liaison via their comm link. "Beth? We're leaving some of the Go-Team in place. Pathology and avionics/powerplant. The rest of us are heading back now. Where are we staying?"

"Um, I'm having a little trouble booking rooms. I hope to have it sorted out by the time you get back." She paused. "Are you sure it's wise to leave some of our people that close to a forest fire?"

"Time's arrow only points one direction," he responded, and checked his diver's watch. It was a little after 8:30 A.M.

"Del Wildman's Rule Number One is pretty clear," Beth said. "First, take no risks."

"Noted," Peter said. "Out."

In fact, Beth Mancini had booked only four rooms so far. She would need upward of eighty within a day or two. She hadn't anticipated the popularity of Helena during hunting season.

CRASH SITE

Lakshmi edged her way into the downed Claremont, a Maglite held up by her shoulder. She moved toward the flight deck. She didn't enter: it was crowded with Jack Goodspeed, Reuben Chaykin, one intact dead pilot, the remains of another dead pilot, and, completely unexpectedly, a deer.

She said, "My."

Jack turned and saw her eyeing the deer carcass. "Yeah, I know. Weird. I think the plane hit once, shredded this wall," he stamped his boot on the rough sod beneath him, "bounced, caught this poor guy," he nodded to the deer, "and scooped him up."

It was growing lighter outside but very little sunlight crept into the flight deck. Jack and Reuben crouched together up front. Reuben's right arm stretched almost completely behind the avionics panel, reaching back for something. Lakshmi said, "Can you get the equipment out of here?"

"Think . . . so . . ." Reuben stretched his arm farther, wincing in discomfort.

Lakshmi stepped over the threshold. She went down on one knee, moved a portion of the severely crumpled right-hand seat. She saw part of the torso of one pilot.

She shifted to the other pilot, played her flash along the gold nameplate over his left-hand pocket. Pilot-in-Charge Miguel Cervantes. He lay on the forest floor, his upper torso leaning on a portion of the flight deck that—in a normally oriented Claremont—would have been the ceiling. From the way his head lolled, she guessed a broken spine. She played the light on his neck, manipulated his skull. Yes. A C4 break.

She studied the rest of the body. Very bad bleeder in his right arm, with a trail of blood that ran forward to where Jack and Reuben were laboring. Lakshmi frowned. She also pulled back his shirt collar to discover a broken clavicle. Common enough injury in airline crashes: the safety harness.

But not with a C4 break.

She looked at the men kneeling up front. Lakshmi did not enjoy physically touching people until she knew them well, a process that could take years.

Steeling herself, she said, "May I?" and wedged herself in closer to the men. Her jeans-clad calf rubbed against Reuben's left arm. There wouldn't have been enough room for a third man up in front but Lakshmi was willow thin and flexible enough to fit, if uncomfortably. She stood, studying the pilot's chair. Yes, there was the telltale blood of the arm bleeder, the smear of blood on the safety harness from the clavicle break. And she studied the buckle of the safety harness. One perfectly fine, bloody thumbprint.

She turned back, shone the light on the pilot. Turned and shone it on the seat.

Reuben said, "Can you give us a little light here?"

She turned the Maglite on the avionics monitors.

"What are you trying to salvage?"

Jack nodded to the monitor nearest his head. "EFIS."

"Which is . . . ?"

"Sorry. Electronic Flight Instrumentation System. Five high-res liquid crystal displays. Some of these Claremonts are retrofitted with heads-up holographic guidance systems, too, but I'm not seeing one here."

"Me, neither." Reuben grunted, still trying to reach some hidden connector in back.

Jack said, "We get this, maybe the TCAS unit. That's got global positioning, traffic alert, and collision avoidance systems, rolled into one. That could tell us if we had a near miss or a missile."

Lakshmi said, "Missile," as if Jack had said *eight tiny reindeer.*

Kneeling, Jack shrugged. "Assume nothing."

And a minute later, three of the avionics monitors fell free.

HELENA

The ambulances carrying Tommy, Kiki, and the six other survivors of Polestar Flight 78 arrived at Big Sky Community Hospital at 8:45 A.M. The Claremont had been on the ground nine hours.

16

MOST OF THE MEMBERS of the Go-Team were ferried back to Helena Regional and found that Beth Mancini and her assistants had rummaged up only a few hotel rooms in different hotels. Beth apologized profusely. Peter Kim recommended that people use their own credit cards to find rooms. They'd get reimbursed later.

It was a bad way to start their first full day on the ground, everyone thought, as they headed their own way to find hotel rooms.

Gene Whitney loved airports. You could almost always get booze. And nobody knew that you hadn't just flown in from Hong Kong, wherever, and it was really happy hour to you. He returned to Helena Regional and found a chain restaurant serving a full menu of drinks. Plenty of time to find a hotel room later.

He hoisted his 250-pound form up onto a stool at the nicked bar. It was wood but no discernible type of wood. Just wood. He ordered a Coors and got a bowl of pretzels without asking.

He didn't get into a fight with the locals for a good hour. It was almost a personal best.

LIMA, MONTANA

Almost due south of the crash on Highway 15, Calendar's man, Cates, stood outside in a motel's parking lot, sipping coffee from a Thermos lid as the sun rose. He leaned against a Ford Escape SUV. Five minutes later, an identical Escape pulled in, facing the other direction, and parked next to it.

The new driver—another of Calendar's soldiers for hire, Dyson, also with the look and bearing of a military man—got out without a word. The men opened the truck doors, looked around to see if they were being observed, then transferred the original black boxes of Flight 78 into the newcomer's truck. Two perfectly identical but fake black boxes went into the first truck.

The drivers nodded to each other, climbed into their respective cabs, and drove away in opposite directions.

Cates opened up a cell phone, hit Redial, and said, "I have the packages." He disconnected the line, hit the power window, and threw the phone into a field.

LANGLEY, VIRGINIA

"I have the packages." *Click.*

In her subbasement listening post, Jenna Scott heard the mercenary's four words and the *click* of his disconnect. She punched in a new number. She sent Barry a text: "Alternative packages en route."

SOUTH OF CRASH SITE

Calendar stood in the bathroom, still naked, and blinked at Andrew Malatesta's empty case. He felt a red haze behind his eyes, tasted coppery adrenaline at the back of his tongue.

Finally, the sound of gurgling water caught his attention. He frowned, glanced around. The bathroom mirror had been shattered. How? He turned to the case again. It still rested between the wall and the toilet, but the toilet had been ruined, the lid on the floor, the reservoir smashed, water flowing out onto the floor, over his bare feet.

He raised his right hand, stared at the HK. He touched the silencer. It was hot. He'd apparently emptied the chamber, although he couldn't remember having done so.

He rotated his wrist. Blood trickled down his forearm from a piece of glass the size of a poker chip embedded in the heel of his hand. Huh. He pulled it out, dropped it to the floor.

He inhaled deeply, held it, let it out through his mouth. Again.

He tilted his head to the left, heard his neck pop. Tilted to the right. Pop-pop. He rotated his shoulders, worked out the kinks.

Calendar ripped a towel and bandaged his hand. He picked up all the shell casings, threw them into his luggage. He got dressed, took the ruined attaché case and his luggage to his stolen Chevy Tahoe. He returned to the motel room with a military-grade flare and kerosene. The flares burned so hot, they would leave no forensic trace of themselves behind. He checked the room carefully, looked in the closet and under the bed, found nothing connected to him. He poured the kerosene on the bathroom floor, walked to the door, lit the flare, tossed it into the bathroom, and was pulling out of the parking lot before the first fire alarm sounded.

HELENA

Gene Whitney was supposed to catch a late-morning flight from Helena back to Washington, D.C. One of his principal tasks was to interview the ground crew at Reagan. But that was before the fistfight with the two drunks in the airport bar.

He'd managed to snag a dirt-cheap room in a down-on-its-luck motel near the airport.

Gene woke around 10:00 A.M., found himself lying in his street clothes on top of the thin bedspread, only two hours after crawling into bed, still drunk, still sore from getting popped in the mouth. He had absolutely no idea what the fight had been about. He'd said something or they'd said something, and one side or the other had taken exception to it. Someone had said, "You wanna step outside, dipshit?" and thinking back, blinking up at the popcorn ceiling, Gene was fairly certain he'd been the one to say that. Anyway, he and two locals who were three and three-quarters sheets to the wind already had stepped out by the Dumpster and gone all testosterone on one another. Gene Whitney was a big man. Fat, for sure, but once upon a time that had been muscle and he still knew how to use it. After the two local dipshits had slunk off, Gene returned to the bar and drank until noon.

He rolled over now, feeling his age, and tasted blood on his teeth. One of the locals had gotten in a punch. Just the one, though.

He staggered to the bathroom, pissed, and squinted at himself in the mirror. He'd missed his wakeup call and his flight to Reagan to interview the ground crew.

"Fuck . . ." he muttered to his reflection, shirt collar up, shirt untucked, bruising around his limp mouth.

He limped back to bed and closed his eyes.

ANNAPOLIS

Renee Malatesta had taken two sleeping pills, which managed only to hold her in an insensate fog of consciousness and limp lassitude that stretched on into the night, minute after minute after agonizing minute.

She must have dozed off in her living room, waking up at 2:00 P.M. with that wonderful, luscious half second of amnesia before she remembered it was likely that Andrew was dead.

She lay on her back, listening to the frogs in the city park, staring at the ceiling. It was a concern to her that she hadn't cried yet. Crying was natural. Right? She loved her husband. Alas, she didn't particularly *like* him.

They hadn't been living together, but they hadn't divorced, either. She had had affairs, yes. Brief, cathartic flings. Never with anyone Andrew knew or who traveled in his circles. God knew, when he was in The Zone, she was essentially a widow for weeks. When he was inventing some contraption, some new micro-whatever, he locked himself away for fourteen, sixteen hours at a time, emerging only to eat, use the bathroom, and play soccer. Andrew had solved many intractable problems by mindlessly kicking a soccer ball against a wall, over and over again, his brain a trillion miles away.

All of which was beside the point. Renee loved her husband. And within the next few hours, she likely would receive a phone call announcing his death.

And she hadn't cried.

Her eyes played about the luxuriously comfortable room, her thoughts, as they often did, turning to the stunning poverty of her youth in Haiti and marveling at where the world had taken her. The bedroom walls were painted a shade of daisy yellow she and Andrew had first seen in the Loire Valley. They had repainted it a half-dozen times to get the color exactly right. The framed photo opposite the headboard showed the two of them, arm in arm, in a winding alley in Toledo, Spain, which reminded her so much of Venice except with steep hills instead of canals.

She squeezed a fistful of the soft, pale-yellow bedsheets, so soft, a thousand-thread count. She turned to look at Andrew's pillow and re-coiled in shock, gasping and rising to her feet, eyes wide, hands squeezed into fists and bunched in front of her throat.

The Colt Pocket Model .25 pistol Andrew had bought her lay on the pillow.

Renee took two steps away from the bed. The small, nickel-plated gun lay on the exact center of the pillow. Like Cinderella's slipper. But how?

She had no memory of getting it down from its box on the high shelf in her closet. The shelf so high that it required using the step stool from the kitchen. She thought back to the combination of Prozac, Vicodin, and liquor she'd taken last night. Was this their combined effect?

She stepped closer to the bed, paused, bent, and picked up the tiny pistol, the barrel as long as the handle, a little V of nickel-plated iron. Andrew had bought it, against her protest, after a break-in by a pair of meth addicts. That had been more than a year ago. Since the day he'd brought it home, this was the first time Renee had touched the semiautomatic. It was cool to the touch, slightly greasy, although when she rubbed her fingertips together, she realized that was an illusion.

Renee thumbed the release, let the small magazine slide out into her right hand. The magazine was fully loaded. Had it been, before? Maybe. She couldn't remember.

She retrieved the step stool from the kitchen and returned the .25 to its box on the high shelf.

She went to the bathroom and found the vials of Prozac and Vicodin. She thumbed off the caps, lifted the toilet-seat lid, and stood, for just the longest time, a vial in each hand. After a while, she put the caps back on, lowered the toilet seat, and returned to the kitchen to make a full pot of coffee.

BIG SKY COMMUNITY HOSPITAL

The ER doctors had put Kiki Duvall on whole blood because she'd bled more from the leg wound than she had realized. They also offered a morphine drip but she declined, telling them, "I may have to stay sharp."

Tommy woke up in the adjacent bed with the aid of a penlight in his right eye; his left eye dilated accordingly, which was good.

A young, female doctor asked him the requisite questions. ("My mom? Ah, Ann. She was Ann . . . Friday. Well, we went down on Thursday. Probably Friday . . . Other medical conditions? Jesus, a plane just fell on my ass!")

The doctor determined that his concussion was mild. He was given a private room and sedated.

In all, eight of the twenty-six passengers and crew survived the crash of Polestar Flight 78. They included the teenage girl with the upper-arm bleeder and the man with the gaping abdominal wound, both of whom Tommy had treated. Other survivors included the woman with the broken ankle, whom Kiki had rescued and Tommy had assisted, and the Middle Eastern man Kiki and someone else had helped carry out of the fuselage.

ANNAPOLIS

Her iPhone rang and Renee snapped it up. "Hello?"

A somber, male voice said, "Is this the home of Andrew Malatesta?"

She dropped to her knees in the middle of the living room. "Yes."

"Are you a member of the family?"

"Yes. I'm his wife. I'm Renee. His wife."

"Mrs. Malatesta, my name is David. I represent Polestar Airlines. Ma'am, I'm afraid I'm calling with very bad news. Your husband's flight? Flight Seven-Eight to Seattle? It crashed last night, outside Helena, Montana."

Renee's peripheral vision dimmed. Her eyes stung, they were so dry. *Why no tears?* she wondered. *Why aren't I crying?*

"Mrs. Malatesta, I regret to inform you that your husband died in the crash."

Renee said, "Oh."

The line was quiet for a while.

"Mrs. Malatesta?"

"Ooooooooohhhh . . ."

"Mrs. Malatesta? There's an e-mail heading your way right now. To the homes of all the families. We're arranging transportation and lodging for everyone who wants to come to Helena."

Her mouth fished open but, with no more air in her lungs, the long, low keening noise died out. She slumped back, sitting on her ankles, the long fingers of her left hand stretching down to touch the blond wooden floor, balancing her.

"The e-mail will explain everything. It has my name and number, a twenty-four-hour hotline. There's a Web site. We are here to do everything in our power to help you in your time of need."

The caller waited a minute. "Okay. Well . . . ma'am, our condolences." And he hung up.

Renee set the phone down gently on the floor. She knelt with her legs under her and steepled her fingers on her lap.

Her eyes were so dry they itched.

WASHINGTON, D.C.

Halcyon/Detweiler's Infrastructure Subcommittee on Deferred Maintenance met at a mom-and-pop coffee shop in Dupont Circle.

Liz Proctor of the Aircraft Division and Admiral Gaelen Parks (retired) of the Military Liaison Division were already seated as Barry Tichnor entered. Both of them eyed Barry with hostility as he went to the counter and ordered a cup of decaf.

He sat, his thick eyeglasses gleaming.

Parks whispered, "What in God's name happened?"

Barry poured a little sugar substitute into his coffee and stirred. They waited. "The first field test was a success."

"Jesus Christ!" Liz exploded, and people at other tables looked over. She lowered her voice and hissed, "Are you fucking kidding me? Seriously? You tested the device on U.S. soil? On a civilian airliner? We don't have a list of survivors yet but there were twenty-six people on that plane! Twenty-six Americans!"

Barry looked at his spoon and considered using it to gouge out her trachea. But he set it down on a square brown napkin, letting it absorb the residue of coffee and sweetener. "If it's at all possible," he said, smiling, "could you avoid using the Lord's name in vain?"

The others stared at him.

"We have a potential buyer," Barry said. "It's a country. An ally, before you ask. They are offering a . . . hefty sum for the device, if it works. We are looking at what I would refer to as a staggering third quarter, if everything pencils out."

"India," Liz said, and got a soft smile from Barry in return. "It's India or South Korea, but my money says India."

Barry shrugged. "The point is, the test was a success. The device works.

Malatesta spoke to a journalist regarding ways to release his knowledge of this operation to the media. In movies it's called The Big Reveal. Very dramatic. He was also writing a speech to be given at a technology expo, saying he was giving up his Pentagon contracts and renouncing Satan— that's us—for experimenting with an illegal device. He hacked into our R-and-D computers. He had rock-solid proof."

Admiral Parks said, "Oh, damn. Damn, damn, damn."

"Yes." Barry nodded. "Damned, indeed." He took a sip and winced when it burned his tongue. Light danced on the refracting lenses of his thick glasses.

The table was quiet for several seconds.

Liz said, "You're using . . . ?"

"Someone quite good. We've used him before."

Parks said, "The speech?"

Barry sipped his coffee. "Secured."

HELENA

The drugs wore off and Tommy Tomzak woke at about 2:30 P.M. on Friday. He slid slowly into consciousness, the firm, comfortable pressure of Kiki Duvall on his left shoulder. She had snuck out of her room around noon and curled up in Tommy's bed.

She shifted, her thigh sliding across his.

"Hey," Tommy muttered, his lips as dry as chalk. He blinked a few times and the penny dropped: the flight, the crash, the whole thing. The general sense of dullness that comes only from Schedule I narcotics washed over him.

A headache and dizziness kicked in. "Jesus."

Kiki kissed his stubbly cheek. "Tommy?"

"Damn, we were . . ." His vision blurred. "I'm concussed. We gotta get me to a hospital."

"Tommy, this is a hospital. In Montana."

He bleared around, realized she was right. "Oh. You okay?"

Kiki leaned into him and reached for the lidded cup on the bed stand. It had a straw. She put it to Tommy's lips and he sipped the stale, warm water.

"Thanks. You okay?"

Kiki kissed him on the lips. Her face was blotchy and swollen, her dusty red hair a mess, her eyes bloodshot. As luck would have it, her boyfriend's vision was so blurry from the concussion, he thought she looked beautiful.

"I love you," he said.

"Tommy? Isaiah didn't make it."

He blinked. "He missed the flight?"

"Isaiah died in the crash. He's dead. Isaiah died."

"But . . . No, he . . ." Tommy's brain scrambled to make sense of the words he had just heard. "Oh my god . . ."

Kiki nestled her face in Tommy's clavicle and cried. He gripped the back of her head in one calloused hand, pulling her close, into his shoulder, and tears poured down his cheeks.

LOS ANGELES

It was not quite 1:30 P.M. Friday, Pacific time, and Ray Calabrese sat in the cafeteria of the Los Angeles field office of the FBI, at a table to himself, coffee untouched and sports page of the L.A. *Times* open but unread. His foul mood was so palpable, others steered clear of him.

The whole situation with Daria Gibron was eating at him. Ray had met her when she was with Israeli intelligence and had uncovered a right-wing plot to assassinate a member of the Israeli Knesset and blame it on a moderate Lebanese minister. Not knowing whom to trust, she'd turned to an FBI team, led by Ray, in Tel Aviv for a law enforcement conference. The plot had been foiled and Daria had taken a bullet to her abdomen. After recuperating at Ramstein, and knowing that people in her own agency had put a price on her head, she'd emigrated to the States. Ray got her a job translating for Los Angeles's thriving Middle Eastern business community. The job had not been a good fit. To say the least.

During the insanity of the Oregon air crashes, Daria's actions had led directly to the death of four Ulster Irish terrorists. Her actions had been brave if foolhardy and the FBI had been more than grateful. The bad news: she hadn't given a damn about the accolades, she wanted to get back into the game.

The FBI had said no. Brave but foolhardy; it worried them. The ATF, on the other hand, liked a little foolhardy. They had an undercover unit working directly with the ultraviolent drug cartels on both sides of the U.S.–Mexico border, trying to cut off the endless river of guns that flow from the United States to the gangs. Daria could pass for Latina and could handle herself in a fight or under the crushing weight of a long-term false persona.

They took her on for a high-risk undercover op. Against the advice of Ray Calabrese's very strongly worded written statement opposing the move.

As Ray sat in the cafeteria and stewed, Henry Deits, recently promoted to special agent in charge of the L.A. field office, set down a Pepsi and a lemon Danish and pulled out a chair. "Hi, Ray. I haven't seen you since you got back. How was your vacation?"

Ray folded the sports section and checked his watch. "Fine. I should—"

"And by *vacation,* I mean: what dumb-ass stunt did you pull in Mexico that has the ATF lobbying mortar rounds into my office?" He took a healthy bite of the Danish and waited.

Ray glowered. Henry continued to wait.

"It's Daria Gibron."

Henry Deits moved the paper plate and the pastry six inches to the side, then bent at the waist and rapped his forehead twice against the tabletop.

"What on God's green earth were you thinking?"

"That operation is a clusterfuck, Henry! The agent in charge is a drug addict. There's a line in the sand that separates law enforcement from vigilantism, and that unit's about three miles past that line! If it was *just* entrapment, that would be unethical and illegal. No, this J. T. Laney character is putting on a road-show production of *Heart of Darkness.* I've investigated. They're not just planting guns and arresting traffickers. They're engaging in open warfare! The death toll is rising and Daria is stuck somewhere between live bait and part of a black ops death squad!"

Henry groaned. "ATF is a fine agency, Ray. They're above reproach."

"Most, yes. I agree. This unit has gone native."

"But they filled out all the right paperwork when they borrowed our asset. Daria built up her reputation as a gunrunner both here and in Israel. Her cover is spotless. Look: she was bored in L.A. She volunteered for this."

"She volunteered to help ATF, not to be part of an illegal wet-works squad!"

"That's your take on things. Fine. I trust you. But you've started a bureaucratic firestorm inside the Justice Department and I got guys from D.C. who want me to bench you pending an investigation."

"Good!" Ray's voice was drawing attention from other tables. "Do it. Start an investigation. Get Laney and his guys back to the States. Get 'em deposed, closed-door hearings, whatever. Let's shed some light on—"

Ray's cell phone chirped. He reached to turn it off but Henry's phone rang as well. Ray changed his mind and answered.

"Agent Calabrese? My name is Nathan Kowalski and I work for Delevan Wildman, director of the—"

"NTSB, I know."

Across the table, Henry's eyebrows rose. "Ray? I got NTSB, too." Into the phone, he said, "What's this about?"

But the voice on Ray's phone drew his attention. "The director asked me to call you and tell you that some friends of yours from our agency have been involved in a plane crash. . . ."

Twenty minutes later, Ray and Henry Deits stood in Ray's office. Ray was checking the contents of an overnight bag he kept there.

"I called the AIC in the Montana field office. She's totally understaffed and has three agents out on medical leave. When I offered you as liaison to the crash investigation, she jumped at it."

"Thanks, Henry." Ray added his service weapon and extra magazines.

"I'm not being a nice guy here. This lets me put off the ATF crap, at least for now."

"I'm not hiding in Montana."

"No, I'm hiding you in Montana. There's a difference."

Ray glowered at the idea.

"Did you know this pilot well?"

"Isaiah? Not well. I saw him pull off some of the most amazing stunts any pilot has ever tried. He saved our lives a couple of times. He was a good man."

Henry offered his hand. "Go. Help if you can."

Ray's instincts told him to stay and get this feud with J. T. Laney and his so-called Wild Boar Brigade out in the open. But with Isaiah Grey dead, Tommy and Kiki injured . . .

He took Henry's hand, pumped it once. "Thanks, boss."

WASHINGTON, D.C.

Nathan Kowalski stepped through the almost-always-open door of Del Wildman's office. "I got that FBI agent in Los Angeles. Tommy's friend.

FBI called back, and Agent Calabrese has been assigned as liaison to the Go-Team in Montana."

Del capped his pen. "Good. That relationship can be dicey. Calabrese's help in Oregon was essential."

Dicey was a nice way to put it. By law, all crash investigations on American soil are investigated by the NTSB, right up to the moment that it can be proved that the crash was the result of an illegal act and not just an accident. Once the illegal act is established, command of the investigation switches from the NTSB to the FBI.

"Anything else, sir?"

Del tapped three blunt fingers on his desktop, ruminating. His aide waited. "Close the door."

Kowalski did so.

"This is Peter Kim's first crash as Investigator in Charge. This is Beth Mancini's first crash as governmental liaison."

The aide nodded.

"With the complication of Tommy, Kiki, and Isaiah . . . Plus, I read Beth's daily report about this forest fire. I don't know."

His voice drifted off.

Kowalski said, "It would be good to have an experienced hand overseeing things. I don't have to tell you how I feel about Peter Kim, sir. He's smart enough, but what an arrogant jackass."

"Hmm." Del didn't deny it.

"You know the one person in this entire agency who could keep him from imploding, sir."

Del made a sour face. "I was the one talked her into taking her husband to Italy for four weeks!"

"I know. Still . . ."

"How would it look to Beth Mancini, me bringing in a relief pitcher?"

"She wouldn't like it. Probably. Then again, you catch your first crash in the supersensitive role as intergovernmental liaison, you've got Peter Kim, you've got dead and wounded crashers." The aide shrugged. "Could be Beth would appreciate the help."

Del pondered it awhile.

"Let's hold off," he said. "At least for now. But get me Susan Tanaka's phone number, just in case."

PORTLAND, OREGON

Later that afternoon, the owner of Dennison Records met Calendar's man, Cates, with his U.S. Marshal's shield at Portland International Airport. "You made good time."

The so-called deputy marshal nodded. "Time's of the essence with these things."

The recording expert signed a receipt saying he had taken possession of the cockpit voice recorder. "We'll get you a digital recording uploaded to the NTSB site inside of an hour."

Calendar's soldier shook the man's hand. "That's outstanding work, sir. Your nation thanks you."

ANNAPOLIS

Renee Malatesta wondered who would inform the other designers at the company and then realized she was supposed to.

She sat on the hardwood floor, staring at the phone. How does one do this, exactly? Is there a script? Are their appropriate colloquialisms? The man on the phone from Polestar had said, *I regret to inform you . . .* That was good, Renee thought. Cliché, admittedly, but clear. Clarity was a blessing. Short and sweet. Cut to the chase.

Andrew is dead. I regret to inform you that Andrew is dead.

She pressed her palms against her clenched eyes so tightly that amorphous, electrochemical lights danced in the darkness. *Andrew's dead! I'm a widow!*

And yet . . .

She rolled over, onto her side, on the floor, palms pressed against her eyes.

WASHINGTON, D.C.

Barry Tichnor returned to his car after his meeting with Gaelen Parks and Liz Proctor. His cell phone rang. He didn't recognize the number.

"Hello?"

"It's me." He recognized the voice of Jenna Scott. "I want to talk to you about something but I don't want to do it at Langley."

Barry was tired of surprises. "Rock Creek Park again?"

"Thank you. Twenty minutes?"

. . .

They met in the lovely, sylvan valley that was Rock Creek Park. Barry waited for her to tell him what was up.

"The speech. The sketch pad," she said. "Calendar didn't recover them."

"Oh." He stared up at her.

She turned to walk, so Barry did, too.

"You're the one now running Calendar. What do you recommend?"

Jenna paused. "I'm not sure."

"I am. NTSB. Their phones, their computers. We need to know what they know."

Jenna bit her lip. "Well, NTSB Go-Teams use communication gear with dedicated bandwidth. Easy enough to get their frequencies. Their computers are tougher."

"How much tougher?"

Jenna scanned the park, saw no one loitering. "It's against the law to conduct signal intelligence missions on another federal agency."

He nodded. "True."

She dug at the grass with one riding boot, fingers snugged into the back pockets of her jeans. Barry waited for her to get there.

"I can get us up on their phones in a day. Give me some time to get into their computers."

Barry Tichnor said, "Thank you."

She glanced up at him, squinting into the sun. "There's something else. I might have to be in the field to make this happen. I don't want to pull anyone from the Agency into this."

Barry shrugged. "You're the spy."

ANNAPOLIS

Renee Malatesta chose a black jacket and pants, white shirt, open at the throat. She added a necklace of pearls and a black pearl bracelet, checked the effect in the mirror. The pearls were too much; she took them off. She wore diamonds in her earlobes every day. She took them out but that looked wrong, and she put them back in. She had bought in early for that season's mile-high-shoe fashion—platforms and heels to match—but not today, not today. Her ballet flats were equally wrong. She had no shoes for telling the company that Andrew was dead. She had boots that would do.

Boots meant the pants had to go, so it was a pencil skirt and a chocolate sweater with three-quarter sleeves. *I regret to inform you* . . . That was good. She'd use that. The boots and pencil meant she was showing a little leg above the knee. Was that all right? It was. She wasn't going on a date. The thought made a little laugh burble to the surface.

I regret to inform you . . .

She went into the office just as the clock struck 6:00 P.M. It was 4:00 P.M. mountain time.

TWIN PINES

While part of the Go-Team struggled to get bodies and evidence out of the field, Beth Mancini organized the first press conference. One of her aides informed her that the media was clustering in the little town of Twin Pines, closer to the crash than Helena.

"Okay. Hey, any luck getting the Go-Team into one hotel for tonight?"

The aide admitted, no, the crashers likely would be spread out around Helena. Beth knew Peter would be steamed about that.

Beth had been hogging Adrienne Starbird's office and found the ops manager of Helena Regional in the airport's staff cafeteria. She had transformed one table into her makeshift office, complete with a laptop, piles of papers, and a Red Bull.

Adrienne sat in one chair, her hiking boots up in the adjacent chair, clacking away at her laptop, earbuds in place and MP3 player in her lap. Beth sat opposite her but had to wave a hand in her eyesight to catch her attention. "Hi."

"Wow!" Adrienne yanked on the white cords and the earbuds popped free. "I am so sorry! I was a mile away."

Beth smiled. "Are you kidding? You've been great. Thank you. I hereby declare my occupation of your office over. The siege ended."

Adrienne smiled back. "Now what?"

"I need to get out to that town you told me about. Twin Pines. I need to organize the first press conference, and that's where they're clustered. The media."

Adrienne slapped down the laptop, shoved it up into the piles of papers, and picked up a ring of keys. "C'mon."

ANNAPOLIS

It was 6:30 P.M. on Friday by the time Renee Malatesta met with Antal Borsa and Terri Loew at Malatesta, Inc.

They gathered in Andrew's office. Antal, who favored double-breasted suits and pocket squares, hand-made shoes, and a ubiquitous bottle of San Pellegrino, and Terri, lithe and intense, blond hair cut Agynnes Deyn–short, as usual in jeans, sneakers, and a Manchester United jersey top.

"I, ah . . ." Renee had brought in a Starbucks cup with five shots of espresso over ice. She drank a couple of those per day. But now she wondered if it sent the wrong signal, standing in line at Starbucks when Andrew was—

I regret to inform you that Andrew is dead.

"It's, ah . . ."

Terri stepped forward and opened her arms and hugged Renee so very hard. Terri was not, by nature, a hugger. This was one of their first, and they'd known each other fifteen years. She held the deep squeeze for ten seconds. When she stepped back, her eyes were red, her nose running.

Antal put his left hand on Renee's shoulder, his right hand on Terri's. "God. I'm sorry. We're sorry. Renee, there's just no words. I . . ." His voice faded away.

So they'd heard. So much for the rehearsal. Renee put down the damning coffee cup. "Thank you. Both of you. This is a tragedy. I haven't—"

She checked her dime-thin gold watch. "Have you heard from Vejay or Christian? Are they on their way in?"

Terri bit her lips so hard that they turned white.

Antal said, "I'm sorry. We thought you knew. They were on the flight with Andrew. They died."

Renee blinked. "They . . . ? They're dead, too?"

The engineers nodded.

The three of them stood in Andrew's toy-cluttered office, his desk adorned, as always, with a Mr. Potato Head and a Rubik's Cube, solved. On the wall was the *Wired* cover showing a young Andrew. Renee had framed it herself at a U-frame-it shop. A picture of the Starting Five, plus Renee, at that little fish-taco stand in the Dominican Republic.

Renee said, "*Keeeeeee . . .*" and it wasn't a word. It was a sound, an exhalation of terror and sorrow and guilt. "*Eeeeeee . . .*" until she fell to her knees and the designers were on their knees, too, a three-way hug, and both were crying; "*Eeeeee . . .*" until the air ran out of her lungs and then it was just good, old-fashioned sobbing until she collapsed, sideways, on the rug, fingers grasping at the nap, barking sobs, the two engineers holding each other still, on their knees, lost.

MONTANA

The remains of most of the dead were taken to Twin Pines, to a cold-storage facility arranged by the mayor.

The bodies of the pilot and copilot went to the office of the Lewis and Clark County medical examiner. At 5:00 P.M. Friday, Dr. Lakshmi Jain stood by and observed as the medical examiner examined what remained of Second Pilot Jed Holley. The body bag contained his right arm, portions of his thorax, and a left shoe.

"We'll do what we can with this, but . . ." The medical examiner shook his head.

He looked at the whisper-thin Indian woman, who nodded solemnly. Her NTSB photo ID was clipped to her belt and her black hair was pulled back in a severe bun. If she felt any emotion about the tangle of ex-human parts in the viscera-stained body bag, she didn't show it.

Together, they moved to the operating table where the body of Miguel Cervantes lay. He had been stripped naked, his clothes in a sealed, plastic container taped shut and properly marked. Cervantes had taken good care of his body. He was trim and muscled. He looked like a runner.

Lakshmi and the medical examiner both knew the cause of death. The C4 break in his spine. But there are proper procedures that must be taken, and nothing in an NTSB investigation is taken for granted.

Lakshmi could have conducted the autopsy but she had confidence in the medical examiner. He began with the classic Y incision to open up the breastplate and gain access to the heart, lungs, liver, stomach, spleen, and the rest. The cuts begin at both shoulders and come together at the lower end of the sternum. The cut then descends in a straight line to the pubis.

The organs were removed and weighed. Blood and other samples were taken for toxicology tests. The contents of Miguel Cervantes's stomach were examined.

Through it all, Dr. Lakshmi Jain said not a word, showed no hint of emotion. It was her job to confirm all available facts about the flight crew. Not to mourn them.

TWIN PINES

For NTSB intergovernmental liaisons, the first week's press conferences were always the worst. Reporters seemed not to understand exactly how little they would know about the crash, and how the investigation itself could be painstakingly slow.

Beth attended without the rest of the crashers, promising Peter Kim she'd keep the media at bay. Adrienne Starbird drove her out to Twin Pines. The two women, in Adrienne's Civic, caught their first glimpse of the small town as they pulled off State Highway 12. It was a small, quiet village snugged up against farmland to the west, scrub brush to the east. Past the scrub brush was the state forest and their downed airliner. The streets of Twin Pines appeared nearly empty and, with the exception of a basketball game between teenagers at the local park, they saw hardly anyone.

"Timber town," Adrienne told Beth. "The industry pretty much has ground to a halt. Towns like this are seeing twenty, maybe thirty percent unemployment. It's pretty sad."

Mayor Art Tibbits had arranged for the media to use a closed Save-More Store as a base camp. Plenty of parking in the store's lot, under old and sun-faded, red, white, and blue bunting hung from the light poles. The store itself was a big box, a perfect, dull rectangle with a 1950s italic-font logo. The old store may have been depressing but Beth thought it was a good location, close enough to the crash. All the major national media was there: a total of thirty newspapers, including blue-chip dailies like the *Washington Post* and *The New York Times*; all the TV news networks; three national radio networks. Reporters from Helena and Missoula were on hand, too. She counted no fewer than fifteen microwave trucks in the grocer's parking lot.

She wished the cameras weren't in the room. Beth considered herself ten pounds overweight and television cameras added another ten.

"Okay," she started from behind the lectern and the fanned-out array of microphones. The round seal on the lectern read TWIN PINES ROTARY CLUB. "I'd like to start with a statement, then I'll take questions."

She gave them the make of the plane and its history. She listed the departure and arrival airports for Flight 78. She gave them the number of dead, the number of wounded. She identified all four crewmembers, because their families already knew. She began to point to a reporter at random but, as she raised her arm, Beth felt moisture in her pits. She made a little nodding gesture instead.

"Do you have theories on the cause of the crash?"

"No. It's far too early to know why the plane crashed. Um, you?"

"Is the Claremont considered a safe plane?"

"It has an outstanding record. Several domestic carriers use fleets of them. My assistant will be handing out statistics on domestic airline crashes. Um, how about you?"

"Have you ruled out pilot error?"

"We have not ruled out anything."

"So it could have been pilot error?"

Beth blinked at the questioner. "Yes. Absolutely."

HELENA

Gene Whitney didn't leave his hotel room until after six. He found a liquor shop, thinking, as he often did, that a bit of the hair of the dog . . . Hey, it's a cliché because it works.

He'd intended to buy just a pint of vodka but there was a sale on Hood River vodka, which he'd never heard of before. He could get two liters for twelve bucks. Who could beat that? So he got that instead, thinking, *Look at the money I'm saving!* Because, after all, he'd be in Helena at least a week.

He got back to the hotel and took a fingerful of the vodka, feeling the ball-peen hammer inside his temple dial back a bit. He went online and made another reservation to fly to Reagan, sipping his second glass, realizing Hood River wasn't top-notch vodka but, again, that price . . . seriously.

Meanwhile, Beth's aides failed miserably at getting the 160 or so people involved in tomorrow's All-Thing settled. Helena, Montana, did not have an overabundance of hotel rooms. The crashers alone were already straining the city's reserves and the copious attendance at the All-Thing stretched it well beyond capacity.

17

T HE TEAM LEADERS GATHERED around a large table at a family-run restaurant near the airport. The only one missing was Gene Whitney, who handled the flight and ground crews, but they knew he was conducting interviews back in D.C.

They gathered at 8:00 P.M. and, for the most part, agreed that cheeseburgers and fries would do the job. Jain had the chopped salad with homemade, fried pita bread rather than croutons, dressing on the side. Peter opted for grilled salmon and a salad.

"Not a bad start," he said, still wearing the natty suit, tie knotted firmly at his throat fourteen hours after he'd put it on.

Teresa Santiago pulled her thick, black hair into a cable behind her neck and fixed a leather clip to it. "Credit goes to Tomzak and Duvall. The site was pristine."

Peter flashed an icy smile. "Yes. Other thoughts?"

Reuben Chaykin *humphed* and raised both hands, palms up, and let them drop. His powerplant was a charred ruin stretching a mile long in the forest. "It's going to take months to put the pieces together. The fire . . ." He shook his head. "Thanks to Jack, we got out about half of the avionics, enough to run a pretty good test on the flight deck. We should be able to tell what was working and what wasn't but we need to get the rest of it."

"Left-hand side of the cockpit," Jack Goodspeed corrected. "The avionics in front of the copilot were pretty smashed up."

Peter turned to Dr. Jain, who picked at her iceberg lettuce. "How are the pilots?"

Lakshmi had a second-language-speaker's habit of waiting a beat before responding. She also rarely smiled. Between the chipper Jack Goodspeed and the flirtatious Teresa Santiago, Peter was pleased to have a more staid team member.

"The copilot's body was badly destroyed. He died before the plane hit the ground. We haven't even found the majority of him and I suspect we never will. He's probably back in the portion of the forest that's on fire. The pilot suffered a broken neck, severe spinal injury. It is he who surprised me."

Hector Villareal poured ketchup on his fries. "How?"

"I . . . I am not sure. I want to go over his postmortem again."

Peter took note of her puzzled frown. "Take your time. Get the pilots' autopsies right."

Lakshmi returned her attention to the salad.

Peter turned to Hector. "Cockpit voice recorder?"

"The digital copy was uploaded to our site a couple of hours ago. We can listen to it after dinner."

"Good, good. Gene's in D.C. He's interviewing the ground crew. He should be back tomorrow."

Beth Mancini nibbled on a fry. "The All-Thing is set for eleven A.M. tomorrow. We look to have a pretty good crowd."

Reuben chowed down on his burger. "Do we have confirmation on the Bembenek Company?"

Beth checked a spiral-bound notepad. "Um . . . Yes. Why?"

The tough little Chicagoan looked glum. "I'm going to need full replicas of the engines and propellers if I have any hope at all of reassembling that mess out there."

Peter turned to Jack Goodspeed. "Speaking of which, are we going to need a reassemble?"

If necessary, Jack's team of engineers could reassemble the destroyed Claremont VLE. Jack squinted up at the ceiling of the diner and considered the question. "I'm gonna guess, no. I want to hear the cockpit voice recorder, see what Teresa makes of the flight data recorder, of course. But at first blush? No reconstruct."

A full reconstruct was the costliest and most time-consuming duty of a Go-Team. Peter knew that if they could avoid it, Chairman Delevan Wildman would be pleased.

Teresa Santiago leaned back. "My black box will tell the tale. The FDR is in awesome shape and it's a DataSave, 1200 Series. Damn good recorder. Not a Gamelan, but the next best thing. Don't you worry your pretty head." She leaned over and ruffled Jack's hair. Jack winked back at her.

Lakshmi blanched a little at their quick friendship and flirtatiousness.

"Good." Peter looked past Reuben's shoulder and saw a waitress point to their table. A big, dark-haired man with an overnight case in his fist began wending his way through tables.

Oh, great, he thought. He patted his lips dry with a napkin and stood. "Agent . . . ?"

"Calabrese. Ray Calabrese." They shook but it wasn't cordial. "Peter Kim, right? Hi."

Peter waved to the table. "Agent Calabrese was the FBI liaison for the crash in Oregon last year. I take it you're our liaison again this year?"

Ray said, "I asked for the gig, after I heard about Tommy and Kiki. And Isaiah." The big guy's eyes were pulled down in a grimace. "God, I am so sorry about Isaiah."

Peter nodded, his stomach acids kicking in. Another player from the insanely screwed-up operation in Oregon. Worse yet: one of the Big Four: the people who'd flown a jetliner into a dune. *Part of the damn legend.*

Beth said, "I'll call one of the hotels, see if I can get you booked."

Teresa Santiago steepled her fingers, elbows on the table, and cradled her chin. She batted her lashes at the big FBI agent. "Hey, if there's no room at the inn, I'm glad to share."

She was pleased to see Ray Calabrese reply with a good-natured smile. She also was perversely pleased to see Peter Kim grimace.

LANGLEY

Jenna Scott decided to handle the signal-intelligence duty herself. First, the Malatesta gig was completely and totally illegal, and there was no one in the entire Central Intelligence Agency she trusted to keep this particular secret. Second, she wasn't a field agent anymore, but when she had been, she'd been a gifted hacker. And it's good to brush off the old skills now and then.

She had the Go-Team's communications locked down. That had been the easy part. She started making digital copies, starting with Beth's call to the hotel. She jotted down the name *Ray Calabrese.*

HELENA

Gene Whitney only woke up because he'd puked a little bit on his pillow. He staggered to the bathroom and threw up properly. He filled the bathroom sink with cold water and dunked his head in. It helped sweep away some of the barbed wire wrapped around his cerebellum.

Gene didn't remember anything about his flight to D.C. Or even getting to this hotel. He knelt over the toilet and dry heaved a little, realizing he must have gone and gotten himself good and pissed last night.

He found his travel kit and brushed his teeth. He did not look at his reflection in the mirror. He gargled with the travel-size bottle of Listerine, spit it out, and slouched back to the main room in his socks, his creased pants, his untucked dress shirt.

He stood with his hands on his hips and squinted around the room for several minutes before he realized two things.

One: he was still in Helena, Montana.

And two: the two-liter bottle of Hood River vodka was half empty.

By the time the team leaders and Ray Calabrese returned to the hotel where Peter and Beth were staying, the cockpit voice recording from Polestar Flight 78 had been uploaded to the NTSB Web site. The team agreed to meet in Beth's room, which was large enough to seat everyone.

"You might as well hear this, too," Beth told Ray as they entered the hotel lobby.

Peter Kim bristled. "I don't think so. Until this is proven to be a crime—if it is a crime—the FBI is here in an advisory capacity only. I think it's better to play this by the rulebook."

Beth blinked in confusion. "I've read the reports from the Oregon crash. Agent Calabrese was really helpful."

"It's okay with me," added Hector, and turning to Ray: "You've heard CVR downloads before?"

"Just the one. In Oregon."

Hector shrugged. "He could be useful."

"No." Peter made a horizontal, sweeping gesture. "Sorry."

Ray studied the slight engineer, and Peter studied him right back. After a beat, Ray hitched the strap of his overnight bag higher on his shoulder. "It's all right. I have to check in, then catch up with the Montana field office. Good luck, folks."

He turned to the reception desk.

The others took the elevator to Beth's suite. There, Hector set up a Bose speaker shaped like a flying saucer and attached an iPod to its dock. He had downloaded the CVR recording to his laptop and from the laptop to the iPod.

Beth opened the minibar. A few of the team took diet sodas or bottled water, then settled in. Teresa Santiago kicked off her shoes and nestled into the couch.

Beth sat, pulled out her cell phone, and sent a text message to Gene Whitney in D.C.: *its beth. how did it go?*

Hector consulted his notepad. "I've cued it up to just the last minute or so. I listened to the full thirty minutes, three times. I can tell you that the pilots ran a tight flight deck. No horsing around, distractions. We're going to hear from, ah, Miguel Cervantes. He's what Polestar calls the Pilot-in-Charge. The other is Jed Holley, copilot or so-called second pilot.

"Holley is first," Hector added, and hit the button.

Holley: We're at, ah, a thousand feet. Passing outer marker for Helena
    Regional.
Cervantes: A thousand?
Holley: Ah . . . yeah.

(beat)

Cervantes: I don't think so. I think we're lower.
Holley: I got a confirm on the altimeter, now reading nine five zero
    feet . . . mark.
Cervantes: Ah, Helena Regional, this is Polestar Seven-Eight, what
    elevation do you have for us?

(beat)

Cervantes: Helena Regional, Polestar Seven-Eight.

(beat)

This feels way low, Jed. We're lower than we think. Helena Regional,
   Pole—
Holley: Trees!
Cervantes: What?
Holley: Trees, trees! Pull up!
Cervantes: Pulling up.
Holley: C'mon . . . climb, baby. Do it!
Cervantes: Okay, pul—
(Crack!)
Holley: Mayday! Mayday!
(CRACK! CRACK!)
Holley: Polestar Seven-Eight! Mayday! We—

End of tape.
The seven crashers sat, ill at ease. No matter how many of these they heard, it still smacked eerily of talking to ghosts.
Jack Goodspeed broke the silence. "Controlled flight into terrain."
Dr. Jain frowned. "Sorry?"
"Likely cause of the crash," Peter explained, leaning back in his chair. "The pilots were uninjured and in full control. They simply flew into the trees."
Lakshmi Jain still frowned. "Is that likely?"
Reuben shrugged. "More common than you'd think. Last twenty years, something like—what, Beth? Fifteen percent of domestic crashes are controlled flight into terrain?"
"About that: fifteen, sixteen percent."
Teresa Santiago jumped in. "In this case, likely a binary glitch. Altimeter was wrong, and they lost radio contact with the tower. I mean, we have a long way to go, to be sure. But I'm betting the flight data recorder backs up that diagnosis. I wish Gene were here."
He was the only pilot among the Go-Team leaders.
Reuben shrugged. "Sounds like a slam dunk. Sure didn't sound like pilot error. The big mystery is going to be the altimeter and the radio. Separate glitches? Or symptoms of another gremlin we haven't discovered yet?"
Peter Kim looked pleased with himself. "Jack, Reuben? Getting as much of the avionics out as you did today is going to be invaluable. Thank you both. Nice job."
Teresa stood and moved to the door. Others rose, too. "My FDR will

fill in the gaps. Five dollars says we'll be sleeping back in our own beds inside of a week."

Reuben said, "Your lips to God's ear."

They were all near the door now, realizing that most of the mystery of Flight 78 had been solved in less than twenty-four hours.

Peter thought—but didn't say—that this would get everyone at the NTSB to stop gabbing about the damn Oregon crash. *Thank God.*

18

PETER KIM CALLED HOME but it went right to voice mail. He left a message saying his team was performing very well and he hoped to be home sooner than anyone anticipated.

He decided a quick drink was in order because the day had gone so well. He checked his diver's watch: closing in on 10:00 P.M.

He had spotted a quaint-looking bar down the street from the hotel. A one-story brick-facade affair that looked like something out of the 1950s, right down to the flickering neon sign.

The saloon itself was dark and neat, with a red leather bar and black-and-white photos of San Francisco cityscapes on the walls. Sinatra played softly. Only a few of the round tables were taken. Two of eight stools at the bar were in use. Peter selected a third.

"What do you have in the way of single-malt Irish whiskeys?"

The bartender pointed to a bottle of Bushmills.

"That'll do."

"Peter?"

He glanced to his left. Jack Goodspeed sat at the bar, a beer in front of him. Peter thinking, *Oh, great.*

Predictably, Jack stood and scooted over to an adjacent stool. He'd changed into jeans and sneakers and a Utah Jazz sweatshirt, sleeves pushed up his muscled forearms. Peter's glass arrived and Jack held his stein up in toast. Peter decided to gulp his whiskey and escape quickly.

"To a good first day," Jack said. "Quick, clean, by the book."

That, actually, was a toast Peter could get behind. They touched glasses and sipped.

"Can I ask you a question?"

Peter said, "Shoot."

"So what's up with everyone's reverence for last year's Oregon crash?"

Peter was surprised. "What do you mean?"

"No offense, here. You guys, that Go-Team. Remarkable work. You saved thousands of lives. I'm just saying: from an outsider's perspective, it appears that absolutely nothing went according to protocol."

Peter decided not to gulp the Bushmills after all. "Honestly? It's worse than you know. We soft-sold some of that absolute clusterfuck to give Del Wildman the political cover to not fire Tomzak and Isaiah Grey."

"No kidding? Hell."

Peter was thinking maybe he'd underestimated the affable Jack Goodspeed.

"Laws were broken, protocol was broken. It was pure dumb luck that solved the crash. But trying telling that to Wildman."

"Why'd they put a pathologist in charge of the team? That'd be like—and again, no offense—Dr. Jain running our investigation. Thanks. I'll pass on that."

"That was Susan Tanaka's stupid idea. Do you know her?"

Jack said, "A little. We haven't caught a crash together."

"She was with Tomzak at the Kentucky crash, three years ago."

"The unsolved crash. I remember."

"Right. She was using Oregon as . . . I don't know. Therapy for Tomzak's bruised ego over not solving Kentucky."

"Well." Jack raised his beer. "Here's to the book. And going by it."

"To the book."

Peter ordered another.

Gene Whitney sent a text message to Beth Mancini that read, *"all looks normal in d.c. see you A.M. tomorrow."*

He sent it from two miles away at a bar—a different bar from the one with the fistfight because, on the ground, what? a day, day and a half, and he'd already been kicked out of one local watering hole. City wasn't that big. And he might be around for a while. Best to slow that shit down.

Gene caught the eye of the cute-as-pie waitress with the spiky hair and full-sleeve tattoos and said, "Hit me."

ANNAPOLIS

At 8:00 A.M. eastern, Saturday, Renee, Antal, and Terri met in the little conference room of the company headquarters. Two full walls were covered in wipe board, with trays of dry-erase markers everywhere. Engineers were encouraged to toss up notions, quotes, mathematical formulas, whatever. The quote nearest the light switch today read: "Outside of a dog, a book is man's best friend. And inside a dog, it's too dark to read—Groucho Marx."

Renee sat on the conference table, her feet in a chair, elbows on her knees, spine curved, hunched in. She hadn't slept and it was obvious. Her voice was thick, as though she had a cold. "There's a plane, going to Helena. Helena, Montana, where . . . Anyway. I can go."

Antal took a sip of fizzy water. "Do you want us to go with you?"

"No. I'll represent us."

Terri reached out and they grasped hands for a moment.

Renee wiped her cheeks. She held a wadded Kleenex in her fist like it was a life raft. She smiled a brittle smile at Terri, thinking, *Were you fucking Andrew? He said you weren't. I think you were.* She said, "The company . . ."

Terri said, "The company's fine. There's nothing we need to do today, tomorrow, that can't wait. We'll come with—"

"We're maintaining our contract with Halcyon."

Terri and Antal exchanged looks. The natty Hungarian engineer cleared his throat. "Ah. Okay. That's a talk for later. We should come with you. To heck with the airline's plane. We'll charter a jet. I'll foot the bill. Let's go to Montana, go get our people."

Renee let a little laugh escape. She smiled at the intense man with wispy blond hair, whom she'd known for fifteen years. Eight in the morning on a Saturday and Antal Borsa's idea of *dressing down* was to put a cashmere turtleneck under his double-breasted suit coat.

Renee had thrown on a burgundy sweater, jeans, JP Todd moccasins. She had pulled her hair back into a ponytail. She'd aged twenty years since yesterday. "I am serious about Halcyon/Detweiler," she said. "Andrew was wrong. I've already informed them. You stay here. You have work to do."

She climbed off the table, wiped her nose with the wadded cloth, walked to the door.

Terri said, "Renee? Andrew didn't want—"

"Yes. I know."

She walked out.

HELENA

Friday morning, Ray Calabrese drove his rental to Big Sky Community Hospital to find Tommy and Kiki.

He located them in Tommy's room. Tommy was in bed wearing hospital PJs and propped up by pillows. Kiki wore powder-blue operating-room scrubs and slippers someone on the staff had dug up for her. These were obviously from the neonatal or pediatrics unit and were adorned with cute patches of teddy bears and giraffes. A metal cane rested against the bed stand.

Kiki's face lit up. "Ray?" She hopped up, weight on her good leg, to take the proffered hug. A half second into it she said, "Broken rib! Broken rib!"

"Damn! Sorry!"

She laughed, and winced when even that hurt.

Tommy looked pale and gaunt, unshaved, with purple bags under his eyes and a large, square bandage adhered to his skull over his right ear. Ray put out a hand to shake.

Tommy said, "How you doing, New York?"

They shook hands. "Docs tell me that thick skull of yours finally paid off." He gripped Kiki's hand in his left and said, "Hey. Isaiah. I am just so damn sorry."

Kiki hugged him again, then perched on the side of Tommy's bed. "Thank you. I haven't processed it yet. I keep wanting to ask him what to do."

Tommy sipped water through a straw. "Is there a proper Go-Team on site?" His voice was as rough as sandpaper.

"Yeah. I met the team. Ah, Peter Kim is IIC."

The two crashers exchanged glances. Tommy drawled, "Well, shit," but then shook his head. "No. Petey's smart. Smart and determined. He's a dick, but that's okay. He'll do good."

Ray produced his ubiquitous notebook and went through the names of the Go-Team members. Some Tommy had worked with. Some Kiki had. For some, neither. There wasn't a bad review for any of them.

Kiki said, "Sounds like Peter has a good team. I can't vouch for Beth Mancini. She's pretty new. But Susan says she has potential."

The hospital-room telephone rang. Kiki leaned over to grab it. "Hello? . . . *Susan!*" To the boys she said, "It's Susan Tanaka!" Then into the phone: "My God! . . . Thank you . . . I know, us, too. Hang on: here's Tommy."

She handed him the receiver. She saw her boyfriend paste a smile onto his face, knowing that Susan would be able to tell otherwise. "Hey."

Ray made an I-should-go gesture. Kiki stood, retrieved her metal cane. "Walk you out."

Tommy lay down as they exited, the phone to his ear.

In the corridor, Kiki said, "Can you pull some strings here? I want to hear the CVR."

Ray said, "Sure. But you're in a lot of pain."

She winced. "Yeah. I'm laying off the painkillers. I want to be sharp. I want to help."

"Their cockpit-voice-recorder guy, Hector Villareal? He seems pretty competent."

She placed her long-fingered, pianist's hand, palm forward, on Ray's chest. "I know. I want to help."

They hugged again, only very softly this time. "I'm on it."

"Thanks." As they separated, Kiki said, "Hey—how's Daria?"

Ray's eyes traveled around the hospital corridor, his brain mulling his options. "She's . . . busy."

"I'm sorry to hear that." She straightened Ray's tie.

He gave her a rueful, crooked grin that was robbed of any humor. "Half a year ago, ATF was working with her in L.A., breaking about a dozen law-enforcement-entrapment rules. I blew the whistle. Federal judge threw out a few convictions. Top ATF people took early retirement. I'm not on ATF's Christmas card list and I . . . Daria is in Mexico. Doing God knows what."

Kiki let the moment linger. "Well, I'm sorry."

He winked. "Hey, let me do what I can on the cockpit recording. Stay off that leg."

In her hotel room, Beth Mancini began filling out a preliminary report on the first day of the investigation. She sat cross-legged on her bed with a can of Diet Coke on the bedside table, her MP3 player locked on Ani DiFranco.

She entered her ten-digit alphanumerical NTSB identification and the date of the crash. Under "Most Critical Injury" she typed: "Fatal."

She added the nearest city/place, Twin Pines, along with the state, zip code, and local time of the accident.

Under "Aircraft Information" she typed the registration number, followed by "Claremont VLE," plus the model serial numbers.

Under "Injury Summary," she typed "18 dead; 8 survivors."

Under "Narrative," she typed: "On August 4, about 2315 mountain standard time, a Polestar Airlines Claremont VLE, d.b.a. Polestar Flight 78, crashed during its descent to runway 5-23 of Helena Regional Airport (HLN). The crash site was approximately 7 nautical miles west of the airport. Four flight crew and 24 passengers were fatally injured and the aircraft was destroyed by impact forces. There were 8 surviving passengers and no ground fatalities. Night visual meteorological conditions prevailed at the time of the accident. The flight was a Code of Federal Regulations (CFR) Part 121 scheduled passenger flight from Ronald Reagan Washington National Airport (DCA) to HLN. Updated on Saturday, August 6.

Beth saved her work, made a pdf of it, and immediately e-mailed a copy to the NTSB mainframe, to Delevan Wildman in Washington, to Peter Kim in Helena, and to her own MobileMe Web-cloud account.

ANNAPOLIS

Renee Malatesta called the airport shuttle service and asked for a ride to Reagan National. She dragged out her matching russet-red suitcase and carry-on satchel. She packed underthings. Three unopened packages of tights, her riding boots, khaki boot-cut trousers, three tops, and a warm jacket. She hadn't checked the weather in Montana, so she walked to the entryway closet and grabbed a small, retractable umbrella. She returned to the bedroom and gave a little shriek.

The nickel-plated Colt .25 sat atop the pile of clothes in her suitcase.

Renee turned to the closet. The step stool sat there; not in the kitchen, where it lived.

Renee's knees buckled and she eased herself onto the bed. She let her fingertips touch the iron, making sure it was real. It wasn't as cold this time—her own hand must have warmed it up, retrieving it. She had no memory of having done so.

Renee sat and stared at the gun, as her eyes brimmed with tears, spilling out, running down her cheeks, the underside of her chin, pooling in her clavicle.

She fell to her knees on the floor and sobbed.

VARENNA, ITALY

Susan and Kirk sat on a bench by the cobblestone pathway that encircled the village. She was reading *The New Yorker* on her iPad. He was up to sitting thirty minutes at a time without aggravating his back injury. He was reading something by Lee Child that he was realizing, just now, was beginning to be uncomfortably familiar. "Crap. I think I've read this," he grumbled.

His wife reached over to rub his thigh through thin, Irish-cotton trousers. "That almost always happens, babe," she said without looking up. The man had many great qualities but he absolutely could not remember any plots.

Kirk popped a Vicodin and stared at the sleeping ducks and the rocking sailboats for a while. The ferry from Menaggio approached the dock. Life went on around them but not quickly. Things took their time in Varenna.

Susan's computer tablet pinged: incoming e-mail. She glanced at the server, frowned. "It's Del Wildman."

"Open it."

Susan turned to him. "We're on vacation, babe. I shouldn't be reading e-mails."

Kirk Tanaka said, "Shut up, dummy." He kissed her bare shoulder. "Ever since you heard about Isaiah, Tommy, and Kiki, you've been tight as a steel drum. It's driving you crazy, not helping. Check Del's e-mail. I'm not going anywhere."

Susan leaned over and kissed her husband on the mouth. He tasted like citrus. "I love you."

"You have remarkable taste in men."

Susan opened the e-mail. A little, vertical frown line formed on her forehead. "It's the day-one prelim from the Montana crash. From Beth Mancini. Del's asking if I could take a look at it."

"Why not? You told me you were worried about Beth catching a complicated crash. I don't mind. Here." He stood, wincing, hand bracing the small of his back. "I'll go grab us some coffee. I need to stretch my back."

As he limped toward the nearest little taverna, Susan began scanning the preliminary report.

WASHINGTON, D.C.

One shift per week, Amy Dreyfus worked as a line editor on the night Metro desk at the *Post*. She was in training to be an editor. Which meant she left work after the top of the eleven o'clock news on Friday and after scanning the wire services one last time. She was the PIC, or Person In Charge, but, upon grabbing her coat, that duty fell to the copy-desk chief.

The second-day follow-up of the Polestar Flight 78 crash in Montana had taken up fourteen column inches on page 7A, the last page that night dedicated to national news. Only one copyeditor had read the story, plus the slot editor. On the Metro desk, Beth mostly read local stories the paper's own reporters had written, although she did scan the wires to see what was moving. She had opened the Polestar story but never got past the second paragraph.

She'd gotten home around 11:45, had a glass of good pinot grigio, read three chapters of a Robert Crais thriller, then climbed into bed next to Ezra Dreyfus at 12:30 Saturday morning.

A patent lawyer who ran his business out of their spare bedroom, Ezra always got up first on Saturdays. He made pancakes for their eight-year-old son Levi who was glued to Saturday morning cartoons. He let his wife sleep in until noon.

Usually.

It was only 10:30 when Ezra sat on her side of the bed and shook her shoulder. She wore a Where's Waldo T and a pair of his boxers. "Hmm?"

"Kidlet? Hey."

She opened her eyes, blinked. "You're a good-looking man," she slurred. When he didn't smile, she got up on one elbow. "Ezra?"

He showed her page 7A of the *Post*. She got to Andrew Malatesta's name in the eighth paragraph and threw her hand over her mouth.

HELENA

A transcript of the Polestar Flight 78 flight data recorder was uploaded to the NTSB high-security server. Teresa Santiago used her pass code to access it, then curled up on the bed in her hotel room with a legal pad, a pen, and a sweetened chai tea. She went through it line by line.

The team leaders met at ten in Beth's suite. She had arranged for coffee, orange juice, apple juice, bottled water, and baked goods. Teresa handed out her one-page summary. She'd kicked off her sandals as soon as she'd entered; one of those people more comfortable barefoot than shod.

Ray Calabrese joined the crashers today. Beth had argued that keeping him out made no sense, since Ray was a trained investigator and had a keen eye for detail. Peter Kim eventually agreed.

Gene Whitney looked pallid and rumpled and had mottled bruising around his lip.

Beth said, "Are you okay?"

He just nodded.

Peter, with his degree in electrical engineering, read the one sheet and got the gist of it first. "Short circuit, second bus panel?"

Teresa nodded. "Yes. Took out the altimeter and their comms. Leveque Aéronautics of Quebec made the system."

Hector said, "Anyone else remember a crash, couple of years ago in Germany? Leveque avionics package shut down by a short circuit?"

Jack Goodspeed sat forward. "Düsseldorf. It was a KLM flight, like, three years ago, yeah."

Reuben Chaykin pushed out his lower lip and nodded. "We maybe got a pattern. Got to love patterns."

Peter's smile tightened. "Good. All right. Jack, did you pull the panel out of the flight deck?"

"No. We'll get that today."

"Thank you. Dr. Jain, did you get tox back?"

The laconic pathologist nodded to her palm-top. "Just now. No poisons, no drugs. Both had a beer the night before with steaks and french fries."

"Thank you. Gene?"

The big man shrugged and leaned forward, holding a coffee in both of his large hands, eyes on the hotel room's carpet. "Pilots had great reputations. I've asked around. Navy fliers. Experienced."

"Fine. And everything was okay with the ground crew in D.C.?"

Gene sipped from his lidded coffee. "Yeah."

Peter made a check mark next to Gene's name.

Most of them had heard the cockpit voice recorder the night before, so he skipped Hector Villareal's name. "Jack?"

"County sheriff's office is giving us off-duty deputies to keep the lookie-loos away from the site. If we don't have to rebuild, and I'm thinking we don't, I want to do a chop-and-haul."

For some crashes, the only way to solve the mystery is to pick up each piece of the downed airliner and rebuild it. But if the cockpit voice recorder and the flight data recorder offer up a culprit—say, a short circuit on the flight deck—then the costly process of rebuilding the craft can be bypassed in favor of a chop-and-haul—separating the plane into sections, loading them on flatbeds, and driving them to a hangar, just to hold on to them until the investigation is over.

Peter said, "I'll take that under advisement. Reuben?"

Reuben Chaykin sighed theatrically. "The damage, the fire, I got debris spread everywhere. It'll take a month, tops, to get all of the pieces to a proper engineering facility, confirm what happened."

"With luck," Peter said, "that won't be necessary. We have—"

"Yes, it will."

"What?"

"It'll take a month at least but we'll do it. I know we have a likely culprit, a binary malfunction. But . . ." He gave the room a broad shrug. "I can't confirm till we do this right."

Peter nodded. It was a good, by-the-book answer and he appreciated it. "Then we'll do it right. Thank you. And if Jack's team isn't going to have to do a rebuild, we could divert some of his people to Powerplant."

Jack gave Reuben the thumbs-up. "Sure thing!" Peter noted that the big, handsome man's bonhomie no longer annoyed him quite so much.

"All right." Peter made his last check mark. "Anything else for the good of the order?"

Beth Mancini put a pen and a condolence card down in front of Peter. "It's for LaToya Grey. I got her flowers, too."

Peter scribbled his name and passed the card and pen to his left. "Anything else?"

Ray Calabrese raised his hand.

"Yes, ah . . . ?"

"Ray. I talked to Kiki. She wants to help. She'd like to hear the cockpit voice recording."

Peter and Hector spoke simultaneously. Peter going with, "That would be against regulations, no." And Hector going with, "Sure. I'll get her . . ."

They turned to each other. Peter made a *tsk* noise. "Ah, no. We're following procedure on this one."

Gene had been sitting quietly, leaning forward, elbows on knees and not making eye contact with anyone. "You shitting me?" He looked up at Peter with bloodshot eyes. "You've seen what Duvall can do with audio. She's the goddamn Sonar Witch."

Hector nodded. "She has that reputation. No, I'd appreciate her ears. Tell her I'll get it to her right away."

Peter frowned. "Was I unclear? Did my words confuse anyone?"

Beth Mancini, thinking, *Oh, God. Here we go.*

Teresa Santiago said, "I worked with Kiki on one other crash. She's amazing. I vote yes."

Peter turned to her, slowly. "I'm sorry. Did you say *vote?*"

Lakshmi Jain was next. "I don't care, one way or another. But it would be outside standard procedures."

Reuben Chaykin shrugged. "She's not a civilian. She's not media. She won't talk out of school. And if she's that good . . ."

The tide in the room quickly turned against Peter, who capped his expensive gold pen and stood, buttoning his suit coat. "Folks?" When they stopped talking, he went on. "This discussion lasted about a minute, which is fifty-five seconds too long. I think we're done here."

He stepped toward the door but stopped when he was in front of Teresa. *"Vote?"* He shook his head, walked out.

Everyone sat quietly, uncomfortable. Gene said, "Well, shit, that went well."

Dr. Jain stood. "He's the Investigator in Charge."

Gene sipped coffee. "He's also a jackass."

Beth jumped in. "Okay. Meeting adjourned. Thanks, everyone. Good work here."

Her cheery smile fooled no one.

CRASH SITE

Calendar lay on his stomach, binoculars to his eyes, and watched the remains of the Claremont VLE. Things couldn't have been much worse.

First, a sheriff's deputy walked the perimeter of the crash site. Calendar had the skills and the weapons to take out the man. But that course of action would alert everyone that the crash had not been an accident.

Second, fire crews were on scene, keeping an eye on the blaze about a mile away. It had died down a bit during the night, during a windless evening. But they were close enough to see the fuselage, further limiting Calendar's offerings.

Finally, a tall, painfully thin woman with jet-black hair in an NTSB windbreaker and ball cap showed up around eleven and started ordering people around.

The crash site was a damn circus.

He checked his watch.

He was only an hour away from Coeur d'Alene, Idaho. Plenty of time.

Lakshmi Jain identified herself to the sheriff's deputy guarding the Claremont VLE. She ducked through the hole in the center of the fuselage, and dug a palm-size flashlight out of the messenger bag she carried over one shoulder. She made her way through the debris, stepped on the torn-out door to the flight deck, and ducked inside.

The bodies had been removed but not the stench of death. Lakshmi ignored it. The dead deer—or about two-thirds of one, she corrected—lay where she'd first seen it. There was no standard protocol for removing or not removing an animal carcass from a crash scene.

She drew a tablet computer from her shoulder bag, activated it, and studied the still photos she'd taken of the pilot, Miguel Cervantes, concentrating on his spinal injury.

She walked gingerly through the cockpit to the sole remaining seat, the left-hand seat of the lead pilot. She studied the bloody thumbprint on the catch of the safety harness, the congealed blood from the arm wound on the seat. She knelt and scanned the floor—which had been a wall—noting the blood drops, their size and shape. Blood from the arm wound had dropped straight down, but hadn't blossomed into large splashes. She imagined Cervantes crawling, on his knees and one good hand, back to where she had found him. He must have stood up. Then he died of his

wounds, fell back against the curved bulkhead and slid to the seated position in which she'd found him.

She studied the tablet again, and the spinal injury.

She sat in the dark for a while and ran the scene over and over in her
head.

HELENA

At 11:15 A.M., Beth Mancini called Peter Kim. He picked up on the first ring.
"Kim."

"Hey. It's Beth. Um, where are you?"

"Ten minutes from the crash site."

She blanched, turned, and looked at the 167 people fidgeting in their
seats in the Burton K. Wheeler Memorial Conference Center. "Peter! The
All-Thing was supposed to start fifteen minutes ago!"

He said, "It hasn't started yet?"

"I'm waiting on you and the others!"

"Oh. Well, don't. Those things are useless. I told everyone to stay away.
Get on with it."

She made eye contact with some of the people in the crowd and smiled.
Whispering, she said, "The Investigator in Charge introduces the All-Thing.
That's the way it works."

"Beth? Reciting to me *the way it works* generally won't get you very far.
A lot of things work poorly. I think the All-Thing is a stupid idea and I've
told Delevan Wildman that to his face."

"But you're the one who insists we work *by the book.*"

"Not when it's a stupid waste of time. The All-Thing is a waste of time.
It's a political carnival and you are our intergovernmental liaison. Have
them introduce themselves, have them get business cards from your assistants, then tell them that if and when I call, to have their teams ready,
double-quick, to do exactly what I tell them to do. Out."

He disconnected.

Beth tucked away her earpiece and voice wand and stepped up to the lectern, on the stage of the downtown conference center. She tapped the end
of the microphone with her fingernail three times. "People? Shall we get
started?"

One hundred sixty-seven filled the first fourteen rows of the auditorium. And many of them were experienced enough in NTSB protocol to recognize that something was off.

"Let's do introductions." Beth beamed positivity. She nodded to one of her aides, who was getting everything on video. It had been Beth's idea to create an NTSB blog, to document the public aspects of the investigation and to give survivors and loved ones up-to-the-minute details of their progress. "Polestar? Do you want to get us started, please?"

Polestar Airlines had brought nineteen people to the All-Thing. The company's vice president for operations stood, but motioned for his people to remain seated. "Miss, ah, Mancini? We don't mind waiting for the Go-Team and the Investigator in Charge. If there's a conflict . . . ?"

Beth blushed and hoped no one could tell. "The Go-Team is on the scene of the crash. Time is of the essence, so I'll be handling the All-Thing today. Would you like to introduce—"

A woman two-thirds of the way toward the back stood, raising one arm high over her perfectly coiffed blond bob. "Ms. Mancini?"

"Um, yes?"

"Veronica Manheim, chief counsel with the Airline Pilots Association. At the media briefing yesterday, you were asked if pilot error was a factor. You are quoted as saying, 'Yes, absolutely.' We would like to know if that was an accurate quote."

Beth felt the room tip under her shoes. As she struggled for an answer, the vice president from Polestar half turned to address the room. "Do we have the floor still?"

The blond lawyer ignored him. "If the quote is accurate, we have serious concerns about the investigation."

Polestar wouldn't be shouted down. "We normally get to meet the Investigator in Charge and the team leaders. I've known Delevan Wildman for fifteen years. There's a protocol to these things."

Beth said, "Folks? Everyone?"

A representative from Leveque Aéronautique, Limited, of Quebec, maker of the aeronautics suite, stood. "Pardon me. Are we meeting the investigators? We're here to help but we were told we were meeting the lead investigators."

A consultant from the engine makers, Bembenek Company, stood, too. "Yeah. We were told that."

Beth tried to apply a smile. "People? Can we do the introductions first?"

The pilots' attorney raised her hand again. "Can you answer our question, Ms. Mancini? We officially protest the rush to judgment we feel your statement to the media represents."

The consultant from Bembenek cut in. "Whoa. Slow down, everyone. If the Go-Team is calling this pilot error, we should assume they know what they're doing."

Leveque Aéronautics jumped into the fray. "Can we hear this from the Investigator in Charge, please?"

Now fully half of the 167 people in the auditorium were on their feet. Voices tumbled over one another like boulders in an avalanche.

"People?" Beth tried to dim the cacophony. "Excuse me? Everyone?"

The All-Thing continued to spin out for the next twenty minutes. Beth's aides caught it all on video for the Web site.

19

ONE OF THE NURSES peeked into the rec room of the Brighten-
wood Retirement Center in Coeur d'Alene, Idaho, and said, "Arlen?"

Colonel Arlen Combs turned from his chess game, thick white eyebrows rising.

"You have a visitor."

He pivoted his wheelchair a quarter turn to the left. The nurse stepped
aside.

Arlen Combs's long, thick-jawed face broke into a craggy smile. "I will
be God damned."

The man behind the nurse stepped forward and offered his hand. "Dad."

They went to the colonel's room, the old man refusing the offer to help
with his wheelchair. "I'm fine, I'm fine," he growled. He'd smoked Camels
for sixty-five of his eighty-one years and they'd left his voice so rough it
sounded as if he were gargling asphalt. He was six-two—fat lot of good it
did him in the damn chair—and his hands were as thick and rough-hewn
as a lumberjack's. His skin was leathery and taut with deep wrinkles.

His private room in the retirement village was as tack-sharp and neat
as a Pentagon briefing room.

"What brings you around?" Arlen wheeled himself to a maple side table and poured two fingers of Jack Daniel's into mismatched, cheap tumblers. He handed one to his son, eyeing him. His only boy had grown into a tall, broad-shouldered man. He stood at parade rest, hands held behind his back until accepting the drink. He wore jeans and lace-up boots and a T-shirt under a brown blazer. His pale blue eyes scanned the room.

"I was in the vicinity." He made eye contact with his dad. "Thought I should drop by."

Arlen Combs took a sip, feeling his ulcer protest and not giving a good shit. "You look good."

"You, too, sir."

"Sit."

His son looked around, found a folding chair pushed up to a table with a three-quarters-finished jigsaw puzzle. He picked up the chair one-handed, spun it around, and sat stiffly, his spine not touching the back of the chair. He had not sipped his drink.

"How goes the war?"

Those pale blue eyes continued to scan the room, although there wasn't much to see. "There are no wars anymore. Just missions."

"Which you can't talk about." Arlen sipped his whiskey.

"No, sir."

The old man smiled a crooked smile. "I sure as hell hope the Special Forces have changed since my day. In Vietnam, they were fucking idiots, the lot of them. Sneaky Pete. Strutting around like their shit don't stink, not giving a good fuck about the grunts who were sweatin' and dyin' in the jungle. Assholes. The lot of them."

His son nodded.

"Being a regular GI wasn't good enough for you?"

His son looked over the room, the untouched whiskey in his left hand. His face turned to his father, his eyes the last to light. "There are different ways to protect America, Dad."

The old man barked a laugh and drained his drink. "Protect America!"

"Threats change. How's your health? After the stroke, you—"

"Like when you boys invaded Puerto Rico?" He laughed and reached for the bottle of Jack.

"It was Grenada. It was—"

Arlen Combs poured himself another drink, his arms still knotted with muscles at this age, pale polo shirt open to show a tuft of white hair on this chest. His son could see the chain that dipped into his shirt, know-ing, even today, his father wore his dog tags.

"What was that asshole's name? Secretary of dee-fense? Dyed black hair?"

"Secretary of Defense Casper—"

"Cap Weinberger! That was him. Jesus H. Christ!" His son bristled a little when Arlen took the Lord's name in vain. "Little tin soldier, telling America we'd done it! We'd rescued all those medical students! Hell, half of them were still in their dorms, watching fucking television when he said it! You boys screwed that one! Hee!"

"That was before my time, Dad."

The old man ignored him and wiped his rheumy eyes. "Invaded a coun-try the size of a Ramada Inn. Yeah, that was a man's war, sure enough."

"Communist forces were—"

The old man said, "Fuck. You want Communist forces? I was a grunt in Korea, boy. And I was a colonel in Vietnam. Now, we had some Communist forces! You had Grenada and, what was it, Panama? Jesus, Joseph, and Mary! What a pussy army. What, Epcot Center was too big a foe? Ha!"

He drained his glass and winced as the ulcer spasmed.

His son sat, back straight, unemotional, still scanning the room as if he could see ghosts. His drink remained untouched.

"Special Forces! You see these?" Arlen wheeled himself four feet to the left, to a picture frame on the wall. Behind the glass was every medal he had ever won, had ever worn on his dress uniform. "You see these? Ask me about any of them. Any goddamn one of them. I can tell you ex-actly how I got it. Protecting America. You, Special Forces? You're just the CIA in khaki. Just the fucking CIA."

His son scanned the room, found a coaster near the jigsaw puzzle, pulled it closer, set down his drink, and stood.

"It was good seeing you, Dad."

"That's it! Run away when the questions get too hot. That's you guys' style. Just like—"

But his son had left the room.

BIG SKY COMMUNITY HOSPITAL

Ray Calabrese returned to the hospital Saturday afternoon and again found Kiki in Tommy's private room. This time, Beth Mancini was there as well.

"... Normally conducts interviews with survivors, but, well, I figured your written report would be every bit as good. You've filled out enough of those." She turned and smiled politely. "It was . . . Ray?"

Ray shook her hand. "Right."

Beth turned back to Kiki. "Here's a report for you and one for Tommy. Though, Tommy, you can wait a day or two, wait for the concussion to subside. Okay, well, thank you."

They chatted a bit, then Beth excused herself.

Kiki rose and bussed Ray on the cheek. "I'm being released."

"I figured as much. I reserved a room for you in my hotel."

She squeezed his arm. "Thank you. Is it the same hotel as the rest of the crashers?"

Ray shrugged. "They're spread out all over town. Hunting season, I guess."

Tommy said, "That sounds inefficient."

Ray turned to Kiki. "Hey, I got no love, regarding the cockpit recorder. I asked, but Peter Kim . . ." He shrugged.

"That jerk! I want to help!"

"I know. Hey, how're you doing, Texas?"

Tommy looked marginally better, with maybe a little more color in his cheeks. "Bored out of my fucking mind. Reading gives me headaches and daytime TV just makes me hate humanity."

Ray smiled. "Bitch and moan, bitch and moan."

All three turned at a knock on the door. A very tall, willow-thin woman stood there.

Ray said, "Hey. Guys, this is the team leader for pathology and, ah, I just absolutely don't remember your name."

"Dr. Lakshmi Jain. Dr. Tomzak?"

"Yeah. Howdy."

Dr. Jain looked uncomfortable. She held herself rigid, her feet close together, a hand on her shoulder bag as if facing muggers.

"I'm Kiki Duvall. Cockpit voice recorder." Kiki limped forward on her metal cane, offered her hand. A brief pause, and Lakshmi took her hand. One formal pump, up and down.

Kiki realized the pathologist's clothes smelled of woodsmoke.

"Dr. Tomzak, I thought it proper to look in on you, to see how you are doing."

"It's Tommy, and that's mighty nice of you. What's the condition of the pilots?"

"The copilot died on impact with trees, not the ground. We have found very little of him. The pilot . . . puzzles me."

Kiki perched on the edge of Tommy's bed. Ray slid the room's one chair over to Dr. Jain, saying, "Yeah?"

Lakshmi sat, looking like she'd been called into the principal's office. "Yes. I . . . Dr. Tomzak, you have a reputation for . . . creative analysis of situations."

"It's Tommy, and thanks. What is it?"

Lakshmi nodded. "By following a thumbprint and a blood trail, it appears the Pilot-in-Charge woke up after the crash, used his left hand to undo his safety harness, rolled or fell out of his seat to the forest floor below. Then probably pushed himself toward the flight-deck door on his knees. His right arm would have been useless at this point, the nerves sheared at the elbow by shrapnel. He . . . likely rose to his feet. When I found him, he was slumped over with a blood smear on the wall that indicated he'd leaned against it and slowly collapsed."

"Okay." Tommy was seeing the scene in his mind.

"Cause of death was a broken neck. C4. And I confirmed in the postmortem that the spinal cord was badly damaged."

Kiki said, "I'm with you so far. It's—"

But Tommy was sitting up now, a hand on his lover's arm. "Whoa, whoa. C4?"

Lakshmi nodded. Ray and Kiki waited. They looked to Tommy.

"No shittin' way. C4 spinal damage and the guy's a quadriplegic. There's no getting out of the harness, dragging your ass back to the door. Certainly no standing up."

"Not just quadriplegic," Lakshmi added softly. "The nerves controlling breathing were badly damaged. There was no way he could breathe."

Ray absorbed all that. "So the lesser injuries were from the crash. But the broken neck . . . ?"

Tommy said, "Happened after the crash."

Kiki said, "What about the deer?"

Ray and Tommy slowly turned to her, Ray going, "The *deer*?"

Kiki nodded. "There was a dead deer on the flight deck. It got scooped up somehow as we were skidding. Could it have killed the pilot?"

Tommy turned to Ray. "Sometime in the not-too-distant future, I'm gonna say to you, *That's the damnedest thing I ever heard.* When I do, you got permission to say, *There was a dead deer on the flight deck.*"

Ray said, "Check."

Lakshmi thought it over. "Perhaps. If it did not die on impact. If it was struggling, it might have hit the pilot, broken his spine."

The others agreed that, yes, it was possible. Weird, unlikely as hell, but possible. One thing was certain: the pilot's severed spine had happened minutes after the crash.

Lakshmi stood up to leave. "I also wish to convey my regrets regarding the death of Isaiah Grey. I had met him but we had not worked on a crash before. He seemed most professional."

Kiki said, "Thank you. Really." She was a hugger by nature but was pretty sure that wouldn't fly with the tense Dr. Jain. "Listen, I'm sorry but I have to know what killed Isaiah."

Lakshmi said, "He had a crushed larynx. He suffoc—"

Tommy said, "Hang on. Crushed larynx?"

Lakshmi nodded. "Yes. Damage was extensive. He—"

"Doc, I don't know you and I don't mean to doubt your autopsy, but I spoke to Isaiah before I passed out. And more importantly, he spoke to me."

Lakshmi said simply, and not unkindly, "No. There is no possibility that he could have spoken with that level of damage. Again, I am sorry."

Tommy's face drained of what little color it had. "But we talked!"

"And that, I am afraid, we must chalk up to your concussion. Dr. Tomzak, Miss Duvall, I wish you a speedy recovery."

She left.

Tommy flopped back against his pillows. "Well, shit."

Kiki gripped his leg under the blanket, gave it a little squeeze. "I'm so sorry, sweetie."

Tommy wiped tears from his eyes. "Dammit. That seemed so real!"

Ray shrugged. "Combo of the concussion and they have you on some pretty strong painkillers. Sorry, man."

After a few beats, Tommy coughed. "Could I, ah, get a few minutes to, you know . . ."

Kiki eased up off the bed. "Sure." She turned to Ray. "What's your plan?"

"I haven't been to the site yet. I'm heading out there. I want to see the crash you two walked away from."

20

THE POLESTAR CHARTER FLIGHT from Dulles to Helena arrived before noon. The corporate Lear held family members of six of the dead, hailing from throughout Virginia, Maryland, and the District of Columbia.

The airline did everything possible to make the dreaded flight as pain-free as possible for mourners. All family members had been picked up at their homes. Their luggage was fast-tracked onto the corporate jet, bypassing TSA security regulations, and nobody had to pass through an invasive scanner or a pat-down procedure. It was agreed that the families had suffered enough.

Other chartered flights from other parts of the country were vectoring to Helena, too.

A charter bus took the family members to the surprisingly ritzy Belvedere Hotel, not far from the capitol building. The hotel manager, assistant manager, and three reservation staffers waited to show the guests immediately to their rooms; there was no need to wait for check-in.

Once safely in her room, Renee lifted her suitcase onto the folding stand near the spacious closet. She got out her hanging clothes and hung them, fluffing out the creases. She slid the Colt Pocket Model .25 out of her folded jeans and held it in both hands. It had seemed uncomfortable, even alien, a few days ago. Now the small V-shaped gun seemed perfectly molded to her hand. She kissed the short barrel. She gripped it tightly in her left hand and conducted the remainder of her unpacking more or less one-handed.

Mayor Art Tibbits of Twin Pines called a meeting for 1:00 P.M. that Saturday. The so-called Twin Pines City Council had five elected council seats but only two were filled because nobody had bothered to run for the other three. The core leadership of the town had dwindled down to Tibbits, Police Chief Paul McKinney, school superintendent Chip Ogilvy, and Joan Tibbits, Art's wife and current chair of the chamber of commerce. They met in Tina's, one of only two coffee shops left standing in the downtown core.

And for once, the place was bustling and the town leaders had to wait for service.

"Oh my god," Joan said, pointing to a table to her left. "He's a reporter for NBC! I've watched him for years!"

Chip Ogilvy listened to the ring of the old-fashioned iron cash register. "Got to admit, Art. Getting the media to stage up here was smart. Tina's gonna see more profit today than she did in all of July."

Chief McKinney nodded. "Agreeing to store the bodies means the mourners are on their way here, too. I told Olaf and he's going to open up his restaurant again."

Chip said, "Didn't the bank already foreclose on Olaf?"

The mayor tried not to look smug. "I had a talk with Roger over at the bank. He's giving Olaf this weekend, see how he does with the influx of folks. Plus, I talked to the state. If the forest fire picks up, they're sending a crew. That's another two or three dozen men."

He turned to his wife. "Artie's hotel is booked up. We need to tell folks to open their homes as bed-and-breakfasts, just for the week or so. We play our cards right, and we're going to get through the third quarter of this year, maybe see some profits before the holidays."

Nobody at the table said it, but they all knew that Art Tibbits's quick thinking had infused some hard cash into a town desperately hard up. But that didn't change the simple dynamic that Twin Pines was dying.

. . .

Three large travel coaches arrived in the tiny timber town around two in the afternoon. A senior member of Polestar's Public Affairs Office stood at the front of each bus as they pulled into town.

The PR guy in the lead bus said, "Folks? This is the town of Twin Pines. Your loved ones are being . . . ah, stored here. We're just a few blocks away." His cohorts were saying the same thing in the second and third buses. "Now, there's no good way to say this. Some of the bodies sustained extreme injuries. We're going to have family members go in five at a time, and we'll use a lottery to see who goes first. Another thing: this isn't a hospital or a morgue, because there's nowhere in this region of Montana large enough. Last night, the NTSB team on site, along with local law enforcements, found a building here in Twin Pines that is temperature-controlled."

He turned to the driver. "Do you see the address?"

"Yeah, right here."

People on the bus started mumbling. Some started crying again. Someone said, "Wait, what . . . ?"

The PR guy leaned down, his head at the same height as the seated passengers'. Then he realized for the first time that the temperature-controlled building bore a sign: Stan's Meat Market! Fresh Meat Daily!

To his left, Renee let loose a quick, small, teary-eyed laugh, then covered her mouth with a bunched-up ball of Kleenex. He knelt and squeezed her hand.

"Mrs. Malatesta? I'm so . . . we're so sorry about this."

Renee offered up a brittle smile and a nod, her vision blurring, losing it but trying not to, feeling her composure dwindling, willing herself to bail out a boat that was filling with salt water.

In the center of Twin Pines, Mayor Art Tibbits hustled down the sidewalk, grinning. He hadn't seen downtown this busy in ages. A shopkeeper gave him a little mock salute. "Mr. Mayor. Lookin' good!"

Tibbits saluted him back.

Calendar, who had been walking in the opposite direction, stopped abruptly and knelt, pretending to tie his boot. It had taken him an hour to return from Coeur d'Alene, Idaho. He considered the situation, then stood and reversed course.

The mayor headed back over to Tina's Diner and realized he'd have to sit at the counter because every table was still occupied. He recognized reporters as well as a handful of people with NTSB ball caps. Tibbits sat and, unbidden, the waitress brought him decaf coffee and a little bowl of creamer packets.

Calendar took the next red-topped stool at a faded Formica counter. "Morning." He nodded.

"Morning." The mayor added a milklike substance to his coffee. "Journalist?"

"Yes, sir," Calendar said. The counter was adorned with napkin dispensers, glass salt-and-pepper shakers, and a sort of standing fork into which three laminated menus stood up like a bouquet. The girl behind the counter smiled at him and he ordered coffee, black.

"Nice town you have here."

Tibbits beamed. "Art Tibbits. Mayor."

"You don't say." They shook hands.

"Anything we can do for the Fifth Estate, you just ask. We're the friendliest town in Big Sky Country!"

Calendar was pretty sure it was the *Fourth Estate* but he didn't correct the mayor. He also smelled bourbon on the man's breath. He tamped down his annoyance at such weak leadership. "So do you know where they're storing the bodies from the plane crash?"

"Sure do. Temperature-controlled warehouse down on Third. Used to be Stan's Meat Market but it folded. We had hopes a co-op would buy the site, setting it up as a meat market again, but . . ." He shrugged.

"That was fast thinking. Being temperature-controlled and all."

Tibbits's boozy smile blossomed. "That was my idea."

"And a fine one," Calendar said as his coffee arrived.

WASHINGTON, D.C.

Delevan Wildman and his chief aide, Nathan Kowalski, watched the video of the All-Thing, the first-day meeting of all of the organizations that would be involved in the investigation. In his long career at the NTSB, Wildman insisted on watching a video of each All-Thing, a legal pad on his knee, eyes peeled like a defense coach breaking down game film of an opposing team.

He had never seen one quite like the spectacle from Helena.

Kowalski waited until his boss hit Pause, then said, "Wow. That was . . . um . . ."

The older man drawled, "You're looking for a hyphenate, son. Starts with *cluster-*."

"Yes, sir. That was the phrase."

VARENNA, ITALY

"He what?"

Susan shrugged and studied the latest e-mail again. "Del wants me to watch the video of the All-Thing. Love, I'm sorry, these things can run up to three hours. This isn't turning into the vacation we—"

Kirk Tanaka set down the *International Herald-Tribune* and bussed her on the forehead. "Del wouldn't ask if it wasn't important. Don't worry about it."

Susan went to the NTSB public Web site and cued up the All-Thing.

It didn't take three hours. The players began streaming out of the auditorium, some shouting in anger, in a little under thirty minutes.

They watched it together, Susan sitting on the bed in their hotel room, Kirk standing by her side, an arm slung around her shoulder. "Wow," he said.

"Pilot error."

"She's quoted as saying, 'absolutely.'"

Susan sat, eyes wide.

"Give me that." Her husband took the iPad from her.

"What are you doing?"

"Responding to Del Wildman. Get packed. You're heading home."

CRASH SITE

Jack Goodspeed said, "You smell smoke?"

Reuben Chaykin deadpanned back, "We're standing in a forest fire: yeah."

"I'm serious, man. I think the wind's changed."

Jack jogged over to the nearest of the sheriff's deputies. "Hey. Excuse me. I'm smelling more smoke. I think the wind's changed."

The deputy looked up into the green canopy. He sniffed. "Well, dammit."

The wind had changed.

Jack and Reuben were on the scene, hoping to dredge loose the last bits of the powerplant and avionics out of the cockpit before the fire changed its mind. They would need this equipment if they were going to prove the theory of the Leveque gremlin. And now the fire had, indeed, changed course.

Jack toggled the comm unit on his belt.

"Kim."

"Peter, it's Jack. The wind's changed. The fire is coming back."

"Okay. You and Reuben get clear while it's safe." Peter disconnected.

BIG SKY COMMUNITY HOSPITAL

Tommy and Kiki were introduced to the chief of surgeons, a Dr. Carol Leitner. Tommy—the last vestiges of vertigo still making him dizzy—came in a wheelchair. Kiki took the chair next to him.

"Thank you for seeing me. I'm compiling histories of our patients and I need to know who you either rescued or treated."

Dr. Leitner sat on the edge of her stunningly cluttered desk and turned her PC monitor so that all three of them could see the screen. "You know, when you get that middle-of-the-night call that an airliner is down, you think: *I'm getting a hundred ER patients, or else I'm getting none and it's the morgue's night of woe.* Getting just eight patients was a weird relief. Okay, these first two are you. This is Annie Boynton, fifteen."

Tommy said, "Right-arm bleeder. Brachial vein. I applied a pressure bandage. She gonna lose that arm?"

Dr. Leitner smiled. "First answer is: HIPAA rules say I cannot discuss the patients. Second answer: No. You made sure of that."

Kiki smiled at Tommy and rubbed his shoulder.

Dr. Leitner reached behind her, hit the Space bar.

"Orysya Bronova. On vacation from Minsk."

Tommy and Kiki exchanged glances. Both shrugged.

"Okay. Ibrahim al-Mahmood."

Kiki nodded. "Another passenger and I carried him out of the Claremont. No obvious injuries. But he was unconscious."

"He's lucky. Sprained wrist, swear to God. Okay, Charles Hamner, crushed knee."

Both shrugged again.

"Anita Fremont—"

Tommy said, "Broken fibula, bone showing. Wasn't a hell of a lot I could do for her."

Dr. Leitner hit Tab. "Gene Cartman?"

"Gut wound. Intestines showing."

Kiki going, "Ewwww!"

"Yeah, that lacked prettiness, hon. I created a pressure bandage with a pillow and my belt. Shit! That belt was a gift from you. I'm sorry."

Dr. Leitner laughed. "You managed to do all that, the two of you, with a concussion, a broken rib, and significant blood loss from a leg wound. That's amazing."

Tommy said, "It was mostly me," so Kiki elbowed him.

"Do I have your permission to tell the *Helena Independent* about your heroics?"

They said "no" in tandem and damn near in key.

"It's a good story. . . ."

Kiki said, "There will be no end of good stories. Thanks, though."

The doctor turned her terminal back around. "Well, thank you for—"

Kiki said, "We're at least one short."

"Excuse me?"

"There's one more survivor. Tall man, silver hair? He helped me carry Mr. al-Mahmood."

Dr. Leitner frowned. "Hmm. We didn't get him. And we're the only certified trauma hospital in the region. Are you sure?"

"Dark sweater, jeans, good hiking boots . . ."

Tommy said, "Silver hair cut short. Yeah, I saw him. Guy was picking up debris."

Dr. Leitner picked up her telephone receiver and dialed a number from memory. "J. J.? Can you tell the sheriff we might have another survivor from Thursday's plane crash?" She described the man. She hung up and turned back to the crashers. "He could have tried walking out. Could have had a delayed reaction to a concussion. If he's out there, they'll find him."

CRASH SITE

Mac Pritchert of the Montana Department of Forestry toured the crash site in a Sikorsky S-76. He could see the downed, wingless aircraft and people in blue windbreakers and baseball caps milling about. He could see the trail of destruction stretching a mile back, plus the fire hot spots where both engines and their fuel served as accelerants. He viewed the fire itself, then called the state meteorologist's office to get a forecast.

He tapped the pilot's shoulder to get his attention, then thrust his thumb back toward the town of Twin Pines.

The pilot put the Sikorsky down, light as a platonic kiss. Peter Kim, Jack Goodspeed, and Teresa Santiago marched down the slight decline to meet it. Chief of Police Paul McKinney joined them as Mac Pritchert, a massive bear of a man, hoisted himself down from the helo. His belt was adorned with a cell phone, bowie knife, flashlight, and a massive ring of keys. He wore a walrus mustache.

"Investigator in Charge?" he asked over the whoosh of the rotors.

"That's me. Peter Kim." They shook hands.

"Mr. Kim, this here is a state-owned forest, and I've been named the fire chief for this thing. That makes me the landlord. The governor was pretty damn clear: I am not to let you guys risk your lives. If I say the fire's coming, your people vamoose. Are we good?"

"If we think you're wrong, we'll try to change your mind."

Pritchert studied him, then nodded. "Fair enough. I've spoken to the state meteorologist. It's our opinion that the wind's gonna die down here real soon. Our prediction: you have this afternoon and tonight and Sunday until maybe noon. Then the winds'll whip up from the east."

Jack grinned. "That'll give us more than enough time. We can get the remainder of the avionics and what's left of the shredded powerplant out tonight, come back tomorrow with flatbeds, carve up the fuselage, haul it out of here."

Peter offered his hand again. "Mr. Pritchert."

"Good luck, fellas. And, ma'am."

Teresa winked at him. "*Fella* works fine, Chief." And Mac Pritchert blushed.

TWIN PINES

Calendar crawled through the alley behind Stan's Meat Market in his stolen SUV. He saw a loading dock with a rolling metal door. It was going on 6:00 P.M. There were no windows in the back. The opposite side of the alley was a cinderblock self-storage facility with no windows.

"Place practically begs you to break in," he muttered.

Pulling out onto the street, he was surprised to see three massive touring coaches. Five sobbing civilians were being led out of the meat market and five more were about to enter.

The bodies were laid out on the floor of the former meatpacking company. On their backs, bedsheets covered their heads and torsos. The loved ones were escorted in, under the watchful eye of two of Chief Paul McKinny's deputies. This was, technically, part of a potential crime scene until the cause of the crash was confirmed.

Sheets were pulled back. Family members fell to their knees or hugged themselves tightly, sobbing. The HR people from Polestar Airlines stood back, crying a little, too; how could you not?

Renee Malatesta didn't need to identify the bodies of Christian Dean and Vejay Mehta. Their families had arrived, too. One of the last sheets to be removed revealed the body of Andrew. His throat had been crushed. His eyes were closed, thank God. A line of blood ran from his nose to his upper lip, then down his cheek to his neck. Renee asked about a bathroom. She was shown the way. She yanked out a square of paper towel, wetted it, returned, knelt, and wiped the blood off Andrew's face and neck. She kissed his cold lips. She pulled the sheet back up, covering him.

She knelt for the longest time. Other mourners—some she knew, others were perfect strangers—walked by, touched her shoulder or knelt by her side, hugged her. She was insensate. She might have been a pillar of salt.

Later, outside, Renee hugged her suede jacket tightly to her body. It was pleasant, about seventy degrees, but she couldn't stop shivering. She found a private place across the street from the meat shop—*It had to be a fucking meat shop?*—and lit a cigarette. She smoked only a few cigarettes a month and only when she was stressed. This seemed like the right time.

"Renee?"

She turned. "Amy?"

Renee had known Amy Dreyfus since Stanford. She'd been Andrew's roommate and best friend. She'd introduced Renee and Andrew. They'd maintained contact over the years, partly because of Amy's high-tech beat at the *Post*. But now was totally the wrong time for an interview. She started to protest when the journalist came to her in a rush. Renee's fevered brain thought about defending herself but the woman crushed her in a hug,

Renee's freshly lit cigarette falling to the pavement. Amy hugged her, crying silently. After the longest time, Renee returned the hug.

"You and Andrew were close. I should have called."

Amy broke the bear hug and used Kleenex to wipe her eyes, then blew her nose. "God, no. No. You had . . . Fuck, don't worry about it. Did you . . ." She gestured toward the meat shop.

Renee nodded. Amy's eyes brimmed. She stood with her weight on one leg. She reminded Renee of some kind of small, light shorebird, especially with that curly mop of cherry-red hair. "Okay. Okay. Wow. This wasn't . . . Hey, are you, y'know . . ."

Renee actually belted out a raggedy little giggle. "No. No. I'm not. No."

Amy hugged her again. "This fucking sucks."

HELENA

Kiki Duvall was checking into the airport hotel as Hector Villareal stepped out of the elevator.

"Hi. Kiki, is it?"

She turned. "You're . . . I'm sorry, Hector . . . ?"

"Hector Villareal. Hi. We met at that conference in Miami."

They shook hands. He said, "Are you all right?"

"Pretty much. They released me."

They shook hands. "Dr. Tomzak?"

"He's okay. Concussed."

"Listen, about Isaiah . . . I'm just . . . We're all of us so sorry."

"Thank you. That's so sweet."

"You need help carrying your luggage?" Then he rolled his eyes. "Of course. Your luggage is in the Claremont."

"Beth Mancini told me she left me an NTSB credit card at the desk. I'll go find some clothes tonight." She lived in Levi's and sweatshirts; the task wasn't daunting.

Hector's eyes traveled around the lobby as if looking for surveillance, and Kiki wondered why he looked guilty. Maybe talking to tall redheads in hotel lobbies did that, she thought, and almost smiled at the vaguely naughty thought.

Hector reached into his windbreaker pocket and withdrew an iPod Nano. "Do me a favor? Don't tell Peter Kim about this."

He placed the device in her palm.

"Oh my god! Is this . . . ?"

"You're the Sonar Witch," Hector said. "I know how good you are. Give it a listen. Tell me what I missed."

She hugged him. "Thank you. I need to help. I need to be useful."

"I know. But that being said: don't tell Peter."

Lakshmi Jain called a meeting of the medical examiner and his staff, plus volunteers who had come from three adjacent counties to help, giving up their Saturdays. But so far there had been no bodies upon which to conduct postmortem examinations.

"We appreciate everyone volunteering," she said, addressing the twelve staff and volunteers in the sterile, white examination room with its three metal tables. Lakshmi disliked public speaking. She held herself stiffly, wearing the eyeglasses she really needed only for reading fine print. She wore them without consciously realizing she used them as a shield.

"Our host," she nodded to the medical examiner, "and I performed autopsies on the pilots immediately because we wanted to rush the lab results. That's standard operating procedure for such events. However, the airline has flown in the families of the dead, and are letting them attain . . . closure, I suppose is the word, before we begin conducting posts."

She checked her cell phone for the time. "That should be happening now. The process won't make any of the families happy, but research shows that it will reduce post-traumatic stress in the months to come. That's why we wait. If there had been overwhelming evidence that a passenger played a pivotal role in the crash—as, say, one might have in a hijacking—then that would necessitate an immediate postmortem.

"I intend to go to . . ." she checked a notepad, "Twin Pines momentarily. My goals are threefold: to make sure the bodies are being properly and humanely stored; to make sure all of the evidence is protected; and to confirm that the families have had the chance to say their goodbyes.

"Once I am satisfied, I shall begin the transfer of bodies here. Doctor?" She turned to the medical examiner. "I will leave you in charge of conducting the postmortems. However, before we begin post, every victim will be scanned, twice, with X-rays. We also will run metal detectors over them."

"Twice?" a volunteer asked, raising one hand.

"Some of the shrapnel from an airliner can be as thin as a sheet of paper. X-rays are conducted from two acute angles to make sure we miss nothing. As we proceed with the autopsies, all foreign items found in the bodies will be photographed, bagged, and tagged. The victims' clothing will be searched as well. I, myself, would hardly recognize any of the shrapnel we find, but my counterparts in other NTSB teams likely would. It is important that we catalog all of the shrapnel. Questions?"

There were none. She thanked the medical personnel again and gathered her things.

In the corridor outside the medical examiner's suite, Lakshmi applied her earpiece and punched the number 2 on her belt communication rig.

"Hi, this is Beth."

"Hallo. This is Dr. Jain." Lakshmi winced, realizing she needn't be so formal. "I am heading out to Twin Pines to check on the bodies."

"Okay." The intergovernmental liaison seemed not to be her usual chipper self.

After a beat, Lakshmi added, "I need a driver."

"A driver?"

"Forgive me, Beth. Since moving to America, I have lived in New York City. I have no need of a car, nor a driver's license."

"Oh. I'm sorry, I'm . . . working on a report regarding the All-Thing. Plus, we're still trying to find out why there were so few passengers on board."

"I wouldn't dream of asking you to drive me. Are other team leaders heading toward the crash site this afternoon?"

Beth said, "Jack and Reuben are there now. I don't think Gene's back yet. Hang on."

Lakshmi heard a hiss, indicating that she was on hold. Beth came back on the line within seconds.

"Teresa is heading that way. Tell me where the medical examiner's office is, and she'll pick you up in ten minutes."

Amy Dreyfus drove Renee from Twin Pines back to Helena. They agreed to have dinner together. It was almost 8:00 P.M. They found a bar near the hotel with black-and-white photos of San Francisco on the walls and Sinatra on the sound system. They took a booth and Amy ordered a vodka gimlet. Renee asked for Haitian Barbancourt rum and the waitress looked at her as if she'd ordered Sheetrock. "Any rum will do."

When they had their drinks and some privacy, Amy said, "Listen, what was it Andrew needed my help with?"

Renee sipped the dreadfully mediocre rum. It tasted like cough syrup. "What do you mean?"

Renee stuffed her hand into her suede jacket and gently gripped the reassuring, hammerless Colt .25. Her hand felt better wrapped around the cold metal. She wasn't sure why she'd brought it but its presence was comforting.

"He called the *Post*. I don't know, Wednesday, I guess. He called and said he needed some help leaking a story and wanted my media expertise."

Renee's mind raced. "Really?"

"Yes. What's going on?"

Renee hunched her shoulders. "I don't know. I don't know. Why would he call you about the media?"

Amy studied Renee.

"I asked him if it was serious and he said, 'life-and-death serious.' What do you think he meant?"

Renee drained the rum. She caught the waitress's attention, pointed to the empty glass. "I don't know."

Amy leaned forward. "Renee! You're his wife. What was he working on that he needed to *out* someone or, whatever, some*thing* to the media?"

The waitress brought another rum and Renee drained it in one long pull.

Amy observed this and, *click*, realized how insensitive she was being. Her eyes glittered with tears. "Oh shit. Oh shit I am so sorry. You're in noooooo condition to put up with my journalism crap. Oh, forgive me, I am so sorry."

Renee Malatesta's eyes remained as dry as sandpaper. She gripped the glass in one hand, her other hand on the .25 semiauto in her suede pocket. "No. It's okay. I can't help you. I don't know why he called. I'm just . . ." She reached across the table and touched the reporter's forearm. "I'm just glad you're here."

When their food came, Renee stared at it for a moment, then stood and walked out of the bar without touching it. Amy Dreyfus cried, the heels of her hands pressed against her eyes.

The waitress sat beside her, one-arm hugged her, and said, "She dump you, honey?"

To her utmost surprise, Amy actually belted a laugh. "Wow, did you guess that one wrong!"

But she hugged the waitress right back. That anyone could bring her a few seconds of laughter was a blessing right now.

HALFWAY TO TWIN PINES

The ride to Twin Pines had been a Bad Idea.

Once in the car, Teresa Santiago never stopped talking. Not even to inhale. Lakshmi Jain was, if possible, chillier. No subject was taboo for Teresa: her energetic love life, her parents' divorce when she was twelve, the lumpectomy her sister had just undergone, the brattiness of said sister's twerpy kids, her dogs. The drive took twenty-five minutes; it just seemed like days.

It was about 8:30 P.M. by the time the crashers arrived in the sleepy little timber town.

TWIN PINES

Calendar walked half the length of the alley and saw no one. He bounded up the two cement steps to the back door of the meat market and picked the lock in seconds.

There was no alarm system to bypass.

He stood in the dark, listening for human sounds and hearing none. He stood in a storage room with a rolling bay door next to the door he'd lock-picked.

He padded through the largely empty room on his rubber-soled boots, checked the corridor. He turned on his Maglite. Empty. He trotted to the end of the hall, checking every unlocked door. He had the place to himself.

The corridor ended at a door that led to a much larger storage room, and this one he did not have to himself.

It was full of corpses.

A dozen bodies, more or less, were on the cement floor with their feet toward the door that led to the street. They were lined up evenly, but some were cocked at five degrees to the left or the right.

Calendar's breath misted as he exhaled. It was about forty degrees in this room.

The bodies lay on their backs. White bedsheets had been spread out, covering them. That had been a kindness, Calendar thought. He was glad someone had done that. A pile of extra sheets was lumped together in the middle of the room.

Beyond the dozen bodies were another dozen rubber body bags with zippers. They were lumpy and misshapen. Partials, Calendar guessed.

Andrew Malatesta's speech, announcing that he would not be working for the Pentagon after all and that a rogue element in Halcyon/Detweiler was experimenting with banned weapons, was either in this room or in the fuselage of Flight 78. Calendar's instructions were clear. Job one: find and destroy the speech. Job two: find Malatesta's sketch pad, with its vast array of innovative weaponry ideas. Halcyon's R&D boys would gorge on that for years. If the sketch pad had been destroyed in the airliner, well, that would be a shame, but Halcyon/Detweiler could survive without it. The speech, on the other hand, had to be destroyed.

Calendar forced his strong hands into tight latex gloves, letting them snap against his forearms. It was difficult getting the glove over the bandage on his right hand.

He picked the body closest to him, knelt, threw off the sheet. It was a woman, midtwenties and pretty, her right arm missing at the shoulder and a massive, tacky contusion at the very top of her skull. Her eyes were open. She was pale—livor mortis had let her blood pool near the floor. She wore capri pants and one Adidas sneaker, the toenails of the other foot painted fuchsia. She wore a Hello Kitty sweatshirt. Calendar felt her pockets, turned them inside out. He lifted her sweatshirt, checked to make sure no documents had been tucked up into her bra—he'd found Malatesta alive; there had been time. He pulled her belt and pants away from her belly and peered down at her legs. Nothing. He turned her partially over; the backs of her arms were livid with pooled blood.

Nothing.

He covered her again, shuffled on his knees to his left, to the next cadaver, threw off the sheet.

A key rattled in the street door. Instinctively, Calendar drew his six-inch MAC-SOG combat knife from its nylon Cordura sheath clipped to his belt.

HELENA

Kiki urgently wanted to listen to the cockpit voice recording but, when she'd switched from hospital togs to her own clothes, the first thing she'd noticed was blood on her left sleeve, near her elbow. She didn't know if it was hers or someone else's, but it was weirding her out. She tossed the iPod Nano onto the hotel room's bed, picked up the NTSB credit card Beth Mancini had left her.

Beth also had left her a little bouquet of flowers, a subtle explosion of pinks and purples. Her gesture was so simple but singularly heartfelt that Kiki teared up a little.

"Tommy . . . I tried to save her. Jesus, man . . ."

"I know. Let's get you outta there. . . ."

Tommy woke up, his head pounding. He sat up in bed, knees up, arms folded over his knees. He wished his head would stop hurting. At least the vertigo was all but gone now.

There was no earthly way that Isaiah Grey could have talked to Tommy with a crushed larynx. Couldn't be done. Which meant it had been a figment of his concussion.

So why did he remember with such vivid detail the girl with the brachial bleeder, the guy with the open gut wound, the woman with the broken bone showing near her bloody sock? He remembered persuading Kiki to help evacuate survivors.

He climbed out of bed. The vertigo ramped up, but just a little. He threw on a robe and left the room, found the nurses' station. A nurse directed him to room 104.

He knocked, peeked in. The fifteen-year-old girl was watching TV. Her right arm was in a full cast. She turned down the sound. "Oh. Hi."

"I'm Tommy. Do you remember me?"

She smiled. "You saved my life. I'm Ann."

Dr. Leitner had called her *Annie* and Tommy noted the difference. "Hey, Ann. Can I ask you something?"

"Sure."

He entered all the way into her room. "That night, after I left you the second time, I went over to these airplane seats to help a guy. Did you see him?"

Ann shook her head. "I couldn't stop looking at the airplane. It was just so . . . weird."

"Yeah. Sure as shit was." He paused. "Sorry."

Ann smiled. "It's okay. How's your head?"

"I got my chimes rung, big time. Still hurts."

"Did they have to shave your hair?"

Tommy's fingers went to the bandage. "You know, I didn't ask. Crap. I bet they did. So where are your folks?"

"They were here but visiting hours are over. Mom's, like, freaking me out worse than the crash did."

Tommy winked at her. "That's understandable. Cut her some slack, she's a mom. Hey, do you remember another survivor? Tall guy, short, silver hair, wore—"

She nodded. "Blue jeans, a sweater, boots?"

Tommy smiled. "Okay, thanks. Last question. And you don't gotta answer it if you don't want to."

She nodded solemnly.

"What are you, fifteen? Why's your doc got you on Prozac?"

"He says it's to even out my disposition."

"How long've you been on it?"

"Since I was eleven."

"Jesus H. Christ."

She said, "He also told me it would help my mental image of myself if I lost ten pounds." She blushed.

If anything, Ann looked undernourished to Tommy. He glanced around the room, found a pen, and ripped off a strip from the back cover of a *People* magazine. "Where do you live?"

"Seattle."

"What's the asshole's name? I'm gonna make 'em yank his license."

After a longish beat, a healthy smile blossomed on Ann's face. "You can do that?"

"Let's find out."

The smile spread. "Cool!"

TWIN PINES

The chatterbox in Teresa Santiago clicked off as they stepped into the frigid storage facility. She gasped. The bodies lay on the floor under white bedsheets. Several smaller, rubber body bags were strewn about, too. She covered her mouth with both hands.

It took Lakshmi Jain a second to realize what Teresa was responding to. "Your first time?"

Teresa, wide-eyed, nodded.

"You can wait outside, if you'd like."

Teresa said, "Split up? You've obviously never seen a slasher movie."

Lakshmi had not, in fact, seen a slasher movie and didn't get the reference. She was just pleased to have some silence.

She went down on her haunches and pulled back the nearest sheet. Teresa averted her eyes.

Teresa jumped. One of the bodies under another sheet seemed to move, just a little. *Estupidez fresa!* she cursed herself. *Get a grip!*

Calendar lay under the sheet and cursed himself. He was sure his foot had moved, just a little. Had these two stupid bitches noticed? If they had, his options were limited. Gut them both, leave them here with the corpses, under two sheets. That would buy him a little time.

The other option, he realized, meant more knife work and the use of the shorter, rubber body bags.

HELENA

The idea of stiff new jeans rubbing against her bandages seemed dumb, so Kiki bought two pairs of identical, cuffed khaki shorts, two pastel T-shirts, a denim shirt, panties and a bra, cotton socks, and lace-up Wolverine boots with rubber soles. It took her twenty minutes. She'd worn the same sizes since high school. She didn't care that the outfit would reveal her leg wound. It was hardly her first.

Kiki took her new purchases back to the hotel room and took a long, hot shower. She dried off, put one foot on the toilet lid, and gingerly replaced the bandage on her leg, hissing in pain a few times. The cut and its sutures looked nasty. She wiped a crescent of steam off the mirror with her palm, turned sideways. She sported a bruise the size, shape, and color of a banana gone bad over her broken rib.

A sudden wave of fatigue hit her so hard and fast that she actually rocked back on her heels. She blinked several times and realized she'd better lie down.

She was asleep within seconds. The iPod Nano with the cockpit voice recording rested by her calf.

TWIN PINES

Lakshmi checked the two nearest cadavers. Both had been set down carefully and were properly covered. Good. She stood and crossed to the wall-mounted thermostat. Forty degrees. Not cold enough to halt all decomposition but cold enough to slow it down considerably. Acceptable.

"This looks fine," she said.

Teresa stared out the window at the darkened street, shivering. "Good. Good."

Lakshmi adjusted her comm unit and slipped on her ear jack. She heard Peter say, "Kim."

"It's Dr. Jain. Teresa and I are in Twin Pines. I wanted to check our makeshift morgue. It all looks acceptable."

"Okay. We've done all that we can for tonight. The field teams are heading into Helena. Can you join us for a debriefing dinner?"

"We'll see you there." She disconnected, turned to the uncomfortable Teresa Santiago. "Peter wants everyone back in Helena. Do you mind?"

"No problem," Teresa said with a shudder and reached into her jacket pocket for the rental keys.

Calendar lay under the sheet and listened as they left.

L'ENFANT PLAZA

The drive from Bellagio to Malpensa Airport was no less taxing than the reverse trip. Susan Tanaka wavered between terrified and livid by the time she got to the United counter. Fortunately, the clerk there was both unfriendly and incompetent, so livid won out. It took Susan exactly seven and one-half minutes with the on-duty United supervisor before she had a seat on the next flight out; it was first class, and it was comped because of Kirk's status as a lead pilot.

From the way the flight attendants glanced nervously at her, Susan thought possibly she had overdone her rant just a tad. As a second glass of golden prosecco arrived, ice-cold, she decided she could live with that error in judgment.

Susan had expected to be exhausted as the Boeing 747 landed at Reagan National but something else took over. She was being called in, like a relief pitcher, to save the game. Susan truly liked Beth Mancini. It absolutely was not her intention to humiliate the first-time intergovernmental liaison. But Susan would have been lying if she'd said she wasn't feeling the adrenaline pumping. She took the Yellow Line from Reagan National to NTSB headquarters. She jogged up to the surface—her suitcase was still back in Varenna with Kirk—and dashed across the square to the building. Her ID got the front door open, even after 10:30 P.M.

Susan took the elevator to her floor, dumped her tote bag on her chair, and called Delevan Wildman's home number to let him know she was back.

"I hated like hell asking you to come home," the director said.

"I understand. And I'm going to stay here in D.C."

"You're not going to Montana?"

"No." Her voice was unyielding. "I can help from here without cutting Beth's legs out from beneath her. At least for now. If I just barge in there, I undermine her authority and piss off Peter Kim. That would just slow us down."

"Fine," Wildman said, his voice deep and warm. "I trust your judgment. Susan? I appreciate this more than I can say."

"Thank you, sir."

She hung up, sat at her desk, and used her superuser access codes to get into the Go-Team's preliminary reports.

HELENA

The Go-Team gathered at a family-style diner with an improbable Hawaiian theme on the walls and bad country-western Muzak. Jack and Reuben reported their joint teams had saved all of the avionics not destroyed in the first moments of the crash. Lakshmi Jain reported that the local crew set to perform the autopsies seemed to be more than competent. She admitted this to no one, but she'd expected Montana to be a *frontier* state, backwards and technologically behind the curve. Privately, she had to admit that her knowledge of the American West was a bit too influenced by Bollywood films.

She did not report the statistical anomaly she had discovered in her initial examination of the bodies: she kept finding crushed throats. She would spend the next few hours after dinner on the secure NTSB servers, exploring the autopsies from the crashes of other similar, midsized carriers and looking for the same odd pattern.

TWIN PINES

Twice on Saturday, a crew from the county coroner's office had come to Stan's Meats to retrieve bodies for autopsies. They were taking them three at a time. Each time Calendar hid in an adjacent room, then returned to his task.

He searched every cadaver in the freezing room and found neither Andrew Malatesta's speech nor his sketch pad. He searched the partial-body bags. The same.

If none of the survivors had smuggled out the speech, and if it wasn't with the dead, then that meant it was on the airplane.

He called it a night and snuck out.

After dinner, Lakshmi sent e-mails to her three favorite pathology professors: one was retired in Mumbai, one was working in London, and one was on a one-year sabbatical studying at Johns Hopkins.

She asked each if he had ever seen an anomaly in a major vehicular accident—plane, train, or bus—in which so many people had ended up with crushed throats.

She had counted six such injuries. Six out of eighteen dead. The number seemed extraordinarily high. Didn't it? Perhaps not. The throat is one of the human body's most vulnerable spots. The thoracic organs are protected by the rib cage. Even the stomach—in most cases—is protected by a layer of fat. Okay, that was true in America and Europe, anyway.

The throat offered very little protection.

She went online and scanned *the American Journal of Pathology*. She looked up some ancillary sites. She logged on to the NTSB server with her password and speed-read every report she could find signed "Tomzak, Leonard."

She did not find the crushed-throat anomaly.

How odd, she thought, and closed her laptop.

21

IN THE MORNING, BARRY Tichnor went directly to the CIA head-quarters in Langley and down to Jenna Scott's subbasement office. He punched in the code to let himself in. The place was painted off-white and was sterile: it held computers and chairs and not much else. Barry noted the tiny metal windmill in the ceiling and assumed it was a fire extinguisher. In fact, if triggered, it would spray a corrosive acid in the event that these computers needed to be purged quickly.

Jenna doffed her headset and smiled ruefully at him.

"No luck with the speech or the sketch pad. Calendar reports they're not in the morgue."

Barry sat. He had anticipated this. "This isn't good news."

"No," she agreed. "The speech is inculpatory. The sketchbook is a gold mine of potential weapons and weapon platforms. At this point, we have to consider them the primary objectives of the mission."

Barry nodded. "I don't know what *inculpatory* means." He did, but it annoyed him when people used legal jargon in conversation.

"Not important, it just means that having the Go-Team's phones isn't enough. We need their office bugged, their hotel rooms bugged, we need their laptops. Everything. I'm going into the field."

He could tell she was not happy about this. "I'm sure you'll be fine."

His tone was patronizing and, given the situation, Jenna let him get away with it. "I've had a call name randomly selected for the situation, and I've uploaded communication protocols to your private account. For the duration of my stay in Montana, my call sign will be Vintner."

"And if I need to communicate with Calendar?"

"No," she said, smiling and shaking her head. "He still reports through me."

"Remind him that we need the prototype and the projectiles back here. Even if he needs to use one of his two men to do it. This is as important as the sketchbook and the speech."

Jenna nodded.

Barry stood. "Thank you. Good luck, Vintner."

TWIN PINES

A deputy sheriff arrived at the crash site at dawn and called Chief of Police Paul McKinney. "Hey, I think this fire's bigger."

McKinney was just getting out of bed and couldn't find his eyeglasses. "Yeah?"

"I volunteer for the fire crews each summer, Chief. I swear she's grown since yesterday."

"Shit. Okay, thanks. Stand by, I'm going to contact the fire chief."

CRASH SITE

Jack Goodspeed held the crook of his elbow against his mouth and nose, his eyes watering from the smoke. It was going on 6:00 A.M., an hour after Chief McKinney had gotten the word. The chief had raced out to the crash site, only to realize that most of the crashers already were there, along with a half-dozen flatbed trucks and small, agile Caterpillar tractors.

"Look!" Paul stepped up to him. "This is not my jurisdiction and I can't order you around, but if the wind picks up, this fire will be right where you're standing in less than an hour! I strongly recommend you evac, now!"

Jack coughed. "Not without my fuselage."

"Yeah, well, lift with your legs, not your back."

"I'm serious, Chief. The clues to this crash are in that tin can. I can't let it burn up."

A firefighter in yellow turnouts jogged up to them. "Look around, fella! We're in a forest. You can't get your flatbeds close enough. It'd take a week, minimum, to chop down enough trees to get 'em in here. You don't have a week."

The firefighter said, "You're talking about getting this plane out?"

Jack nodded, coughed.

The firefighter said, "You could fly it out."

"Yeah, that's a sidesplitter, buddy."

The firefighter shrugged. "I wasn't kidding. You want that plane? Let's fly it out."

L'ENFANT PLAZA

Dmitri Stepanovich Zhirkov, a computer-reconstruction expert for the NTSB, arrived at 8:30 A.M., went directly to the basement and shoved his aged backpack into his messy cubicle. The garbage can was stuffed with fast-food containers. He shoved a long, wild mop of blond hair away from his eyes, dug an antique Walkman out of his backpack. He chose an Aerosmith cassette tape for this morning's work. Twenty-five, angular, and thin, he owned no fewer than eight Walkman tape players, half older than he was. He felt there was something missing from digital, downloaded music.

He sat on the side of his desk and stuffed his size-twelve feet into in-line skates. He found it easier to glide through the main computer room, which ran the length of the headquarters building. He was lacing them up as the security door to the mainframe room hissed open.

"Go away!" he shouted, eyes on his laces. "I am without caffeine!"

"Dee?"

He turned. "Susan!"

Susan Tanaka stepped forward and hugged him. Standing on the in-line skates, he towered over her and had to bend at the waist for the hug. "What are you doing here? You are supposed to be in Italy."

"It's this thing in Montana. Delevan—"

Dmitri cut her off. "Isaiah and the others. I know. Is tragedy." He had lived in the States for a decade but his accent was still marked.

"I have a huge favor to ask."

Dmitri reached into the old, camouflage backpack and dragged out an energy drink, cracking the lid and glugging the lurid liquid. "Of course!"

"This is just between the two of us, okay? I'm worried about the Go-Team. I'm worried about, well, Peter Kim."

Dmitri said, "Yes. Is dick."

"Right. Is dick. But beyond that, I just have this gut feeling that not everything out there is what it appears to be. I'd like to watch over the crashers' backs, make sure they're okay."

"You have the hunch?"

"Little things," she said. "On my flight back, I ran through the Go-Team's dailies. Do you know Gene Whitney, the crew-team leader?"

Dmitri shrugged. "Not well."

"He's accessed his NTSB credit card to head back to D.C., to interview the ground crew. In fact, he did it twice. But he's never bought a ticket back to Montana. How's a guy do that? Plus three or four coincidences left Flight Seven-Eight more than half empty. That could be freakish good luck but . . ."

"But your famous saying: no coincidences in crash. Okay. But look, you left a beautiful man in beautiful part of Italy. What is the word Tommy Tomzak uses? Mesh . . . ?"

"Meshuga. And yes. I'm doing this *for* Tommy. And Kiki and Isaiah."

The kid gulped his energy drink. "For you, I do anything. You get me this job, yes? Bring me your iPad. This is not the biggie."

She grinned. "I thought you were going to tell me this breaks every protocol at the NTSB."

"Pfffff." Dmitri made a dismissive wave of his hand. "I spy on your Go-Teams all the time."

TWIN PINES

Peter Kim stepped out of the rental. He couldn't see smoke but he thought he could smell it. He checked his watch: 8:30 A.M.

The state fire crews had set up shop in the police station to take advantage of the department's high-speed Internet and communications system. The station took up a third of a brick building that looked straight out of the 1920s. It looked like any small-town police station: cluttered, utilitarian, with corkboards up on every available wall for posters and flyers ranging from the feds' "most wanted" to auditions for the Twin Pines Methodist Church Choir. There was no Plexiglas safety partition to protect the staff and no key-card-protected security doors. Nobody had ever entered the police station with malice aforethought.

The rest of the squat, square building included city hall and related city offices.

Mac Pritchert, the state fire chief, shook Peter's hand. "Mr. Kim, was it?"

"Yes. I spoke to the hospital. There's a possibility that we have a missing survivor. He could still be in there."

"Let's hope not," Pritchert said. "That bitch of a fire just turned our way."

HELENA

Ray Calabrese was bored. He'd packed so quickly in Los Angeles, he'd forgotten to grab a novel. There was nothing to watch on television, and Peter Kim had made it clear that he didn't want Ray hanging out at the crash site or *bothering* the crashers. He'd found a *Time* and an *Economist* at the grocery story, plus a book of crossword puzzles. It was going on 9:00 A.M. Sunday. He was wondering what the hell he was doing in Montana when his cell phone beeped.

"Calabrese."

Kiki Duvall's voice came back over the line, but higher-pitched than usual and clipped. "Oh, thank God I got you!"

Ray found himself standing. "Are you okay? Did you open your wounds or—?"

"The cockpit voice recorder!" she cut him off. "Ray, I don't know who those men are, but they weren't our pilots!"

Fifteen minutes later, Ray barged his way up to Tommy Tomzak's room. "Get dressed, Texas. Kiki needs us."

Tommy stood and moved to the room's closet without asking why. A duty nurse frowned. "He can't just leave, he—"

Ray flashed his tin. "FBI business, ma'am."

Ray explained en route to the hotel. They stopped at a Radio Shack and bought a small, portable speaker designed to work with an iPod.

Kiki, barefoot in cuffed khaki shorts and a white T-shirt, opened her hotel-room door and hurried them in. Ray made a valiant effort not to notice her flat stomach or the concave curves where her hip bones disappeared into her shorts.

"You are *not* going to believe this!" she said, grabbing the electronic gadget from Tommy's hand.

She hooked up the Nano and the speaker. Kiki hit Play.

> Holley: We're at, ah, a thousand feet. Passing outer marker for Helena Regional.
> Cervantes: A thousand?
> Holley: Ah . . . yeah.
>
> (beat)
>
> Cervantes: I don't think so. I think we're lower.
> Holley: I got a confirm on the altimeter, now reading nine five zero feet . . . mark.
> Cervantes: Ah, Helena Regional, this is Polestar Seven-Eight, what elevation do you have for us?
>
> (beat)
>
> Cervantes: Helena Regional, Polestar Seven-Eight.
>
> (beat)
>
> This feels way low, Jed. We're lower than we think. Helena Regional, Pole—
> Holley: Trees!

Kiki hit Pause.

"I'm not one hundred percent certain about the pilot. He could be our guy, although I don't think he is. The copilot? Definitely not ours. Ours was born and raised in New York City. This guy is from Boston."

Ray said, "Standard operating procedure, the CVR goes from the crash site into the custody of NTSB. From there, a U.S. Marshal's deputy takes—"

She brushed her hair from her face with an angry swoop of one open palm. "I know the SOP, Ray! I wrote the SOP!"

Ray raised both hands. "Hey. Not doubting you here. What I'm saying is: I've got to get to the Marshal's Service, get confirmation that the hand-off went according to Hoyle. I'll call the Portland field office, get someone over to the recording studio. If this is a fake, we should be able to track down where it was switched."

Tommy cut in: "Does the Go-Team have a cause yet?"

"Short circuit somewhere in the cockpit, is all I know. Took out the, what do you call it, the altimeter. Plus the radio. Some of the guys recall that another airplane, same make and model, um . . ."

Kiki said, "Claremont VLE."

"Right. What's VLE stand for?"

Tommy said, "Very Little Elbow room."

Kiki said, "Initials of the three engineers who started the company, back in the thirties."

Tommy stood up to pace and immediately his vertigo flared. He lost his balance, sliding back down onto the bed beside Kiki. "Whoa. Sorry about that. Look, we got us another problem, gang. Short circuit on the flight deck? No altimeter? Fine, but I was awake when we lost power. Cabin lights, engines. Even the reading-thingie I bought. Boom. Nada. A massive and complete power loss. Not only are those guys bogus," and he jammed a pugnacious finger at the iPod, "but they lay out a scenario that don't match the facts."

Ray turned to Kiki, eyebrows rising.

"Sorry. I was asleep. Tommy had me down between seats and was on me before . . . Wow." She blushed and put a hand over her lips. "That came out so much naughtier than I was going for."

Ray smiled at her. "No worries. I got where you were going with that. But I need another witness. The other six surviv—"

Tommy said, "You got a witness. Get Peter on the horn."

Ray shook his head. "Can't. You're a crappy witness, Doc."

Tommy's face clouded over. "Says who?"

"Says your concussion, jackass. You got your clock cleaned out there."

Kiki put a hand on Tommy's forearm. "At one point, after you blacked out, you said to me, 'Don't tell Mom.'"

"I did? Crap. Okay, I hear you. Petey is never gonna buy me alone. But he's got to believe Kiki's ears." He turned his hand over, took her hand, looked lovingly into her eyes. "When it comes to sound, my gal is Wolfgang Amadeus Motherfucking Mozart."

"Sweetie? Later, when this is all over? We're going to work on your compliments."

"Anything for you, babe. But, guys, there's more. The Indian chick—"

"Dr. Jain," Ray provided.

"Right. She has the pilot getting up and waltzin' around the flight deck with a C4 tear in his spinal cord. Ain't happening. She's got Isaiah with a crushed larynx and I know—*I know*—he spoke to me. I've been denying it, last coupla days. But, dammit, I remember you evacing the survivors and me field-dressing their wounds. Isaiah said he'd tried to save the flight attendant. Said he was stuck. I knelt and ran my hands over his legs and torso, looking for blood. He was jammed down, lying between four seats, like—"

"Oh my god!" The men turned to Kiki. "Isaiah wasn't lying between the seats when he died. He was sitting up when I found him! He was sitting in one of the seats!"

"Well, shit, hon. There you go. What I'm saying. Oh, and hey: remember the teenage girl with the brachial bleeder? Name's Ann. She remembers the silver-haired guy, too. That's three of us."

Ray pulled out his ubiquitous sealskin notebook. "Describe him."

Tommy and Kiki looked at each other. She said, "Um, six feet, six-one. Late forties, early fifties. Looked pretty athletic. Silver hair, cut short . . . Um . . ."

"Ah, navy sweater," Tommy cut in, "jeans, um, boots—"

"Good boots. Thick rubber soles, lace-up. They looked new."

Ray said, "Military boots?"

Kiki nodded. "The perfect boots for stomping around in a forest."

Ray blinked at her.

Tommy said, "What?"

"Lots of my work takes good, sturdy boots. But I always pack them in my checked luggage. Since nine/eleven, I fly in loafers. Gets me through TSA quicker."

Kiki nodded. "I do the same. Top-Siders for the flight, boots for once I land."

Ray checked earlier notes in his pad. "There were twenty-six people on that plane. Twenty-six *souls,* as you crashers put it. Two pilots, two flight crew. Accounted for. Eight survivors, that's twelve. Fourteen passengers dead: that's twenty-six. Everyone's accounted for. So who's Silver Hair?"

Tommy and Kiki shrugged.

"Do either of you remember seeing this guy at the airport or on the plane?"

They both shook their heads. Kiki gave a little shudder. "Are you saying he wasn't on the plane? He was on the ground? Waiting for us?"

Tommy waved her off. "No, wait. That makes no sense. For the guy to be waiting for us, he'd have to know where the plane was crashing."

He glanced at Ray and Kiki, realized they were staring at him. Kiki's eyes were wide with fright.

"What?"

Ray repeated Tommy's words at half-speed. "He'd have to know . . ."

And Tommy suddenly got it. ". . . Where the goddamn plane was crashing? Holy shit! I do not goddamn believe this. Only way that works is: he brought that bird down!"

Ray shook his head. "We're getting ahead of ourselves. Did either of you talk to him?"

"Yes." Kiki nodded. "He helped me carry out a survivor from the cabin. He asked me what happened to the aircraft, why it crashed. I said I didn't know, I'd been asleep."

Tommy said, "You know, he asked me that, too. And he asked Ann, the girl."

Ray said, "What did you tell him?"

"I said, 'Damned if I know.'"

Ray sat, thinking, his eyes darting randomly to different spots on the room's carpet. Tommy opened his mouth but Kiki squeezed his hand. She could practically hear the gears churning in Ray Calabrese's head.

Ray's eyes narrowed. "You wear a watch, Texas?"

"Yeah, but it's busted." Tommy reached into his trouser pocket and withdrew his battered Timex. He showed the LED face to Ray. "Bupkes."

Kiki said, "My watch broke, too."

"Was it a winder or digital?"

"Digital."

Tommy thought he caught a glimmer of where the agent was going. He turned to Kiki. "You said my penlight didn't work that night?"

She nodded.

Ray stood. "All right. You make an airliner fall out of the sky by destroying every electronic circuit on board. That includes watches, and penlights, and reading devices. You fake two black boxes to cover your tracks. You've got enough juice to pull in guys with fake Marshal's creds—and I'm just spitballing there, we've got no evidence of that. The plane hits the ground. There are survivors. What do you do next?"

Tommy lifted Kiki's hand and kissed her knuckles. He looked more grim than ever. "You get a guy dressed for working in a forest to ask the survivors: what happened? If they don't know, you leave 'em alone."

Kiki gasped, getting there. "Oh my god. Oh my god! If they do know. If they know about the power loss, if they can contradict the black boxes . . ." Her eyes glittered with tears.

Tommy's voice dropped a half octave out of pure rage. "We got two instances of fatal injuries occurring *after* the crash. Pilot, for sure he don't get to walk out."

Kiki was crying for real now. Her shoulders hunched and her knees rose, contracting her body into a tight ball of pain. "Isaiah."

"I woke him up. I called out to him. A pilot, veteran crasher, no way he didn't realize how quiet the plane got with no engines. Even during the fall, he'd've diagnosed the situation."

He hugged Kiki. "Jesus. I got Isaiah killed. This is my fault."

Ray sat again and let them drown in their grief. They needed the time. And Ray needed to write a whole new playbook.

CRASH SITE

The firefighter with the bright idea of flying the Claremont out borrowed an NTSB–issued tablet computer and showed Jack and Reuben what he had in mind. "See? We can fly the plane out."

Reuben let his glasses hang from their lanyard and craned his neck to see the tablet, nestled in the firefighter's forearm. "With a zeppelin?"

"An airship. We've been using 'em for more than a decade in the logging industry. Cut down a big tree, no way to get a Cat in those tight spaces, so you rig heavy-lift cables, attach them to the airship, and float them out."

Jack said, "What's the lift capacity?"

"Forty tons. Skyhook and Boeing collaborated on this bad boy."

"And it's nearby?"

"Logging camp, three miles north. I work there when it isn't fire season."

Jack adjusted his comm unit. "What the heck. Go get it. I'll call the boss."

Reuben jogged toward the nose of the fuselage. When he was done,

Jack called his number-two guy on the airframe team and got the word that the team was on its way with the supplies they'd need.

Reuben Chaykin hurried back, a handkerchief tied over his nose and mouth, bandit-style. "There's a path, about eight or nine degrees clockwise from the nose. If we can get the fuselage off the ground and turn it just a little, I think we can snake it between the trees. Eighty, maybe a hundred feet straight west, and we're out of the woods."

Jack said, "As it were." He slapped Reuben on the back. "Sorry we couldn't get at my wings or your engines."

Reuben sighed forlornly.

Chief Paul McKinney hurried up to them, coughing. "We can try this crazy stunt, and if it works, great. But I just talked to the guy running the fire crews. He gave me authority to make the call and evacuate your people."

Reuben said, "Fair enough. Just let us take a shot."

Jack Goodspeed's airframe team broke land-speed records getting to the site in a massive truck and trailer. In the back were metal mesh straps, five feet wide and one hundred feet long, capable of lifting a Boeing or an Airbus wide-body off the ground; more than strong enough to lift a midsize carrier like a Claremont.

If . . . of course. *If* the structural integrity of the fuselage was stable enough. If not, it would crack into pieces as soon as it left the ground.

Although the Go-Team now had a pretty good idea of what had caused the crash—a short in the avionics suite—there was still much to learn by examining the aircraft. What had broken and what had not would be invaluable information and could help the designers of the next generation of aircraft to build them to be even safer.

Jack's crews took shovels and pickaxes and started looking for places on the forest floor where they could create tunnels under the fuselage for the straps.

Another truck arrived, this one with Beth Mancini. She oversaw a crew that brought food and bottled water, plus arc lights for working in the shade of the forest. Plus hazmat turnouts that, by adding a self-contained breathing apparatus, could serve as rudimentary firefighter suits.

"That won't help you if the fire line gets here," Chief McKinney warned Beth, as she climbed into the one-piece suit.

"Understood. They might buy us some time, though."

McKinney had to admit that the crashers were brave enough. Just a little foolhardy.

Reuben stepped into one of the moon suits. "Did you find out why the plane was so light?"

"Polestar Airlines is working on it. A computer glitch wouldn't let any of the airplane-ticket Web sites mesh with that particular flight. Also, a connector that was supposed to land at Reagan got diverted to Dulles. No one seems sure why."

Reuben said. "Wow. Lucky break."

It was. But it still nagged at Beth. She said "Tanaka's Law of Coincidence," and Reuben nodded.

"Got you. In a crash: no such damn thing."

One of the airframe team finished digging a tunnel under the midsection of the ship and stood. "Okay, straps are gonna work. What the devil are we going to lift this bitch with?"

Jack pointed westward and upward. "That."

Casper the Friendly Airship floated into view. Fifty feet long, and fat, the bright white airship was powered by downward- and rearward-facing propellers.

Casper's controller, Ginger LaFrance, knew that her name made her sound more like an exotic dancer than a civil engineer with a pilot's license, but that's what she was. Now, she sat in the passenger seat of a firefighter's Ford F-150, the remote control for Casper in her lap, pacing the giant airship that floated directly parallel with the truck. There was no space for a crew on board; Ginger ran the ship from the box on her lap with toggles and two joysticks.

22

AMY DREYFUS FILED HER story for the *Post,* sitting on the floor of her bed-and-breakfast room in Twin Pines, her Compaq Presario balanced on her upturned knees. She wore one of Ezra's casual cotton shirts and her favorite fluffy socks. The shirt smelled like her husband and helped center her when she traveled.

The *Post* had sent her to Helena because a handful of microelectronics firms' executives had been on board that plane, en route to the Northwest Tech Expo.

She interviewed a number of the mourners, talked about their loved ones' lives. It was a human-interest piece, and business reporters don't get that many opportunities to do human interest.

She closed the lid on the computer, leaned against the wall for a while, rubbing a kink in her neck. She felt guilty about her aborted dinner with Renee Malatesta, about the way Renee had bolted down her drink and fled.

She reopened the computer and checked her Sources file. She scrolled to the Ms.

Renee Malatesta sat on the edge of her freshly made hotel-room bed. She was naked, still-wet hair brushed straight back. She felt occasional rivulets of shower water run from her hair down the hollow of her spine.

She cradled the Colt .25 in both hands. Such a small and seemingly delicate weapon. She stared at it for some time.

Andrew had picked out the weapon for her. It fit her hand perfectly.

Renee removed the magazine, set it on her bare, tanned thigh. She ratcheted the slide to confirm there was no round in the two-inch barrel.

She tried pulling the trigger a few times, to see how it felt. She measured the tension against her forefinger. *Snap. Snap. Snap.*

Words were etched into the metal near the trigger. She turned and swiveled the gun, letting light bounce off the tiny tip. MADE IN SPAIN. How odd. The Colt sounded like such an all-American creation.

She tugged on the trigger, thinking of the *plaza mayor* in Segovia, the pink-lit cathedral, the bandstand, the glasses of good, golden cava she and Andrew had shared.

Snap. Snap. Snap.

She liked the heft of the weapon. It felt right in her hands. She pressed the short barrel against her right thigh. *Snap.*

She felt the sting, even without any bullets. She moved the barrel to her abdomen, right under her rib cage. *Snap.*

She imagined how different it would be when it was loaded.

If it were loaded. She'd meant *if.*

Her cell phone rang. She watched it, unsure how to react.

Snap. Ring. Snap. Ring.

She picked up the phone with her free, left hand. "Hello?"

"Hey. It's Amy. Look, I'm sorry about earlier. I was being so thoughtless, what with—"

Renee appreciated the drag on the trigger, the pressure it took before the hammer fell. "Where are you?"

"I couldn't find a hotel room in Helena. I'm in a b-and-b in Twin Pines. It's where the NTSB press briefings are."

Renee surprised herself. "Meet me for lunch?"

"Um . . . really?"

"Please. Lunch."

"Okay. Where?"

Snap.

. . .

An hour later, Amy and Renee sat in a booth in Café Artemis, in the Park Plaza Hotel. Both were surprised by how tony the place was.

Renee ordered a Wray & Nephew white rum, a very strong drink with a hint of sulfur in the smell. Many rum drinkers couldn't handle the aroma but Renee loved it. Amy ordered a pinot noir.

Renee took a sip of rum and sighed. "Did you bring a recorder?"

Amy pulled a digital recorder out of her tote bag. "Sure. Did you want . . . Is this an interview?"

Renee sipped the strong drink. "Yes."

"Okay, but, again, can I say—"

"Thank you. Andrew and I always appreciated your accurate reporting. You cover all the angles. You get your facts correct. We appreciated that. I appreciate that."

Amy nodded and activated the recorder. She also dug out a narrow reporter's notepad and a cheap Pilot pen. Like most reporters, she had a distrust of recording devices. "Andrew told me he was going to make a major announcement at the Tech Expo. Can you tell me about that?"

"Malatesta, Inc., has signed a multiyear agreement with the Pentagon to implement research into offensive and defensive weapons platforms."

"Wow. That would be a sea change for you. Weapons."

"Yes," Renee said. "We have been in negotiations for two years. I came from severe poverty in Haiti. America opened its arms to me, and today I am a successful lawyer and businesswoman. My husband felt much the same way about the opportunities granted to us. This is the direction he had turned the company before he died in the crash."

Her voice did not quiver. Her eyes did not twinkle with tears. She spoke with no emotion, almost by rote. Amy wondered what kind of medication she was on.

"What sort of weaponry?"

Renee tilted her head to the right. *"Sea change?"*

Amy looked up. "Excuse me?"

"You said *sea change*. I wonder where that phrase comes from."

"Um . . ."

"Never mind. I'm not at liberty to talk about the work. It's classified. Andrew had been up at all hours, working around the clock, coming up with some of his most innovative ideas yet. Ideas that will keep America safe."

Amy thinking, *Can't talk about the weapons. Great.* "This contract: can I ask what the impact on company earnings will be?"

"We lost three of our five top engineers, including our president and founder. That will have a larger immediate impact on earnings than the Pentagon contract."

"Of course. Sorry. Um . . ." *Couldn't talk about the weapons, couldn't talk about the money.* "You must have had a time line. Their deaths will surely slow that down."

Renee sipped her drink. "It will. We still have to have memorial services. I need to convene a meeting of the company, talk to our people. Let them know where we go from here. There are steps to grieving. Not just for me. I . . . I suspect, but I don't know, that the entire company will go through post-traumatic stress disorder for the next year. Or years. But we're good people. We're patriots."

She smiled but it was a wan thing and quickly faded away. Renee sat with one hand hovering over the rum, the other shoved into the pocket of her long sweater, as if her hand was chilled. Amy underlined that word in her notepad: *patriots.*

She asked a few more questions but didn't get much. When she thought she had enough for a short, online story, she stopped the recorder and capped her pen. "I guess that's that. Thank you."

Renee said, "No, thank you."

Amy took her first sip of the red wine. "Um, *The Tempest.* The cliché, 'sea change'? It's from *The Tempest.*"

Renee looked at her—possibly for the first time—and frowned. "I didn't know that. I thought perhaps it was a reference to how slowly big ships turn in the water."

"No. Ariel says it to what's-his-name, the prince."

Renee smiled, the tanned skin around her eyes crinkling. It was a true smile, and now, too, her eyes finally glittered with tears.

Amy heard a faint *snap snap* from somewhere near the table. She glanced around, looking for one of those candle-lighting wands that waiters use, but saw nothing.

"Thank you, Amy. I appreciate knowing that."

Amy thought that maybe she was the first person since Thursday to tell Renee Malatesta a single thing that didn't ache.

Tommy was showering and Kiki picked up the phone when it rang. It was Susan Tanaka.

Kiki sat on the bed and proceeded to tell Susan the theory that they had brewed up.

Tommy stepped out, towel around his waist, eyebrows raised.

"It's Susan."

Tommy smiled and walked back into the bathroom.

Over the line, Susan said, "I knew it. I knew something was off. Look, don't tell a soul on the Go-Team, but I'm not in Italy. I'm in L'Enfant Plaza."

"But . . . ?"

"I know. Still. Del has been keeping me posted. Between Peter Kim's arrogance and Beth's lack of experience, the investigation is spiraling out of control. Now, with what you just told me. . . . I'm treading softly here, though. I don't want to undermine Beth."

"Okay. I understand."

"Do you know Dmitri Zhirkov, in the tech center? Twenty-something, long, crazy blond hair?"

Kiki could picture him. "Travels around the NTSB on in-line skates?"

Susan said, "That's him. He's a major-league computer expert. He handles a lot of the computer reconstruction we have to do after a crash. I, ah, I took the liberty of asking him to hack in to the Go-Team's computers and comm systems."

Kiki said, "Susan!"

"Well, I want to know what's going on! Please, I have to—"

Kiki said, "You were about to say, *please, I have to help.* Susan, I totally understand."

Tommy again stepped out of the steamy bathroom, this time clad only in jeans. He had applied shaving cream to the left side of his face. "What?"

"It's Susan. She has our backs."

Tommy started lathering up the right side. "Course Susan has our backs. Duh."

CRASH SITE

Peter decided he needed to see this stunt for himself. He asked Teresa Santiago and Lakshmi Jain to stay in Twin Pines with the few crew chiefs, monitoring the fire, as he drove to the crash site. Lakshmi agreed quickly, saying something about checking e-mails for information on an injury anomaly. Peter wasn't really listening.

Approaching the state forest, the first thing that caught his eye was

Casper the Friendly Airship. Roughly the size and shape of a humpback whale, its white belly glowed brightly, reflecting the arc lights below.

He cocked his head. No one at the NTSB had ever moved a fuselage with an airship before; the trick would never have occurred to him. He thought about that for a moment. The idea was innovative. It was creative.

The next thought curdled his soul: *That bastard Tomzak might have thought of this.*

Ginger LaFrance's remote control was a flat box that hung horizontally from straps over her shoulders, much like a guy hawking beer in a baseball park. She stood between Reuben Chaykin and Beth Mancini. She hit a toggle and three heavy-lift cables began descending from the glowing white blob in the sky.

Jack Goodspeed stood atop the fuselage, his boots between two windows that had, until a few days ago, faced the portside wings. It was dangerous on top of the wreckage like this, but Jack hadn't wanted to ask any of his airframe crew to do something that he, himself, wasn't willing to do.

The smoke was thicker twenty-eight feet off the ground, and Jack wore a fully contained hazmat suit with an air tank and a helmet of soft Tyvek and a Plexiglas face shield. His comm unit's ear jack and voice wand fit inside the suit.

His crews had dug tunnels under the keeled-over jet to pass through the thick mesh belts. They used two narrow, long-reach forklifts that could turn on a dime and dart nimbly between trees. The forklifts were made by a company called Skyjack, which the crashers agreed was as bad-karma-inducing a name as any in the aviation industry. The long-reach lifts gathered the metal mesh belts and lifted them up on Jack's left and right. He attached them to the first of Casper's three cables, using two heavy bolts to assemble it all.

Peter approached the cluster of people around the remote operator, Ginger LaFrance. "Who authorized Goodspeed to get up there? He could fall and break his neck."

Beth said, "It was his idea. He's as athletic as anyone on the Go-Team."

Jack attached the belts and cable, then carefully walked a third of the way down the fuselage, stepping on the stylized logo of Polestar Airlines.

"I hope this works." Peter turned to Ginger LaFrance. "You're controlling?"

She kept her eyes glued to Jack and the cable. "That's what my ex says."

Peter was the wrong audience for droll. "The airship. You're controlling the airship."

"Uh-huh."

"How much weight can it lift?"

"Pretty much just itself."

Peter blinked. "I don't understand."

Ginger glanced his way, then back to Jack's steeplejack act. "Casper maintains enough buoyancy to keep itself in the air. The downward propellers provide enough lift for the cargo."

"So again: how much?"

She shrugged. "He's been tested at eighty-six thousand pounds. Just shy of forty tons. So what's this thing weigh?"

Peter peered at the ruins of the Claremont and did the math in his head. With the wings and the turboprops, he figured twenty-five thousand, twenty-six thousand kilograms. That's about fifty-six thousand pounds. Without the wings . . . Peter said, "I'd say . . . roughly thirty-five thousand pounds."

Ginger LaFrance blew a gum bubble and kept her eyes glued on Jack. "Then this should be a walk in the park."

Jack got the last of the three cables hooked up. Beth had arranged for Ginger to have an extra headset. Jack set his comm unit for All. "Okay. Let's try lifting her straight up, about six inches."

Peter said, "Get down first."

"No. This works, someone's going to have to play navigator. I'll hold on to the airship cables and I'm standing on the steel O-ring. I'll be okay."

Beth turned to Peter. "O-ring?"

"The Claremont is built with two sturdy, solid-state O-rings, one-third and two-thirds of the way back toward the empennage. The fuselage is moved down the assembly line at the manufacturing plant, hoisted at those two rings. Goodspeed's standing on one of them."

Jack said, "Miss LaFrance? Ready?"

Ginger wore fingerless, weight-lifter's gloves. She gripped the joystick and said, "Six inches, straight up."

The metal-mesh belts grew taut against the fuselage. The crashers and firefighters held their breath. The Claremont let loose a long, low groan, almost like a mortally wounded giant. Something went *snap!* within. The airframe shuddered.

With more low keening and the shriek of rent aluminum somewhere inside, the Claremont VLE lifted off the forest floor. Ginger applied more thrust and the fuselage rose two more inches.

It didn't break in half.

More upthrust brought the Claremont six inches off the forest floor. Things began falling out of the ruptured downward-facing starboard portions of the fuselage: luggage, jackets, pillows, bits of ruined aircraft. A human hand. A Sony laptop. A roll of toilet paper bounced free and rolled toward the crashers, unspooling in its wake. It came to rest against Peter Kim's shoe.

Then the noises from the aircraft stopped.

The Claremont floated. Silent. Peter got down on one knee and looked under it. "Amazing," he whispered to himself.

Reuben Chaykin coughed and said, *"Oy vey iz mir."*

Jack, standing atop the levitating airliner, laughed over the communications gear. "I will be a son of a gun. Miss LaFrance? Outstanding."

She popped a gum bubble. "It's just Ginger, boys."

"Ginger it is. Now, here's the tricky part. The Claremont was never designed to be carried while tilted ninety degrees off its axis. We need to put her right-side up."

Ginger tried to wave smoke away from her face. "What about you?"

"Montana girl, I'd think you'd have seen men running on logs in the water before."

Ginger laughed. "It's the twenty-first century. This isn't *Seven Brides for Seven Brothers.*"

"I love that film. Okay, go slow."

Ginger adjusted controls on her box, and the hooks beneath Casper began letting out the thick straps, slowly, the strap to the left of the airship slacking and the straps to the right tightening.

Beneath Jack's feet, the fuselage slowly rotated a few inches. Holding on to the hooks over his head, he took two steps to his right, staying at the "top" of the steel O-ring.

"Okay. Little more . . ."

Things crash-tumbled inside the Claremont. More items fell out of the holes in the fuselage onto the dry earth below.

"Good . . ." Jack chanted, stepping gingerly as the O-ring turned beneath his boots. "That's it. . . . Nice and easy . . ."

More groaning from the cadaverous aircraft. Things knocked against one another.

Peter Kim dashed forward to watch it all from the perspective of the nose of the plane. It slowly turned counterclockwise, Jack riding it, walking the curved surface.

Jack, chanting, "Good . . . uh-huh . . . that's it . . ."

Peter raised his arms over his head, palms open.

". . . Steady . . . Good . . ."

Ginger LaFrance's eyes danced from the rotating fuselage to Peter's raised hands.

". . . That's it . . ."

Peter made fists. "Stop!"

Ginger released the controls.

Jack laughed out loud. "Not bad!"

The Claremont hung in the air, right-side up.

Jack's grin could light up a small city. "Damn. Never done that before. Alrighty then, Ginger, want to try forward movement?"

She popped a gum bubble. "I'm game if you are."

"First, we've got to turn to about one o'clock. There's a more or less straight path out of the forest."

Ginger made minute adjustments to the remote controls. With another loud moan, the Claremont turned clockwise, five degrees. Casper did, too, but with the cadaver of the airliner off the ground, nobody's eyes were anywhere else. "Good. Okay, try moving her forward," Jack called out

Another adjustment from Ginger and the ruined fuselage floated to the left a couple of inches. Then a foot.

The crashers took two steps in the same direction, keeping pace with the eerie, floating apparition.

For reasons that she could not explain, Beth Mancini felt compelled to reach out and touch the aluminum skin of the devastated craft. As if she'd stumbled into a beached whale.

Peter snapped his fingers. He motioned to Jack's airframe group. "You guys. Hey, guys! Anything falls out of the aircraft, pick it up and bring it along. Anything at all! We—"

He jumped as, *thud,* a deer carcass fell out of the cockpit.

"Okay," he said. "Not that."

.   .   .

The forklifts led the way, breaking off branches where necessary. Jack, riding the aluminum leviathan, called out minor changes in vector. "Little to the left. Little more. Okay, good."

Peter, Beth, Chief McKinney, and Ginger LaFrance walked slowly out of the forest, keeping up with the floating wreckage. From time to time it groaned, and, again, Beth kept imagining a beached whale.

Beth's team started dismantling the floodlights but she shouted back, "Leave 'em! Help Jack's guys pick up debris!"

At almost exactly 2:00 P.M. on Sunday, Polestar Flight 78 left the Helena State Forest and began floating its way to the town of Twin Pines.

23

KIKI HELPED TOMMY GET discharged from the hospital and checked in to her hotel room around two that Sunday. He needed toiletries and Kiki needed what she called *girl stuff*—Tommy didn't ask—so they hit a PayLess Drug Store in Helena. Kiki had wound her hair into twin pigtails because it was easier to manage.

Susan Tanaka would have been horrified. Tommy thought the pigtails looked cute.

They were walking out, hand in hand, when Tommy pulled away and said, "Hey!"

A big man, twenty paces away, was lighting a cigarette with a disposable lighter. He glanced their way.

Tommy marched over to him. Kiki thinking, *Oh, hell* . . . Susan Tanaka had informed them that Gene Whitney had faked his interviews with the Reagan National ground crew.

The bear of a man loomed over Tommy. "Yeah?"

"Tomzak. We met at a thing in D.C. You're Gene Whitney."

Gene blinked. "Don't remember you."

"The fuck are you doing, faking interviews with the ground crews at Reagan?"

Gene took a drag from his Camel. If he was surprised by the question, or by Tommy's knowledge, he didn't show it. "What'd you say your name was again?"

Kiki had caught up to Tommy. "This isn't the right time or place for—"

"It's all right," Gene said, his voice gray and sullen. "I was fucking with your boy Tomzak here."

He turned to Tommy again. "You need something?"

"I need to know why you're screwing with Peter Kim's Go-Team. I need to know why you're half-assing your way through this investigation."

Kiki touched his shoulder. "Hey, come on . . ."

Gene sucked smoke into his lungs, held it, wincing. His eyes roamed the Helena cityscape. "Your official title in this Go-Team is *crash victim*. You been Investigator in Charge twice and one was Kentucky, which you clusterfucked nicely, I'm told. I need to tell you shit, why?"

"Because one of our best people died in this crash. And he deserves your A-game."

Gene nodded, as if to an inner dialogue. He said, "You went and got yourself a concussion, Doctor. You wanna watch your temper. You don't want to . . . what's the word I'm looking for?"

Tommy ground his teeth. "I'm serious as—"

"*Exacerbate,*" Gene said. "You don't want to exacerbate your concussion."

Kiki stepped forward. "Tommy, come on."

Tommy had eyes only for Gene Whitney. "You don't know me, bub. You don't have any reason to listen to me, but I'm telling you, you run the risk of screwin' up this investigation. You're falsifying official reports and lying to your team leader. Petey ain't my favorite guy on Earth, but what the hell, man?"

The big man flicked his cigarette butt to the sidewalk. "And you don't know me, so you don't know that I don't give a flying fuck about either of you or the Reagan ground crew. Me flying there and asking them a bunch of stupid questions that they could lie about? That's masturbation." He scanned the buildings again. "Guy could go blind doing that."

Tommy was livid. "Jesus Harold Angel Christ! Where do you—"

"You don't know me, Doc. So you figure I wouldn't deck you 'cause I got a hundred pounds on you and six inches and you got a boo-boo on your cortex and you got an M.D. and this long, cool drink of water here protecting you." He reached up to pick a flake of tobacco off his tongue. "Which means: you don't know shit."

Gene Whitney turned and ambled away.

Tommy tensed and Kiki grabbed his arm. "He isn't wrong," she whispered. "About the concussion, I mean."

Whitney was almost a block away before Tommy dragged his eyes off the man's slumped shoulders, hands the size of fryer chickens jammed into his pants pocket, his head bowed.

Tommy shook his head. "What a jackass. I should call Del and—"

"No." Kiki kissed his cheek. "Love, he's not inept. Or stupid. Or lazy. He's drunk."

"You're kidding!"

"It's in his voice. He's been on a serious binge."

TWIN PINES

Calendar sat in a booth at Tina's Diner. He'd ordered coffee and apple pie with vanilla ice cream. There were flecks of actual vanilla in the ice cream and the golden, flaky piecrust had been pinched by hand.

A very blond, very tall woman, midthirties, walked in. She wore a sweater, jeans, flats, and sunglasses. All perfectly nondescript. She slid into the other end of the C-shaped booth. She carried a large tote bag, sealed, which she slid around the C to Calendar's side. He slid it closer to his hip. "Hi."

The waitress came by and the woman ordered coffee. When they were alone, she leaned over the table and spoke in a whisper. "I'm Vintner. We have their communications frequencies. I'll be setting up both passive and aggressive wiretap protocols for—"

Calendar said, "Vintner? Why are you doing that?"

She blinked at him. "Excuse me?"

"Leaning in. Whispering. You look suspicious. You're the most suspicious-looking person in the room. Also, ditch the sunglasses indoors. And order some pie. It's really good."

The blond woman leaned back. Her coffee came but she made no eye contact with the waitress. She removed her sunglasses.

"Their computers?"

The woman said, "Not yet," and Calendar could tell she was hurt by his critique of her field skills. "We're working on that. Normally, I'd piggy-back onto their hotel's telephone circuit boards, but they're split up all over the city. Once they set up a headquarters near the crash—and it's SOP to do just that—I'll have to bug that site as well. No problem there."

Calendar said, "Do you want some pie? It's really good."

Vintner stared at him. Then she slid her glasses over her eyes, stood, and left the diner.

When the waitress refilled his cup, Calendar smiled up at her. "This is really good."

ANNAPOLIS

Terri Loew rapped on the door to the Malatesta, Inc., break room. Antal Borsa came here to play air hockey, often all by himself, just slapping the puck around as his brain processed data.

He looked up. She entered and noticed that they had the break room to themselves.

"Did you go online, see the *Post* article?"

He whacked at the puck a few times, watched it bounce off felt and float back home. Antal's shirt was finely starched and his tie was an origi-nal designed by a small, family-owned business back home in Hungary. He owned twenty of their ties and no others. "I did."

Terri sat on the break-room table, brought her Nike cross-trainers up onto one of the chairs, hugged her knees. "It says Andrew was excited about working with the military. Making weapons."

Whack! The puck zoomed out and back. An open bottle of San Pelegrino stood by his elbow. He did not respond.

She let a full minute slip by.

Terri finally shrugged. "If it was a typo, a—"

"Amy Dreyfus? You've been interviewed by her."

She said, "I haven't, actually, but I know. She's good."

"She is. She was Andrew's roommate at Stanford. They were good friends. The quotes are accurate. They came from Renee."

"But they're not true."

Antal stopped playing, sipped his water. Terri got off the table, started making herself a cup of tea. Or at least fiddling with the kettle and cups, to give her fingers something to do.

Antal said, "This is what I wanted. This is what you wanted. This is what Renee wanted. Wants. And we're left."

"But Andrew never said—"

"Terri. She just lost the love of her life, and that would send anyone over the edge. But she also just lost the sheer genius of Andrew Malatesta. You know . . . you *know* that every million-dollar contract we've ever had started with an idea in his head."

"We've contributed plenty." She glared over her shoulder. "You gave us the—"

"Yes, but they all started with Andrew. All our designs. We're good. We're extremely good. But, to use a baseball metaphor, we were born on third base. We've never hit a triple in our lives."

She stopped playing with the accoutrements, turned off the burner.

"Think about it. Renee lost her husband, yes, but she lost the goose that laid the golden egg. She lost three-fifths of her senior designers. She's got mouths to feed, and a new building about to break ground in Maryland, and she's scared."

Terri turned. They both stared at the floor. A receptionist entered. "I'm sorry. Are you . . . ?"

Neither of them had noticed her. "No," Terri said. "We're good."

TWIN PINES

The police station was jammed to the gills, playing host to the first of the state fire crews and expecting two more crews later that day.

Peter Kim and Beth Mancini, with the help of Mayor Art Tibbits, trolled slowly through town and found many abandoned businesses, including a recently closed real estate office that would do nicely as a temporary headquarters.

Casper the Friendly Airship hovered in the distance, a little obscured by a scrim of white forest-fire smoke.

"Where are we storing the Claremont?" Peter asked.

"An auto-parts shop. It has high fences, barbed wire. It should be secure enough." Beth wrote down the address on a notepad, ripped out the page, and handed it to him.

Peter surprised her by saying, "That'll do. You did well. What's our status with the media?"

"It's funny, but the forest fire flaring up is distracting the media from the cause du jour. This morning's press conference, not a single person asked me about al Qaeda."

Peter actually laughed.

HELENA

Amy Dreyfus was in the Firetower Coffee House on Last Chance Gulch. She'd had to check twice before believing that, yes, they'd named the street "Last Chance Gulch." It sounded like the kind of place Uncle Donald took Huey, Dewey, and Louie for an adventure.

Amy was simultaneously pouring creamer into a coffee go-cup with two shots of espresso, stirring, paying, and calling the *Washington Post*, phone cradled between ear and her shoulder.

"It's Amy. Is Big-Time in? Thank you." She got her receipt and mouthed a thank-you to the clerk.

"Ames! You just bought a coffee with two shots of espresso and you just poured in half-and-half."

She licked the stir stick. "I did not! I'm not anywhere nearly that predictable!"

The editor laughed. "What's happening?"

Amy shoved her cherry-red hair away from her eyebrows. "It's the Malatesta, Inc., thing I filed."

"The widow? How is she?"

She moved to the front window of the coffee shop for some privacy. "We had drinks the other night and I thought she was made of spun glass. I tap her, she'd shatter."

"Grief. What do you expect?"

"Look, it's about her husband, Andrew. We've been friends since college. I bought him his first boilermaker. He called me a couple of days before the crash. He said he wanted to break something big to the media and he wanted my help."

"What?"

"I don't know! The fucking schmuck didn't tell me!" She felt herself tear up again and willed herself to get a hold.

"Amy?" He had heard it in her voice.

"Ah, he wanted to know if I was going to Seattle for that high-tech expo, but it was Ezra's birthday. Jesus, I've been going psycho, trying to figure out what he was being so mysterious about!" She was about to take a sip of coffee but realized he might hear it. She had just denied being the Clockwork Girl.

"But you know what it was. Right? The wife told you about some multimillion dollar deal to be a Pentagon contractor. This guy was about to become an arms merchant."

"No. I don't think so. This wasn't about promoting their new contact. He told me it was *life-or-death* serious! He wanted my help in breaking something. If it was a damn press release, he wouldn't have sounded so . . ."

Big said, "So . . . ?"

"I don't know. I just know—I knew Andrew. He wanted to break huge news. Dangerous news. I just know it."

Big-Time chuckled. "So earn your keep. Go figure it out."

WASHINGTON, D.C.

Dmitri Zhirkov rollerbladed into the main server room. He slowed to a crawl, reached out to type one-handed on a keyboard, then glided to the far end of the room and typed on another. His headset was blasting the Beatles' *White Album* loudly enough that, had anyone else been in the NTSB server room, they could have sung along.

He turned off the vintage Walkman, pulled the headphones down to his scrawny shoulders, and picked up his cell phone. He had learned Susan Tanaka's cell phone number once, three years earlier, and, like every other number in his life, it came to him when he needed it.

"Hello?"

He chomped on a Red Vine. "Is Dmitri. Can you come down? Bring your tablet."

Susan said, "Ninety seconds."

It took seventy. She began by hugging the lanky Russian. "Thank you so much for this. What have you got for me?"

"The Montana Go-Team's computers. I wrote a program that will let you snoop around in real time."

She whistled and he grinned. "You're a criminal genius."

"Is true. Also, did you know the comm units have GPS trackers? Also their tablets and smartphones."

"Yes?"

"Yes. Boot up your computer."

She handed over the tablet computer. Dmitri slouched in a rolling chair, his Rollerblades up on a desk, crossed at the ankle. He'd brought a Thermos of hot, sweet Russian tea from home—just like his mom made it—and poured himself a cup. He dipped his Red Vine in the tea and then bit that hunk off.

"I've got it," Susan said.

"Open up your browser."

"Ooookay, I'm there."

"You are seeing a download, yes?"

"Uh-huh."

He dipped the candy, chewed on it.

"It's complete. And, it's . . . ah . . . Oh my gosh!"

He beamed. "You like? You can see where the crashers are. It looks like some are in Helena and others in a small town." He twisted in the chair to peer at the computer nestled in the crook of Susan's arm. "Twin Pines?"

"Yes. Twin Pines. Dee, you're my hero."

His smile blended with a blush. "Isaiah Grey was always nice to me. Was good fella, yes?"

TWIN PINES

Ray, Tommy, and Kiki hit town around three and noticed the vague, white haze. They could smell smoke, but just barely.

They found the police station and were rerouted to the real estate office. Kiki climbed out and tried the door, which was locked. She put her hands on the glass, parentheses around her eyes, and peered in.

"It's the right place," she said. "I see NTSB jackets. They must be out investigating."

"Wonder when the crew gathers for the daily powwow?" Tommy asked.

"C'mon," Ray said, checking his watch. "There's a coffee shop around the corner. I'm buying."

Inside the real estate office, Jenna Scott knelt behind a high-back office chair and exhaled deeply as she watched the FBI agent and two crash survivors walk to the coffee shop. That had been close.

She returned to planting the electronic bugs throughout the building.

HELENA

Back at her hotel, Renee poured three fingers from the bottle of rum she'd bought off the restaurant, then booted up her computer. She did a Google search for *sea change, Tempest,* and *Shakespeare.*

> *Full fathom five thy father lies;*
> *Of his bones are coral made;*
> *Those are pearls that were his eyes;*
> *Nothing of him that doth fade,*
> *But doth suffer a sea-change*
> *Into something rich and strange.*

She sipped the overproofed rum. *Those are pearls that were his eyes.* She thought about the body on the floor of the meat market in Twin Pines. There had been no sign of Andrew's soul there. Nothing to indicate the complicated, mercurial man, the inventive lover, the harsh self-critic, the sangfroid-laden pessimist.

Nothing of him that doth fade, but doth suffer a sea-change into something rich and strange.

She poured more rum and cried. Andrew was gone, too, but Andrew had changed before he died. He'd changed. Long before Renee made that late-night call to Barry Tichnor, he had begun to fade. He had suffered a sea change.

BOOK THREE

THE TEMPEST

24

TWIN PINES

At 3:30 P.M., all the team leaders came together. Tommy, Kiki, and Ray also showed up. They asked to address the Go-Team.

Peter, in a natty pin-striped suit, made a show of checking his watch. "We're a little busy here, so . . . make it quick."

By agreement, Ray Calabrese had been designated to tell them what they knew: the sudden loss of power for every system on the plane, including watches and hand-held devices; the silver-haired guy with hiking boots; the strange, postimpact wounds of Captain Cervantes and Isaiah Grey; Tommy's conversation with Isaiah, Kiki, and the black-box recording.

"What we're saying is: the plane was sabotaged, the black boxes switched with fakes, and the guy on the ground was there to make sure nobody could vouch for what really happened."

The crashers sat, stunned. Except for Peter Kim, who sat back, legs crossed at the knee. "That's good. No, really. Just enough verisimilitude to avoid sounding like the lunatic ravings of a conspiracy nut."

Tommy said, "Jesus, Peter. We—"

"Look, everyone! The saviors from the Oregon crash have done it again! Protected us poor, dumb engineers from ourselves!"

The crashers exchanged self-conscious glances. Gene Whitney hunkered in the corner, arms crossed over his thick chest. He stared at the floor.

Jack Goodspeed rubbed his neck and smiled weakly at Ray Calabrese. "This story? This is . . . guys, I don't mean to sound disrespectful, but I mean, hell!"

Hector Villareal leaned forward. "Peter, I gave Kiki a copy of the cockpit voice recording. She really is that good. I thought—"

"You're off the investigation." Peter stood up and buttoned his suit coat. "Head home. Please file a report with Wildman's office, explaining the breach of protocol."

No one spoke for a few seconds. Beth was trying to figure a stratagem for changing Peter's mind. Hector just shrugged. "Sure."

Peter turned back to Ray. "Calabrese, I don't know you. I don't know if you've been suckered in or not. Kiki, I suspect you've actually come to believe your own hype. Tomzak? Go fuck yourself."

Kiki fired back first. "Why, you idiot! Are you even listening to yourself? Tommy saw the power die!"

"So he says."

Ray pulled a twice-folded sheet of paper out of his blazer pocket. "Signed statement by Orysya Bronova, the Russian woman who survived the crash. She says the lights went out and the propellers stopped twirling long before the crash."

Peter turned slowly to Gene Whitney, whose job included debriefing survivors.

Gene kept staring at the floor and gave the room a generic shrug. "She doesn't speak English. I'm meeting a translator from Missoula tomorrow."

Ray handed the paper to Peter. "I found an orderly who speaks Russian. Here."

Kiki had built up quite a head of steam. "Did you say *my hype*?"

Peter shrugged. "Yes."

"Look, you pompous jackass, you immigrated to the United States when you were no older than five. I know this because I know from voices."

She looked around the room. "How many of you have I ever had conversations with before today? You." She pointed at Jack. "You grew up in urban Nebraska. Hector, you had a speech impediment when you were a boy, probably a stutter. Reuben, your grandparents never taught you any Yiddish and the little you do speak you picked up from movies and TV, and you're a little embarrassed by that. And as for you," she pointed at

Teresa Santiago, "your family has lived in New Mexico for at least four generations, probably longer. Your people never crossed the border to get into the States. The border crossed you!"

She turned and glared at Peter Kim.

Teresa held up her hand, fingers splayed. "Five generations."

Jack said, "Lincoln, Nebraska."

Reuben gave Kiki a what-are-ya-gonna-do shrug.

Hector said, "Stutter."

Beth, repressing a smile, stood and patted Peter on the shoulder. "And I've read your bio. You were three."

Peter glowered back at Kiki. "Nice carnival act. But—"

She barreled right over him. "At Reagan, the copilot said he was *having a catch* with a little boy, not *playing catch*. Then he asked us to stand *on line* with our boarding passes. Not *in line*. There's only one city in America where people use those colloquialisms: New York City. The copilot on the CVR is from Boston. The recording's a fake, jackass."

Tommy shook his head, grinning. There were maybe twenty people in the world who knew exactly how good the Sonar Witch was. That list had just grown.

Peter smiled indulgently. "I concede the point, Kiki. You're the Jascha Heifetz of voices. Brava. But it still doesn't mean Tomzak's theory isn't full of holes. This total-power-loss thing? There is, in fact, a technology that could cut power to the plane as well as personal electronics. It's called a nuclear bomb. The electromagnetic pulse of a nuke would do what you've hypothesized. But I'm thinking someone would have noticed that."

Ray shrugged. "So maybe there's another way to generate this pulse."

"Well, there's not."

"Easy way to prove you're right, Petey." Tommy, oddly enough, had remained the calmest of the bunch. "Dr. Jain? Check all the bodies. Whitney, check the survivors. Find out if any of them have an MP3 player, a digital watch, a camera, a cell phone, what-the-fuck-ever. Who's got the airframe?"

Jack raised his hand.

"Check the luggage. Same thing. If you find one electronic device that's working, then we're all zebra-shit crazy. But, you do a survey and they all are broken, then we got us a ball game."

Ray said to Peter, "I'm already rolling on the black boxes and chain of evidence. I'll report what I find directly to you. You're the Investigator in Charge. For now."

The threat was implicit: by federal law, the NTSB is the chief investigative agency in the event of a plane crash. Right up to the moment that a crime could be proved. If that happened, the FBI would take over. And Peter would be answering to Ray Calabrese.

Peter nodded. "Jack, Gene, Lakshmi: please check all of the electronic equipment on the Claremont, the survivors, the bodies. In the meantime," he turned to the interlopers, "you three stay away from the fuselage and stay away from the other survivors. You are interfering with a federal investigation. Meeting adjourned."

Tommy shrugged. "Fair enough. But work quick. You're wasting clock."

Kiki took a step forward, into Peter's personal space. "And the next time you disrespect me in public, I will knock you to the ground."

They glared at each other.

Tommy nudged Ray, cocked a thumb at Kiki. "I'm nuts about her."

When they were gone, Peter checked his watch. "Look, it's Sunday. Everyone has done a great job. Go back to your hotels, get some rest. Get some food. Call your families. First thing in the morning, I want, in my hand, one working cell phone from that plane. I just want one, and that smirking son of a bitch is done."

L'ENFANT PLAZA

Susan called Dmitri Zhirkov from her office. "Dee, it's me. Am I catching you at a bad time?"

She heard the Russian laugh. "Am using a three-point-four million dollar mainframe computer, paid for by taxpayers, to playing Dragon Age. God, I love America."

She smiled. He really was incorrigible. "I have a question about the program you loaded, to let me monitor the Go-Team's computers."

"Shoot."

She sat and frowned at her tablet computer. "In the left-hand column, there are blue dots under the heading 'Nodes.'"

She heard a vaguely positive grunt over the line.

"That represents the people with access to the server here in D.C. The one designated for the Montana crash, right?"

"Bingo." He pronounced it "bean go."

"Okay, so there are eleven blue dots. One of them is me and I assume one of them is you. There are eight team leaders. That's ten. Who else is monitoring this investigation?"

The Russian said, "Hold on," and she heard a hiss. It took her a second to realize that it was the sound of his in-line skates crossing the floor of the server room. Susan waited. She could hear the Russian muttering to himself.

"Dee? I'm on my way down."

She hung up, hit her office door at full clip. She was in the elevator, then in the basement, her ID card on its lanyard gaining her access to the mainframe room as Dmitri grabbed the telephone receiver. "Susan? Hallo?"

"I'm here," she said and he turned to her. The Russian looked paler than usual.

"*Bozhe moi* . . ."

"Excuse me?"

"This shouldn't be."

She could see the tension in Dmitri's face. "What?"

"The eleventh node. It's not one of ours. The Go-Team has been hacked."

TWIN PINES

Tommy, Kiki, and Ray sat in Ray's rental outside the real estate office–turned crasher central. Tommy shook his head in awe. "Why, that snarky rat asshole. Can you believe that guy? Okay, what's next?"

Ray extended his hand. "Shake." Tommy, perplexed, hesitated, then shook. Ray offered his hand to Kiki, too.

"Welcome to the first meeting of the Other Go-Team."

Kiki smiled. "Like a shadow government, shadow cabinet in England. I like it. Shadow crashers."

"First, I've got FBI agents in Oregon and D.C. already digging into the deputy marshals who got the black boxes. That's the easy part. Those guys had to sign a document. We'll match the signatures with the real marshals, find out if those guys flew to Montana on Monday."

Tommy's fingers probed gingerly around his head wound. "You got any experts can tell us if some kinda electro-whatever weapon exists?"

Ray beat a little ditty on the steering wheel with his thumbs. "Maybe. I know a guy. I'll call him."

Kiki said, "Silver Hair is an assassin. An assassin with enough power to create fake black boxes. I can't believe there are a million people in the world doing that for a living. I can't believe there are a hundred. Is there, I don't know, a clearinghouse for assassins? An FBI team dedicated to watching guys like that? Somebody who might know this guy?"

Ray leaned back against the headrest and sighed. "Yeah. I know who'd know. Crap."

Tommy and Kiki looked at each other and said, in unison, "Daria."

Ray nodded glumly. "Daria."

Gene Whitney and Beth Mancini walked toward the row of parallel-parked rental cars. Beth coughed into her fist. "Um, Gene?"

The big man jammed his fists into the pockets of his windbreaker, turned to her.

She wanted to ask about the interview with the ground crew at Reagan, but equally, she wanted to trust her teammates.

He said, "What?"

"Um . . ." At the last minute, she changed tack. "Tommy and Kiki? This crazy theory of theirs."

Gene was working a wad of bubble gum, his lantern jaw rolling. She thought the bags under his eyes had grown deeper.

He winced as if in pain. "Straight up?"

Beth nodded.

"Duvall's auditory skills are for real. The cockpit voice recording is a fake if she says it's a fake."

She hadn't anticipated that. "Really?"

He shrugged, testing the shoulder seams of his windbreaker. "The whole thing about the power outage? I think Tomzak's an ass but he's got no reason to lie. Our team's being fuckin' played."

HELENA

Peter Kim returned to his room at the airport hotel and called home. "Hey, honey. It's been a day," he said, grabbing a bottled water out of the minibar. "Is Pete there?"

"He's at the roller park," Janice said, her voice neutral.

"You will never believe what we did with the fuselage of the plane today."

"Did you remember he had a game this morning?"

"Pete? No. How'd they do?"

"They won. Pete had a double and a single."

"That's great. He's—"

"He was so disappointed you weren't here."

Peter gulped water. "He understands about my job. We're investigating a crash to make all airliners safer in the future. Today, for instance, we actually flew a wingless—"

"He's twelve, Peter. What he understands is, you weren't here."

The conversation—if it could be called such—went on for another five minutes of recriminations.

Hanging up, Peter checked his watch. A bit after five. He rolled up his sleeves, sat, booted up his computer, and checked the other crashers' preliminary reports. That done, he pulled out a yellow legal pad and a monogrammed pen and began planning his report for Delevan Wildman and the board. That took an hour, because Peter's reports were always meticulously accurate and clear.

When he was satisfied with it, he returned to the computer, typed his report in Word. He ran spell-check, reread it twice, then copied and pasted it to Hotmail. He shot a copy to Wildman's in-basket, one to his own home in-basket, and one to Beth Mancini.

That task complete, Peter remembered how good the Irish whiskey had been the night before. He threw on his suit coat and headed back down to the ground floor.

He ran into Jack Goodspeed, who had purchased a copy of ESPN's magazine in the lobby gift shop. Impulsively (and Peter Kim was anything but impulsive), he said, "That was good work today with the fuselage."

"Thanks, boss." Jack with his perpetual grin.

"I'm going to grab a drink. I'm buying."

Jack nodded. "Why not?"

Tommy's cell rang when he, Kiki, and Ray were halfway back to Helena.

He grinned. "It's Susan," he told the others, then listened.

He was quiet for a time. Ray and Kiki heard him say, "Sure. He's right here. Kiki, too. What's up?"

Ray drove. Kiki, sitting shotgun, turned in her seat and watched. Tommy listened, said, "Uh-huh," a couple of times, nodded as if Susan could see him.

He lowered his phone away from his lips. "Hey, New York? It's Suze.

She wants to know whether, if you hear about a crime, you're obligated to report it."

Ray smiled into the rearview mirror. "Tell her yes, I'm obligated to report it."

"Yes, he's obligated." Tommy listened some more. A furrow grew between his eyebrows. Kiki reached back and brushed the comma of black hair off his forehead. He loved it when she did that, the whisperlike feel of her fingertips against his skin. He winked at her.

He lowered the phone. "Ray? Suze hacked the Go-Team's computers. She's monitoring the investigation. Illegally."

Kiki whistled, high-low. "I love it!"

"It gets better. She wasn't the first one in. Someone else is monitoring 'em, too."

Ray slapped the steering wheel. "Whoa. Back up. There's someone else in the NTSB computers?"

"Nah. Suze says just the computers assigned to this crash. The Go-Team's been hacked."

Ray drove, fingers tapping on the steering wheel. "Shit. Guess that makes sense. Say you've got the wherewithal to hire an assassin to wait on the ground and finish off witnesses. It's not a stretch to think, if you could do that, you could hack the investigation, figure out who knows what."

"That's scary," Kiki said.

"No, what's scary is that I didn't think to suggest this possibility in the first place," Ray grumbled. "If we're right about what this is all about, we gotta stop underestimating whoever's behind this."

He and Kiki listened as Tommy explained their working theory, including the bit about the silver-haired assassin.

"This is good," Tommy said to the people in the car as much as to Susan Tanaka, seven time zones away. "Let the bastards hack the Go-Team. We're running our own, parallel investigation and we don't got computers to hack. With the help of a little misdirection, we'll catch the bastards nappin'."

Kiki reached back and tousled his hair. "I like it."

"Hey, Suze: another thing. Kiki and I ran into Gene Whitney. He's a serious head case."

"Anger issues," Susan said. "I've been checking with past Go-Teams. Plus two ex-wives. But, Tommy? I called up an off-duty investigator to conduct the interviews at Reagan National that Whitney didn't do. On the

QT. They found nothing. Whitney may be incompetent, but the secret of this investigation isn't at National. It's with you in Montana."

"Yeah. I been thinking the same. We love you. Bye."

He hung up.

"Shit," Tommy said to those in the front seat. "An assassin on the ground waiting. Someone hacking the Go-Team. This is the damnedest thing I ever heard of."

Ray said, "In your hotel room, you asked that if you ID'd anything as *the damnedest thing ever,* I was to repeat this back to you: *There's a dead deer on the flight deck.*"

Tommy rolled his eyes. "Okay, I walked into that one."

Like Peter Kim, Beth Mancini typed up her daily preliminary report and sent copies to Delevan Wildman, Peter Kim, and her own e-mail account.

Unlike Peter, she described, in detail, the far-fetched theory of the crash recounted to them by the FBI's Ray Calabrese.

TWIN PINES

Jenna Scott was still stinging from Calendar's off-putting critique of her fieldwork. She sat in the surveillance van in Twin Pines, reading Beth's prelim report.

She got to the part about the theory of an electromagnetic pulse and slid on her headset to call Barry Tichnor.

She connected almost immediately with Barry's cell, but he wasn't picking up. Which meant he likely was in public.

Jenna thought about it for a moment, then hung up and called Calendar.

"Yes?"

She spoke briskly. "Vintner. Intercepted a communication from the Go-Team. The investigators heard a report today that mentioned you, not by name, but describing you pretty accurately. They knew about the device, too, if not the details."

She listened to the distorted hiss of the encryption software.

"Are you there?"

His mechanical voice said, "Yes. Names?"

She checked Beth's report again. "A Dr. Leonard Tomzak and a Katherine Duvall. Plus, the FBI liaison to the case, Special Agent Ray Calabrese.

Right now, these three are being considered as crazy. The Go-Team is not buying in on it. *Right now*."

Calendar said, "Understood," and rang off.

HELENA

Teresa Santiago called Hector Villareal and told him she'd found a Catholic church in town that was celebrating a rare Sunday evening Mass. She could tell that he was pleased by the call. He offered to drive.

Reuben Chaykin had dinner with two engineers from the Bembenek Company, maker of the twin turboprop engines on the Claremont. They spread blueprints out over a red-checked tablecloth and tried not to drip pizza sauce on any of it.

Gene Whitney found a sports pub and sat at the oak bar, knocking back Coors and watching soccer on the Fox Soccer Channel. He hated soccer but watched it anyway as the beers came and went.

Calendar used his satellite phone to route the calls through the same chain he'd used before—Thailand to Prague to Nebraska—and called back his two soldiers, Dyson and Cates. They had stayed in close proximity, in case their services were needed again.

Jenna Scott completed the job of leapfrogging onto the frequency of the Go-Team's comm units. She had their personal cell phones, she had their laptops and the server in D.C. dedicated to this investigation, and she had their rally point in Twin Pines.

Now she just hoped Calendar wouldn't screw up anymore.

"The thing is," Peter said, "the discipline it takes to play the cello is exactly the same discipline it takes to be a crash investigator."

Jack Goodspeed made a "one-more" gesture to the bartender wearing a Caterpillar hat and a Willie Nelson T-shirt. He took away their empty glasses.

"Cello?"

"Yes. I don't blame Tomzak for being creative. And I don't blame him for being a self-starter. That's all good."

The waiter, shaped more or less like a wine barrel, brought a third whiskey for Peter and a second Coors Light for Jack. The bar was almost empty tonight. Last night's Sinatra had been replaced by Bobby Darin.

"It's his lack of discipline. His crappy teamwork."

"So you play cello?"

"Since I was three."

Jack palmed a fistful of pretzels. "You still play?"

Peter took an appreciative sip. He'd loosened his collar and rolled up his sleeves, something that no other member of this Go-Team had ever seen. "A little. You know. My job, my family. I have a son, twelve."

"He must be proud of you."

Peter didn't like talking about his family. "How about you? You're married?"

Jack shrugged. "No. There's a cliché; what is it? . . . serial monogamy. I'm pretty serious when I'm in a relationship. They just tend not to last."

"You should do something about that." This was unlike Peter, giving someone unwanted advice or, for that matter, even asking personal questions.

Jack smiled. "Elephant-in-the-room time. You know I'm gay. Right?"

Peter blinked.

"I mean, we're drifting into the realm of mixed signals here."

Peter said. "But . . . you're from Utah." Then winced.

Jack belted out a laugh. "Yeah, we're a small but enthusiastic bunch."

Peter's brain whiplash intensified. "Ah. No mixed signals here. Nope. Just two colleagues blowing . . ." He'd been going for *off steam*. "Not blowing. Not blowing anything."

Jack smiled, sipped his beer. "Good, then."

Peter threw a couple of twenties on the bar. "I probably ought to go."

"Gonna finish your drink, boss?"

"You know what? I'm good." Peter held out his hand and they shook. He exited quickly.

Jack just shook his head as the burly bartender in the Cat hat picked up the money and the half-finished whiskey. "For what it's worth," he drawled. "I thought he was cute."

Jack said. "Yeah, but wound a little tight."

25

LAKSHMI JAIN ROSE AT 5:00 A.M. on Monday. She had to wait until 6:00 A.M. to call the office of the Lewis and Clark County Coroner and confirm that more bodies would be arriving for autopsies. She asked that all electronic devices be checked, to see if any of them were functioning. Satisfied that things were working well there, she volunteered to go to the makeshift morgue and check the rest of the bodies.

I just need one, Peter had said the night before.

Jack and Hector had volunteered to go to the auto-parts shop and check luggage, so they offered her a lift.

Ray called in many, many markers and found out that ATF still had Daria Gibron working south of the Mexican border. He eventually rustled up the phone number for a DEA agent with whom he was on okay terms. "ATF and the Mexico caper," he said. "I know you're the liaison for the drug side. ATF is using Daria Gibron. You remember her."

After a longish beat, the DEA agent said, "Shit, Calabrese. I'd like to help you, but she don't want to see you down there and neither do I."

"Got a pen? Just tell her Tommy Tomzak and Kiki Duvall crashed again."

Ray hung up, checked his contacts list, and found a number in D.C. for a CIA analyst who had helped him out a couple of other times.

"Hi, this is John Broom." The guy sounded like a late-night talk-show host greeting his audience.

Ray held the cell in one hand and packed his overnight case with the other. "Hi. My name is Ray Calabrese. I'm an FBI agen—"

"Hey, Ray. After that comic-opera thing you and the NTSB pulled off in the Mojave? I remember you. What can we do for you?"

"I recall that your areas of expertise include weapons and weapon platforms."

"Plus, I'm a snappy dresser."

Ray smiled. "You know that airliner crash Thursday in Montana? We've got some witnesses saying all power went out as they were on approach to Helena. Engines, interior lights, palm-top devices, watches—everything."

Broom laughed. "You called them *witnesses,* not *survivors.* You making another run at the NTSB, Agent Calabrese? Last time you did that, I seem to recall something about you driving a jetliner into a sand dune."

"Nothing even remotely like that happened, Mr. Broom," he said. "It was a mesa."

"See? Bad intel. That's our problem here in D.C."

Ray was liking this guy. "We're working on a scenario for how the plane crashed. We're looking at instantaneous power loss to the jet, but also to all electronic devices on board. Watches, computers, everything. Now, a roomful of engineers just told me the culprit for something like that would be an electromagnetic pulse. My question to you is: short of a nuclear bomb, is there another weapon that could generate that pulse?"

Broom said, "Nope."

The quick answer startled him. "Just like that? You're for sure?"

"By international treaty. A revamping of the old START talks. At an arms convention in Bruges, Belgium, the United States became a signatory to the ban on EMP weapons."

"How come?"

"Nuclear proliferation. If our Strangeloves invented a pulse weapon, other countries' Strangeloves might be tempted to counter with suitcase nukes. The Bruges Accord even bans research into pulse weapons."

Ray felt let down. The fake cause of the crash—the short circuit in the cabin—was the tent pole of their theory. If no such weapon existed, the theory was shot.

"Okay. Well, thanks, Mr. Broom."

"You sound like you wanted a bicycle for Christmas and got knitted socks."

Ray chuckled. "That obvious? Yeah, you busted up a pet theory. Listen, I appreciate the help."

"No sweat. Good luck." They rang off.

Ray thought about the problem for a while. Tommy's description had been so vivid! He looked up the speed-dial number for his boss, Henry Deits, and hit Send.

Henry was in. "How is it there?"

"Way fewer casualties than the Oregon crash," Ray said. "Look, we've got a puzzle."

He described the power loss, told Henry what the CIA analyst had relayed regarding the Bruges protocols.

"We got a guy we sometimes use as a source," Henry said. He sounded glum. "I'm not happy about it, but the guy's been pretty good about predicting theoretical weapons. Stuff that's on the horizon. If anyone's experimenting with pulse weapons, he's the guy we should talk to."

"Yeah?"

"Conspiracy nut in the Valley. He's got an online magazine, calls it *Pentagon or Pentagram?* Stanley Katz. The guy's full of hokum when it comes to who killed JFK and Elvis, but when it comes to predicting weapons, the guy's eerily accurate. He called that Syria was designing FAJR 7s for Hezbollah. He called the new generation of BM-28 Grads in Chechnya."

Ray wrote it all down, thanked his boss, and hung up.

He checked his cell. He'd missed one call. It was his DEA contact. He called the man back.

"Son of a bitch, Calabrese. I got a hold of Gibron. Believe it or not, she said yes. Follow these directions."

TWIN PINES

Jack and Hector got back to Twin Pines and dropped Lakshmi off at the makeshift morgue, then headed over to the auto-parts-storage facility. They got there at the stroke of 7:00 A.M. Monday. The smoke was definitely worse today. The police officer guarding the parts store unlocked the padlock and pulled back the rolling gate to let them in.

Hector said, "You understand, Peter fired me."

Jack said, "I understand it's his first time as Investigator in Charge. He was wrong to fire you and I'm going to talk him out of it. Now, c'mon. I need your help."

They walked around the Quonset hut, then gasped.

The Claremont sat in the middle of the back lot, as if teleported there from the forest. Battered, wingless, paint scratched, aluminum either dented or fully rent. Casper the Friendly Airship still loomed overhead. Jack's crews hadn't removed the massive, metal-mesh belts tethering the airship to Flight 78.

"That," Hector whispered, "is the stuff of legend."

"No kidding."

They borrowed a hammer and chisel from the auto-parts stockyard and got busy opening all the locked luggage retrieved from the forest floor and the cargo deck. Their actions were legally dodgy but they didn't see a lot of options.

The FBI agent and the two crash survivors had offered up a theory that was far too improbable to be true. But the Go-Team's job was to follow the evidence, no matter how unlikely the outcome.

Hector Villareal came up with the first cell phone. He hit the Power button and waited.

Nothing happened.

Jack found a man's toiletry kit with an electric shaver. He thumbed the On switch.

Nothing.

Hector and Jack exchanged glances. Hector whistled, high-low.

Jack said, "Keep looking, man."

Ray Calabrese, ex-air force, used his military service record and his FBI connections to get the Montana National Guard to fly him to San Diego in a B-1B Lancer. It was his first time in the sleek bomber and he loved it.

From San Diego, he grabbed a new rental and badged his way across the border into Mexico.

TWIN PINES

Lakshmi Jain entered the converted meat shop to check for electronic devices that had been with the corpses. She nodded politely to the deputy guarding the front door, which he unlocked for her.

"Ma'am? Are they talking about evacuating the town?"

The question startled her. "I have no idea. Should they?"

The deputy shrugged, but he looked worried. And now, so, too, did Lakshmi.

She started to enter the freezing building when an SUV pulled up and a man rolled down his window. "Pardon?"

He stepped out. He wore a somber black suit and black tie. He produced a folding wallet with a shield.

"You're with the NTSB team?"

Lakshmi nodded.

"Bob Sonntag, U.S. Marshal's Service. Hi."

"Hullo."

"I'm checking up on some paperwork regarding the crash. Do you know if any of the luggage was recovered before the fire got to it?"

"Yes. All of it."

The big man did a double take. "Beg your pardon?"

"I am told that the fuselage was secured, including its contents."

Deputy Sonntag said, "Wow. I didn't think that was possible."

Lakshmi waited.

"Do you know where the plane is being held?"

"I'm sorry, I don't." She pointed. "The rest of our team is in a real estate office, two blocks that way. You will find it by looking for a large collection of rental cars."

"Thank you, ma'am. Hey: this is where the bodies are being stored?"

She nodded.

"Have you uncovered a saddlebag? Actually, a messenger bag, but it looks like an old, scratched-up saddlebag?"

She said, "Not that I recall. What did you do to your hand?"

The big man with close-cropped silver hair looked at the bandage on his right hand, shook his head with woe. "Stupid. Tried to clean grass out of my lawn mower, sliced me up good. Anyway, thank you."

HELENA

The red message light was flashing on Renee Malatesta's hotel-room phone. She read the directions on the phone, then dialed her voice mail.

She had sixteen requests from reporters for follow-up stories regarding the company and the defense contract. A lot of reporters were chasing Amy Dreyfus of the *Post,* it seemed.

Renee took two Vicodins and washed them down with rum. She called the concierge desk and asked if the hotel had a conference room and if she could schedule a press conference for later in the day.

TWIN PINES

Teresa Santiago had just hit the edge of Twin Pines when she realized she was out of cash and deeply in need of a chocolate fix. She'd noticed a convenience store a few blocks away and decided to hit the ATM and get a stash of M&Ms.

She was climbing out of her car when she noticed that the smell of smoke had grown stronger. A white haze was visible when she looked at buildings three or more blocks away.

An SUV pulled into the parking lot next to her, window descending. A silver-haired man flashed a badge across the top of her car. "Excuse me, ma'am?"

"Yes?"

"Bob Sonntag, Marshal's Service. Do you know where they're storing the fuselage?"

He was good-looking, she thought. She crossed to the passenger's side of her car, rested her hands on his driver's side window. "Auto-parts facility, right at the town border on the main drag. You're part of the investigation?"

He smiled. "Nine-tenths of what I do is paperwork. Just crossing Ts, dotting Is."

She laughed and tossed her hair. The deputy marshal looked to be in good shape and his hair was cut short and well kept. She liked that in a man. The silver hair gave him . . .

Her smile guttered.

He said, "You okay, ma'am? You look like you've seen a ghost."

In her mind, she heard Agent Calabrese's description of the assassin.

"I'm good. I'm fine. I've got to get back to the team." She began back-pedaling but quickly bumped into the side panel of her rental car.

Calendar's eyebrows rose in concern. "Everything's okay?"

"Yes. Of course. I . . ." She shrugged.

"Who's your Investigator in Charge?"

"Peter Kim."

"Is he around?"

She nodded. Calendar pulled a business card out of his breast pocket, held it out between two extended fingers of his left hand. "Give him this, ask him to call me. 'Kay?"

Teresa reached out for the card. Calendar grabbed her wrist and yanked. She stumbled forward into the driver's door, the force sending his MAC-SOG combat knife so hard into her chest that it broke her sternum before breaching a full five inches into her heart.

She gasped, eyes wide, looking down at the polymer handle sticking out of her blouse, thinking, *What's this?*

Calendar held on to her arm and laughed at something, as if she'd just cracked him up. He held her there until a passing car turned out of sight. Still holding her tight against the side of the car, he scanned the windows of the convenience store. A clerk had her back to the parking lot. The lot was otherwise empty.

Teresa's mouth fished open but no sound emerged.

Calendar opened the door, holding Teresa's body taut against the metal, sidled out, opened the driver's side back door, and shoved her in. He was back in the driver's seat and pulling out as Teresa took her last breath and died.

Because Calendar had kept the sturdy combat knife pressed hard against Teresa's chest, she'd bled internally but hardly at all externally. He drove out into the rural countryside, into farmland. He found a ditch surrounded by trees and dumped the body.

But he retrieved the knife first. He loved that knife.

26

RAY MET DEA AGENT Gustavo Rojas in Ensenada. Rojas was a nondescript man, small-boned, in clothes that seemed two sizes too large. He chewed his fingernails and had a smoker's pallor. He fit nicely into crowds, which made him an exceptional undercover agent. They had known each other for a dozen years and had never been friends.

Rojas said, "Calabrese."

Ray shook his hand. "Thanks for doing this."

Rojas scanned the dusty streets, a toothpick between his lips. "J. T. Laney at ATF just about shit a brick when he heard you were here. You are not the most popular guy in Mexico today, Raymondo."

Ray climbed into the man's Explorer. "Since when did this job become about being popular?"

Rojas checked in both with ATF's Wild Boar Brigade and with his own bosses at the DEA, but not with the corruption-racked Mexican Army or police. He confirmed to the friendlies that he was ferrying a federal agent across Mexican soil. He and Ray took Mexican Highway 2 past La Joya and Playas de Rosarito, cutting inland and climbing quickly to one thousand feet, to the town of San Jeronimo. They didn't chat.

It's possible that the village of San Jeronimo had never had its heyday, but, if it had, it was decades ago. The streets showed the vague remnants of once being paved. The "downtown" was a gas station, a bar, a city hall, a bar, a grocery store, and a bar. Other than Rojas's truck, the only other vehicles were steel-reinforced jeeps favored by the *narcotraficante*. Plus, a tireless El Dorado on its rims.

It was easily ninety-five degrees at noon. Ray, in a polo shirt and jeans, climbed out of the Grand Cherokee with a mismatched right front quarter panel. Rojas picked a copy of *The New Yorker* off the floor of the cab and said, "I'll be here."

Ray walked into El Perro Fumando, sat at the empty bar, and ordered a tequila with lime juice.

It was an odd place to find a former Israeli soldier and spy. Then again, this was Daria Gibron. A lot about her was odd.

Ray had just finished the first sip of his drink when two beefy, unshaven men entered and took tables at the far end of the saloon, flanking him. He recognized them as the men who'd been positioned outside the bar when he'd tried to find Daria a week or so ago. Both wore untucked shirts.

Ray nursed his drink.

Thirty seconds later, the saloon-style doors opened and Daria Gibron entered.

Daria, always dark-skinned, had grown more tanned. She wore her black hair cut very short and a bit spiky, making her round face look even more so. She wore a sleeveless tank that revealed sharply muscled arms and shoulders. Her khakis and hiking boots were well worn and dusty. She looked tougher than Ray remembered. Harder.

Ray started to say hello but the word stuck in his throat. He opened his mouth, closed it.

Daria gestured to the bartender, who brought two shot glasses and a bottle of Tequila Uno. She poured, downed hers in a gulp. "Is good to see you, too."

TWIN PINES

Jack and Hector tried cell phones. They tried MP3 players. Cameras, computer game stations, travel alarm clocks, digital audio recorders, laptops, electric razors. Hector even unearthed a vibrating dildo. He hid it from Jack and tested it.

But it, like all the rest, was inoperable.

Hector said, "You don't think . . . ?"

Jack scratched his head. "I didn't two hours ago."

In the makeshift morgue, Lakshmi Jain found the same results. But she found something far more disturbing.

She went to the front door and the officer whom Chief McKinney had posted. "Excuse me. Other than myself, who's been in here?"

"Todd from the coroner's office. Him and one of the EMTs loaded up some more bodies this morning. Also, that tall looker you brung yesterday."

Lakshmi said, "No one else?"

"Not on my watch."

"Very well." She adjusted her ear jack. "If you could avoid sexist comments around me, I would appreciate it."

"Um . . . okay?"

She stepped back inside.

"This is Kim."

"Mr. Kim. It's Lakshmi Jain."

"You're bringing me a working cell phone? One which I can then use to beat Tomzak over the head with?"

"No. They're all dysfunctional. But there's something else. These bodies have been searched. Their pockets are turned out."

SAN JERONIMO, MEXICO

Daria Gibron looked comfortable in the heat. Her taut skin was dry. Ray's cornflower-blue polo shirt was soggy with sweat.

"What are you doing here?" he asked.

"Last time you showed up, you weren't looking for conversation. No?"

"I'd had you under surveillance for four days. I saw the holes in J. T. Laney's plans that you could drive a tank through. I didn't see a way to talk him down, so . . ." Ray shrugged.

"I am grateful you were there."

"You haven't answered my question. What are you doing?"

She smiled, cocked her head. "Finding loads and loads of guns."

"And selling some, too?"

She shrugged and knocked back a shot of tequila. "We like to call it chumming the waters. They said your friends were *in* a plane crash?"

"Yeah. Tommy's got a mild concussion and Kiki's banged up a little."

Daria shook her head. "They investigate crashes. How—"

"Will you believe me if I say there's no variation of that conversation I haven't had? They did. Both are okay. Do you remember Isaiah Grey?"

"The pilot in the Mojave."

"Yeah. He died. And we're not sure it wasn't murder."

She nodded. "Tell me."

"I will. But . . . how are you? Are you good?"

She smiled wryly and nudged Ray's shoulder with her own. She felt densely packed and solid. Ray's heart fluttered and his poker face tried to hold still. She poured more amber booze. "I am alive. Sitting in L.A., in posh clothes, translating for princes and bankers, I was going fucking insane."

With her Israeli accent, she had always had trouble with that word. It came out *fakking.*

"Down here . . . you Americans have a saying about being in one's element. Yes?"

Ray said, "Yes," and sipped his drink.

"What do you need?"

"Kiki and Tommy have a theory that someone brought down their plane and an assassin was waiting in the woods to pick off any survivors who could prove that the cover story—a cockpit malfunction—was a hoax. Whoever did this had the juice to create false black boxes, too. The assassin was a guy, six feet, six-one. Close-cropped silver hair, put together like an athlete. Probably late forties, early fifties. Handsome. Wondering where I'd start looking for a guy like that."

Daria said, "Thailand. He lives there. His nom de guerre is Calendar."

Ray wiped sweat off his neck. "No way. You know this guy?"

"There are few people in the world who can do what Calendar does. He's expensive. I was involved in a CIA situation, six months before you and I met. He handled the wet work."

She sneaked a glimpse at her burly handlers, sitting behind them. Softly, she added, "My new friends occasionally need a woman with—how do you say—a certain skill set. That is me. Once or twice, when they need a man with the same skill set, they hire Calendar. But I charge a lot less, I think."

Ray's blood pressure spiked. He forced his fingers to relax around the shot glass. "These ATF assholes have you playing assassin?"

"Not *playing*, no."

Ray downed his drink, hearing a hum inside his ears. "And this Calendar works for them."

She shook her head. "Calendar works exclusively for American intelligence, military assets, corporations. He considers himself the patriot. He is on no one's personnel rosters. He is what they call . . . what is the phrase, in English . . . deniable . . ."

Ray said, "Plausible deniability."

"Yes. Thank you. Just like me."

Ray seethed. "Jesus Christ," he whispered. "You don't have to do this. You don't have to *be* this! Come home. I have contacts in military intelligence. If it's an adrenaline high you're after, we can find a way to do that and to buy back your soul!"

Daria looked at him. He wanted to punch someone so bad. Anyone. Daria linked her arm around his, rested her forehead against his biceps.

After a moment, she looked up, eyes too bright, smile too wide. She slid off her stool and kissed Ray on the cheek.

"I will see you around, Ray."

"Where do I find Calendar?"

"If his work is finished, you don't. He is the ghost. If his work isn't, you won't have to look far. He'll be there." She drained her last shot glass. "Also, has a team."

Swell, Ray thought. "Size?"

"Small, two to four at the outside. Experienced."

"You know or your suspect?"

Daria took the longest time before answering. "He offered me the job."

Despite the heat, Ray felt his body temperature drop. "And you turned it down because . . . ?"

"Because I was otherwise occupied. Ray? Tread carefully. He is the sociopath but very good at his work."

She kissed him again, ran a hand through his close-cropped hair.

"Goodbye."

TWIN PINES

Tommy and Kiki treated themselves to a lunch of burgers and fries at an A&W that hadn't been remodeled since the sixties. It was noon, Monday.

Tommy pounded an upside-down ketchup bottle over Kiki's fries, so that she didn't have to tax her broken rib. "You're a very nice boyfriend."

"You know, I really am."

They scarfed down the food, well rid of hospital meals. No burgers had ever tasted better.

"So. That was a neat trick with the crashers' voices and their histories. I thought poor Petey's head was gonna explode."

"Jerk."

"Silver Hair: where's he from?"

A french fry was halfway to Kiki's lips when she froze. She stared over Tommy's shoulder, into the middle distance.

"Hon?"

She *ssshhh*ed him, still staring.

She finally turned her gaze to Tommy's eyes. "You know I couldn't tell you."

"Well, a plane had just fallen on you. Plus, your hunky, gorgeous boyfriend was leaking blood like it was—"

"No. It's not that. I can hear him. He asked me, 'Hey, are you okay?' and later, 'What happened to the airplane?' It's just . . ." She stared into space again.

Tommy pointed to her burger. "You gonna finish that?"

"Yes. It's like I can't tell you where he was from because he wouldn't tell me. There was no regional accent. No dropped sounds, no cultural signposts. There was no *there* there. Like what he presented was so tightly controlled. He gave away nothing."

Tommy reached out, took her hand in his. "It don't matter. Ray Calabrese's all over this. We find out about the chain of possession on the black boxes, Ray's people ID the . . . whatever, the pulse weapon. We'll call Delevan Wildman, call Isaiah, get—"

He squeezed his lips together, grimacing at the mistake, averting his eyes.

Kiki gripped his hand tighter. "I do that all the time. When Peter was being a brat, I wanted to ask Isaiah how best to handle him."

Tears glistened in Tommy's brown eyes. He got out of his side of the booth, sat on hers, and hugged her softly.

"Silver Hair and his friends killed Isaiah. We are going to fuck them over like nobody's been fucked over. Not never."

She kissed him. "Promise?"

"Promise. Asshole's killin' days are behind him."

.   .   .

Lakshmi Jain got a call from the coroner's office in Helena. They had checked the bodies that were there waiting to be autopsied for electric devices.

They had found several, but none of them was functional.

Peter Kim met Police Chief Paul McKinney at the morgue. The assigned officer unlocked the door, let them in.

McKinney pulled back the sheets on five bodies. It was obvious that they'd been searched.

"Goddammit." Peter was livid. "You assured us these bodies would be protected."

"You saw my guy out there. I have another one posted at the remains of your airplane. I have four men on day-shift duty and you've got two of them. You think I have unlimited personnel?"

"I think someone broke in here and searched these bodies. I think that makes our jobs much, much harder. I also think the hotels of Helena are chock-full of bereaved loved ones, and I'm wondering what to tell them."

McKinney looked around and shivered in the cold. "Um, any reason they have to know?"

"Chief . . . Jesus Christ." Peter was close to unspooling. "Yes, they have to know. I have to assume items were stolen. I have to know how much the passengers took out of their ATMs before the flight. I have to ask about expensive jewelry, watches. I— Fuck it! I want that officer posted inside!"

"It's forty degrees in here!"

"Get him a parka!"

They were toe-to-toe now.

"No. I tell you what. Here's a better idea: get these goddamn bodies out of my town. Do it now."

Peter stepped closer. "This is a federal investigation!"

"I don't care if it's being conducted by the Detroit Red Wings! The bodies! Out! Now!"

Peter saw red.

McKinney said, "Swing, and I will arrest you, Mr. Investigator in Charge. I kid you not."

Peter turned and marched out.

Halfway back to the real estate office, he realized he really should have brought Beth Mancini along.

LOS ANGELES

For the second time that month, Ray Calabrese returned to Los Angeles from Mexico. Neither trip had been much fun. He took a cool shower in his own condo, traded worn clothes for new travel clothes. He wolfed down two scrambled eggs with an English muffin, washed his dishes.

He checked his e-mail. His office mates had looked up the address of Stanley Katz, the conspiracy theorist with the *Pentagon or Pentagram?* online magazine Henry had told him about. Ray threw his satchel into his trunk and drove out into the Valley.

TWIN PINES

Calendar drove carefully around the perimeter of the auto-parts-storage yard. A quarter acre surrounded by tall Cyclone fencing topped with barbed wire. Not impossible to break into but tough. He wondered if there were dogs. A lot of chop shops kept dogs to hold off meth addicts looking to steal metal.

The luggage in the fuselage was his last chance to secure Andrew Malatesta's speech and sketch pad. Unfortunately, he saw too many people walking in and out of the shop in their NTSB windbreakers.

He'd have to wait to break in.

ORANGE COUNTY, CALIFORNIA

Ray found the address in a shabby neighborhood just off Interstate 5. The houses were one-story, two-bedroom clones of one another, with wire fences around dingy brown yards strewn with children's toys. The cars were a decade old. The starter homes needed new aluminum siding, new roofs.

Still in his car, on his cell, Ray said, "Everything you can find, yeah."

Henry Deits, director of the FBI's Los Angeles field office, said, "His name's Calendar?"

"No, that's a DBA."

"And he specializes in freelancing for U.S. intelligence agencies?"

"So my source says."

"Good source?"

Henry had specifically warned Ray to steer clear of Daria and the rogue ATF operation in Mexico. "It's a source I trust."

"Okay. So are we assuming command of the investigation?"

"Not yet, I think. I don't have the conclusive evidence. Trust me on this: the current Investigator in Charge is going to want the Is dotted and Ts crossed. This isn't like Oregon, where Tommy was IIC and was willing to bend the rules a little."

Henry Deits didn't seem mollified. "Cryin' out loud, Ray. If there's an assassin involved . . ."

"I don't have any reason to believe he's lurking around. Likely he did his job and moved on." That wasn't precisely what Daria had told him, but Ray thought it sounded reasonable.

"Okay. You got the boots on the ground. I trust your judgment."

"Thanks, boss. I'm at this guy Katz's place. Call when I'm done."

Stanley Katz was a small-boned man, five-three, with a hunched back and spindly arms and legs. He used a walker to get around. From the name, Ray had anticipated a Jewish man. Stanley Katz was African American; Ray thinking, *Well, they're not mutually exclusive.*

Stanley led the agent through the demonically cluttered one-story house, past the precarious stacks of newspapers and periodicals as high as Ray's thighs. Ray noted that Scotch tape adhered wires to the windows, the wires linked to an oscilloscope.

Stanley saw Ray's glance. "Noticed that? They beam lasers off my windows, try and catch audio, a couple times a year. Faggots. Who gave you my name?"

"A big fan."

"Nah-nah nah-nah, man. Keep your secrets. FBI man comes to my door, keeping secrets, means he's not lying to me. That's a start, Agent Calabrese. If that is your real name."

"You got ice water or something? It's, like, eight hundred degrees out there."

Stanley Katz, in a wife-beater and frayed chinos, looked all sinew and bone. Ray put his age anywhere from thirty-five to sixty-five. He wore an Afro and a jazz patch. He said, "I got home-brewed iced tea."

"That'd work."

Stanley filled two tumblers with ice up to the brim, then poured from a pitcher in the fridge. One glass was adorned with Boris Badenov, the other with Snidely Whiplash. Ray eyed the yellowed Commodore computer on the kitchen table, the stacks of *Omni* magazine back issues.

Stanley saw him looking. "Nobody hacks a Commodore. Nobody writes virus for that, for sure. Here."

Ray sipped. It was delicious. "What's this I'm tasting? Vanilla?"

"Yeah, yeah. Vanilla bean from a farmers market in Encino. What am I doing you for, Mr. FBI?"

"That airline crash on Thursday in Montana?"

"An airliner?"

"You heard about this, right?"

"The news is mostly faked, Mr. FBI."

Ray's hopes for the interview tumbled. "Okay, well, a midsized airliner crashed in Montana last week. I've got witnesses saying all the electricity stopped. Engines, hand-held gadgets, watches. Boom: gone."

"Nobody cooked off a nuke in Big Sky Country, right? I mean, you woulda led with that."

"Right."

"Bruges protocols say: no pulse weps."

"I'm told."

"An' you're wondering, how's that? Huh?"

Ray waited, sipped tea. He tried to keep a poker face but, damn, this was good tea.

Stanley Katz waved his fingers in the air to make a circle, filled by a diagonal slash through it: the international symbol for *no*. "No pulse weapons, man. It's not just good sense, it's the motherfuckin' law."

"So nobody has a weapon that could do that?"

"I di'nt say that, did I? Did you hear me say that?" Stanley, grinning now.

"I did not." Ray, playing along.

"They's this cat, he got mad weapons. Designs only. Vaporware. They say this guy's got a design for an EMP weapon. Fired from a shoulder-mounted launch tube. Laser-guided. It's clay, two containers of chemicals inside. Hit a target, a tank, a helo, what you got, it sticks to it. The binary chemicals blend together: wham. Electro-goddamn-magnetic pulse. And the lights go off all over the fucking world."

Stanley winked, grinning.

"Is this weapon for real?"

The hunched man shrugged. "Nah. Paper only. In the man's brainpan. But what I hear? This cat's the da Vinci of new weapons. Gonna revolutionize war. He's Bill and Melinda Gates from the mirror universe. Spock with a Vandyke, yeah? He's *Chitty Chitty Bang Bang* but with less chitty, more bang."

Stanley laughing now, cutting up.

"This guy got a name?"

"Malatesta. Andrew Malatesta. And you make of this what you want, Mr. FBI, but in Eye-talian, that translates to *bad head*."

Ray wrote down the name. "Mr. Katz, this is the best goddamn iced tea I have ever had."

Stanley nodded. "You like that, you should try my house-brewed gin."

Ray checked his watch. "Hit me."

TWIN PINES

Jack Goodspeed sat on a food service cart, drinking from a bottle of seltzer that hadn't broken in the crash. It was, strictly speaking, evidence, so drinking it was breaking protocol. Jack didn't particularly care. It was hot.

He said, "You are one tenacious dude."

Hector Villareal flashed him a shy smile. Only three suitcases were left and Hector was determined to check every one of them. "Got to be sure."

"Hector, we're sure. It's going on one o'clock! We've been here for four hours! We've tried, what? Forty electronic devices? Fifty? Not one, man. Not. One. I've got an engineering degree. You've got an engineering degree. What are the odds that every contraption with a circuit board for a heart would go belly-up on this flight? Hm? The plane landed on its side. The cargo bay was largely undamaged. Some of these suitcases don't even look scuffed up. And nothing works? C'mon."

Hector retrieved an MP3 player. He tried it. Zip.

Jack had found the oddest thing: an old, scratched saddlebag stuffed into a bin that usually held pretzels. He pulled it out. Inside was a portfolio. He eyed it, bored now, then started scanning the printed document with the pencil scribbles in the margins. "Tenacious. That's what we're going to start calling you from now on. Tenacious H. That's . . ."

Hector looked up. "Jack?"

"Hey. I know who this guy is."

Hector found a penlight. He clicked it. Nope. "What guy?"

"I found a speech by a guy named Andrew Malatesta. I heard him speak at a Chautauqua at Harvard last year. World-class brainiac. Some really out-of-the-box stuff. He's got the patent on some amazing, holographic heads-up-display avionics."

Jack turned back to the speech. "I think this guy was going to Northwest Tech. He was going to denounce Halcyon/Detweiler. Which, I'm just saying, I got stock in. Says here—"

Beeeeep.

At the sound, Jack glanced up from the portfolio and aged saddlebag. A few feet away knelt a suddenly grinning Hector Villareal, holding a woman's clutch purse in one hand, a cell phone in the other.

And the LED face on the phone was lit up. It showed three bars of reception.

Jack jumped off the cart. "No way!"

Hector nodded.

Jack immediately lost interest in the speech from the saddlebag. He stuffed his findings back into the pretzel bin, for lack of anywhere better to put them. He adjusted his ear jack and hit buttons on his belt-mounted comm unit.

"This is Kim."

Police Chief Paul McKinney and Mac Pritchert, the state-assigned fire-crew chief, stepped out onto the roof of the Pure-Pride Tool and Dye Building. Both carried binoculars and Pritchert had a walkie-talkie.

He toggled the Send switch. "Jillian, what do you got? Over."

McKinney jogged to the eastern end of the tarmac roof and raised the lenses to his eyes.

The radio squealed. The voice on the other end shouted over the din of helicopter rotors and an engine, "Mac? The fire has reached the crash site. It's definitely moving faster today. Over."

Pritchert hit the switch again. "Copy that. Jonah, it's Mac. Is the firebreak gonna hold? Over."

A different voice this time. "Ah, that's a negative, base. Winds really picking up and the fire is crown-jumping." It wasn't just surviving on ground cover anymore, but had climbed into the trees. "On the western face of the fire, we do not—repeat, *do not*—have containment. Over."

Chief McKinney lowered his glasses. "It's your call, but I think we *encourage* an evacuation. For now. Wait an hour, see if it needs to be mandatory."

Pritchert looked into his binoculars. "Yeah. Make the call."

TWIN PINES

Peter Kim was ebullient. "A meeting, today. All team leaders."

Beth Mancini perched on the edge of desk in the former real estate office and started to jot notes. "Agenda?"

"Putting Tomzak in his place. Invite him, Duvall, Agent Calabrese. We're going to put an end to this insanity once and for all."

"When and where?"

"Four. Here."

She reeled back. "They're evacuating the town! We've got to get—"

"It's a voluntary evacuation. We're not leaving the fuselage or the remaining bodies. But get going on the meeting, please. Top priority."

Beth set down her pen and pad. "About the bodies. The police chief called and told me you'd been in a shouting match. I talked him out of kicking us out of our morgue, but it wasn't easy. Peter, you've got to let me do my job and run interference for you. It's—"

"You're right."

Beth hadn't seen that coming.

"No, absolutely. I blew that badly. Thank you for calming the chief down."

"I . . . You're welcome," she said, thinking, *What have you done to the real Peter Kim?*

"Sure. Now, please set up the meeting. Slapping Tomzak down is priority number one."

Kiki and Tommy went down to the hotel dining room for coffee. It was going on 2:00 P.M.

"Ray's flying back today," Tommy said, fiddling with a miniature white porcelain pitcher of half-and-half. "Here's hoping he brings good news."

Kiki's comm unit buzzed. Beth had left her one in their hotel room, without informing Peter. She activated it. "Hello? . . . Hi."

She listened for a minute, frowning. "We'll be there. Thank you."

She disconnected. "That was Beth. Peter's called a team meeting for four at the real estate office in Twin Pines. We're invited. Ray, too, if he's back in time."

"And he ain't worried about, you know, the damn town burning down?"

"Peter is anything but impetuous. It must be okay. Anyway, Beth says it's about the power loss on board the Claremont."

"You think we actually got through to Petey?" Tommy sounded incredulous.

"Well . . . maybe?"

Neither Kiki nor Tommy noticed the driver in the baseball cap and sunglasses, in the Ford Escort, parked outside their hotel and watching them through military-surplus binoculars.

TWIN PINES

Jenna Scott listened in on Beth Mancini's call to Kiki.

They were going to discuss the Malatesta prototype. So far, only the two crash victims, Duvall and Tomzak, plus their FBI liaison, had lent any validity to the power-loss scenario. That looked likely to change.

She immediately called Calendar. "It's Vintner. The team is meeting in Twin Pines, in two hours. Tomzak and Duvall will be there. It is imperative that they be intercepted before that meeting."

Calendar just replied, "Copy." And the line went dead.

Mac Pritchert, the fire chief, was using the Twin Pines Police Station as his rally point. He made the call to bring in the air tankers once he realized his crew could not put a firebreak between the flames and Twin Pines.

He had called for "any birds" and was hoping to get Tanker 910s, converted McDonnell Douglas DC-10s that are among the largest air tankers in the world for this sort of work. But he was stunned when the Canadians called to up Ilyushin II-76-Ps.

"Tell me you're joking!" he said into the telephone.

"Nope," the voice came back. "Ilyushin II-76-Ps. We got four of them, and they're yours if you need them."

"Hot dog! We'll take them and we're grateful for the offer! What kinda runways do those beasts need?"

The Canadian said, "They can land on only about five hundred meters but, full up, they need a good nine hundred for takeoff."

Pritchert dug a pen out of his shirt pocket and did the math. They needed close to three thousand feet for takeoff. Helena Regional had that to spare.

"Send them bad boys on down! And again: thank you!"

Chief McKinney walked up with two coffee cups, one held backward, the handle extended. Pritchert took it, grinning.

"Good news?"

Pritchert's smile blossomed. "We're getting Ilyushins!"

Paul McKinney misheard the word. "Ah . . . okay. Of . . . ?"

Ginger LeFrance's phone chirped and she flipped it open. "Hello?"

"Ginger? It's Jack Goodspeed. From the NTSB crash team."

"Hey." The big, good-looking guy. This was a surprise. She was pretty sure he was gay.

"We might have to move the fuselage again. Can Casper come out and play?"

"You bet. I'll be there in ten."

Peter Kim said, "What do you mean, *not answering?*"

Beth frowned. "Teresa's comm unit seems to be working. She's just not answering."

HELENA

Reporters throughout the country wanted a part of the Malatesta story, following Amy Dreyfus's story in the *Washington Post*. Since so many were in Montana covering the crash already, Renee Malatesta held a brief press event in the hotel's conference room, confirming that Malatesta, Inc., was in the arms business.

She wore sunglasses throughout. It could have been to hide either her tears or her wildly dilated eyes. She wore a long, white Missoni sweater that reached her knees, her hands jammed into the sweater pockets. She looked pale, brittle.

She answered their questions lucidly but with a chilling lack of emotion. She was a humanoid, a cybernetic being. One of Andrew's microelectronic creations.

Her left fist curled around the nickel-plated Colt .25 in the sweater pocket.

Amy Dreyfus listened in, standing with a good friend from the Business desk of the *Wall Street Journal*. Amy tapped a drumbeat on her notepad with her pen. "Something's not adding up here," she whispered.

The *Journal* reporter leaned in. "What?"

"Where are the other two?"

"Other two what?"

Amy said, "The chief engineers of Malatesta, Inc. Andrew Malatesta used to call them the Starting Five: himself and four other engineers he'd known since they were undergrads. They were really tight."

"Yeah?"

"Two of them died in the crash with Andrew. Christian Dean and Vejay Mehta. I knew Christian, a little. The others are all that remain of Malatesta's engineering brain trust. Wouldn't you think they'd be here for this? Or that they'd have called the press conference back in Maryland? This isn't adding up."

The *Journal* reporter just shrugged.

Amy said to herself, *I gotta get to Maryland. Pronto.*

Ray Calabrese flew back to Montana and drove directly to the crashers' hotel. He rapped on the door to Kiki and Tommy's room. They were in.

Tommy said, "You look like shit, hoss."

"It's not an illusion, Texas."

Tommy knelt—a little vertigo; not bad—and drew two tiny scotch bottles from the minibar.

Kiki looked at the pale band around her wrist—no watch—then glanced at the bedroom alarm clock. "Is that a good idea, this close to the Go-Team meeting?"

"Trust me, hon. Man's on Mexico time."

Kiki looked unsure.

They sat as Ray cracked them open, drained them into a tumbler. "Good news and bad news."

Kiki said, "I always start with the bad."

"Guy I know who's an expert in the field says there are no EMP weapons. They're forbidden by international treaty."

Tommy was crestfallen. "What the hell. I know what I saw on the plane."

"My boss also hooked me up with another guy. This guy's pretty knowledgeable. He says there may be this one engineer who's been working on the theory of a pulse weapon, but it's just on paper."

The trio was glum. Kiki said, "And the good news?"

"I lied. It's pretty bad, too. First, you two aren't crazy. Daria ID'd Silver Hair. Goes by the code name Calendar."

Tommy and Kiki slapped palms.

"Don't celebrate. He's an assassin. He's damn good. And she says he's a psycho. If his job's not one hundred percent done, then . . ." Ray shrugged. "And it gets worse."

"It gets worse'n a psycho assassin who's good at his fucking job?"

"Yeah. He freelances for U.S. intelligence and military agencies. Exclusively."

He drained the booze.

A very long silence. Tommy started a couple of sentences, but they died, stillborn. He finally got, "Are you saying . . . Is Daria . . . ? Is it possible we might've been brought down by a federal agency? This could be some sort of domestic spy shit?"

"Yeah."

"Is that even possible?"

Ray said, "I'm FBI. That means I'm a cop in a good suit. I don't know jack about the espionage world. Is it possible? Yeah, Texas, maybe. What can I tell you?"

Kiki turned to Tommy. "Please tell me there's more scotch in there."

TWIN PINES

The town had only twelve hundred residents, but when four-fifths of them agreed to the recommended evacuation, the route to the highway quickly jammed.

State police turned both lanes of the highway into westbound lanes, right outside the town limits. Two of Paul McKinney's four dayside officers helped direct traffic; the other two were guarding the makeshift morgue and the parts shop with the ruined fuselage. Pickups and SUVs quickly jammed the western edge of the town, turning the freeway on-ramp into a parking lot.

. . .

Ray, Tommy, and Kiki had to drive on the shoulder of the highway to get back into town. They were joined by a phalanx of fire trucks and Caterpillar bulldozers heading toward the conflagration. Neither Ray nor the crashers noticed the Ford Escort following them, a mile back.

Beth Mancini finally got through to the U.S. marshal for the District of Columbia. "I'm looking for Marshal Tyson Beck," she said. She explained who she was, why she was calling: that she was tracking down the truth behind two signatures.

The woman on the other end said, "Marshal Beck will have to get back to you. He's in a meeting with the attorney general."

Beth gave the woman her number and hung up.

At that very instant, Ray Calabrese said, "Marshal Tyson Beck. Yes, please. It's about the crash."

Ray didn't like talking on a cell phone while driving. He didn't like driving on the shoulder of a highway, facing an unending sea of trucks and cars going the other way. He didn't like dodging the massive, daisy-yellow Caterpillar dozers. It's the reason he hadn't spotted his tail, yet.

"Beck. You're calling about the crash in Montana?"

"Yes, sir. Two black boxes were recovered from the crash. One went to Portland, Oregon. The other to NTSB headquarters in L'Enfant Plaza. They were signed for by, ah . . ." He blanked on the name. Kiki dug out the notes, which Susan Tanaka had provided them. She showed them to Ray. "Ah, Deputy Marshal Robert Sonntag."

He waited. He heard nothing. Cars coming out of Twin Pines honked at him, as if he didn't know he was driving toward a forest fire.

Marshal Tyson Beck said, "Is this a joke?"

"No, sir. Sonntag signed for both of the black boxes."

"What is your name again? Your field office?"

"Ray Calabrese, FBI field office for Southern California. My SAC is Henry Deits."

The man said, "I know Henry. So I suspect this isn't a joke."

"It isn't, sir."

"Bob Sonntag died of pancreatic cancer three months ago."

. . .

Ray hung up as, three miles to the east, Beth's comm unit chimed. "Beth Mancini."

"Miss Mancini, this is the U.S. Marshal's Service in Washington. We spoke a few moments ago?"

In her surveillance van, Jenna Scott said, ". . . We spoke a few minutes ago?"

Beth Mancini said, "Oh, yes. Thank you for getting back so quickly."

"Not at all. One moment for Marshal Tyson Beck, please."

She put the Mancini woman on hold, adjusted her headset. "Barry? Your name is Tyson Beck. Ready?"

LANGLEY

Barry Tichnor said, "This is Marshal Beck."

"My name is Beth Mancini. I'm—"

"My aide told me. You're calling from Montana. What can the U.S. Marshal Service do for you, Miss Mancini?"

"Two black boxes were signed for, night of the crash, by a Deputy Marshal Robert Sonntag. I need to confirm that he actually came to Montana, came to the crash site."

Barry said, "Can you hold a moment?" He put her on hold, studied the new Degas print he'd seen the weekend before and just had to have. It certainly brightened up his office. He reconnected. "Miss Mancini?"

"Yes?"

"I spoke to Bob. He confirms. He picked up your packages."

He heard a sigh. "That is a huge relief. Thank you. Good day."

"Good luck out there."

As soon as Beth hung up, Barry heard Jenna's voice in his ear: "Hook, line, and sinker."

TWIN PINES

Calendar met up with his two ex-Special Forces soldiers, Cates and Dyson, less than three blocks from the crashers' new meeting space. Calendar laid out the new goal, told them they'd be using the forest fire as cover. These were soldiers he'd worked with before. Guys he knew could do the deed, quickly and cleanly, then evaporate like dew.

Ray said, "I don't know if it's the fire, but now I'm getting nothing but static."

He folded his cell.

Tommy checked the dashboard clock. "We're early. Look, there's the real estate office. You go use their landlines or, I don't know, someone's comm unit. Me, I'd kill for an aspirin."

Kiki said, "Me, too."

Ray parked and undid his seat belt. Tommy said, "I'll drive," and the other two laughed.

"Hey, Concussion Boy. Kiki's driving."

She moved to the front seat, bussing Ray's cheek en passant. She pulled out, heading for a convenience store they'd noticed the day before.

Calendar's man, Cates, sat in a Chevy pickup a block away. "Targets are separating from Guard Dog. Repeat: Guard Dog is out of the picture."

Calendar heard that message through his ear jack. He was just approaching the auto-parts facility with the destroyed aircraft. The fat, white airship hung over the facility's fenced-off backyard, looking vaguely like a prop from a 1950s science fiction story. As he watched, vans arrived and more than a dozen members of Jack Goodspeed's airframe team began securing the detritus of the Claremont crash.

27

AT THE DRUGSTORE, KIKI fished the NTSB credit card out of her hip pocket. "I say we get slushies on the taxpayers' dime. There are very few opportunities for good, honest graft in the . . . Tommy?"

He was staring down at a point on the tarmac before his shoes. Slowly, he went down on his haunches.

"What is it?"

"Blood."

Kiki circled the car and knelt, her thigh wound protesting. She saw it now, too. A small, tight cluster of round, coagulated drops.

Tommy said, "Hmph."

"What?"

"Funny splatter pattern."

"Funny how?"

He scratched his chin, which he often did when calculating in his head. "Both too much and too little. Like, I don't know, you cut an artery, a really good bleeder, then put a pressure bandage on it right quick."

She peered at it but didn't see the same signs Tommy did. "Is it fresh?"

"Not too old. See how round these are? Fell straight down."

"Do you think it's germane to all this?" Kiki made a twirling motion, taking in their whole situation.

Tommy looked her in the eye and reached out one hand. Kiki took it, palm to palm. "Nah. Blood splatter, convenience store parking lot? I don't see how. Except for Tanaka's Law."

They stood, Kiki quoting Susan: "In a crash, there's no such thing as coincidence."

Jack put two fingers to his lips and whistled. The fifteen people on his airframe team stopped chattering in the auto-parts facility, turned in his direction.

"Listen up! Normally, in a crash, *where* stuff landed is vital. But this case is different. We've already moved everything once."

The team members nodded.

"The fire's coming this way. We escaped it once and it looks like we'll have to again. Take everything you picked up off the forest floor and stow it back inside the Claremont. Doesn't matter where. Ginger, here, is going to fly everything out at once."

Ginger LaFrance waved to the crew.

Jack clapped twice, like the quarterback he used to be. "All right! Let's book!"

His crew starting hauling artifacts of the crash from outside and into the Claremont's ruined fuselage.

Tommy asked the store clerk about the blood in the parking lot. She said, "Oh, gross!" but knew nothing helpful. Kiki paid for Extra Strength Tylenol and two bottled waters. Plus a bag of Fritos because she was feeling salt deficient.

Stepping outside, they found a big white guy in a suit, carrying a clipboard and standing by the rental. Kiki smiled politely at him.

"Katherine Duvall? Leonard Tomzak?"

They nodded.

He turned the clipboard forty-five degrees to reveal a 9-millimeter Glock auto with a long, charcoal-gray silencer.

"Lieutenant, the driver's seat, please. Doctor, the passenger side."

"The fuck do you think—"

"Dr. Tomzak," the guy cut in. "I will gut-shoot the redhead unless you do you exactly what I say. Understood?"

They noticed the doors were open an inch. They climbed in, and the big guy got in the back behind Kiki.

Kiki put the car in gear and pulled out of the parking lot.

The Ford Escort, a half block away, fell into formation.

A firefighter brought his Caterpillar D11T crawler-dozer to a halt and hauled up on the hand brake. He lowered the massive forward blade, which could handle six cubic yards of debris at a pass. He climbed down from the cab, removing his hardhat and wiping sweat from his forehead.

A black guy who looked like a fullback, wearing an identical orange safety vest and hardhat, walked his way. "Pardon?"

The firefighter stopped.

The black guy held out his hand to shake. As they did, he swung his left hand fast, straight as a sword, clocking the firefighter in the throat. He fell like his strings had been clipped.

With ridiculous ease, Calendar's man, Dyson, hefted him over one shoulder, climbed up on the tank treads and into the cab, and dumped the firefighter inside with him.

Tommy said, "So, this is about the late library books?"

The big blond guy, Cates, nodded. "That's good. I like that. Turn here. Left."

Kiki turned. "Why are you doing this?"

"To keep America safe."

Tommy snorted a laugh. "Horseshit. You brought down a goddamn airliner filled with Americans."

"Collateral damage. Sometimes—"

Tommy reached into the 7-Eleven bag in his lap. Cates cocked his Glock 9. "Pull your hand out of the bag. Slowly."

Tommy turned in his seat, stared into the assassin's eyes. "Fuck you, you cocksuckin' piece-of-shit errand boy." He pulled out the box of Tylenol. He opened it, broke eye contact long enough to line up the cap and thumb it off, then stared at the guy again as his thumbnail rent the foil cover. Tommy dry-swallowed three pills.

He turned back to face forward.

Kiki said, "I love you."

"Me, too, babe."

Peter Kim checked his watch. "Teresa's been missing for hours. Something's wrong."

Chief Paul McKinney shrugged. "And I'd like to help but we're evacuating a town here. The fire is picking up speed. There could not be a worse time to conduct a missing-person investigation than right here, right now."

Peter started to protest when a deep rumbling sound filled the former real estate office. It was so loud and so low, he could feel his clavicle vibrate.

"What the heck is that?" He shouted to be heard.

"Air tankers!" McKinney shouted back. "Biggest damn birds I ever seen! They just got here from Vancouver! They're gonna start dumping water on the fire!"

The Ilyushin II-76-P's had been constructed originally for the Soviet military as well as civilian traffic. They'd seen service for the Soviets in Afghanistan, and for NATO in Sarajevo. With a wingspan of 165 feet and an empty weight of almost two hundred thousand pounds, the massive, four-engine aircraft were the largest air tankers in the world (the *P* stood for *Pozhahrniy*, or "Firefighter").

And the airborne monsters were dropping water at the western front of the fire, trying to slow its remorseless march on Twin Pines.

Cates directed Kiki to the south end of Twin Pines, to a warehouse that looked like it hadn't been used in years. The building was three stories tall and the aluminum siding had turned a sickly gray. A sign over the door read AMER AN S ORAGE AN ENTAL. It looked like Esperanto to Kiki.

The tall gate was open and an old padlock had been sheared through. She drove in, pulling onto hard-packed dirt with yellow, waxy sage grass sprouting up here and there. The rear side of the acreage ended with a twelve-foot-high cliff wall. Atop the cliff, they could see more sage grass.

"Park here," Cates ordered at the base of the cliff.

She did. "What's here?"

Cates ignored her. "Keys."

She cut the engine, handed the keys back over her right shoulder. The big man grabbed them. "Now, stay put and—"

An enormous, four-engine Ilyushin cleared the cliff and zoomed away, not one hundred feet over their heads. The bellow of the beast hit the car like a physical blow. Everyone flinched.

Tommy twisted in his seat and darted for the gun.

The hit man may have outweighed him by eighty pounds, but he also was twice as fast. His fist caught Tommy in the jaw before Tommy's hand was halfway to the Glock.

Tommy slumped forward until his seat belt pulled taut, his vision blurring, drooling blood out of a split lip.

Kiki contemplated making a move but didn't see any.

"That's for *errand boy,*" Cates growled. "Now, sit here and be good."

He climbed out.

Atop the cliff, and twenty-five feet to the west, a bright yellow Caterpillar bulldozer hove into view. It was a behemoth, thirty-six feet long and fifteen feet high. Weighing 115 tons, it moved on two tank treads that rotated through a wedge-shaped frame. The deeply concave universal blade alone was larger than the crashers' rental car. Seen from below, the dozer looked positively prehistoric.

Kiki took Tommy by the shoulder. "Baby?"

He leaned forward, head over his knees. "I'm all right," he mumbled, wiping blood from his lips with the back of his hand. "Gimme a minute."

"Your concussion?"

He nodded slightly.

Kiki leaned forward, looking up and out of the windshield, as exhaust belched from the upward-facing exhaust pipes atop the mammoth Cat. Its front shovel gleamed in the sun. It began rolling forward, drawing closer and parallel to the cliff. Within seconds it would be directly overhead, but perilously close to the cliff edge. *If that fool isn't careful, he's going to topple right over the cliff,* Kiki thought.

Then she gasped, realizing that was precisely the plan.

The mercenaries, Dyson in the tractor-dozer and Cates holding the crashers at gunpoint, weren't using sophisticated comms for so simple a mission.

Cates made a very broad head bob to confirm that the targets were in position. Dyson, in the glass-and-iron cabin so tall he could operate the Cat standing up, gave his partner a thumbs-up.

Dyson brought the tractor-dozer to the very edge of the grassy cliff, now fifteen feet from being straight over the NTSB rental car. He watched clay crumble away as the massive tank tread drew closer, finally peeking over the edge.

Kiki reached for her door handle and saw the blond guy, a dozen feet away, draw his Glock and aim it at her head. The crashers were stuck in the car.

Tommy peered up but his vision was blurred.

Kiki looked up again. About four inches of the left-side tank treads were visible over the edge of the cliff now. The Cat was ten feet away from being directly over their car.

The Ford Escort that had followed the crash investigators since Helena pulled slowly into the warehouse yard. The driver paused, brake lights flashing. Then the compact pulled forward, picking up speed.

Kiki's military training kicked in. *They're going to use that bulldozer to crush us to death. If we stay in the car, it will look like a weird accident. If I step out of the car, that blond bastard will shoot me and I'll die and my autopsy will be proof of our conspiracy theory.*

She reached for her door handle.

The blond hit man turned, saw the Ford Escort zooming toward him, gaining speed. He raised his weapon, left hand bracing his right, and fired at the quickly accelerating car.

The windshield starred as his bullet hit home. He fired again and it shattered.

Kiki opened her door in time to see the big, blond man turn away from her and fire his weapon at the oncoming car.

· · ·

Cates had never known an opponent he couldn't put down with a good handgun. He fired and fired at the Ford Escort. He didn't run. He knew his weapon would save him, as it had on battlefields around the globe.

The Escort hit him doing sixty.

He rag-dolled over the hood, slamming into the already-destroyed windshield and up onto the roof, rolling, spinning, limbs no longer constrained by knee or elbow joints. He was a limp washrag in a nice suit, more fluid than solid, as he rolled off the trunk and onto the hard-packed dirt.

The Escort threw a rooster tail of dust and gravel and weeds, spinning ninety degrees, brakes keening. An arm extended through the shattered windshield, a silver automatic aimed high at the Cat, squeezing off four shots as the car continued to spin.

Kiki grabbed Tommy's shirt collar as she hip-checked the driver's side door. It sprang open and she stepped out, long, rangy muscles garnered in a sailboat and on the packed sand of volleyball courts bunching as she dragged Tommy over the emergency brake, the driver's seat, and out through the door.

She backpedaled, dragging him in her wake.

Still dizzy from the blow to his head, Tommy's feet scrambled for purchase but his brain ground gears. "Come *on!*" Kiki huffed, stutter-stepping backward, dragging him away from the car.

Up above, in the cabin of the bulldozer, Dyson watched his associate die under the impact of the Ford. "Dammit!" he bellowed and drew his Heckler & Koch .45, firing at the still-spinning Escort, below. He got off only one shot before the scary-accurate return fire made him flinch back.

The Cat hovered at the edge, more than half of the left-hand tank tread now over empty air. Dyson thought about returning fire, but he was out of time. He crawled over the dead firefighter to get to the passenger door of the cab.

The Escort screeched to a halt, rocked on its shock absorbers, the rooster tail of dust and debris catching up, waving past. The driver stepped out into that dust devil, obscured by flying grit.

The driver fired at the dozer cabin two more times.

. . .

Kiki heard the booming shots and turned to see a handgun fall from the driver's right hand; left hand rising with an identical pistol, slide ratcheting, snapping off five more bullets in such close formation that one bullet left the chamber before the bullet in front of it hit the Cat.

Four of the last six bullets shattered the Cat's windshield. One of them slammed into Dyson's shoulder, just as he felt the cabin yaw madly to the left.

He was halfway out of the cab but fell back in.

The Cat rumbled off the cliff, taking a wide swath of clay and sage grass with it. The iron beast toppled and twisted. Upside down, it slammed into the rental car. Kiki caught a brief glimpse of a stranger in the cab, his shoulder blood soaked, upside down, scrambling madly to escape.

He didn't.

The car was crushed flat. The tall cab of the bulldozer pancaked in on itself.

Under the impact of 115 tons of mostly iron falling a dozen feet, a surge of dust and dirt escaped in all directions, moving with such force that, when it reached Kiki, ten feet away, she was lifted off her feet and landed two feet back, on her ass, Tommy landing atop her.

He coughed and hacked up blood and dust, rolling off her, groaning, flopping onto his back on the hard-packed earth and squinting, unbelieving, at the massive wreck.

Coughing in pain, her barely mended rib cracked again, Kiki rose on her elbows, turned to the Escort as the rooster tail of dust subsided, revealing the driver.

The driver holstered the weapon. "Hallo, Kiki."

"Daria?"

28

IT WAS GOING ON 6:00 P.M. in the Malatesta, Inc., headquarters. Terri Loew was packing her tote bag, getting ready to head home, when the receptionist knocked on her office door. "Terri? There's someone here."

Terri turned and saw a small, vaguely familiar woman with artificially red hair cut in a shoulder-length bob.

"Hi. Terri Loew, right?" The woman extended her hand. "Amy Drey-fus, *Washington Post.* Remember me? I was Andrew's best—"

"Of course I remember you. Hi. It was . . . Amy Shinberg?" They shook hands

"Yeah, it was." Amy flashed a small, modest wedding ring. "Andrew and I kept in touch. Not just because of my job, I mean. He spoke so highly of you. Of all of you. He called his designers the Starting Five."

Terri's eyes brimmed with tears. "I know. I loved that. We were such a family here."

"Can I talk to you about Andrew? I . . . really need some answers."

Terri called in Antal Borsa, who never left the office before 8:00 P.M. They chose Terri's office and closed the door.

Antal said. "You did yesterday's online piece about Andrew and the Halcyon subcontract."

"Yes. Renee told me you guys had signed on to build weapons."

A pregnant silence filled the office.

Terri and Antal exchanged glances. Antal said, "I know it's not politically correct, but would anyone mind if I smoked?" He pulled a packet of German-made Ernte 23 cigarettes out of his double-breasted suit jacket.

Amy said, "Can I bum one off you?" She smoked maybe four cigarettes per year and only in interviews. She knew that interviewees who smoke sometimes answer questions more honestly with a reporter who shares the vice. Antal lit both cigarettes with an antique Ronson lighter.

"Andrew called me. He said he needed my help breaking a story to the media. I asked him if it was serious and he said, 'Life-and-death serious.' I'm quoting here: life-and-death. I'm such an idiot, I didn't press him then. He said we'd talk when he got to Seattle for the Northwest Tech."

She blew smoke toward the ceiling. "Andrew was going to break something very important to him. And, I'm sorry, but I don't think it was to announce he was becoming Iron Man or whatever. I think it was something so secretive, he hadn't even told Renee."

Terri pulled Kleenex out of a decorative box on her desk and began crying in earnest. Antal Borsa adjusted the crease in his impeccable trousers, eyes avoiding contact with anyone. A halo of blue smoke surrounded his head.

He said, "Is this on the record?"

Amy reached into the tote for her digital recorder and a slim reporter's pad. She set them both on the desk for the engineers to see. She pulled out a pen and uncapped it.

"Yes," she said. "Absolutely."

LANGLEY

Bloomberg's cable channel played a clip of Renee Malatesta's press conference, in which she confirmed that the software company had signed a deal with the nation's number-one defense contractor, Halcyon/Detweiler, to become part of the military/industrial complex.

Liz Proctor called Barry Tichnor's office. "Hello?"

She said, "Are you watching?"

"Yes." He sounded tired.

"Barry? Did things just get better or did things just get worse?"

Renee Malatesta looked half awake and as brittle as a moth's wing.

TWIN PINES

MSNBC played a different clip of Renee's press conference. Wearing wide Dolce & Gabbana sunglasses, she sounded like someone in a sleep-deprivation clinical study.

In the break room of the former real estate office, Jack Goodspeed watched the taped press conference. "Hey. Listen to this."

Hector Villareal sniffed the sleeve of his shirt. It reeked of woodsmoke. "What?"

"This. She's the wife of the guy."

Hector turned to him. "The guy?"

"I was telling you about. Chautauqua, Harvard. The saddlebag in the food services cart. Andrew Malatesta."

Hector said, "Six degrees . . ."

"No, no, man. Listen."

They did.

Jack shook his head. "That's not what the guy's speech said. I'm . . . I think it's almost exactly opposite of what the guy was gonna say."

In the front of the realty office, Ray Calabrese hung up the phone and turned to the Go-Team leaders. Peter Kim was present, along with Beth Mancini, Reuben Chaykin, Gene Whitney, and Lakshmi Jain.

Hector and Jack emerged from the break room, Jack saying, "We should call her. Tell her."

"It's none of our business."

Peter Kim checked his watch. It was 4:15 P.M. Monday. "They're late."

Ray perched on the edge of a desk. "They went to get aspirin. Look, we're now in a position to prove, at least in part, that there's a conspiracy here."

Peter buttoned his suit coat. "And we're now in a position to prove that Tomzak has his head so firmly ensconced up his ass that he can see his spleen. That makes you either a dupe or part of his Area 51 Alien Conspiracy Fan Club."

Beth rolled her eyes. "Peter! Come on. We can agree to disagree but—"

Another Ilyushin air tanker roared overhead, and everyone winced until it had passed on. Peter said, "God, those are annoying. Look, we cannot simultaneously investigate this crash, outrun a forest fire, and stave off Tomzak's lunatic need to be center stage."

Ray fought down his impulse to pop this guy in the mouth. He smiled, nodded. "The good thing about working in a huge bureaucracy like the FBI is, you get immune to nausea when dealing with arrogant, bantam-weight demigods with a false sense of adequacy."

Peter glared at him for two seconds, then, unintentionally, let a brief smile flicker. He turned to Gene Whitney. "At some level, you have to admire the complexity of that insult."

Gene shrugged. "Had a poetic quality."

Peter turned back. "And fuck you, too, Ray." He checked his diver's watch again. "Where are they?"

Ray shrugged. "Jesus Christ, Kim! We've got false federal agents, a wingless airliner flying under a balloon, air tankers barnstorming us every five minutes, a missing crasher, and a forest fire at the back door. Absolutely nothing could surprise me today."

The bell over the front door tinkled. Tommy and Kiki entered, escorted by Daria Gibron with twin .40-caliber Browning Hi Power autos strapped to her thighs.

Gene Whitney turned to Ray. "I was you, I'd stop saying shit like that, man."

29

RAY STOOD, STUNNED. DARIA offered a small nod.

Tommy looked a little dazed and his lower lip was split. Kiki held an arm curled around her middle, under her breasts, hand in back supporting the rebroken rib. They looked like hell, their hair and clothes dusty, Kiki's denim shirt ripped along one seam.

Kiki started in. "Peter, we can prove it! We—"

"And we can disprove it!" he shouted back.

Tommy said, "Hey. You wanna watch your tone, buddy."

Reuben Chaykin stepped in. "Tommy, Kiki, we've been patient because you're our people, but your story's full of holes. I'm sorry, but there it is."

And as people began to shout over one another, Dr. Lakshmi Jain cast a glance around the room, saw two aluminum Open House signs. She picked them up, one in each hand, and brought them together like cymbals.

Ka-lang!

Everyone in the room jumped. Hector, nearest to her, covered his ears. "Ow!"

"Enough! All of you! I have put up with your unprofessional, childish outbursts, but no more! Mr. Kim: you are our leader. Start acting like one!"

It was as if she'd physically slugged him. "I beg your pardon?"

Lakshmi went eye-to-eye with him. "You heard me."

She turned to Tommy. "And your cowboy antics end here and now. Our investigation has disproved portions of your conspiracy theory. We are minutes away from evacuating this site. Please, in thirty seconds, give us one good reason we should lend credence to anything you say."

"Okay," Tommy said, rubbing his swollen jaw. "This here's Daria Gibron. She just stopped two hit men from killing Kiki and me. She ran over one of 'em and she clobbered the other one with a bulldozer."

Silence reigned for almost five seconds. Finally, Reuben Chaykin said, "Are you guys for real?"

Daria smiled a languid smile and shrugged.

Ray, still staring at her, said, "Hey."

She rolled chocolate eyes in his direction. "Hallo, Ray."

"Thank you."

She nodded.

Beth Mancini studied the newcomer, decked out in a cropped tank, jeans, and dusty boots, a holster belt snugged around her slim hips, twin, saddle-brown holsters tied with leather thongs to both thighs. Beth could not remember ever meeting a woman more solidly muscled than this one with her spiky, boyish haircut.

Beth said, "Everyone? They are going to evac this town any minute now. I—"

She was drowned out by another air tanker, maybe eighty feet off the ground.

Tommy dry-swallowed two more Tylenol, handed the bottle to Kiki.

"Sorry. They are going to evac any minute. I recommend we debrief each other. Quickly, while we still can. Agent Calabrese, why don't you start."

Peter nodded his approval and turned to Hector, who held the still-working cell phone from the luggage compartment.

Jack Goodspeed stepped into the office's break room and returned with a twelve-pack of bottled water, handed them out, starting with the newcomers.

Ray said, "Okay, this is Daria Gibron. She's attached to ATF and . . . I didn't realize you'd followed me."

"Calendar," she said, and only three other people in the room knew what she meant.

"Right. Tommy said you took out two hitters . . . ?"

"Not him." She sipped water. "But he's still here."

Peter cleared his throat. "Could we try this in English?"

Ray nodded. "The silver-haired guy that Tommy and Kiki saw at the crash site is an assassin. He works under the name of Calendar. He free-lances for American military and intelligence agencies."

Reuben Chaykin shrugged. "This is for real?"

"Yes." Kiki swept hair off her forehead with an open palm. "This is really, really for real."

Ray said, "Second, I just got off the phone with the U.S. marshal for the District of Columbia."

Beth frowned. "Me, too."

"He told me that the agent who signed for the black boxes died of cancer three weeks ago."

Beth felt the blood rush to her cheeks. "No. The marshal's name is Tyson Beck. I talked to him, too. The deputy marshal, um . . ."

Ray said, "Robert Sonntag."

"Yes. Beck spoke to Sonntag while I was on hold. He confirmed the story."

"No," Ray said softly. "He didn't."

"Excuse me." Lakshmi Jain held up one hand, as if still a schoolgirl. "I met a deputy marshal yesterday at the morgue. He identified himself as Robert Sonntag."

Tommy said, "Describe him."

"Ah, fifty, perhaps. Large, not fat. One hundred eighty centimeters—"

Tommy throwing in, "Six feet."

"Yes. Ah, broad-shouldered, short, silver hair . . ." She froze.

Hector Villareal made the sign of the cross. "Holy Mary, mother of God."

Beth touched Peter Kim's arm. "Teresa!"

Peter blanched. "Oh. No . . ."

To Kiki's and Tommy's confused looks, Gene said, "We lost us a team member. Teresa Santiago. She's been off her comms all day."

Ray Calabrese pinched his nose, willed himself to calm down. "Ah, God. Kim? You and I aren't friends. But please take this in: your comms are compromised. Your team member is dead. Don't believe me, use my cell, call the Marshal Service back, confirm—"

"No." Peter's voice barely rose above a whisper. "You're right. I know."

He cleared his throat, eyed the tiled floor, hands on his hips, buying himself a little time. "Ah, everyone? Jack, collect everyone's comms, please. They're compromised."

After a stunned beat, the crashers reached for their belt units and ear jacks. Jack used a discarded Krispy Kreme box to gather the electronic gadgets.

Kiki said, "Peter, we are so sorry."

30

IT'S AMY. HI. YEAH, get me Big-Time, please."

Amy Dreyfus was typing on her Compaq, phone tucked against her ear. On the other side of the office, Terri Loew and Antal Borsa were huddled together.

"Big-Time? Hey. I have a story. I have two sources. It's huge. . . . No, boss, seriously. We need to post it online now. I'll transmit it to your Hotmail account in, I don't know, five minutes. Chief? The editorial meeting is in twenty minutes. Go fight for the front page. Above the fold . . . I kid you not."

TWIN PINES

Peter Kim pressed the heels of his hands against his eyes, bit his lips. He gathered himself. "Okay. The conspiracy's real. The assassins are real. The black boxes are fakes. That still leaves us asking: what brought down Flight Seven-Eight? And why?"

"All power died. Like that." Tommy snapped his fingers.

Peter shook his head. "One cell phone. That's all it would take to disprove your electromagnetic-pulse theory. Hector?"

Wiping his cheeks, Hector Villareal produced the cell phone and the gold-painted, chain-metal clutch purse from the luggage bay. He set them both down on a desk. The purse was small but heavy, and clanked as it hit the desk. He hit Power and the cell phone sang a little mechanical ditty.

"From the Claremont," he said, his voice husky with tears. "We found it in this."

He pointed to the clutch fashioned from intermeshed metal links.

Tommy couldn't believe his eyes. The one theory that made sense was crushed to dust. "But . . . I was sure—"

Peter Kim said, "What the fuck?"

Everyone paused. They'd expected him to sound triumphant. But Peter looked like he'd seen a ghost. He pointed to the little purse. "What the hell is that?"

Lakshmi shrugged. "It's a purse."

Beth said, "A clutch. A purse without a handle or shoulder strap. Women carry them—"

"Holy crap!" Peter spun to Jack, then to Hector. "The phone was in *that?*"

They nodded.

Beth was lost. "Peter, it's a clutch. What—"

"It's a fucking Faraday cage!"

Reuben, an engineer, got it right away. "Wow!"

Jack was next. "Oh, man . . ."

Tommy said, "You're over my head, fellas."

Peter, livid with rage at himself, crossed to a wipe board on the wall of the office and grabbed a marker. He started drawing with vicious stabs at the board. He drew a sphere, made of connected hexagonal links around a box marked with an X.

He turned to Jack. "How many other electrical devices did you guys check?"

"Dozens," Jack said. "Phones, gaming devices, shavers, whatever. None of them worked."

"Dammit!" Peter continued to draw. He turned and stabbed one finger toward the chain-link purse. "This purse, this clutch, acted as a goddamn Faraday cage! Look, an electromagnetic pulse shuts down all electrical circuits. Right? The only known way to block an EMP is to build an enclosure of conducting metal, or a mesh of such metal." He pointed again to the metal-mesh purse.

"An external static-electrical field should have short-circuited that phone. Like it did everything else on Flight Seven-Eight. But inside the chain-metal clutch? Inside a damn Faraday cage? The static field caused the electrical charges naturally in the cage to redistribute themselves. It cancels the external field, protecting the device within the purse!"

Tommy's eyes went from the crude drawing to the purse on the desk. "God*damn!*"

"A Faraday cage." Peter capped the marker and hurled it overhanded, harmlessly, against the office's front window. "Proof positive, Tomzak: you were right and . . . I was wrong."

WASHINGTON, D.C.

An aide to Admiral Gaelen Parks, director of Halcyon's Military Liaison Division, caught the *Washington Post's* online story about the Malatestas.

"Dammit!" he muttered, then dashed from his cubicle, down the corridor, to the office of the admiral.

Gaelen Parks's secretary said, "Hi, Captain," then frowned. "Hey, he's got someone in—"

The aide ignored her, stalked into the admiral's office. Gaelen Parks sat on the big, green leather love seat, across a low coffee table from two high-ranking Pentagon officers.

A lowly captain could expect to get reamed out for interrupting the brass like this, but Parks had relied on this man for years. He stood. "Gentlemen, I think this may be something I need to take care of. Can you give me a minute?"

The two officers rose and stepped out without questions. Parks turned to his aide.

"Barry Tichnor, sir. Two of the senior engineers at Malatesta, Inc., just outed him to the *Washington Post*. They know about the Bruges Accord and the prototype."

Gaelen Parks was not a man who panicked. "That was always a threat. Okay. Start severing every conceivable tie between that prick Tichnor's R-and-D Division and this office. If we can isolate the crisis to his division, we might be able to keep the rest of the firm off the hook."

He picked up his phone and called Liz Proctor.

TWIN PINES

Tommy's headache appeared to be Tylenol–proof. "Look, Petey. Don't get me wrong. I'm thrilled to have you say I was right and you were wrong.

Thing is: I wasn't right. Ray talked to two experts. There ain't no such thing as a pulse weapon."

Ray took up the narrative. "I got a CIA analyst who specializes in weapons of mass destruction. He says the Bruges Accord outlaws even researching pulse weapons. Another guy—and, I admit, he's a piece of work—says some engineer's been working in secret on a theoretical model for a pulse weapon. But it's vaporware. It's—"

Peter had had it with ambiguity. Every time he'd lacked a specific bit of information, it had come back to bite him in the ass. "Which engineer? What's the name?"

Ray consulted his notebook, flipping pages. "Ah . . . Malatesta. Andrew Malatesta."

"Shit!" Gene Whitney scrambled for a three-ring binder he'd brought from Helena. He found a page his finger descending a list. "Malatesta. Andrew Malatesta. He was on Flight Seven-Eight, Reagan to Sea-Tac. Seat Seven-A."

Kiki tried to reassemble the jigsaw puzzle of facts in her head. "Wait, wait. A guy on the plane was researching a weapon that, had it been real, could have brought down the plane? That . . . that makes no earthly sense."

Tommy turned to Lakshmi. "How did this Malatesta guy die?"

She said, "I believe he's part of my anomaly. Let me check." Before Tommy could ask *what anomaly?*, she dug the coroner's telephone number out of her NTSB jacket pocket, along with a cell phone that was not part of the crashers' comm units. She stepped into the break room for some quiet and made a call.

Peter Kim said, "Tomzak, at the crash site, how is it this Calendar guy didn't kill you? I've only worked with you once and I already want to kill you."

"He asked us what happened to the plane. I was concussed and all, and didn't feel like conversing. Kiki'd been asleep and really didn't know."

Peter nodded. "So you couldn't contradict the faked black boxes. Isaiah . . . he must have told him the power went out. So he killed him."

Lakshmi stepped back in. "I was right. I have been running statistical analyses through every M-and-M database I could find."

Jack looked askance. "Eminem?"

"Morbidity and Mortality studies. In a crash of this magnitude, theoretically we would have seen two throat injuries. Here, we have six. Andrew Malatesta was one. His postmortem happened yesterday. He died of a crushed larynx. And yes, before you ask, the wound was almost exactly like that of Isaiah Grey. Plus one of Dr. Malatesta's research associates."

Tommy ground his teeth, which made his jaw ache all the more. "Odds of the death are up three hundred percent and half of them are connected with this investigation. Motherfucker's mode of killing. All it proves is, their throats got hit by somethin' moving fast. In an airliner crash, it's the perfect murder."

All of a sudden, Jack Goodspeed's brain almost literally went *ping!*

"Jeez. Oh, man. Oh, God."

Every eye turned to him.

"I think I know why the plane was sabotaged. And who's behind it. Me and Hector, we found a speech this Malatesta guy was going to give at the Tech Expo. The speech says one thing, but just now, like a minute ago, I heard his wife on TV. She was saying the exact opposite."

"You know this Malatesta?" Peter cut in.

"I heard him speak at a thing, this one time. So I was curious, read his speech. He was outing Halcyon/Detweiler for producing illegal weapons. He had a whole bunch of pages with Halcyon letterhead in his bag, too. He was going to tell everyone at that tech conference in Seattle."

Ray Calabrese turned to him. "Where is it now, this speech?"

Jack glanced at his watch. It was a quarter past five. "I put it back where I found it. In a food-services cart, back on board the Claremont. That thing could be airborne at any minute. We're evacing it with the airship again."

Tommy said, "How?"

Peter said, "We're flying it out."

Tommy's eyebrows rose. "I'm sorry. You're flying out the plane Kiki and I climbed out of on Thursday? The one without wings? That's the damnedest thing I ever—"

Ray said, *"There's a—"*

"Dead deer, yeah, yeah." Tommy waved him off.

In a white panel truck two blocks away, Jenna Scott played back the last few seconds of the audio captured by the array of bugs she'd planted in the real estate office. Things were much worse than she previously believed. It was the worst-case scenario.

She reached for her headset and called Tichnor.

Once the encryption kicked in on both sides, she said, "Target A and target B are still alive. And they also know about the asset." That would be Renee Malatesta. "Listen to me: they have our man's name!"

She waited. The line hissed.

"Confirm transmi—"

"I'm here." Barry sounded calm. "This is still fixable. There is a way out. Please hold your position."

"If you see a way out of this, that makes one of us."

"Just . . . Please hold."

L'ENFANT PLAZA

"Spokane International Airport, this is Fallon."

"Eileen? It's Susan Tanaka. Kirk's wife."

The woman on the other line said, "Hi! How are you? Are you in Spokane?"

A third voice rode over her question. "Hey, Eileen?"

"Kirk?"

"Eileen, I'm calling from the Lake Country in Italy. Susan is in D.C. It's a conference call."

"Italy? What in the world?"

Kirk said, "We're calling to ask a huge, huge favor of you."

He and Eileen Fallon had flown together when they were both with United and had become close friends. He had served as best man at her wedding.

"Name it."

"No, no. I mean, it's a *big* favor."

Just a little of the glee left her voice. But her response was, "Bring it."

He said, "Susan?"

Susan took over the narrative. "There's an NTSB Go-Team in Helena, working that—"

"Polestar crash, sure."

"Eileen, I have really, awfully, seriously good reason to know their comms have been compromised. Their computers, too. They're being monitored by someone who doesn't want this investigation to succeed."

She waited. After a few beats, Eileen said, "Go on."

"We keep a supply of NTSB communication gear in about fifty airports around the nation. Spokane is one of them. I need you to get someone, anyone, to fly new comm gear to Helena, as quickly as possible. But here's the thing: I don't want my supervisors in D.C. to know. Our headquarters has been compromised, too. The Go-Team is being screwed with. I need to get them back on their feet before we go global with this."

Susan waited. A couple of thousand miles eastward, Kirk Tanaka did the same.

Eileen said, "We can have your gear there in a half hour."

TWIN PINES

Chief of Police Paul McKinney addressed a crowd of about twenty towns-folk. "Fellas? Everyone? We haven't called for a mandatory evacuation yet but my money says the governor's office is gonna make that call, and soon. If I were you, I'd pack up and get out of town now. These air tankers might turn things around; we'll see. If I'm wrong, you can always come on back home. But what I'm saying is: better safe than sorry."

Everyone flinched as yet another Ilyushin air tanker roared overhead, shrieking toward the wall of fire. The crowd, looking frightened, headed back to their homes or their businesses. The smell of woodsmoke was stronger now, the white haze only about thirty feet over their heads.

Calendar knelt in the hard-packed soil and studied the misshapen bag of flesh that was his soldier, Cates. None of his long bones had survived after the car hit him. Both knees and one elbow were shattered. Calendar's phone vibrated and he flipped it open, kneeling and reaching for the cheap, mass-produced St. Christopher medallion Cates always wore as a good-luck token.

He heard Barry Tichnor's distorted voice: "They have it. The crash investigators. All of it. There's only one play left."

Calendar stood and crossed to the upside-down, daisy-yellow tractor-dozer atop the rented car. He peered into gaps between the metal, circling the ruined vehicles until he spied the severed arm of Dyson, his other soldier.

"Go ahead," Calendar said into the phone.

Dyson's good-luck piece was a shiny, flat river rock, about the size of a quarter, he had picked up in Tikrit years earlier. Calendar would very much have liked to find that little rock and bring it, with the St. Christopher, back to his home in Thailand. He had collected a few such tokens over the years in honor of good soldiers who had fallen.

Barry said, "We have someone, right now, falsifying a suicide note for Renee Malatesta. She'll take all the blame. Surveillance tells us she's still in Helena. Our contact will meet you in the lobby of her hotel, get you the note. Go make it look good."

Calendar's vision was hazy with a red glow that came not from the nearby fire but from synapses popping discordantly inside his head. "No," he said.

After a beat, Barry said, "Say again?"

"No. I've got to finish some business here, first."

Barry Tichnor said, "No! Get to it now. We—"

Calendar broke his cell phone in two, tossed the parts into the wreckage, and turned away.

He knew that Cates, from Alabama, had served with honor as a U.S. Army Ranger and had been awarded three Purple Hearts. He knew that Dyson, a Pennsylvanian, had been a SEAL and left behind a kid sister who waited tables and attended Penn State. He knew that both soldiers had expected to someday die with their boots on. He knew for a fact that Cates and Dyson had been Christians. It's why he'd picked them.

From Calendar's point of view, Barry Tichnor's mission was part and parcel of the war on terrorism. Anything that made America stronger made the terrorists weaker. Anyone who stood in the way of that stood with the terrorists. It was as cut-and-dried as that.

What he did not know was who in this godforsaken town had killed these two good men. He could think of only one way to make sure the right person was punished.

31

JACK GOODSPEED CALLED ONE of his crew at the auto-parts store. Within a minute, Jack had his phone on Speaker and the crew member was reading them the Andrew Malatesta speech.

Ray said, "Deal like that? Could be worth hundreds of millions. That's a motive."

Peter Kim said, "Yes, but we're in the fortunate position of not caring." When others looked at him oddly, he said, "We're crash investigators! We don't care about *why*. We care about *how*. That's all we care about. And right now, we have a potential *how*. That's a win, people."

He turned to the sturdy FBI agent, noting that Ray rarely moved when he didn't need to. "Calabrese. You got yourself proof of a crime. The crash is yours."

Ray looked around the real estate office, sized up the situation. Other members of the Go-Team studied him as well, waiting to see how their lives were about to change.

"Nah." Ray waved it off. "Your crashers don't know me. You keep the baton, let the suits in D.C. decide who's in charge later."

Peter nodded, thinking not how gallant Ray's gesture had been but how surprised he was at the agent's use of logic. "Okay. Lakshmi, arrange to get the rest of the bodies out. Beth?"

"The number of bodies left unautopsied has been whittled down enough so that the county morgue can now handle the remains. I called them. They're expecting us."

"Right. Agent Calabrese, coordinate with the chief of police, please. His name's Paul McKinney. He needs to know about this Calendar and that we suspect Teresa has been murdered. Tell him about the bodies of the hit men. Jack, Reu—"

An air tanker attacked their eardrums yet again. Peter shouting, "What are those?"

Gene said, "Ilyushin Seven-Six. Damn things can carry forty-four tons of water. And they're flying gas cans. Stays in the air for about four thousand miles, even fully loaded. And the reason they're so loud is, they're so low. Taking on water at Helena Regional, I'm guessing, then cruising at eighty, a hundred feet over this town before hitting the fire lines."

Peter blinked at him. "When I said, 'what are those,' I was being rhetorical. Jack, Reuben, Hector: go secure the Claremont. Get it airborne before the fire gets here. Get everything back on board the fuselage."

Peter turned to Beth. "You and Lakshmi supervise moving out the last few bodies. At this stage, preserving all evidence is our number-one task. Everyone good with that?"

Gene Whitney hacked a wet cough. "Anybody know where the babe with the guns went?"

Ray turned. The others, too. Daria had been standing by the door. Now she wasn't.

Peter Kim turned to Tommy. "You go with Calabrese. The police station is crammed with firefighters and emergency-med techs. Have someone check your head."

"Nothing wrong with my head, Petey."

"Hey, you could be bleeding into your brainpan right this second and I'd sleep like a baby tonight. But you croak, and I'll have Duvall in my face again. Which, you know . . . Pass." Peter turned to her. "Kiki. About what I said earlier. Sorry."

She nodded but did not smile.

"Fair nuff." Tommy stepped forward, proffered his hand.

After a moment, Peter took it.

.   .   .

Calendar marched stiff-legged back to his SUV but didn't realize he was doing so. Later on, he wouldn't remember starting the truck, driving across town to the abandoned feed store he'd hidden his gear in. He wouldn't remember climbing out of the cab. One minute he was staring at the yellow dozer, the next at the spiderwebbed store. A Russian-made cargolifter roared overhead but he didn't hear it.

Only three bodies from Polestar Flight 78 flight were left in town. The rest had been taken to Helena for autopsies. While there were more than enough ambulances to get those three bodies out, the traffic jam of evacuees at the town's edge would make it tough to get ambulances into town.

Chief McKinney pleaded his case to the superintendent of the Twin Pines/Martin's Ferry School District, who had finally consented to let Lakshmi transform one of his school buses into a hearse. Again.

Chip Ogilvy waved a finger in Paul McKinney's face. "The students would think it's cool, but if the parents find out, they'll go ape shit. This never gets out, Paul! Never!"

HELENA REGIONAL

Dorina Hande had feared she would never again feel the rush of flying a fighter jet after she'd left the Canadian Air Force.

Following the first Gulf War, she and a contingent of pilots from the air force, within the Défense Nationale, had been attached to the U.S. Fifty-fifth Expeditionary Fighter Squadron, flying out of Incirlik Air Base in Turkey and keeping Saddam's jets out of the Northern No-Fly Zone. She'd been locked on countless times by antiaircraft batteries. Had been fired on by fire-and-forget missiles, only to climb well out of their range.

Good times.

Three weeks after becoming a civilian, Dorina Hande received a flyer in the mail about a career as an air-tanker pilot. She hadn't been hopeful, but when she shown up at the airport outside Vancouver and taken her first look at the mammoth Ilyushin Il-76, with its 165-feet wingspan, it had been love at first sight.

She was as happy as she'd been over the sands of Iraq, only now she slept in her own bed at night with her partner of seventeen years and two Labrador retrievers.

The radio embedded in her Mickey Mouse ears crackled. "Hotel Juliet One One Three, you are filled and ready to fly."

She saw the water truck pulling away from her Ilyushin. She had more than forty-four tons of water, and she had a map with highlighted coordinates.

"Ah, roger that, Helena Regional. Be back soon. Over."

"Runway Five-Two-Three is yours, One One Three. Go get 'em. Over."

She peered out her windshield, and back over her left shoulder, as three more converted Ilyushins lined up behind her, ready to sprint.

Police Chief McKinney had his hands full with the slow-going evacuation of his town. Learning about the silver-haired assassin, Calendar, didn't improve his mood much. He was equally unhappy to learn about the two killers and the overturned dozer. He wasn't all that thrilled that Daria Gibron with her twin hand-cannons was doing a road-show version of *Tomb Raider* and nobody knew where she was.

He stood with Ray Calabrese in the bustling police station, which was serving as the temporary HQ for the state firefighting team. Kiki Duvall had led Tommy a few feet away to find a medic.

Paul McKinney said, "I'm sorry, you said this woman is Israeli intelligence?"

Ray said, "Not anymore."

"So she's what, again? ATF?"

"Not really, no."

"FBI?"

"Uh-uh."

"Then what?"

"Utility infielder."

McKinney grunted. "Great." He went to put out the all-points bulletin on Calendar. Not that his handful of police officers weren't already up to their eyeballs in alligators.

Tommy was getting his vision checked by an EMT-3. Kiki had hoisted herself up onto a counter in the police station to take pressure off her leg. She nudged Ray's arm when he approached. "Are you all right?"

"What do you mean?"

She smiled. "Raymond . . . ?"

He shot her a sheepish grin. "I'm okay. Rattled, seeing her. But also . . . I was worried about her soul. ATF's got her doing some fucked-up shit down in Mexico. Coming back here, bird-dogging you and Texas. It's a relief. It means she's still in there somewhere."

HELENA

Renee Malatesta had spent hours watching local television newsfeeds, describing the oncoming forest fire that was threatening the town of Twin Pines.

Finally, she took a hit of rum, washed her face, and asked the front desk to call her a cab.

When it arrived, she climbed into the back. "Take me to Twin Pines, please."

"It'll be expen—" The diver was cut off when she stuck three fifties through the Plexiglas screen.

Renee knew this little town. She'd been taken there in a coach to see the body of Andrew. Which had transformed into something rich and strange. The bodies of Christian and Vejay, too, and they were her fault every bit as much as Andrew's body was.

As far as she knew, this was Andrew's last resting place. As far as she knew, this was where the investigators were, too. The ones who sought the truth about Andrew's death.

TWIN PINES

Jack, Hector, and Reuben got to the auto-parts-storage facility on the eastern edge of Twin Pines and were surprised to see that Ginger LaFrance and Casper the Friendly Airship had already raised the Claremont two feet off the ground. The smoke was thicker out here.

"That fire's coming awfully fast," Ginger said. She'd added a Jack Daniel's baseball cap to her ensemble. "I made the call to get her airborne. I hope—"

"No, good call. Hey, who has this Malatesta dude's speech?"

One of Jack's guys raised his hand.

A be-on-the-lookout bulletin went out for Calendar, but, with police units helping with the traffic logjam or escorting fire equipment, nobody was honestly looking for him.

Ironically, Calendar pulled into an alley not a full block from the police station.

He walked to the back of the vehicle and opened the hatch. He reached in and pulled forward a charcoal-gray box, opened it to reveal a nest of black foam rubber and a shoulder-mounted launch tube.

Emotionless, he pulled out the pieces of the launcher and assembled it.

Calendar reached back into the SUV and pulled a second, identical box closer to him, just as a Twin Pines cop passed the entrance to the alley, turned, and noticed him.

"Hey! You!" the cop shouted. He began jogging down the alley, reaching for his service revolver, unhooking the holster flap.

Calendar drew his silenced HK .45 and put a bullet through the officer's chest before the officer's hand got anywhere near his pistol grip. The officer fell straight back, arms and legs akimbo, looking like he was trying to make a snow angel in the middle of the pavement in August.

Calendar watched him for a while, cocked his head a little. He holstered his weapon, walked down the alley, and went to his haunches at the officer's side.

The wound pulsed a deep red. The cop's mouth opened and closed silently. His right lung had been destroyed and blood seeped into his airway. His eyes were wide, wild.

"I hate this town." Calendar spoke softly. He reached down, unpinned the cop's slightly crooked, five-pointed badge, and repositioned it so that the top point of the star pointed straight up, relative to his torso. It was a small detail, but a good microcosm for Calendar's perspective of Twin Pines.

"This town is weak and falling apart," he explained. "Your mayor is a drunk. Two good, Christian soldiers, both real-life war heroes, were murdered in such a way that they won't get an open casket. My good friend Dyson, I doubt they'll find enough of him to even cremate. And all because we came to this town."

The officer turned his wide eyes toward the man speaking to him, although it was unclear if he understood the words.

"This town is keeping me from making sure enemies don't have weapons they should not have. This town reeks of death and decay."

Calendar spoke softly and slowly, as if instructing a child. He brushed dandruff off the officer's shoulder. "We never did what we did for the media elite or the fat cats on Wall Street or the Gomorrah-corrupt administrations that come and go. No, we fought for hometown America. For places like this. But . . . ?"

Calendar glanced around, sighed. "I hate this town so very much. I hate that this may be the future of the American heartland. Killing you won't end the tumor in America's soul. But, Officer? It's a start."

The officer died, his last pink-bubbled breath hissing free, eyes fixed.

Calendar stood, returned to the prototype pulse weapon. He opened the second box in the back of the SUV. It, too, was filled with black foam rubber. The rubber had been drilled with six cylindrical holes.

One of the holes was empty.

The other five were not. They contained the beta-tested electromagnetic weapons Barry Tichnor's R&D boys had whipped up from Andrew Malatesta's designs.

They looked like gigantic Good & Plenty candies, Calendar thought. Or suppositories from hell. Long and convex at both ends, they were five inches in diameter and color coded, red end forward, black end backward. Stenciled on the side was THIS END FORWARD.

He removed one, hefted it in his hands. He could feel, more than hear, liquids slosh inside the front and hind ends of the projectile. It contained two separate sections. The chemicals within were foreign to Calendar but he knew that when they intermixed, they created an electromagnetic pulse with a range of only eighty meters.

The equivalent of a micronuclear bomb. Enough energy to stop all electric impulses, but over such a remarkably small radius.

He gently slid the projectile into the launch tube, the same way one loads a rocket-propelled grenade. The launch tube was shoulder-mounted with a sighting system to peer through.

Calendar walked out into the street, stepping over the dead body of the officer. The street was empty, thanks to the evacuation. He walked to a thrift store, kicked in the door, searched around until he found stairs, then climbed to the second floor. He found a ladder retracted into the ceiling, pulled it down, and climbed up onto the roof.

There, he hefted the launch tube to his shoulder.

A phalanx of four Russian-made air tankers flew low toward downtown Twin Pines from the west.

Calendar put his eye to the crosshairs of the site. With no emotion whatsoever, he said, "I truly hate this town."

32

EIGHTY FEET OVER TWIN Pines, Dorina Hande heard a thump through the aluminum skin of her Ilyushin. A second later, all power on the flight deck died.

The four Soloviev D-30KP turbofan engines flamed out.

"Hey. No. What the heck . . ." She toggled the ignition switch. She checked the A/C backup battery. Nothing.

"Helena Regional! Mayday! This is Hotel Juliet One One Three, declaring an emergency! Over!"

But she got no squelch back. The radio was as dead as everything else.

The insanely heavy tanker nosed over, heading for downtown Twin Pines. Dorina planted her boots on the deck and hauled on the yoke for all she was worth.

An image snatched for her attention, at the very corner of her eye. She glanced over.

It was Hotel Juliet 114. It, too, was falling from the sky.

The EMT told Tommy, "You're fine, sir. Try to get some—"

The young paramedic stopped talking as yet another roaring jet cruised over the town. People were getting used to it, at least.

Only this time, instead of diminishing along a Doppler curve, the roaring just . . . stopped.

Everyone in the police station quit talking, glancing around, trying to pinpoint how and why this flyover sounded different. They could hear the drone of another jet, not too far off, getting close, and it, too . . .

. . . stopped.

Tommy's eyes bulged. "Holy fucking shit! I've heard this before!"

He sprinted for the front door, Ray Calabrese right on his ass, drawing his service weapon.

Out on the street, Tommy got five paces and staggered to a halt. Three blocks to the west, a twenty-foot-tall, four-jet cargolifter with silent engines sank below the town's roofline, falling fast, clipping power lines and, a second later, smashing into the U-Store-It facility behind Stan's Meat Market.

It was two blocks to the north and two blocks to the west but the sound of the crash was horrifyingly loud. Tommy went to one knee, hands over his ears. Kiki was out now, mouth agape, followed by police officers and state firefighters.

Ray shouted, "Look!" and pointed.

Another Ilyushin, six blocks away, sank out of sight and, a moment later, a gusher of dust and smoke and flames rushed into the sky.

From the direction of the first crash, a rumbling force field of dust and debris roared into the air, a psychedelic hurricane of destruction bearing down First Street toward the police station. Tommy grabbed Kiki and yanked her to the ground, lying atop her (yet again) as the debris field hit them like a sleet storm.

Ray held his ground. Others fell. The crook of his elbow over his eyes and a hand over his mouth, Ray squinted as the maelstrom rushed by.

And as it passed them, Kiki's supersensitive hearing picked up another roar.

"Tommy!" she shouted.

Forty-four tons of water cascaded down First Street toward them.

Half the bodies in the morgue had been transferred from Stan's Meats to a school bus when Hotel Juliet 113 hit the U-Store-It across the alley. The explosion toppled the bus and sent it sliding into an empty engraver's office. A fireball rose from the doomed cargolifter.

Its port wing sheared off the roof and most of the second floor of Stan's Meats, sending walls, ceilings, floors, and tons of masonry into the first floor.

Where Beth Mancini and Lakshmi Jain were.

The wall of water was six feet high and traveling at forty miles per hour when it hit the police and firefighters. Tommy, on the ground, locked his arms around Kiki's chest and wrapped his legs around hers as they were swept down First Street.

Ray Calabrese was thrown back into the plate-glass window of the police station. It shattered from the impact.

As he lost consciousness, a third, powerless Ilyushin swept down from above, not thirty feet over their heads, gliding silently, straight toward the auto-parts shop.

Jack Goodspeed, outside in the fenced-off storage yard, saw the first two jets augur into the town, then saw the third vectoring his way, and the fourth lose power and nose over.

He spun to Ginger LaFrance and shouted, "Go! Go! Get the fuselage outta here!"

Ginger hit the toggle and Casper began pivoting counterclockwise. She pushed the joystick and the rear-facing rotors hummed to life.

The Claremont began moving at one mile per hour.

Ginger hit the up-thrusters on the airship, but too late. The Claremont was only four feet off the ground when it bumped into the Cyclone fence. It sat there for a moment. Then, with a sickening groan, the entire south-side fence keeled over.

The whalelike airship and the cadaverous fuselage below it began drifting away.

Just then, Hotel Juliet 112 nosed into the street, fuel igniting a fireball thirty yards wide. The front wall of the auto-parts shop crumbled inward, the roof collapsing.

After the fireball came the tail section, pinwheeling down the street, smashing cars and pickups.

Jack and Ginger, in the back, were buffered from the explosion. They watched, stunned, as the empennage danced down the street, an alien child's game of jacks.

After that came the forty-four-ton wall of water.

From his rooftop, Calendar watched as a fourth Ilyushin zoomed into the town of Twin Pines.

He walked to the edge of the roof, peered down at the blocks of utter devastation.

"Good," he said. "That's better."

Movement caught his eye. It was the airship. And the wingless cadaver of Flight 78.

They were on the move.

In the real estate office, Gene Whitney saw the water a half block away. He grabbed Peter Kim by the arm and literally carried him into the break room, shouting, *"Gogogogogogogogo!"*

The five-foot tsunami smashed the office's windows and ripped out the door, the waves crash-banging together, chopping the hell out of the outer office.

The two crashers were swept off their feet and deluged.

L'ENFANT PLAZA

It was just past 7:30 P.M. when Susan Tanaka took the elevator to the basement mainframe room. She dashed down the hall and swiped her ID card to gain entrance.

"How is it you can run in stilettos?" Dmitri asked, but his smile faltered as he saw the look on Susan's face.

"The eleven nodes," she said. "The computers monitoring the crash. Nine of them just went dead."

Dmitri nudged himself across the room, bent at the waist, and tapped quickly on his keyboard.

"I am seeing this, too. What in hell?"

"I just tried connecting to Beth's comm unit. It's dead. I tried her cell phone, too. No good."

Dmitri said, *"Bozhe moi."*

TWIN PINES

At Stan's Meats, Beth Mancini tried to rise, keening in pain. She lay on her back. Parts of her body worked and others didn't. She was choking on smoke and dust, and her eyes stung. Coughing felt like it was burning her lungs.

She grunted in pain, found a chunk of masonry that was stable enough to use as leverage, pulled herself up to a sitting position.

As a little of the dust cleared, Beth saw that a piece of rebar had pierced her right thigh and protruded about eight inches in both directions.

She was bleeding badly.

She could not see Lakshmi Jain.

Twin Pines had a nice little park at the end of First Street, with a softly rising, grassy hill, perfect for putting out a blanket and setting up a picnic. The chamber of commerce had hosted live music every Wednesday night, June through August, back before the lumber industry had collapsed. There was even a white-painted bandstand with red, white, and blue bunting.

It was the grassy park that saved Kiki and Tommy; they rolled for close to eighty yards with the horrifying torrent of water, but more than half of that had been over grass in a nice little park at the end of First Street, not asphalt.

Tommy never let go of Kiki—not like the last time, on board the Claremont. When Kiki's arm hit a vertical railing of the park's bandstand, she held on fiercely as the onslaught passed them by.

Soaked, exhausted, coughing up water, they lay on the grass. Tommy reached out, grasped her hand. Kiki squeezed back for all she was worth.

In the yard of the auto-parts store, the water wall hefted Jack off his feet and carried him, at close to fifty miles per hour, into a stack of truck fenders, which toppled under his mass and the blast of water. He barked in pain, getting a mouthful of water for his trouble. His head caromed off a chrome trailer hitch and he lost consciousness.

The same watery onslaught drove an axle from a 1972 Chrysler Town and Country station wagon through the abdomen of Ginger LaFrance. She was dead before she hit the ground.

Her remote-control box shorted and died upon impact with the water.

Casper the Friendly Airship knew none of this. It just crept slowly to the southwest, hitting about three miles an hour now.

Unconscious on his pile of fenders, Jack did not see the twenty-one thousand gallons of jet fuel from Hotel Juliet 112 turn the auto-parts store into an inferno.

Ray Calabrese lay, spread-eagled, on Chief McKinney's desk. The water had shoved him through the plate-glass window etched with the symbol of the Twin Pines Police Department. He was plastered with water and the left side of his face and neck were tacky with blood. A jagged shard of window glass had sliced a four-inch gouge from his ear to his chin line.

He moaned, eyes fluttering.

Inside the auto-parts store, Hector Villareal threw a faux-fur seat cover over himself and dashed through a wall of flames, singeing his lungs. He fell to the poured-concrete floor, hacking, reaching out and turning Reuben Chaykin over onto his back.

Reuben's eyes were open, his mouth agape, a wound the size of his fist where his heart should have been.

Eyes watering from smoke and sorrow, Hector covered himself in the fur seat cover, rose, and sprinted to the back door of the shop. His right pant leg caught fire. He hit the door so hard that it sprang off its hinges and turned into a sled, gliding on the four inches of water that remained on the ground, carrying Hector away from the slaughterhouse.

Kiki's broken rib punished her with every breath. She'd reopened her leg wound, too. A rivulet of blood ran the length of her arm and she hissed as she pulled a rusty three-inch nail out of her shoulder.

Tommy tried to stand, failed, and instead knelt, leaning against the bandstand, hacking up water. "You . . . okay . . . ?"

She nodded, soaked red hair plastered to her face and skull.

"Calendar," she wheezed. "Pulse . . . weapon."

"Yeah." Tommy picked a Montana State University T-shirt off the ground, wrung it out, knelt, and dabbed at Kiki's shoulder wound.

"We gotta find the others . . . see who lived."

Kiki said, "Look," and jutted her chin to the south.

Tommy turned. The white airship floated out of town, the fuselage of the Claremont just barely visible from their hillock.

"They . . . got it out." He coughed again. "Out-freakin'-standing."

Daria Gibron waited out the deluge in her Ford Escort, which the water had shoved into the storefront of a yarn-and-beads shop.

When the storm passed, she kicked out the remains of the windshield that Cates had shot out and climbed out. A little burble of a laugh escaped her lips. She couldn't help it.

She grabbed her backpack and splashed out into the street.

The same paramedic who had checked Tommy's concussion cleaned Ray's facial wound, applied sixteen stitches, cleaned it all again, and adhered a wide, white bandage to it. "There. Just sit back and relax."

Ray checked that he still had his Glock. "Tank you," he said without moving his jaw. He stood.

"Hey, man. Seriously. You can't—"

Ray said, "'Kay," through clenched teeth and splashed out into First Street.

HELENA

They directed the call to Sergeant Major Kinnison, the highest-ranking noncom on duty with the Montana Army National Guard. A solid cube of a man, he whisked off his cap and picked up the receiver in the Emergency Protocol Communications Center. "Say again, ma'am?"

"My name is Susan Tanaka. I am a chief investigator for the National Transportation Safety Board. I am calling from our headquarters in Washington, D.C. We have a team investigating Thursday's crash of a Claremont aircraft near the town of Twin Pines, Montana. That team has come under hostile assault."

Kinnison's bushy eyebrows rose. "Hostile assault?"

He could hear computer keys clacking in the background. "You have in your possession a phalanx of Chinook helicopters. I want two of them airborne in five minutes, en route to Twin Pines. I want someone to call me back at this number in three minutes with a status update."

Kinnison looked at his watch. "I'm not sure I—"

The woman said, "Do it!"

Kinnison gulped. "Yes, ma'am!"

TWIN PINES

Beth Mancini removed her belt, lashed it around her right thigh, and cinched it tight, wincing. The dust had settled. She glanced around, saw a four-foot length of copper pipe. She scooted her butt to the right, reached out as far as she could, fingertips scraping the pipe. It rolled a little. She pulled it her way.

Grunting in pain, she levered herself up onto the bit of masonry, then used the copper pipe to stand on her left leg.

Using the pipe as a cane, she dragged her right leg and its length of rebar after her. A step at a time. She coughed. She touched the top of her head, her fingers coming back wet with blood. She had more injuries than she'd realized, but the twenty inches of rebar in her thigh was the big problem.

She took a fifth step, a sixth. Her copper cane was working. She neared the door to the street. And as she looked down, careful to find a place to set her pipe cane, she saw the remains of Lakshmi Jain. A good portion of her skull was missing.

Beth sobbed. She felt guilty that her first emotion had been self-pity: *I'd hoped Lakshmi would rescue me!* She wiped her eyes with her sooty sleeve, opened the door, and limped out onto the three stairs and the street.

"I know you!"

Daria Gibron stopped and turned at the sound of a deep, male voice.

Calendar stood on a second-story balcony of a building, elbows on the railing, one foot up. He shouted down, "We've met."

She waggled her fingers at him. "You're Calendar."

"You're DEA. No . . . ATF. You used to work with Israeli intelligence."

She smiled sweetly and waved. "Hallo. I killed your boys."

The knowing smile on Calendar's face turned chalky and brittle. "Those were good men."

She grunted a laugh. "It was not difficult."

His fists tightened on the railing. "Who's paying you? Who's targeting my op?"

"Today, it's— *Boo!*"

The shout and her abracadabra gesture startled Calendar enough that he flinched. And in that instant, she ghosted. The spot where Daria had stood, below his window, was, strictly speaking, Daria-less.

He blinked. He set aside the rocket-launch tube and drew his Heckler & Koch .45 auto, unscrewing the silencer.

Downstairs, in the same building, Daria drew her massive, matte-finished Browning Hi Power autos out of her thigh holsters. Their .45-caliber bullets could stop a Buick.

She grinned, canine teeth exposed, eyes twinkling.

Tommy and Kiki trudged back up First Street, surveying the complete devastation. No storefront was intact, no ground-floor window unshattered. Smoke roiled from four distinct fires throughout the small downtown area; three to the east of them, one to the west.

A block from the police station they saw Ray Calabrese standing in the middle of the street. His shoulders dropped as he spotted them. He waved, then hunched over, hands on his knees, barely staying upright.

Behind Ray, a Sikorsky helicopter touched down.

Gene Whitney said, "Would you stay still? Okay, on three."

Peter Kim nodded. One-half of a pair of scissors—half the handle and half the cutting surface—had jammed a good four inches of itself into his right calf. He lay in a pinkish puddle of blood and water on the floor of the real estate office's break room, his ever-neat suit a limp rag. Gene knelt by his side, a hand on the scissor, the other on Peter's knee.

"Okay. One. Two—"

He yanked it out. Peter barking, "Aaagh! God! Damn!"

Gene wrapped a dish towel around the wound, cinched it tight. Peter growling, "What the hell happened to *three*?"

"Sorry. C'mon." He stood, offered a hand. Peter hopped up onto his good leg, an arm over Gene's shoulders.

"Do we know what happened?"

"I think this silver-haired guy Tomzak was telling us about? Calendar? I think he brought down one of the air tankers."

Peter thought about it. "Explains the flood. Son of a bitch."

They trudged out into the street.

Peter and Gene found Beth a few minutes later, on her pipe crutch, a length of rebar stabbed through her right thigh. Peter muttered, "Thank God I drew the scissors."

They got her seated on an upside-down white plastic pail that had washed out into the street. Gene confirmed that the belt around her thigh had lessened the bleeding.

Peter spotted an overturned Honda, its hood detached and lying on the sidewalk. "Hey. We could rig a . . . There's a word for it. Thing to drag behind us, like a gurney without wheels."

Beth said, "Peter? Lakshmi. She's . . ." Tears spilled out onto her cheeks.

Standing behind her, Peter wrapped his arms around her shoulders. Beth leaned her head back against his stomach and sobbed.

Hector Villareal slapped Jack Goodspeed softly on the cheek. "Hey. You in there?"

Jack's eyes fluttered open. "What . . . Where are we?"

"In Montana. I think one of the firefighting jets must have crashed. Here." He helped Jack sit up.

Jack moaned, "No, man. They *all* crashed."

"For real? Holy mother of God."

Jack felt the goose egg on the back of his head, winced. "You okay?"

"Burns." Hector held up his left hand; it was lobster red. "Reuben's dead."

"Ah, God."

"And, Jack? Where's our fuselage?"

Ray Calabrese tried to hug Kiki but the hug turned into his keeling over, Kiki and Tommy helping the big man to sit on the pavement in the middle of the wet street.

Tommy dug through his pockets for his ever-present penlight, then remembered he'd lost it during the crash. The first crash, a thousand years ago. He stared into Ray's eyes.

"I ain't seeing any concussion. But I'm betting you lost a hell of a lot of blood. That accounts for the dizziness."

Ray spoke through clenched teeth. "Dis sucks."

"I hear you. It was the pulse weapon. Calendar brought down all four of the tankers. The police are . . . I don't know. Drowned or busy. We gotta find him."

"I'll get him," Ray said.

Kiki said, "No way. Not in your condition."

Ray's eyes seethed with anger but he also came close to passing out.

A man with a bulging, leather shoulder pack approached from the Sikorsky that had just landed. "Excuse me? What the hell happened here?"

Kiki said, "It's a long story."

"Okay. Um, is there a Tomzak here?"

The three friends glanced at one another. Tommy raised his hand. "Yeah?"

"I'm assigned to the Emergency Response Unit at Spokane International Airport. I'm supposed to give you this."

He slid his pack off his shoulder and opened it. Tommy reached in and pulled out an NTSB comm unit.

"Some woman named, um, Tanaka, called my boss."

As more survivors arrived at city hall and the police station, Kiki and Tommy helped Ray Calabrese to his feet, escorted him back into the police station and down onto the swamped floor, his back against the wall.

Kiki adjusted her voice wand and said, "We got them. We love you."

In her ear, Susan Tanaka said, "I assume it's bad."

Kiki shook water off her boot and looked out at the town's former library, which was completely engulfed in engine-fuel-fed flames. "It's Old Testament bad. The EMP weapon is for real. This assassin just crashed four water-filled air tankers into the town!"

Susan said, "Oh, Lord! Okay, the Montana National Guard is en route. Good luck."

Tommy sat on the floor next to Ray, both their backs against the wall. "Damn. This thing went way south."

Ray actually laughed a little, which hurt his cheek. "Here," he said, unsnapping his holster and drawing his Glock semiauto. He handed it butt-first to Tommy.

"You expect me to carry a gun?"

Ray snorted. "Not you. Her." He nodded to Kiki. "Go."

"'Kay." Tommy hoisted himself up, squeezed Ray's shoulder. "Hang tight, New York. We'll try to find Daria. She'll—"

They heard the report of a deep, distant gunshot.

Without moving his jaw, Ray said, "Dat's her."

33

THE ASSOCIATED PRESS QUICKLY picked up the *Post*'s story on Andrew Malatesta and had it out on its wire service before 6:00 P.M. mountain time. *The New York Times* had it next at 6:05. CNN and MSNBC picked it up next and quoted directly from the story carrying Amy Dreyfus's byline.

Amy's cell phone chirped. It was a producer for National Public Radio's *All Things Considered*.

HALCYON/DETWEILER HEADQUARTERS

Admiral Gaelen Parks of the Military Liaison Division shredded files in his fifth-floor office.

Two stories below him, in the Aircraft Division's inner offices, Liz Proctor's people used degaussing magnets to obliterate data on hard drives.

HALCYON/DETWEILER RESEARCH DIVISION, VIRGINIA

Barry Tichnor was packing his cheap, Naugahyde briefcase with the evidence that would back up Parks's and Proctor's involvement in the Infrastructure Subcommittee on Deferred Maintenance, as well as the field test of the Malatesta device.

TWIN PINES

Daria dropped her backpack at the front door of the thrift shop and realized she had the place to herself. She sprinted left, boot soles wet and squeaking; nothing she could do about that. The building had been a grocery store in another life and was one giant room, the far wall wired for refrigerated cases, a meat case at the western wall with glass fronts canted forty-five degrees off horizontal. Most of the room was filled with eight-foot-high metal shelves that ran the length of the room. The shelves were categorized by the items for sale there: women's clothes, men's clothes, children's clothes, baby clothing; home appliances, toys, lawn and garden equipment.

The front window had shattered when the belly of Hotel Juliet 114 exploded, releasing its deadly cargo. Daria dashed down an aisle nearest the front of the store and fell to her knees, hydroplaning on the water for the last six feet, spinning a little, as she heard Calendar descend the stairs. He might not have abandoned whatever rocket-propelled weapon he'd used against the four airplanes, she realized. The Brownings are massive handguns but she was underarmed for a firefight against rockets.

"You're in here!" Calendar's voice echoed off the cinder-block walls. "You were using the call sign Argent, that time in Amsterdam."

She knelt behind a tall rack of used, nicked exercise equipment, ranging from free weights to complicated contraptions with wires and pulleys. "This isn't like you," she yelled. "Killing Americans."

"I killed as few as possible. There's a war on, Argent. Americans have forgotten what it means to sacrifice. That's what I like about you Israelis. You've lived in wartime for decades. You understand sacrifice."

Daria holstered her weapons. She put her hands on the wet floor and lowered her head until her ear felt the water. She peered under her row of shelves, looking for his boots.

She didn't see them but saw a puddle of water ripple. She stood quickly, ignored the cold water that drizzled down the back of her tank top. She drew one of the Browning hand-cannons, guessed where he was, aimed at the rack of exercise gloves and sweatbands, and fired.

The entire rack, twenty-five feet long, wobbled under the impact. The bullet tore a gouge through the thin sheet metal, ripped through the next aisle over, and the next after that.

Calendar neither grunted nor dropped his weapon, so she assumed she hadn't hit him. She turned and ran full speed to the end of the aisle. She fell to her haunches and risked a quick glance around the end.

Calendar had had a fifty-fifty chance of guessing which end she'd run to and he'd guessed right. But he was aiming his HK .45 five and a half feet up. By the time he lowered his aim, Daria had scrambled back, rising to her feet. His .45 slug caromed off the floor, throwing up a dust storm of tile and plaster and the underlying wooden slats.

Good, she thought. *No rockets.*

She danced backward, gun aimed the way she'd come. Calendar never peeked around the corner.

"Who's paying you?" Calendar barked. "Why did you kill my men?"

Daria laughed. "You should not have tried to kill my friends."

"Is that what this is about? You're fighting over friendship?" She couldn't tell where he was but he sounded incredulous. It bothered her that he knew where she was.

"Love and hate are the only acceptable reasons to kill."

She heard him grunt and, a second later, the tall row of metal shelves wobbled badly as if from a terrific impact. The entire thing threatened to topple over onto her. Exercise equipment tumbled to the floor. Shirts and sweats and yoga mats fell on her head. A ten-pound dumbbell dinged off her knee and, as her leg gave out in pain, jump ropes entwined themselves around her ankles.

If she had been Calendar, she would have gone back to the hole she had first blown in the shelves, about halfway to either end, to peer through to catch a glimpse of the opponent. Down on one knee, Daria glanced around, located that bullet hole again and shot at the same place.

This time she definitely heard him stutter-step away. Again, she doubted she'd hit him.

She rose, left leg numb, and tried the same trick. She fired blindly into the metal shelf, hoping she could keep him moving, keep him on the defensive.

She heard a splash, thought maybe he'd fallen. It had come from her right; she limped to her left. The leg felt bad but only because the dumbbell had clipped the small, protruding bone on the outside of her knee. Nothing felt broken. Still, her mobility was a new problem.

"Is that a Browning?" He sounded farther away, but his voice echoed madly off the walls. "I've never used one."

"Would you like to try one?"

"That's very collegial of you. Aren't they heavy?"

Daria sank to her good knee. "Only if you're weak." She'd initially glanced under the shelf to find Calendar's boots. Now she set the Browning on the floor, muzzle facing the shelf, held it firmly, and fired. She turned it five degrees and fired again. Again. Again, like a lawn sprinkler, covering a prescribed arc. She heard clanging on the other side, sensed movement. She was keeping him on defense.

A new voice sounded, seemingly coming from the broken window. "You! Hey, stop!"

Daria recognized the voice: Kiki Duvall.

Calendar's .45 barked and a bullet pinged off the wall, over by Kiki. Daria heard a man spit out, "Shit!" Then new gunfire; someone shooting at Calendar.

Daria aimed the Browning at the rack of exercise equipment, three feet off the floor, and blasted another hole in it. The Browning was empty. Ambidextrous, she holstered the first weapon and drew the second simultaneously, firing off two more shots through the thin metal cabinet.

She recognized the next sound: a boot hitting a door, the door ricocheting off a brick wall. All coming from the back of the store. Calendar, she thought, knew the weakness of a crossfire position. He had retreated.

Daria stood, untangling herself from the jump ropes. "Kiki? Don't fire. Is me."

Kiki and Tommy entered the thrift store, Tommy calling out, "*Dee!* You okay?"

She limped over to them. Kiki said, "I saw him. Silver-Hair! I think he—"

Daria scooped up her backpack. "He's gone. " She drew her first gun, depressed the release. She shoved a new magazine into the handle before the first magazine hit the floor. Her almond eyes narrowed as she noted Kiki's Glock. The long-legged redhead with the funny-looking pigtails held it firmly in both hands, her boots shoulder-width apart, and she looked professional as hell. Daria had not realized Kiki had military training, but it appeared that she had. "Is that Ray's?"

"Yes. He's banged up and lost some blood but he's going to be fine. The police have their hands full with the fires and the floods. We're trying to stop Calendar."

"You two?" Now it was Daria who sounded incredulous.

Tommy nodded. "Why not? Kiki's armed and I'm good-looking. You're limping?"

Daria flexed her knee and felt it twinge, but not much. "I'm fine."

Kiki peered out through the broken window at the sodden, shattered storefronts. "This makes no sense. The man's an assassin. He must have specific targets. Why drown an entire town?"

Daria rooted through her backpack, mentally noting her weapons and supplies. "No, you understand him well. He would have a specific target. In this case: me."

The other two glanced at each other. When Daria looked up, she seemed neither angry nor fearful. Just patient.

"Someone in this town killed his two men. Calendar is the psychopath, yes? But also the good solder. And officer. His men were killed in such a way that their bodies weren't just wounded, they were slaughtered. Plus, they were on a bloodletting mission on American soil, so none of his old contacts, his old cohorts, can do a thing to help. He wanted revenge and he didn't know upon whom. He punished Twin Pines."

After a chilling beat, Tommy said, "That there's a pretty spooky world you live in."

Daria smiled, and the smile was somewhere between charming and predatory. "I find it easier if you categorize it into Good Guys and Bad Guys."

Tommy said, "And you are . . . ?"

"Today?"

He nodded.

"Good Guy."

Kiki wasn't all that sure she agreed. "Okay. Now Calendar knows you killed his men?"

"He does."

"So you're his primary target?"

Daria perched on the edge of a product-display table and rubbed her bruised knee. "That's the line between madman and good soldier. He's not so crazy that he let himself stay in a pincer between our guns. He still possesses self-preservation instincts. Also, he and I work in a very small world. If he wants me dead, he can track me down in six months or a year. No, I think he . . . how do you say, slides back. Chutes and Snakes, yes?"

Tommy said, "Chutes and Ladders, and I follow you, but I got a better metaphor. In video games, you get boxed down or killed, you hit Reset. He went full-on nut-job after finding his guys killed. He needs to find out whodunit. That accomplished, he goes back to the plan."

Kiki said, "The speech. The saddlebag. He's going back to the auto-parts store?"

"No. Petey ordered the guys on the structure team to load everything back on board the Claremont fuselage and to get it outta harm's way. Again. And we saw the fuselage floating to never-never land after the flood. We find the Claremont, we find the speech. We find the speech, maybe we find the silver-haired prick."

Kiki turned to Daria. "If we find a car that's right-side up, can you hotwire it?"

"I could do that at age five." She laughed and limped out into the street.

The three of them sloshed out onto the soggy streets, looking for a car that was right-side up. Before they could, Kiki pointed to the southwest. "The airship!"

It hung, unmoving, maybe five blocks from their position. At least it seemed unmoving. As they watched, the rear end of the blimp swung in their direction, paused, then swung back.

"The fuselage," Tommy said. "It's stuck on something. C'mon."

Daria slung her backpack. "There are fires between us and the aircraft."

"Yeah, but the airship's engines are still working. If it works the Claremont free, this chase'll get a lot more complicated."

Daria spotted an overturned white van and deftly scrambled up on its side. She scanned the battle-scarred street in both directions, then the columns of oily black smoke. Three of the Ilyushins had crashed on the west end of the town, with a fourth to the east, closer to the forest fire. From her perspective, every direction looked perilous.

"We head south, toward the edge of town. That should keep us well away from the fires."

Kiki said, "Will Calendar pick the same route?"

"No. He's less sane than I. He'll move between those two fires." She pointed to two of the three raging hot spots that demarcated the western portion of the town.

Tommy said, "How much less sane?"

Daria turned and gave him a sloe-gin smile. Then she seemed to spot something at her feet. She frowned.

"You okay?" Tommy called up.

"Microwave transceiver. This is a surveillance truck."

As she climbed down, Tommy tried the back door and it fell open.

Sure enough, it was crammed with surveillance equipment. Plus a little blood.

"It wasn't empty when it fell over," Tommy said, and glanced around the soggy street, looking for a survivor. Kiki ducked into the van. Daria hopped down onto the street.

"Tommy?" She picked up a flash drive, one of several stuffed into USB ports. MANCINI was written on the side. She grabbed another: KITCHEN.

Tommy picked up a sodden sweater. It belonged to a woman.

"Shit. Looks like Calendar had more backup than them two guys Daria capped. This is how they kept ahead of Peter's crashers. He didn't just have their comms, he musta had their headquarters, too. Sumbitch."

Daria eyed the smoke columns again. "Come," she said, and started south. The crashers exited the van and followed her.

Half a block away, Jenna Scott watched the three who had discovered her surveillance van. She used one hand to unbutton her overshirt and shrugged out of it. When the van toppled, one of the surveillance racks had gouged a nasty-looking tear in her left shoulder. She used her sleeve to wipe blood away and realized it was a flesh wound, the muscle beneath unscathed.

She used a pocketknife to rip the shirtsleeve and turn it into a fair-to-passing bandage, using her right hand and teeth. She adjusted her camisole, checked to make sure her Sten submachine pistol was fully loaded. She'd jammed a second magazine into the back pocket of her jeans. She stepped out into the now-deserted street and looked around at the carnage.

She spotted the hovering airship. That would be Calendar's target. No question. Same for the crash investigators.

Jenna couldn't believe that the psychotic mercenary had actually used the EMP device on four firefighting planes. No one could have predicted he would act so insanely. Oh, sure. The Agency more or less understood that sweaty dynamite lined the inside of his brainpan. The Agency rolled the dice that Calendar could keep his psychosis in check. After all, he'd been a reliable freelancer for close to a decade.

Clearly, things had changed.

That left Jenna a couple of missions. First and foremost, make sure Calendar was good and dead, and could never tell anyone who he freelanced for. And second, find Andrew Malatesta's saddlebag.

CHANTILLY, VIRGINIA

Barry Tichnor had backed up files of his communications with the Infra-structure Committee on Deferred Maintenance on a server at the head-quarters of the National Reconnaissance Office—the folks responsible for the nation's spy satellites. If he were to go down, it would not be alone.

He stepped out of the elevator into the third-floor lobby and saw that three staffers had gathered around a flat-screen TV tuned to CNN. Barry peered through his thick glasses and saw an aerial view of a town. Some-where flat. He could see smoke in the air and what looked to be a flood in process.

He stepped closer and the caption came into view: TWIN PINES, MONTANA.

Barry cleared his throat. The receptionist turned and blushed. "Oh, I'm so sorry! I didn't realize you were—"

"What happened?" Barry nodded toward the TV.

One of the young analysts in a white shirt and tie, sleeves bunched up, answered without taking his eyes off the screen, "A bunch of air tankers just crashed in some small town in Montana. Weirdest thing. CNN says there were, like, three or four of them on the ground."

Three or four airplanes had crashed. Simultaneously. In the town where Calendar was operating.

Another analyst said, "You know why the CNN crews were on the scene so fast? This is only a couple miles from that Polestar crash last week."

The receptionist crossed to her desk and bent at the waist, reaching for the receiver and hitting one of the buttons. She paused. "Mr. Gelfer? You have an appointment with Mr. Tichnor?"

She turned, smiled brightly. Her smile guttered. "Hey. Where'd that guy go?"

The two analysts glued to CNN shrugged their shoulders.

TWIN PINES

One could not say that Captain Maryssa Loveless was inexperienced. She had been commissioned through the Montana State University Army ROTC and held a bachelor's degree in political science. Upon completion of the Field Artillery Basic Course at Fort Sill, Oklahoma, she had been assigned to the second battalion, 175th Artillery at Camp Hovey in South Korea. After that had come Iraq. A lot of Iraq. Including an IED that had shredded her Stryker and cost her the use of her left hamstring for almost nine months. Despite her experience, when her Chinook dropped down on Main Street, landing as quick and hard as a sucker punch, she looked around at the buildings on fire, the flooding, the oncoming forest fire, and said, honestly, "What the almighty fuck?"

The rotors created perfect, concentric waves in the ankle-deep water. The captain's boots splashed down and she raced over to a cluster of men who seemed to be in charge. One of them, a civilian, was tall and put together, with a bandage on one cheek and an empty holster on his hip. She picked him. "Sir? Captain Loveless, Montana National Guard. What is your situation, sir?"

Without moving his mouth much, he said, "Shit storm. You guys didn't waste any time getting here."

"Yessir. A woman named Susan Tanaka told us to get airborne ASAP. Guess she knew what she was talking about."

The jet-fuel-fed fire at the auto-parts store looked like it would burn for hours. Eleven of Jack's airframe team had been outside with the fuselage and survived with nothing worse than a couple of broken arms. Four other guys inside had died with Reuben Chaykin.

There didn't appear to be any reason to wait, so Jack, Hector, and the remains of the airframe team started walking toward the police station.

Gene Whitney found some rope, and Peter, ever the engineer, rigged it to the hood of the Honda, turning it into a sled. Soon they were trudging up the debris-littered street, Peter limping on his wound, Beth towed behind, her leg elevated on the plastic pail they'd found.

Three blocks from the police station, Gene said, *"Travois."*

"Yes! Right. Thank you. Trying to remember that word was driving me nuts."

Casper the Friendly Airship had been ordered to fly, and fly it did. But with Ginger LaFrance dead and her remote control destroyed, the airship meandered aimlessly, pushed this way and that by the winds.

Fortunately, the same winds that blew the forest fire toward Twin Pines pushed the airship to the west—away from the fire.

That ended at the southwest tip of Twin Pines, as Casper dragged the Frankenstein version of a Claremont VLE through the heavy-duty fence surrounding the Helena Valley Energy Co-op substation. It held the flight deck of the dead ship, forming a shape like a soccer net, binding it in place. As the forward-thrust engines of the airship struggled, the nose of the Claremont edged within a foot of the substation's massive step-down transformers. But the thick fence held, and, with a metal-on-metal groan, the Claremont slid backward three feet.

Above it, Casper began oscillating, its butt end swinging left, then right.

Daria set a grueling pace but got them around the three west-side fires. The southern edge of Twin Pines was defined by two perfectly straight lines of railroad tracks, elevated on an eight-foot berm. Tommy was winded and his head ached but he kept quiet about it. Kiki limped on her wounded leg. The three of them snuck behind a ranch-style home with peeled aluminum siding and a vast array of broken and disheveled children's toys in a yard of packed dirt, gorse, and a curved trail, front to back, pounded into the ground by a largish dog that had paced incessantly for years.

Daria went to one knee, motioned the others to pause, and glanced around the corner of the house.

The graceless, battered airplane fuselage hung four feet off the ground, its nose cone jammed under the top bar of a sturdy security fence that surrounded a power station. The fence's top bar had been horizontal but now curved upward over the shattered windows of the flight deck, the coiled razor wire atop the fence looking like a crown of thorns.

Above the substation, the bulbous white airship groaned and struggled, its tail end swinging, trying to obey the last orders of its mistress: *Fly.*

Kiki whispered, "You see him?"

Daria shook her head. She scanned the street, mostly residential save for the energy substation. The houses were identical, each a mid-1970s design. Four of nine homes had For Sale signs in the yards. The signs were sun-faded. Not much water from the massive tankers had made it out this way but the smoke from the downed air tankers was drifting west and swirled among the low-slung, single-story homes. The street was abandoned.

Tommy glanced around. "You gals cover me. I'm going in."

Kiki said, "Why you?"

"First, 'cause I always wanted to say that. Second, 'cause Dee here doesn't know what we're looking for. And third, 'cause the way you been holding your side, you cracked open that rib again. Plus, your leg's bleeding."

Daria said, "Calendar could be inside already."

"I don't think so. Guy makes his presence known, y'know?"

Daria nodded. She pointed the Browning Hi Power in her left fist toward another house, the next one to the north. "Kiki. Stay here. I'll head that way. If Calendar comes from between the two nearest fires, he'll emerge between us."

With that, Daria darted around the corner and disappeared. When she was gone, Tommy said, "There are times I'm glad she's on our side."

Kiki said, "And yet . . ."

"Yeah. You ready?"

He stepped out from the shadow of the ranch house and jogged across the dusty, poorly paved street toward the substation. Tommy had served as a field surgeon in Kuwait, and while the idea of running while knowing that someone might shoot you wasn't new to him, it was as sickeningly horrifying as it had always been. He bit back the surge of panic, the acidic taste of adrenaline at the back of his tongue making him want to wretch.

Bedraggled and limping, Jack, Hector, and the remains of the airframe team arrived at the police station, walking from the east, coughing in the smoke, just as Peter and Gene arrived from the west, Beth Mancini's leg elevated on the travois.

News media helicopters circled the scene, although all the smoke was making their job difficult. Chief Paul McKinney hadn't been found yet and a sergeant had gathered the surviving, noninjured officers. But all three said they planned to go find loved ones and inspect their homes.

The sergeant looked around at the utter destruction and the deploying guardsmen. "Yeah," he said, nodding to his men in resignation. "We're done here."

He meant it. The last, sad remnants of an already undermanned police department disbursed.

The Montana National Guard team set up a field hospital. They got

Beth into the makeshift hospital—it used to be a Ford dealership—cut off her pant leg, and sterilized the entry and exit wounds.

"Bet you've never seen this before," Beth said, her face shiny with sweat, the shock wearing off and the pain ratcheting up. She thought the EMT-3 looked to be all of eighteen years old.

He smiled up at her and said, "Rebar through the leg? You're my third."

Tommy made it to the fuselage. This close, he could see its end section swaying, arcing back and forth, struggling to push forward or escape the trap of the heavy security fence. The fence itself moaned in protest. Tommy put both hands on the floor of the amidships door—the one he, Kiki, and Isaiah Grey had walked through, just a few days ago—and hoisted himself up onto his stomach.

As he did, a sickening *crack!* echoed close. A gunshot? No, deeper, less metallic. Tommy glanced over his right shoulder and saw that one of the vertical support poles for the substation security fence had wrenched itself half out of the ground, its rough arrowhead of cement one-third emerged from the sidewalk.

He felt the Claremont nudge forward a few inches, struggling to take advantage, like a snared lion sensing which edge of the net was weakest.

Your ass is hanging out in the street! Tommy reminded himself. He swung one knee up and tumbled into the fuselage.

Relative to the Claremont fuselage, Daria was at five o'clock and Kiki was at seven o'clock. Both had tail-cone perspectives. Thus, neither realized that, as the security fence began to give, the nose of the fuselage inched closer to a hulking, iron, step-down transformer the size of a UPS truck, if it stood on its hind end, grille to the sky.

Jenna Scott had gambled that she could get to the Claremont first by scrambling between two of the aircraft pyres, rather than circling around them. It had proven to be a mistake and almost a fatal one. The jet-fuel fires were spreading laterally.

With one arm of her shirt turned into a bandage, Jenna cut off the other sleeve and turned it into a bandanna for her nose and mouth to block the smoke. She was grimy and soot-covered by the time she emerged to the west of the fires, closer now to the airship.

A block away, she spotted one of the crashers, the tall redheaded woman who held an arm wrapped around her rib cage, her other hand hefting a professional-looking Glock.

The redhead glanced her way. She turned, raising her weapon.

Jenna put her Sten on Single-Fire and snapped off a bullet.

Kiki saw the tall, soot-covered figure in the bandit-style bandanna fire at her. She ducked back behind the ranch house, firing instinctively but not aiming. The newcomer's fire pinged against the aluminum siding, not three inches from where Kiki's head had been.

Inside the fuselage, massive holes in the starboard side and roof let in plenty of late-afternoon light. Jack's airframe guys had tossed bits of evidence into the fuselage topsy-turvy to get everything out of harm's way.

It was the first time Tommy had seen the fuselage in daylight since the crash. Blood was everywhere, along with dirt and mud and bits of foliage from the forest floor.

He stepped forward just as the double clap of gunfire erupted outside.

He hit the wall of the fuselage, pressed tight, just inside the amidships door. He tapped his comm unit. "What the fuck!"

He heard more gunfire. He recognized it as Daria's Browning.

Please God in heaven . . . he chanted to himself, until, with a click, Kiki's voice came back.

"It's Calendar! He's a block to the east. I think we have him pinned down. Tommy, hurry!"

Tommy reached into his shirt, removed the Star of David that hung from a simple steel chain, and kissed it. "Gotcha, babe. Hang on. Keep the bastard busy."

He scrambled over boxes and computers and bits of electronic gadgetry, the nature of which he could not guess. When the aisle was too cluttered, he climbed over seats. He stepped on the seats he and Kiki had been assigned. He thought of her, barefoot, long legs stretched under his, sleeping serenely as they flew.

He spotted the food-service cart, hiked over a pile of suitcases. He sat on a Samsonite hard-sided case and began to open drawers. He found water, soft drinks, juices, wine, and beer. He found little packets of peanuts. He cracked open a water and half drained it. *Evidence, shmevidence.*

He heard more exchanges of gunfire outside.

In the drawer that held pretzels he found an aged saddlebag. He pulled it out, opened it, and withdrew a leather portfolio. It contained three sheets of Malatesta, Inc., letterhead, a hand-edited speech.

Tommy said, "Gotcha."

He pulled a sketch pad out of the saddlebag and thumbed through it. It contained page after page of weaponry designs.

Behind him, Calendar cocked his gun.

Jenna, blond hair worn short, six feet tall, wearing jeans, boots, and a now-grimy camisole, plus the bandanna around her mouth, was easily mistaken amid the smoke for the silver-haired assassin. Daria and Kiki kept her pinned down behind an overturned wheelbarrow, so neither got a terribly good look at her.

Tommy turned, still sitting on the luggage. The silver-haired man leaned against a row of seats. His gun was pointed at Tommy's back.

"Do you mind removing your communications device?"

Tommy paused, then pulled out the ear jack and removed the controls at his belt, set them on the deck.

"Thank you," Calendar said, his voice neutral. "I never heard where they'd found the speech and sketchbook."

Tommy said, "You're Calendar. I thought my friends were in a shoot-out with you."

"Not me. It's Montana. Plenty of guns. Who are you?"

"Dr. Leonard Tomzak. Pathologist, NTSB. And while I'm not sure, you might just be the most fucked-up mercenary. Ever."

Calendar smiled serenely. "You think?"

They heard more gunfire close-by.

Tommy said, "Job was to kill this Malatesta guy, make it look like an accident, right? Coulda done it in his home, in his car. Whole Foods, make it look like, whatever, fifteen-grain pasta fell on his ass. But no. You bring down a goddamn airliner. You kill a bunch of folks, but not the right ones. Then you start killin' crashers. Meanwhile, every passing hour, we learn more and more because, hoss, that's what we do. We learn stuff. Finally, you have an assassin's wet dream and pretty much kill a whole town."

Calendar said, "I really do hate this town. May I have that bag, please?"

"You're the Paris Hilton of assassins. You'll be famous for being famous."

He pointed the gun at Tommy's head.

"You know, our jobs have a lot in common."

Calendar paused. He smiled. "Well, no. They really don't."

"You kill people to shut 'em up. I cut up dead people to make 'em talk."

"That's . . . one way to look at it. The bag, please?"

"You killed the pilot, right? But the other pathologist, Dr. Jain? She got him to tell her he was up and walking around the flight deck. That was after the crash resulted in a significant spinal injury at the fourth cervical disk." Tommy snorted a laugh. "Yeah, right. You killed a fella named Isaiah and he told me all about you. You see, you keep killing folks, then we draw the noose closer and closer. So, again, and I'm not trying to be mean here, but you're the worst bad guy in history. Your father must be proud of—"

Calendar shot Tommy.

34

DARIA DIDN'T HAVE ONE of the communications rigs the crashers carried, and she was too separated from Kiki to shout out a plan. But she knew a little about winning firefights.

It had come to her attention that the opponent was carrying a Sten gun. Calendar hadn't been carrying the popular British 9-millimeter submachine gun. He was also a somewhat better shot than their current opponent. But if Calendar wasn't shooting at them, he had to be somewhere nearby. This fight could go quickly from two-on-one to even-steven, as the Americans say.

Kiki was proving an adequate distraction if not an actual threat. She was brave enough but inexperienced with the Glock. Still, she was keeping the bandanna-wearing shooter pinned down and unable to relocate to a better angle.

Daria crouched behind two garbage cans, waited until this shooter switched targets to fire at Kiki. When the moment hit, she rose as if spring-loaded, taut brown arms pistoning, well-worn combat boots churning up dirt. She sprinted to the driveway of the dilapidated ranch house, twenty feet closer to the shooter.

Kiki apparently saw Daria's gambit and let off three bullets in a row, pinning down the shooter. Daria slid, feet first, weight on her right hip, and made it to the body of a Camaro up on cinder blocks, right front corner panel missing altogether, the frame covered in more Bondo than paint.

The three opponents made a triangle: Daria's move widened the side of the triangle between herself and Kiki, shortened the side between herself and the shooter. It also narrowed the space behind the overturned wheelbarrow, which their tango had been using for cover.

Then she heard the boom of a fourth weapon. The sound came from behind her. From the direction of the Claremont. Daria sat with her back to one of the cinder blocks, scanning the neighborhood. If Calendar had them in a pincer, the odds had just gotten considerably worse.

She didn't see him. But she did see Kiki's eyes go wide.

"That came from the plane!" she shouted.

Oh good, Daria thought. *Please alert our opponent to your primary concern. That helps.*

The shooter understood that Daria's move worsened the situation and shifted from single-shot fire to rapid fire. Bullets pinged off the other side of the Camaro, a few landing in the dirt and bouncing up into the metal chassis.

Daria watched Kiki turn from the fight and launch herself, limping but fast, toward the aircraft like a *futbol* striker heading for the goal. Daria assumed the better-armed shooter could see the tall redhead leave the engagement. Even-steven.

Daria took three very quick, very deep breaths, grabbed a rusty hubcap off the ground, and rose to her feet, hurling the hubcap like a Frisbee, as hard as she could. The dull aluminum glinted in the smoke-dimmed sunlight, arcing to Daria's right, to the shooter's left.

Daria gambled that the shooter would see the movement and track the hubcap, if only for a few meters. A flicker of the eye or wrist, that was all she needed. She emerged from around the grille of the Camaro, diving sideways, gaining sight, if only for a split second, of the shooter's legs. The opponent lay prone. Daria fired as she fell, her left hip and ribs taking the impact.

Tommy lay on the deck of the fuselage, the saddlebag by his knees, his right hand bleeding badly, cradled in his left hand. His eyes were squeezed tight.

"There are a lot of bones in the human hand," Calendar said. "And I just broke a whole bunch of them. Don't really know what that's going to mean for your career. Not really my problem."

He stepped forward, gun aimed.

Tommy keened, "Fucking . . . bastard . . ."

"Don't get me wrong." Calendar cocked his gun. "I'm going to kill you. I just wanted to hurt you first."

He stepped on Tommy's hand, bones crackling. Tommy screamed.

Kiki was still twenty paces from the dangling fuselage when another of the upright posts of the security fence gave way, an inverted cone of cement groaning as it pulled free. It sounded like a Norse frost giant on the hunt.

The Claremont surged forward another foot and the broken, dented nose cone slammed into the Helena Valley Co-op's step-down transformer.

A corona of sparks blossomed like Independence Day fireworks. Bits of flaming shrapnel arced in every direction.

Kiki pulled up so fast that she ended up flat on her ass, broken ribs grinding together, the crook of one arm thrown over her eyes.

Inside the fuselage, sparks snapped, electricity arced and popped, and the smell of sulfur filled the space. Calendar ducked, arms over his head. Tommy blindly flailed both legs, got lucky, connecting with Calendar's knees. The assassin stumbled back into the food-service cart, overturning it, becoming entangled in it and the pile of luggage. Tommy rolled to his side, grabbed the shoulder strap of the saddlebag, got one foot under himself, and dragged his sorry ass toward the rear of the ship, to one of the ragged holes in the fuselage wall. His ruined hand against his chest, he leaped out, hitting the street four feet below him, landing with all the grace of a brick.

Ten feet away, Kiki sat, legs spread, looking stunned.

When Calendar's head appeared in the doorway, Kiki lifted Ray Calabrese's service weapon and snapped off a single shot. It ricocheted off the fuselage.

Calendar ducked back inside.

They heard another roar from the damaged security fence and, with a metal-on-metal scraping groan, Casper the Friendly Airship finally yanked the Claremont fuselage free of the substation. The ship came about, twirling and slowly sailing away to the west.

The transformer continued to shoot out halos of damage-plagued sparks. Dried shrubbery around the substation caught fire like the road to Damascus on crack.

Kiki fired twice more into the fuselage. She hadn't a hope of hitting Calendar but she could keep him in hiding. "C'mon!" she shouted. Tommy struggled to his feet, right arm tight against his chest, the saddlebag dragging behind him. Kiki rose, too, and they limped/rushed back toward the firefight.

Which had grown quiet.

The .40-caliber bullet hadn't made much of an entrance wound in Jenna Scott's right thigh but the exit wound removed a chunk of muscle the size of a game hen. It also shattered her femur, leaving behind radial trails of fine cracks from hip to knee.

From there, the bullet had entered her left leg, shattering her knee in too many pieces to count, before changing angles by thirty degrees and flying off into the deserted neighborhood.

Jenna's body jolted as if electrified; arms, torso, neck, and legs jerking in spasm. Her brain went into immediate shock.

Daria used her boot to nudge aside the wheelbarrow, gun trained on the downed opponent. She wasn't surprised to find it was a woman; Daria was from Israel, the land of equal opportunity warriors.

She turned and saw the bedraggled Kiki and Tommy, each looking worse than the other, stagger around the corner of the first house. Tommy's back hit the wall and he slid to his ass in the waxy grass, right arm against his chest. Daria turned to the blond woman bleeding out in the dirt. She wondered, if only for a moment, who she was.

Daria took the Sten gun and the extra clip. She walked over to Kiki and Tommy, shouldering the subautomatic weapon, and saw blood staining his cotton shirt. Both of them were gasping as if they had run a marathon.

Kiki crouched by Tommy, glancing back at the fuselage as the airship flew away.

"Who was shooting at us?" she asked.

Daria shrugged. "Who cares?" She turned her attention to Tommy. "Looks bad."

Kiki looked back and, only then, realized how badly Tommy's right hand was spurting blood.

"Oh my god oh my god oh my god . . . !"

"Damn . . . prick . . ." Tommy spoke through clenched teeth.

Behind them, more sparks coruscated from the substation.

Daria drew one of her Brownings and turned toward the escaping fuselage.

"Leave him," Tommy said. "We got the saddlebag. Everyone's read the speech. He's done."

Daria stood and studied the war-weary couple sitting at her feet. Her dark eyes turned to the white airship and the fuselage, which were slowly sailing away. She knelt, dug around in her backpack, and pulled out an olive-drab cloth used for cleaning her guns. "Wrap it around your hand. We need to get you a hospital."

The body of Police Chief Paul McKinney was finally located under an Impala.

Mayor Tibbett's corpse was next, folded in half and slumped against a long-closed Best Aid store.

Inside the half of the municipal building dedicated to the police station, Ray Calabrese organized an ad hoc committee on What Do We Do Next, including Montana Guard Captain Maryssa Loveless, Mac Pritchert of the state fire team, and Peter Kim. They also had Susan Tanaka, two time zones away, on their headsets. "I've informed Del Wildman and the NTSB," she said into their ears. "Ray, I've contacted the FBI. Teams are on their way."

Pritchert smoothed his handlebar mustache forlornly. "Bottom line: the air tankers were taking water to the forest fire. They didn't get there. This dang fire is still advancing, and we gotta evac anyone still left in town. Now."

"This is a crime scene." Ray spoke without moving his jaw too much. "Is there any way, any way at all, to stop the fire, save the town?"

Pritchert shook his head. "The Illyushins were the biggest guns in our holster. Without them, and without a decent firebreak, the forest fire will morph into a brush fire. It'll pick up speed—no trees to block the wind on the prairie. It'll be here in a half hour, tops. Plus . . ." He gestured around to the buildings already on fire, thanks to jet fuel from the air tankers.

Captain Loveless turned to Ray. Nobody had voted that the FBI was in charge of the scene; Ray Calabrese just had that effect on people. "So we airlift everyone out, sir?"

"With one Chinook?"

"Negative. We have three more birds inbound."

Ray said, "Do it," through clenched teeth.

In their ears, Susan Tanaka said, "Captain? I've contacted every trauma hospital in a three-state region. A man named Dmitri Zhirkov is patching me into your pilots' comms now. They'll have coordinates for which hospitals are expecting them in ninety seconds. Out."

Captain Loveless turned to Ray. "Who the hell is this Susan Tanaka chick?"

Ray didn't hesitate. "Right hand of God."

Her walkie chirped. "Captain? We're full up."

Loveless hit Send. "Copy. There in a minute."

As she spoke, a beautiful if bedraggled woman with dark hair and skin entered the police station. Her stylish jeans were wet to her knees, as was the long hem of her sweater. Her hands were jammed into the sweater pockets. "Pardon me?"

They turned to her. Peter Kim said, "If you're injured, they've set up a temporary hospital just down the block. You see that big helicopter out there? More of them are en route. When they tell you to—"

"I caused this."

Ray and Peter froze. Ray said, "Pardon?"

"My name is Renee Malatesta. My husband was Andrew. People crashed that airplane, caused the fire, to shut him up. And . . . I told them it would be okay."

No emotion. No flickering of her eyelids. Renee swayed just a little, slightly uneven on her feet.

Peter Kim turned to Ray and said, "Huh."

Kiki toggled her comms, got Ray Calabrese.

"Tommy has the speech, the notepad, but he's been shot."

"I ain't shot!" Tommy shouted loud enough to be heard over Kiki's gear. He'd lost his on board the fuselage. "I got nicked!"

Ray's voice came back to her. "The fire's still coming. The National Guard is evac'ing the town. Is Daria there? Put her on."

Kiki handed over her comms.

Ray's voice sounded four feet away. "What's your threat assessment on Calendar?"

Daria squinted, gave herself a few seconds to ponder the question. "Let us say I am Calendar. First job is to kill the engineer."

Ray said, "Malatesta."

"Yes. Job two is to kill witnesses on the airplane. Job three is to steal some sort of speech, which is in a leather bag. Make sure no one sees it, yes? Finally, I have a team of mercenaries. As leader, my final job is to get my team to safety."

Ray said, "Okay. So what's his game plan now?"

"Malatesta is dead. The witnesses are dead. The speech is out and everybody has read it. And all three team members are dead."

Ray cut in. "Hang on: three? You got another one of his goons?"

Daria frowned. She turned to Tommy and Kiki, and covered the voice wand with her palm. "Is *goons* like three men in black-and-white movies, hit each other? The poking in the eyes . . . ?"

Despite shock setting in, Tommy actually managed to snort a laugh. "Stooges, Dee. Those are stooges."

"And stooges are not goons?"

Kiki shrugged. "They can be. The words—"

Tommy leaned forward. "Ladies? Hand . . . bleeding . . . out!"

"Sorry." Daria readjusted her ear jack for Ray's attention. "Yes, I killed his stooges. Which means Calendar has no more mission here."

Ray said, "Okay, listen. We have the wife of the original target, Malatesta. She's here, she's involved, and she's naming names. But the names are corporation fat cats. She doesn't seem to know Silver-Hair or anything about him."

"Then Calendar is the ghost," Daria said. "No one to kill, nothing to steal, no team members left to save. He is crazy, not stupid. This area: police, search-and-rescue, National Guard, FBI . . . this town just became a fortress. Plus, there is the fire."

Ray absorbed that. "Okay. How's Tomzak?"

"Losing blood."

"Okay, we have a field hospital. Get him and that saddlebag here. After the medics get a look at him, the Guard can airlift him to a hospital."

Daria handed the communications device back to Kiki. She made a hand gesture that, on any battlefield, means *we are pulling out.*

Tommy let out a weak laugh. "Honey, guess what. We're walking back toward the forest fire."

Kiki kissed him on the cheek. "That sounds about right for us."

In the floating fuselage, Calendar listened to the exchange using Tommy's comm unit.

Malatesta dead. Witnesses dead. Speech forfeit. Saddlebag heading to the freaking equivalent of Camp Lejeune. Calendar's people dead (he hadn't known about Vintner but she wasn't his people, anyway). The Malatesta bitch was in Twin Pines. Naming names but so what? Calendar's wouldn't be among them.

The mission was a wash. There were no more wins to be had. None from the original mission, at least.

And yet, there is something to be said about seeing a job well done.

35

IT TOOK THREE OF them almost twenty minutes to make it back to Ray and the base camp. As they approached, three twin-rotor heavy-lifts touched down on Main Street, one-two-three, like Balanchine-trained dancers, a block from the police station.

Ray Calabrese was on his comm unit talking to Susan Tanaka. "Barry Tichnor . . . yeah, Halcyon/Detweiler. My boss in L.A. has put in a call to the D.C. field office. They got a BOLO out on this guy. They'll find him . . . Hey, Tommy and Kiki are here. . . . Okay, bye."

Ray—long of arm and Italian of heritage—hugged all three of them in a massive if overenthused demonstration. Both Tommy and Kiki winced.

Kiki said, "Um, I think I dropped your gun back there. It's empty anyway, but . . ."

"It'll be molten by morning." He turned to Daria. "Didn't figure everyone would make it. Thank you. Again."

She nodded, quiet.

Tommy let the saddlebag strap drop off his left shoulder. He grabbed the strap, handed it to Ray. "The *why*."

"Malatesta? The weapons designs?"

"Yeah. This is the wife?"

Peter Kim was holding a woman by her upper arm. Peter's right pant leg was cut off at the knee, a pressure bandage around his calf. Rene Malatesta seemed out of it, swaying, eyes staring into the vague distance. She had a soot smudge on her cheek and her long white sweater was sooty and soaked to the waist with floodwater.

Kiki balled her sleeve into her fist, stooped to get the cloth wet, and wiped soot from the woman's cheek. "Hi. I'm Kiki. You're . . . ?"

Rene blinked, made eye contact with her, and shivered. "I had my husband killed."

"I know. Here." Kiki removed the dazed woman's sodden sweater—Susan Tanaka would have recognized it as a Missoni and expensive; Kiki just thought it felt heavy and off-kilter. Rene stood like a mannequin.

Renee stumbled a little and Peter Kim caught her elbow. Ray took a look at Tommy's hand. With the town all but empty, the National Guard had dismantled most of its MASH unit. "There's a decent med kit in the cop shop."

Daria said, "I'll get it." She threw one strap of her backpack over her left shoulder and set out at an easy jog. She had an ulterior motive: it was a police station and she was running low on ammunition. Combat instinct told her to see what she could scrounge.

As she moved away, Kiki and Ray exchanged looks. "You know she saved our lives. Again."

Daria swung into the police station and rounded the corner toward the desks as Calendar hit her square in the stomach with a police baton he'd borrowed from one of the dead. He swung it like a baseball bat but one-handed, and she folded around it.

Daria grunted and fell, her momentum making her slide forward across the half-inch-deep water that covered the linoleum floor. Her back slammed into a desk. The big man deftly hooked the toe of his boot through her backpack strap and kicked it the length of her arm, skidding it across the floor. Daria came to rest curled in the fetal position, vision blurring.

Two of the massive helicopters lifted off, spraying floodwater in every direction. They both banked west, away from the fire.

The last helicopter hadn't revved up its twin rotors yet, conserving fuel. Kiki—the Sonar Witch—turned abruptly toward the municipal building.

Tommy said, "What?" He'd come to read her like no one else.

"Who else is in there?"

Ray shook his head and coughed over the smoke. "We're it."

Kiki bunched Rene Malatesta's long sweater in her hands, wringing water out of it, the tension obvious in her knuckles. "I thought I . . ."

She paused, frowned.

"Hon?"

From the pocket, Kiki withdrew a small, nickel-plated .22.

"She was armed."

"Is it loaded?" Tommy asked, his eyes now raking over the all-but-catatonic Renee Malatesta.

Kiki checked. "No. No bullets in her pockets, either. Still . . ."

"Yeah."

Captain Loveless hacked a smoky cough. "Agent Calabrese?"

He turned and she pointed. Two blocks away, a couple of civilians limped their way. They had their arms over each other's shoulders and, at a quick look, Ray judged them both to have leg wounds.

"I'll get them," Loveless said.

"Captain? This is your command, but can I ask a favor?"

She nodded.

"This helo is the last ferry out. You're armed. You guard the bird. I'll get the civilians."

She didn't hesitate. "Yessir."

Ray turned. "Kiki, go get Daria and the med kit. Oh, and hey: ask her not to steal too much weaponry, okay? She didn't go in there to make sure Texas here ever plays the piano again."

Ray began jogging toward the limping civilians as Kiki and Tommy headed toward the municipal building.

Calendar shrugged out of his own backpack and set it down on a police officer's desk. He withdrew his beloved MAC-SOG army knife and, with one stroke, sliced an inch-deep gash through Daria's right shoulder. The finely honed blade shredded skin and muscle as if they were soft cheese. Daria didn't even try for a defensive move, lying on her side, no air in her lungs, her dominant arm bleeding. She hissed in agony.

"You're a consummate pro." Calendar kept his voice low. "You of all people should guard your comms better. Malatesta's dead. Witnesses are dead. Can't do shit about the speech. Can't save my two guys. But when you said *no more targets* . . . ? I owe you for the good men you slaughtered. For the fact they can't even have open-casket funerals."

Daria coughed, trying to rise and failing.

"You got friends outside so let's do this quietlike."

He deftly spun the combat knife from the forefinger-up position to pointing downward. The police baton hovered only inches from her skull, should she try some ninja-shit move.

Through clenched teeth, Daria whispered, "C-Combs."

Calendar had begun the downstroke, heading straight for her throat. He froze.

"Combs," she wheezed.

"What?"

"Your name. It's . . . important. I know your name." Blood pulsed from her shoulder and tears of pain blurred her vision. "Combs."

Calendar smiled. "Gosh. You are the good little spy. So what?"

Daria panted, wincing in pain. "Your father. Ar . . . Arlen Combs."

Calendar blanched. "What about him?"

"When . . ." Daria spit floodwater from her mouth. She looked up through sopping wet hair, made eye contact with Calendar. "When this is done, I'll do him, too. Just for spite."

Calendar felt the blood-tide return. His vision narrowed and the overhead lights on the police station turned crimson. A hollow ringing filled his ears. He recognized the symptoms. He was about to go into one of his killing-fugue states.

He didn't care.

He drew back the long knife.

"Okay! Whoa! Hold up!"

Calendar turned. He recognized the pathologist, hand held awkwardly against his chest, face gunmetal gray, shirt turning crusty brown from dried blood. The tall redhead to the doc's right had shot at him earlier. She was one of them. One of the enemy.

Tommy said, "Stop, man! Just . . . be cool!"

Calendar willed himself to stay in the here and now, not to slip totally into the fugue state of total destruction. That he would have to kill all three of them was obvious, but he wanted to be aware of it as it happened.

He heard his own voice, but as if through a far-off AM radio station, tinny and hollow. "I only want the bitch who killed my men. You two are free to go," he lied. "Deal?"

Kiki said, "No," and pulled a handgun out of a limp, wet sweater in her hands.

It was a tiny thing. A girl's gun. Calendar figured it for a .22. He was a lifelong soldier. Probably the smallest-caliber weapon ever aimed at him had been a 9-millimeter. The largest had been a rocket-propelled grenade. Calendar thought a .22 was a *gun* to the same degree that a Segway was a *car*.

Tommy was a poker player of some note. He worked really hard not to show two emotions: *A: I'm about to pass out, and B: that peashooter ain't loaded.*

Kiki dropped the sweater and assumed a two-handed grip on Renee Malatesta's little gun, boots shoulder-width apart, barrel aimed at Calendar's heart.

"She'll do it, hoss," Tommy bluffed, his voice cracking. "You got a knife. She's got a gun. Do the fuckin' math."

Daria keened in pain at Calendar's feet. She worked her right knee up under her, shifted her left arm under her chest.

"Oh . . . okay." Calendar said, barely holding on to his slim, sliding edge of sanity. The lights in the room shifted from crimson to Chianti red. He felt his heartbeat slow down. "Fine. You win. I give—"

Calendar let go of the combat knife. It began to fall toward the watery floor. Handle-heavy, the blade tilted upward as it fell.

Calendar wore a Blackhawk carbon fiber holster over his right kidney. His hand whipped around, snagged his massive .45 Heckler & Koch. The Blackhawk holster eschews the traditional thumb-break release for a faster draw.

Kiki forgot she was bluffing and pulled the trigger on Renee's pocketbook gun. *Snap.* Nothing.

Daria rose to one knee, pushing up off the floor with her good left arm.

Calendar brought his .45 around in an arc, thumbing off the safety.

In her right hand, Daria caught the combat knife in midair and grunted, rising up on her knees. In one fluid motion, she buried Calendar's own blade into his groin, driving it fully to the hilt, slicing deep into his femoral artery. His blood began gushing down her arm, joining the blood pulsing from her shoulder wound to form a single red sleeve.

The shock hit Calendar's central nervous system, his long muscles locking rigidly.

Daria twisted the knife forty-five degrees and Calendar spasmed as if hit by an electrical current.

His arm rose and his .45 flew from his grip.

His spine jolted. He landed on his back, head ricocheting off the linoleum, floodwater splashing, back arched with only his head, shoulders, and heels on the floor.

Tears of pain poured down her cheeks as Daria yanked out the knife and blood gushed from Calendar's wound. Its pink slick quickly spread in the half inch of water, washing against Daria's jeans.

She crawled forward on her good left arm and one knee, caught her breath, deftly spun the knife in her fist, and slit Calendar's throat.

Tommy and Kiki stood, arms locked, stunned. They watched as Calendar twitched and spasmed, and bled out.

Kneeling, panting, bleeding, soaking wet, Daria turned to them. The knife and her hand and forearm dripped blood. From behind sodden strands of hair, her eyes blazed.

The rest was a bit more chaos in a day generally ruled by a biblical level of chaos. Ray Calabrese and Captain Loveless helped the last two survivors of Twin Pines onto the Chinook heavy-lift. Peter Kim secured the catatonic Renee Malatesta in the back of the helicopter. He patted her down for more weapons but didn't find any. Kiki returned with Tommy, his hand properly bandaged. He'd dry-swallowed three Vicodin as well. The forest fire had become a brush fire and had reached the edge of town. It had met up with the fire at the auto-parts warehouse. It seemed eager to join up with the rest of its jet-fuel-fed brethren on the west end of the town.

Ray's eyes watered as he peered through the growing smoke. "Daria?"

Tommy laid his left hand on his shoulder. "Get on board, New York. We're outta here."

"Bullshit. Where's Daria?"

Kiki kissed Tommy gently. "Hop up. We'll be right back."

She led Ray back to the police station. Fully a third of the water-soaked floor was pink with Calendar's blood. He lay spread-eagled. His skin was the color of parchment.

Ray tried to study the scene clinically, as a trained criminologist. His brain vapor-locked.

"He had a backpack," Kiki said, holding Ray's upper arm. "She said it was important. She said to take off. She'd find her own way out."

"No."

"Ray. She's gone."

"No."

She rested her cheek on his shoulder for a second. "Okay. I'll be at the helicopter. We'll wait for you."

Ray searched the municipal building. Every room. He went out back, checked the alley. He sloshed through the street.

As he rounded the building, the fire chief, Mac Pritchert, grabbed him by the forearm as the Chinook's Textron engine spooled up and its twin sets of massive blades began fanning. The Best-Aid store, a block away, exploded in flames. Ray could feel the searing heat three blocks away.

"The fire's here!" Pritchert shouted. "We gotta go! Now!"

Under the baton of Captain Loveless, the last Chinook lifted off the pavement of Main Street. "We're it!" she shouted over the rotors. "Last flight out of Saigon!"

As the Chinook hit thirty feet, Tommy held Kiki and watched as the town of Twin Pines went up in flames.

Free Public Library of Monroe Township
713 Marsha Ave.
Williamstown, NJ 08094

EPILOGUE

DARIA GIBRON BOUGHT AN ice cream. Two flavors: lemon and vanilla.

She used to favor French vanilla until reading an article in an in-flight magazine that said the difference between vanilla and French vanilla is a raw egg. That sounded dangerous and Daria was averse to taking risks.

She licked the ice cream as the sun set over the Oudezijds Achterburgwal, past the Erotich Museum, in the heart of Amsterdam's red-light district. One of the things she loved about Amsterdam was that the people had spent tax money to build a museum to honor eroticism, and they had placed it in the prostitution zone. If you grew tired of paying for sex, you could pay money to study the history of sex.

Daria enjoyed irony as much as the next person, but still . . .

She entered the Hotel Frisian and waggled her fingers at the young man behind the night desk, with his biology textbook and iPod. The clerk blushed and nodded, trying not to be obvious about studying her body.

Daria went up to room 406, let herself in using the swipe card, and tossed out the remains of the ice cream. She checked the fresh bandage on her right shoulder. It looked clean. She pulled her laptop out of her tote bag, set it on the bed pillows, slipped off her stilettos, lay down on her stomach, propped up by her elbows, and surfed online news channels.

CNN was reporting the denouement of last week's biggest story—the annihilation of a small town in Montana by flood and fire.

The body of an NTSB investigator, Teresa Santiago, had been found in a gulley. Based on an examination of the wound, she had been stabbed through the heart with a combat knife.

A brand-new Go-Team from the NTSB was on the scene, investigating the downing of four air tankers. The new Investigator in Charge, Walter Mulroney, informed the media that an illegal EMP weapon might have been deployed to cause the crashes. The FBI and Interpol had been called in to investigate.

In the picture, standing next to Mulroney was a petite Asian woman in a tamale-red Dolce & Gabbana suit and red-soled Louboutin heels. Was that the famous Susan Tanaka? Daria wondered. They had never met.

Daria went to Haartez.com, scanned the Israeli news site. She moved on to *The New York Times*. She tried the *Washington Post* and found a story featuring an Amy Dreyfus byline. Congressional hearings had been called and two high-ranking officials with Halcyon/Detweiler, the massive Pentagon contractor, had been subpoenaed. Admiral Gaelen Parks and Liz Proctor were testifying and, according to unnamed sources, both faced criminal charges. Prosecutors were being cagey but made reference to a laptop and documents found in a backpack, which had been left in the lobby of the FBI headquarters in Washington. The contents of the backpack had been damning, apparently, but so far the evidence suggested that Parks and Proctor had been working without the knowledge of their superiors or the company at large. It looked like Halcyon/Detweiler might escape further scrutiny. The Dow Jones Industrial Average ended a tick up on that news.

A man named Barry Tichnor—and it was unclear exactly who he was and for whom he worked—had been named in documents in the backpack. He was found in a hotel room in Bethesda, in a bathtub of lukewarm water. Both wrists had been slashed with what appeared to be a long, sharp blade. Possibly a combat knife.

Renee Malatesta, widow of Andrew Malatesta, had suffered a complete nervous breakdown. She was tabula rasa. It was doubtful she would ever recover.

Daria switched to CNN's Web site and read a profile on Dr. Leonard "Tommy" Tomzak, of Austin, who had declined to be interviewed for the article. It seemed that Tomzak had suffered life-changing injuries during the investigation of the Montana air crashes, his right hand badly damaged, and it was unlikely that he would ever hold a scalpel again.

She checked the *Los Angeles Times* and found that investigators in Twin Pines had discovered the body of a tall blond woman, both legs smashed to bits. Again, the mysterious backpack left at FBI headquarters was mentioned in passing. The CIA was not responding to initial reports that she had been an agent. So far, her presence in Montana had not been explained.

The body of a tall, silver-haired man had been autopsied. Cause of death was complete exsanguination. He remained unidentified.

Someone knocked on the door to room 406.

"Kom in de," Daria sang out. She had left the latch open.

A smallish, tightly packed man entered and smiled broadly at seeing the girl in the miniskirt, barefoot, lying on her stomach and surfing the Internet.

He closed the door. "Chica," he said.

Daria closed the laptop and turned over on one elbow, smiling enticingly at the man.

His smile faltered, eyes narrowing.

Daria drew the MAC-SOG combat knife from beneath a pillow.

She batted her eyelashes.

"Carlos the War Dog," Daria purred. "We have unfinished business."